TURN
OFF
THE
LIGHT

Also by Jacquie Walters

Dearest

TURN OFF THE LIGHT

A Novel

JACQUIE WALTERS

MULHOLLAND BOOKS
LITTLE, BROWN AND COMPANY
NEW YORK BOSTON LONDON

The characters and events in this book are fictitious. Any similarity to real persons, living or dead, is coincidental and not intended by the author.

Copyright © 2026 by Jacquie Walters

Hachette Book Group supports the right to free expression and the value of copyright. The purpose of copyright is to encourage writers and artists to produce the creative works that enrich our culture.

The scanning, uploading, and distribution of this book without permission is a theft of the author's intellectual property. If you would like permission to use material from the book (other than for review purposes), please contact permissions@hbgusa.com. Thank you for your support of the author's rights.

Mulholland Books / Little, Brown and Company
Hachette Book Group
1290 Avenue of the Americas, New York, NY 10104
mulhollandbooks.com

First Edition: March 2026

Mulholland Books is an imprint of Little, Brown and Company, a division of Hachette Book Group, Inc. The Mulholland Books name and logo are trademarks of Hachette Book Group, Inc.

The publisher is not responsible for websites (or their content) that are not owned by the publisher.

The Hachette Speakers Bureau provides a wide range of authors for speaking events. To find out more, go to hachettespeakersbureau.com or email hachettespeakers@hbgusa.com.

Little, Brown and Company books may be purchased in bulk for business, educational, or promotional use. For information, please contact your local bookseller or the Hachette Book Group Special Markets Department at special.markets@hbgusa.com.

ISBN 9780316580328
LCCN is available at the Library of Congress

10 9 8 7 6 5 4 3 2 1

MRQ-T

Printed in Canada

For Marco,
who lovingly wrangles the chickens so I can write

TURN OFF THE LIGHT

1

EDITH

1630

The apple is an omen.

She does not yet know why, but she is sure of it.

The moment Edith finds it near the hearth, she pauses, a stillness overcoming her body. And then she cannot help but reach for it, pick it up, twist it this way and that in the window's early-morning light.

She wonders if her husband has left it here for her. But that would be curious for David, who is a practical man. Not uncaring, not unkind, but also not preoccupied with the happiness of others. And anyway, she does not know where he would have gotten it. She has heard of only one neighbor, farther north, who has an apple tree in the garden. The low-lying, sandy ground of the Shore does not provide the right climate for growing apple trees.

And yet here she is, holding the firm red thing in her hand.

A part of her consciousness tugs at her like a small child at the hem of her dress. Desperate to be heard. But she snuffs out that voice with her logical brain, a habit she has honed over the years.

It is just an apple. When she sinks her teeth in, juice travels down her chin and through the space between her fingers. She has never tasted anything like it. The flavor is complex, at once biting and soft.

The ominous feeling persists, but she convinces herself she is making monsters of mist and wind after yesterday's sermon. The minister spoke of Eve and the apple, and now she is conflating a religious lesson with an innocent piece of fruit—one that was likely ferried here by an animal from her northern neighbor's property and dropped through her open window. Nothing mysterious about it.

She quickly braids her long, thin brown hair to keep it out of her face as she warms a late breakfast of cornmeal mush over the fire. She takes a few more bites from the apple's yellowish flesh, and with each new burst of flavor, the hollow feeling in her stomach recedes. The apple is, indeed, just an apple. She thinks of her father, whose voice often bounces between her temples, reminding her that practicality and logic should always win over feelings. Perhaps he could see even when Edith was a child that she would forever be tempted by instinct.

A knock startles her from her thoughts. At once, her mouth is dry. She looks at the door, and though she resists it, the ominous feeling returns.

Another knock.

"A moment," she says as she mixes the mush before abandoning it for her visitor. She slips the apple in her apron pocket and heaves the door open.

It's Grace, Edith's closest neighbor and friend. Her eyes are rimmed with red, her face flushed. She must have run the nearly two miles here. Her long, light hair, which usually falls effortlessly to below her breasts, is tied haphazardly at the nape of her neck, loose tendrils stuck to the sides of her sweaty face.

TURN OFF THE LIGHT

"Come," she says between heavy breaths. "Please."

"Calm. Breathe," Edith tells her, placing a hand on Grace's shoulder to help steady her. "You should sit."

Grace shakes her head. The whites of her eyes are so red from crying that it makes the blue of her irises pop. "Bring your herbs," she says. "My husband. His summer sickness—we need you." Her body begins to convulse, the emotion of it all and the toll of the trip setting in.

Edith gets Grace settled in a chair. "Take a moment," she instructs. "And then tell me."

Grace nods and swallows. "Fever, surely. He was shivering when I left. Shivering! In this heat!"

Edith nods solemnly.

"And a rash," Grace continues. "On his neck, his upper back. His eyes look different somehow. And he says it's like fire in his throat." Her own eyes fill, but she presses them closed forcefully in an effort to stave off tears.

"Okay," Edith says. "Wait here while I gather my things."

She needs to find David, who is somewhere on their forty acres, to inform him of her task. But first, she rushes to the corner of the main room just beyond the hearth. There, flush with the wide wooden floorboards, is the door to the root cellar, its rough-hewn planks growing softer each day with damp. Edith crouches low and wraps her fingers around the iron ring hammered into the door's surface.

The wood, swollen from the humid sea air, groans as she pulls upward, the hinges squealing as if alive. A breath of cool, earthy air rises to greet her. She takes the lantern from its hook by the hearth, lights it with practiced care, and descends.

The steps are uneven, carved roughly from stone. The flickering light catches on shelves lined with clay pots and bundles of dried herbs and plants. The cellar is small, only about six feet by ten feet, but it is Edith's favorite place. Filled with her treasures. She prefers plants to people. Roots are more honest than men. And they never ask questions she does not wish to answer.

The damp wraps around her like a friend in greeting. Her eyes scan the shelves as she carefully considers what remedies to bring for her sick neighbor. She must be well prepared; the journey is not short. There can be no quick return for a forgotten item.

She gathers the necessary jars, wooden bowls for mixing, and her mortar and pestle. Then she turns back and climbs slowly, the lantern trailing shadows down the stairwell behind her. When she has resurfaced, she closes the trapdoor and latches it. She spots her shears near the hearth and, in case she needs to harvest anything on the journey, slides them into her apron.

As she does, her fingers rediscover the apple in her front pocket. With her back to Grace, she holds it up to her face as if examining it for clues. The hollow feeling in her stomach returns. And when she throws the half-eaten fruit in the fire, she swears she sees the flames jump.

As the women walk through the woods, Edith's bottles and jugs bump against one another, a chorus in her sack. She mentally rehearses her plans for Grace's husband. Edith has packed boneset for his fever and body aches, as well as wild cherry for his cough. She has brought pokeweed but hopes not to have to use it, as it can be toxic if she makes even the smallest mistake.

"Pluck it while it's young," her aunt told her when she was little and just beginning her training. "Or it'll cost you your life."

They were bent over a pair of juvenile shoots that had sprung up earlier that year. Young and bright-eyed, Edith marveled at the plant that would, within months, become poisonous.

"Just like people," she mused.

"How do you mean?" Aunt Joan asked.

"Innocent in youth but deadly with age."

Aunt Joan guffawed her loud, unapologetic laugh. "You're a wise one, Edie, girl."

Now, nearly ten years later and with her aunt Joan dead and gone, Edith feels far from wise. Apart from Grace, she has no friends. Everyone on the Shore looks at her as if she has two heads. They come to her when they bleed but never to break bread at her table. She wishes she could understand why, wishes she could read people the way she reads the marsh sedge — by the sharpness of its edges, its bending toward the morning light, the way it curls before a storm. But while she is attuned to such subtle signs in nature, the subtleties of mankind evade her.

Edith steps with purpose through the trees. The sun is relentless, its heat bearing down on them even in the somewhat shaded woods. The air is thick and balmy, exerting a constant pressure on anything that dares brave it. If this weren't an emergency, she'd save the journey for just after sunrise or closer to dusk.

"I thought he was better," Grace says as she huffs along.

"Summer sickness is unpredictable," Edith admits.

The truth is, it could be a multitude of things. In her experience as a healer, someone might be sick for weeks, recover, then have recurring bouts for months; someone else might suffer only a few days before succumbing.

"Was he outside in the heat yesterday?" she asks. "Or this morning?"

Grace barks a laugh. "It's August, Edie. It's the hardest part of the growing season. He was out there all day yesterday topping the tobacco." Her voice is strained, her thick eyebrows furrowed together.

"David will help harvest while Jacob is sick," Edith assures her friend. She knows how valuable the crop is; they can't afford to lose the income.

"Thank you," Grace says, sighing a little.

A silence descends, heavy as the air. Neither of them addresses what will happen if Jacob succumbs to the illness, how drastically life would change for Grace. She arrived on the Eastern Shore only last year after being recruited by a company for a bride shipment from London. She has few practical talents; she is a gifted artist, but that does little to provide for a life.

Edith stops suddenly.

"What is it?" Grace asks, turning.

"Do you have a rag?" Edith asks. She is wet between the legs, and while she first thought it might be sweat, she now realizes it must be her monthly bleed.

Grace frowns. "Oh, no, I don't."

Edith considers her options. She could free bleed into her shift and petticoat, but a rag would be more comfortable. She feels around in her sack for a stray cloth and, mercifully, her hands graze the uneven edges of a linen scrap. She loosens her apron and reaches through the layers to place the rag to catch the blood.

When she straightens up again, her body sways. She is light-headed, the oppressive heat only making it worse.

"There will be trouble tonight," she admits to Grace as they resume their journey. "When I tell David."

"So don't," Grace says with a sly smile and shrug.

Edith admires her friend's cheekiness. Maybe she is bolder because she comes from a bustling city. If Grace is shiny silver, Edith feels like tarnished copper in comparison.

"I suppose I don't have to tell him right away," she says. "But he will soon realize, regardless."

Her husband knows little of pregnancy and childbirth, but he understands that if she has gotten her monthly, she is not with child.

"That's nine months now we have failed to conceive."

"It will happen," Grace says. "It has to. Did you place the stone under your bed?"

Edith nods. Grace gave her rose quartz to promote fertility last month.

"It can take time," Grace tells her reassuringly.

But Edith is not so confident. As the season tilts toward autumn, she fears fertility will decline as the cold weather cools the womb. She thinks again of her aunt Joan, who would likely have made her a sachet of red clover to wear under her clothes. Aunt Joan, like Grace, was a superstitious woman.

Edith feels a tug in her heart. For a moment, she is a girl again, pale and freckle-faced, walking through the woods as her aunt points to various plants and shrubs, explaining their uses and properties. She longs for an afternoon of the two of them tending the family garden. Aunt Joan understood Edith on a level no one else seems able to.

"It will be okay," Grace says, noting her friend's pained expression.

And Edith simply nods, because how does she tell her what she is really thinking? How does she tell her that she is longing for another time? A time long ago, in childhood; the only period in her life when she felt seen.

"I found an apple this morning," she says instead, the words spilling out of her.

"That's curious," Grace muses.

They are nearly there. The trees are thinning out, and Edith can see the shore of the inlet that marks the northernmost edge of Grace's property.

"Unless," Grace says, a thought occurring to her, "you planted a tree last season?"

"No," Edith says. "I don't know where it came from. Perhaps an animal carried it and dropped it in the window."

"That's lovely," Grace says. "See? It's a sign. Your luck is turning already!"

And Edith nods again, because she also senses a shift, a wrinkle in the cosmic curtains of the universe. But the tightening in her gut confirms that while she agrees her luck is turning, she does not believe it is for the better.

2
CLAIRE

Present Day

Claire pulls into the driveway of her childhood home.

"Are we here, Mama?" her four-year-old asks from the back seat.

Claire catches Julia's eye in the rearview mirror, and the girl's smile warms her from the inside. She feels the familiar tug of the invisible string that connects them. But a heaviness quickly sets in at the edges of her awareness. Bringing her daughter here should be a momentous occasion, a meaningful braiding of worlds. Instead, it feels like bricks sewn into her hemline. Weight with no relief.

"We're here," Claire confirms, cutting the engine of the rental car.

Even after all this time, the house looks the same. The stately two-story red-brick structure is a standout here on the Eastern Shore, not only because most homes in the remote seaside barrier islands are constructed of wood and insulated siding, but also because this is one of the oldest properties, from the seventeenth century—though it has, of course, been renovated and expanded over the years. She notices for the first time how the roof appears from the front to be all triangles, like a picture her daughter would draw.

"That was a really long bridge," Julia says.

"Eighteen miles," Claire repeats for the third time. Julia is fascinated by the Chesapeake Bay Bridge-Tunnel that connects the detached Eastern Shore to the mainland of Virginia.

"You ready?" Claire asks. She wonders what her daughter will think of this place, which is nothing like their home in Los Angeles. There, they are two specks in a sea of millions. Here, in Claire's hometown of Cape Chase, they are two in only two thousand.

"I want to get down," Julia whines.

"Okay, okay," Claire says as she climbs out of the rental. She can't blame the girl for complaining; she has been strapped into planes and car seats all day to make it from one coast to the other.

"Can we have pasta?" Julia asks.

Claire laughs. "We have to see. I don't know what Aunt Tilly made for dinner, okay?"

Even when Julia frowns, she is so beautiful. Her eyes are golden and large and round, while Claire's are an unenthusiastic brown. Julia's hair is thin and delicate and curls into sweet ringlets at the end; Claire's is an unruly mess of waves that appeared in the wake of postpartum hormones. Many of Julia's features, like the smooth button nose and pointy chin, come from her father.

Claire allows herself to feel briefly annoyed that she shoulders the weight of parenting alone. Her ex dipped out early on. This was no surprise to Claire, who is accustomed to the people she loves disappearing, but she occasionally fantasizes about having a partner. Someone to help research pediatricians and music classes and parenting techniques, to help ferry Julia to vaccinations and playdates and dentist appointments, to order new leggings when the old ones get holes, and to keep the other informed when Julia turns sour on a snack she used to love. At times, the mental load feels unbearable.

"You could get a nanny. Or a mother's helper," one of Claire's coworkers told her last week. But Claire bristled at the thought. Entrusting a stranger with the literal life of the most important person in the world—no.

"Not an option, unfortunately," Claire said, shaking her head.

"You know," the coworker continued, "over-independence is a trauma response."

"That's so interesting," Claire said before pretending to get a phone call.

Now, as she approaches the front door of her childhood home, she is immensely grateful to have her daughter here, even if it does feel like a glitch in the matrix, the crossing of two disparate lives.

Her brother-in-law, Peter, answers the door. His blue eyes still pop, though his receding hairline has become more pronounced since the last time she saw him, and his white polo clings near his belly's center. An altogether different vibe from the lanky skater boy they all knew growing up.

"Claire," he says, going in for a hug. It's awkward with the suitcase and bag and Julia, who has koala'd herself around her mother's right leg.

"Hey, Peter," Claire says, attempting to return the hug.

His eyes crinkle at the corners in sincerity when he pulls away. "I'm glad you're here. I hate the *reason* you're here, but—"

"Yeah, same," she agrees as she looks around. "Dad's . . . somewhere?"

Tilly's voice echoes in Claire's head. The ominous tone with which she told Claire on the phone last night that their father was nearing the end. "It's time," she'd said.

Peter nods toward the downstairs bedroom. "He's sleeping." He stares at the door for an extra second as if in some kind of trance, then turns back to his guests. "Well, come in, come in!"

Claire reaches for Julia, who is still holding on to her leg. "Come on, love," she says.

Peter's eyebrows shoot up when he sees the girl. "Hi, Julia! I haven't seen you since you were this big." He holds his thumb and index finger a mere inch apart, his eyes playfully wide.

Julia cracks a small smile. "I was never *that* little!" she says.

"I don't know," Peter teases. "I guess it's just been too long. I don't remember."

"I see you on the phone," Julia reminds him.

"You're right," he says. "Video calls. Practically the same thing these days, huh?"

Peter takes their bags, which frees Claire to pry her daughter from her leg, pick her up, and carry her balanced on her hip. Her whole body aches from the day of travel and hauling this tiny human through airports.

"You okay?" she whispers to Julia, leaning in so they touch foreheads. Julia nods.

The inside of the house has barely changed. In the foyer, the wide staircase wraps around in a curve along the wall. This was always their mother's favorite spot to take pictures. Looking at the steps, she can see in her mind photos from Christmas with cousins, from prom with friends in fancy dresses.

This area is part of the original home, so the floors are composed of very wide boards with irregular gaps from seasonal swelling and shrinking. Hand-forged nails with square heads line the ends of each piece of wood. Many of the gaps have been filled with oakum, old rope saturated with pine tar to make it waterproof and durable. Though the material was typically reserved for caulking ships, homeowners in the maritime community of the Shore adapted it as needed to keep out moisture and bugs.

And to Claire's left, the crown jewel of the house: the original seventeenth-century inglenook fireplace. The exposed brickwork and timber beams have survived from those earliest days, though the modern addition of a wood-burning stove makes the hearth functional. Along the left side, there's a subtle tilt, just enough to suggest something once shifted deep beneath the house. A long-ago quake, maybe. The kind no one alive remembers but that the house can't forget. One corner sags slightly, and the mortar has fractured into fine, spidery lines. Like wrinkles on a face indicating years of stress and worry.

And only a few feet from all that is the trapdoor that leads underground. Her parents had grand plans to renovate the space and make it into a wine cellar, but it was never upgraded from general storage.

Claire shivers just looking at that trapdoor.

She hates the cellar.

"Tilly is putting clean sheets on the bed," Peter says. Then another idea comes to him. "We assumed you and Julia would want to be together, so we put you both in the guest room, but—"

"Yes, we'd like that," Claire confirms quickly.

As Peter puts out food for them, Claire thinks about her dad. The last time she saw him was when Julia was born; he flew to Los Angeles and slept on an air mattress for an entire week. He did little to care for the baby, but he cared for Claire with a kindness that makes her teary to think about now. Preparing her meals, warming up her coffee when it would inevitably sit cold for hours, washing burp cloths and dishes.

Not long after, he was diagnosed with dementia. Things deteriorated quickly. About a year ago, Tilly and Peter moved in to help care for him. And Claire, in the craziness of newborn life and then toddler life, had been in touch with her father only via a weekly FaceTime. No trips back to the East Coast, no support for Tilly in her new role as caretaker other than gifting her takeout and housekeeper services.

The sisters have grown apart. Lately, their conversations revolve solely around medical decisions and end-of-life logistics. The longer Claire is away from the Eastern Shore, the more she feels that life disappear. Like a rug that loses its color after years in the sun. A fading, a slow letting-go.

Which somehow makes it seem even harder to return. Going back is like stumbling for a light switch in the dark; in a room she doesn't know; in a house she isn't even sure has electricity at all.

Claire leaves Julia downstairs to feast on snacks with Peter and heads up to the guest room. She finds her sister Tilly standing at the far wall, where there's a small alcove with a window that overlooks the backyard. She's turned away from Claire, one hand across her body and the other rubbing her neck mindlessly.

"Hey," Claire says.

Tilly startles. "Oh," she says, "you're here! Sorry, I didn't hear you guys come in."

Her energy is frenetic as she crosses the room with her arms wide for a hug. As they hold each other, swaying back and forth, Claire realizes that even with the built-up resentment between them, Tilly is the only person on earth who knows what it feels like to be losing their dad. The only person whose grief might potentially match her own.

"You look good," Claire says as she pulls away to inspect her little sister. Short, bouncy blond hair that hovers above her shoulders.

TURN OFF THE LIGHT

Comfy sweats and an old oversize T-shirt that swallows her small frame. Bright green eyes that scan Claire's body just as intently.

Tilly rolls her eyes. "I look *tired*," she replies.

"Yeah, well," Claire says, modeling her own matching athleisure set, "*tired* is just kinda my vibe these days. A four-year-old will do that to you."

"I bet," Tilly says.

Silence hovers between them.

"Okay, well," Tilly starts just as Claire asks, "Anything I can help with here?"

Tilly laughs at the awkwardness. Their bodies have forgotten how to occupy the same space.

"No, no, it's done," she says. "I mean, it's nothing fancy. Just some clean sheets and a good vacuum."

"Well, I *am* expecting mints on the pillow," Claire says. "Otherwise I'm writing a shitty review."

"Ha-ha," Tilly replies. "I figured you'd want to be here where you have your own bathroom rather than sharing with us." She gestures to the small adjoining toilet and shower, then to the room above the garage. "Plus, this way you have the playroom for Julia too."

She does not mention the real reason she has put them here: because the alternative is Gabby's old room.

"Dad's asleep now, otherwise I'd . . ." Tilly's voice trails off.

"No, yeah, it's late, of course. I'll see him in the morning."

Another charged moment of silence.

"His nurse," Claire says, "she's the one who thinks he's near the end?"

Tilly bites her lip. "It's not good, Claire. He's lost fifteen pounds in the past month."

"Jesus." Claire shakes her head.

Tilly shifts her weight. Then takes a deep breath. "Should we get you some food? You must be starving."

Without waiting for an answer, she claps her hands together and exits the room as if it's too small to contain her nervous energy. A whiff of lavender conditioner lingers in her wake. Claire stands briefly in the solitude — something she guesses she will have very little of in the coming days. She breathes. Presses her thumbnail to the pad of her index finger, then the pad of her middle finger, then the ring finger, then the pinkie. A calming ritual she picked up as a teenager. She cracks each of her knuckles with the thumb of the same hand.

When she feels centered, she turns—

And sees the framed drawing on top of the dresser. A caricature portrait of the sisters her dad bought in the tourist part of Cape Chase. She was twelve. Tilly was ten.

And their oldest sister, Gabby, was fourteen.

Seeing this cartoon rendition is almost more painful than an actual photograph. The artist accentuated Gabby's most prominent features, as a caricaturist does: her wide smile that showed off too much of her gums; the dimple on her left cheek; even the glimmer in Gabby's eye. As if the artist could tell she *sparkled*.

Claire's body freezes. Her fingertips are suddenly cold, as if all the blood has drained from them.

The three sisters were inseparable, like individual limbs of a single unit. And then, the summer Gabby turned eighteen, all of that fractured. What started as a small crack on the surface enlarged over time, fanning out and webbing over Claire and Tilly's remaining sisterhood.

Until even that was just another broken thing.

Claire proceeds with her nightly rituals despite the new setting. She checks the front door to be sure it's locked, then the side and back doors. She closes a window in the kitchen and latches it, fighting the warped wood. Then she circles around to the front door again for good measure. The floor beams groan and creak loudly beneath her feet, mostly in the same places they always have, though the house has aged like all the rest of them. New spots here and there complain under her weight with low laments. She is careful not to look toward the hearth and trapdoor. The only thing she hates more than the cellar is the cellar at nighttime.

Upstairs, she ensures the path from the bed to the bathroom is clear for Julia, that she won't trip on a stray toy or shoe in her middle-of-the-night journey to the toilet. She also lines Julia's edge of the bed with pillows to keep the girl from falling.

Finally, they lie there together, Julia half asleep as Claire rubs her back.

"Mama," Julia whispers, "what's wrong with Grandpa?"

Claire's fingers pause. "He's sick," she says gently.

"Can't you give him medicine?" Julia asks.

Claire feels her throat open up like she's about to cry. "Oh, honey," she says. "They *do* give him medicine. But sometimes medicine isn't enough."

Claire knew the death talk would have to happen at some point on this trip, but she didn't anticipate it would be this soon. She hasn't had time yet to research as meticulously as she'd like, to read up on conversation techniques and listen to podcasts with child psychologists. She hasn't been able to find a kids' book that conveys the message through a story. Claire likes to be prepared. *Needs* to be prepared.

"Why the medicine not enough?" Julia asks.

"Sometimes," Claire says carefully, "even when we try really hard to fix them, our bodies stop working."

Claire lies there until Julia's breaths move in a steady, pulsing rhythm. Her right thumb, which she has been sucking, slips from her mouth. Her grip on her bunny lovey, a soft gray rabbit attached to a blanketlike soother, loosens.

Despite the long day, Claire is alert. A nagging voice tells her she cannot go to sleep without seeing her father. Without at least laying eyes on him. So she rolls gingerly from bed and pads through the playroom, down the hall past Tilly's and Gabby's rooms, to the front swooping staircase that leads downstairs.

Her father's bedroom is brighter than she anticipated; the curtains on the windows that overlook the front yard are drawn open so the moonlight spills in freely. Her father lies in the king-size bed that sits against the back wall. Claire wrinkles her nose. The room smells like a hospital, antiseptic chemicals mixing with stale air. Death's favorite perfume.

She stands at the end of the bed, careful not to bump it, and watches her father. She can't make out the details of his face in the dimness, but she is struck by how small his frame appears on the large mattress, how he is swallowed by the fluffy duvet.

And then—the covers move forcefully. Right where she imagines his belly must be, like his arms are flailing under there. She hears a *click-click-click* and realizes he is clenching and unclenching his jaw. Bursts of air escape through his lips in fits.

His head jerks from side to side. Is he having a bad dream? Claire considers placing her hands on his feet to calm him, but then she worries that will wake him and make it worse. She steps closer and stands over him dumbly, her eyes frantically scanning his covered body.

Should she get Tilly?

Her father whimpers, his eyes still closed, his brows furrowed together in stress. Claire steps to the head of his bed, her back to the windows, her body casting a shadow over her father's face. He winces, clearly in pain. She holds her hands above his chest, is just about to lay her palms there to calm him—

But then he goes completely still. Limp. His body a slack, empty sack.

The jarring difference between two seconds ago and now is chilling. Claire feels uneasy. She thinks about checking his pulse but finally sees the comforter move again in a steady breathing rhythm.

She looks around the room once more. Nothing has physically changed, but the near darkness now carries an eerie weight. The stale air is suffocating, winding its way around her neck, pushing her toward the door with a warning: *You are not wanted here.*

3
EDITH

"You told him that? Square in the eye?" David asks.

Edith sits with her husband at the table, both of them bent over plates of white fish.

"Of course not," Edith says, chewing a crusty bit of stale bread. "But I told Grace so that she might be prepared."

"Six days?" he asks. "That's what you told her? That he will die in six days?"

Edith shrugs, suddenly self-conscious. "Well, six to eight. That was my estimation."

She has recounted the day's happenings to her husband: the return of their neighbor's summer sickness, her long journey in the heat to his home, the protocol she followed after her arrival. But Jacob's body did not respond to the herbs like it had during the last bout. This time, she does not see a way through.

"How can you know the number of days?" David asks, harping on this point. A small flake of fish rests on his upper lip, distracting her.

"I cannot know for certain," she says, feeling as though she is being interrogated. "But I make an estimation based on past experiences."

"With your father, you mean? Your aunt?" he asks.

She nods. "Them as well as the others. All the ones I could not save."

Aunt Joan always told her that being a healer was a blessing. That she would know more about the natural world and the human connection to it than anyone. But her aunt failed to mention the pain that would accompany the role. Being a healer meant being there in the hardest moments and seeing the patients through to the other side — no matter which side they chose.

David has never asked about her work. Edith may be young, but she has already held eleven hands as they went slack with death. "I have started to recognize the signs of when the end is near," she tells him.

In addition to the settlers she has treated, she was also present when her father succumbed to the ague. Too many years breathing the bad air of the Eastern Shore swamps. And then she watched as Aunt Joan withered away from dysentery. Edith tried everything, but the bloody flux won in the end.

"Eerie, that is," David says, finally wiping his mouth clean of the stray fish flake. "What are they? The signs, I mean."

Edith's appetite sours with the conversation. She pushes her food away, and David reaches across the table to claim it as his own. His cheeks are red, perhaps from his long day in the sun. His eyes seem more sunken than usual. The season is taking its toll on his body. And now with their neighbor Jacob sick, there is even more work to be done, as David helps tend the man's tobacco crop.

"The signs of death . . ." She struggles to explain these to David. The unquantifiable markers of life's end. She does not know how to tell him that it is, above all, a feeling. Something intangible that she can sense. The energy heavy and thick, but the air so thin, you could suffocate. As if it were being sucked into some other realm. And a darkness that becomes more alive as the body slips closer to oblivion.

When she described these things to her father once, she was met with a disapproving scowl. He was always nudging her toward the practical, afraid that others would find her odd. And now she sees that he was right. Sitting here under the scrutiny of her husband, she feels like an outcast in her own home.

"The signs of death," she says again, channeling her father's advice to be practical, "are mostly what you would expect: a slowing heart, shallow breath, yellowing skin."

David shakes his head, his mouth full of food again. "I don't know how you do it," he says.

They have all seen their share of death in the colonies; her husband probably wonders why, then, she would seek it out. But this is yet another inexplicable thing. So she shrugs and allows him to finish his meal in relative silence save for the occasional distant clucking of their chickens and the nearby sputtering of the table's candles.

Her father arranged their marriage. "He's a builder," he had said when he first told her about the man who would be her husband. "Works with wood. Bad weather or bugs can ruin a crop, but nothing will stop people from needing boats. Not out here on the Shore." Her father had always been a forward thinker. Wise. At least in the ways of business.

And then, two months after handing Edith off, her father was dead.

She watches David as he rips a chunk of bread from the loaf. His strong hands and bulging veins communicate violence, but she has also seen the thoughtful care with which they shape wood. Even though she has known her husband for only a short time, she has observed how he closes one eye when sanding a rough edge, how he bites his knuckles when deep in thought, how he falls asleep on his side but always ends up on his back.

Still, she wonders what secrets he holds. He must have them. Everyone does. After all, there is so much about *her* that he does not know. And yet, here they sit, sharing a table, a home, a life.

"My sister died when I was very young," David says, breaking the silence.

Edith looks at him, unable to hide her shock. It is as if he has read her mind in deciding to share something so private and vulnerable.

"I didn't know," she says dumbly.

He continues, his mind preoccupied with its own machinations. "It was fast. None of those signs you describe," he says. "She was just here one minute and gone the next. Bee sting."

Edith's heart catches in her chest like a snag in a sweater. "That's horrible."

"It was," he agrees.

She wonders briefly if he is about to cry, but then he clears his throat and coughs. Reaches for his beer and busies himself with finishing the cup, getting the last dregs. She considers placing a hand on his or at least adjusting her chair to be nearer to him. Anything that might encourage closeness, since she feels his sharing something from childhood could be an opportunity for a tighter bond.

But she is afraid these gestures will be seen as an invitation to bed, and she remembers the blood in her petticoats. The still-looming conversation about their failure, yet again, to conceive. So, instead, she clears the cups and plates and douses the fire, where a stray apple seed still sits in the embers, mocking her from the ash.

David falls asleep almost immediately. But Edith is too hot. She frees her feet from the blanket and sits up slowly. This is the fourth night in a row that she has had trouble sleeping. Her mind insists on rehashing the events of the day or ruminating on the possibilities of tomorrow.

She abandons the bedroom and heads off to make a cup of tea. She still has some wild cherry remaining from the trip to Jacob's earlier today. She gets the water going and then opens the wooden shutters of the window. The moon is big and bright, illuminating the bay behind their home so it sparkles.

Just then, Edith hears a dull thud and feels breath on her neck. She turns, startled that David is awake after being so deeply asleep only moments ago—but David is not there. The room is empty.

Pop!

The fire's flames dance and lick the pot of water.

She turns her attention back to the outside, which is still held captive by thick, balmy air despite the sun's disappearance. Even so, she shivers, feeling suddenly exposed, and wraps her arms around herself.

Edith closes the shutters and sits near the fire as if it could offer some kind of protection. Her fingers graze the side of her neck in the exact spot she felt a puff of air, that gentle exhale. Despite moving position, she cannot shake the feeling that someone is near, watching her. Has someone sneaked into the house? She looks again to the wooden shutters, which are latched. But were they closed before? She struggles to remember.

Edith checks the door, sees that it is locked. She surveys the darker corners of the room before convincing herself that she has simply been spooked like a horse and nothing more.

She again sits by the fire, her back to the window, her eyes fixed on the pot of water as it warms. Her fingers find her leather cord necklace and worry the edges of the flint stone pendant. One side has been worn smooth from years of mindless rubbing.

Edith wears the necklace every day; it is the only thing she inherited from her mother. The dark flint glistens with veins of smoky gray and iron. Tied beside it is a small nub of steel. Together, flint and steel produce spark and flame. The pendant is both a talisman and a tool. Fire whenever she needs it—for warmth, survival, defense.

She stares at the pot of water until tiny bubbles form at the base and vibrate and wiggle their way to the surface. After steeping the wild cherry bark, Edith sips her tea. It's earthy and slightly bitter. She tries to focus on the steaming cup, the hot liquid as it travels down her throat and warms her chest. But she knows sleep is futile now. Her mind is awake, and so, too, is her heart, still pattering with a steady rhythm of fear.

Edith turns back toward the window and—

The shutters. They are open again.

She sets the tea aside and slowly steps toward the moonlight, her heart picking up speed. There is no wind tonight, so the weather cannot be the culprit. And surely she would have heard someone slip in? She can think of no logical explanation.

Finally, her fingers graze the edge of the shutters, and she leans her body out the window, checking that no person or animal hides on the other side. When she again confirms she is alone, she closes the shutters deliberately and narrates her actions out loud.

"The hook is latched—there—*locked*."

By the time she returns to her tea, the liquid has cooled enough that the bitter taste lingers on her tongue long after she has finished the cup.

4
CLAIRE

After the strange visit with her dad, Claire finds Tilly still awake in the kitchen. She does not tell her sister what happened with their father. She figures Tilly will be mad she went in the room at all.

"Want one?" Tilly asks, holding up a plate of brownies. "I baked them this morning."

Claire nods, so they migrate to the living room with their treats and settle on the couch. Her father's door looms in her periphery.

"Oh my God," Claire gushes after tasting the brownie. The sugar crystals of the gooey center dissolve on her tongue. "Not fair that I didn't get this gene."

"This was a product of nurture, not nature," Tilly says. There's an edge to her voice, like maybe she is offended that Claire has undercut her baking efforts.

Claire doesn't take the bait. Instead, she asks, "You got any wine? I could use a glass."

Tilly nods toward the kitchen, where Claire retrieves a malbec and two glasses and returns to the couch.

"It's so weird," she finally says. "Being here."

"Right?" Tilly agrees, and they both exhale. "I guess Peter and I always thought we would eventually move into this house, but we were happy in our tiny apartment by the marina, you know? We definitely didn't think we'd be moving in here while Dad was still alive."

Claire looks toward his bedroom. "It won't be weird for you when he dies?" she asks. "I mean, could you really sleep in that room?"

Tilly shakes her head. "We have plans to renovate. Nothing major or structural, mostly cosmetic," she says. "But still, enough that it will feel like our own. Although, yeah. It might be weird when the time comes. Since we didn't expect it to happen this way. I've spent a lot of hours in that room with Dad the past few months."

"Maybe we just sell," Claire says. "You guys can get a fresh start."

Tilly looks at her like she's speaking a foreign language. "Sell? I didn't... I don't want to do that. I love this house. And the location is amazing. Right on the beach."

"Yeah, sure," Claire says.

Annoyance claws at her chest. This should be a joint decision. If Tilly stays here, she will owe Claire half the value of the property. Claire can't afford to forfeit that money; she's a single mom living in one of the most expensive cities in the country.

But she can't start her trip by talking about inheritance. That's not why she's here. So she swallows her thoughts and shelves the conversation for another moment. Takes a long sip of her wine and feels the effects of it warm her cheeks.

"It's been pretty intense, I guess? With Dad?" Claire asks, picking at the crusty part of her brownie's edge.

Tilly blows out a puff of air. "Yeah. Mostly depressing. It's really hard watching him slowly disappear. You know? I mean, you hear horror stories about things dementia patients do, and luckily it hasn't been anything like that. Dad hasn't been violent or mean, he's just kinda... slipping away. Every day, there's less of him."

"Awful," Claire says. "And to be taking care of him on top of it. That's a lot for you."

"Full-time job without the pay," Tilly says. Her words are laced with acid.

Claire winces, then cocks her head to the side as if trying to work out an equation. "I told you I would contribute to putting him in a home or for more hours of care."

"Yeah," Tilly says, "you made it very clear you'd be fine with our father in a home. But no way could I have stomached that."

Claire snorts. "Yes, Tilly, how *immoral* of me to suggest Dad could live in a care facility like millions of other people."

"And as far as nurses go," Tilly continues, ignoring Claire's comment, "they're super-expensive and most don't even come out here to the Eastern Shore. Not regularly, anyway. Hospice care was hard enough to organize."

Tilly returns her attention to her brownie as the sisters sit in silence.

Finally, Claire sighs. "I'm sorry I'm so far away and can't help more."

"By choice," Tilly says quietly.

"What?"

Tilly sips her malbec and tries to backtrack, waving her comment off as unimportant. "I'm just saying, you living in Los Angeles is a choice."

Ah, yes. Here it is. The refrain Claire tired of years ago. The subtle and not-so-subtle jabs and jokes about her big-city life. The judgment of her escape. As if those who stay on the Eastern Shore assume she must look down on them, so they need to preempt her judgment with their own.

"Yes. A choice," she says. "Los Angeles is where I choose to live. I'm not sure where you're going with this point?"

"No, it just . . . sounds nice." Tilly says these words into her glass.

"You have a choice too," Claire says.

Tilly raises one shoulder. "No, I don't. Not *really*. Who would take care of Dad if I left?"

"And now we're back full circle. Because I would say we can put him somewhere."

"*Put* him somewhere, like he's—I don't know—a stray cat or something!" Tilly whisper-yells this, as if their dad might hear from his room.

And then, suddenly, Tilly is crying. Soft tears that flow effortlessly. When she reaches a hand up to wipe them away, Claire's heart breaks a little. But she also finds these tears annoying, frankly. Tilly acts like her life is already written for her. Like she is perpetually at the whims of everyone else. And she has done this since childhood.

Stuck between empathy and exasperation, Claire sits, paralyzed, watching her sister cry.

"Sorry," Tilly says, pressing her palms to her eyes to stop the flow. "It's like all my feelings are *right here* these days." She holds her hands in front of her face. "Right at the surface. The tiniest little thing can set me off."

"You don't have to apologize," Claire says, still physically a block of stone.

"I just can't believe he's dying." Tilly stares at her fingers.

This softens Claire. "Me neither," she admits. She is not accustomed to witnessing such emotion from her sister, and it makes her profoundly grateful that Tilly has Peter. That she hasn't been doing this alone.

When they were teenagers, Peter spent half his days with the sisters. It started one summer when his father, a contractor, worked on the Fern house. At first, Peter came to help, but after the work was done, he just kept coming until he became like a surrogate brother. He was at the house so often that Claire's mother bought groceries for four kids instead of three.

At least, she did until Gabby disappeared.

It happened two summers after Peter started coming over, shortly after Gabby turned eighteen. Their family unraveled at the seams, and many of their friendships fell apart too. Including the friendship with Peter. Or that's what Claire assumed, anyway. Until she got a call from Tilly about ten years ago, when they were both still in their twenties.

"Peter and I are together," she said over the phone. Her voice was even, as if she were telling Claire she had replaced an old car.

"Like, *together*-together?" Claire asked.

Tilly murmured an *mm-hmm*. "Don't make it weird," she said.

Claire resented that. As if she were unreasonable for finding it strange that the boy whom they'd known since adolescence was now permanently fucking her sister.

Tilly's voice interrupts her thoughts. "You talk to Mom recently?"

"Mom's still alive?" Claire deadpans.

Tilly frowns. "It's messed up. They were together for thirty-some years. Don't you think she should care how Dad's doing? Check in every once in a while?"

"Don't you think she should care how *we're* doing? Her *daughters*?"

Tilly shakes her head. "Good point. She never did like talking about the hard stuff, huh?"

"That's the understatement of the year." Claire snorts. Their English mother was never one to show her emotions. Or have any sort of reflective conversation.

Claire refills her wineglass.

"You and Peter," she says. "You guys are doing well? Is he okay with all this?" She gestures around the room to indicate their living situation.

Tilly shrugs. "It's not ideal. But you know how much he loves Dad." She hesitates, then pretends to be interested in inspecting her nails.

"What is it?" Claire asks.

Tilly looks up, her eyes filling again with tears. She opens her mouth as if she's about to admit something, but then she closes it again and shakes her head. "I'm just tired," she says, pointing to her tear-stricken face. "Obviously."

A classic Fern-family move: Dismiss the emotion and write it off as exhaustion.

"Yeah," Claire says. "Me too."

"Let's get to bed, then."

And there's one brief second when both sisters pause, as if they know this is their chance to step into something deeper, to find a real sense of connection after all the missed opportunities over the years.

But they don't.

Instead, they let the moment pass. And Claire just nods. Because being back in this house has rewound her emotional intelligence to that of a teenager.

As tired as Claire is, she can't sleep.

Julia has been moving around on the mattress like a buoy bobbing in the ocean, flipping from one side to the other. At this moment, her head is where her feet should be.

Claire is on her back, staring at the ceiling. A small crack of light comes from the bathroom to her left, where Tilly has installed a unicorn nightlight for Julia. To her right is the small alcove with the window that overlooks the backyard. Bright moonlight shines through, and Claire can make out the tops of trees from where she lies. A bat squiggles through the air, then disappears into the night. Claire is momentarily transported. It's as if this very second could be any of the ones she has already lived, staring at the ceiling unable to quiet her overworked mind.

She grabs her phone from the nightstand, opens up a web browser, and types *dementia end-of-life timeline* into the search bar.

Confused about place, time, or people . . . Pulse speeds up or slows down . . . Sleeps most of the time . . . Is restless . . .

Claire frowns. This contradictory information is useless. Does the pulse speed up or slow down? Are they restless or exhausted?

She's about to open a mindless social media app when she hears something. A whisper? Her limbs instinctively freeze, even though logically she knows it must be Julia.

"What, sweetie?" she asks quietly.

Claire props herself up on her forearms to get a better look at Julia, whose head is still at the opposite end of the bed. But her daughter doesn't move. She must have been talking in her sleep. Claire lies back down to scroll through her phone.

And then there it is again. Except now the noise is slightly more distinct. A hollow sound.

Thup. Thup. Thup.

"Hello?" she whispers into the dark. "Tilly?"

Is someone standing outside the room? She watches for moving shadows in the small crack beneath the door, but she sees only darkness.

Claire lies impossibly still, her body on high alert. The noise is gone now, but her mind is convincing her of terrible things. She won't be able to sleep until she checks the house.

She slowly climbs out of the bed and adjusts her pillows to

protect Julia from falling. Then she very carefully pries the door open. The hinges squeak in the same spot they always have, and Claire winces, swiveling her head to ensure she hasn't woken Julia. But the girl doesn't react.

Claire pads through the playroom and considers her next move. She could walk up through the hall toward Tilly's room, or she could descend the back stairs to the sunroom and kitchen.

Before she can decide, she hears a clattering downstairs. The tinny sound of what might be a fork dropping in the sink. Her heart hammers as her feet carry her toward the narrow staircase. She descends slowly, muscle memory working to carefully avoid the creaky step halfway down. And then she sees the silhouette of a figure in the kitchen.

She inhales sharply. Then narrows her eyes, trying to make out who it is. Too tall to be Tilly. Too thin to be Peter. Claire reaches the bottom of the stairs and crosses to the kitchen.

"Dad?" she says. Her voice cracks.

The figure turns, and Claire sees his face. It's ghoulish in the moonlight from the windows. His eyes are sunken, his eyebrows unruly, their long white hairs sticking out in all directions. The skin on his face is wrinkled and loose, highlighting his recent weight loss. His large nose is slightly purple, and his thin lips are surrounded by short white facial hair. Something about the shadowy dark of the kitchen makes his ears look abnormally large.

"Dad?" Claire says again. "It's me."

He stares at her blankly. And then Claire sees what he holds in his hands: a pair of extra-large kitchen shears.

"What are you—" she starts, taking a step toward him.

The sudden movement startles him, and he recoils, holding the sharp shears in front of his chest defensively.

"Not any closer," he says. His voice is raspy, as if it's hard for him to get out the words.

"Dad," she says, holding up her hands in surrender. "What are you doing with those?"

He looks at the shears as if he forgot they were in his hands. And then he seems to remember his task. He returns to the sink, bends over the edge, and maneuvers the shears so the sharp blades are on either side of his left wrist.

As if he is about to cut off his entire hand.

"Dad!" Claire shouts, lunging forward.

The large scissors slip and slice a shallow cut into her father's forearm. His skin tears like weathered tissue paper, frail and thin. Blood trails quickly down his arm to his elbow and the floor below.

"Oh God," Claire says, picking up a tea towel and pressing it against his wound.

"I have to cut it out," he says, pulling away from her.

"Dad," she says, trying to keep her voice calm, "you're bleeding. We need to put pressure on it."

"I have to cut it out!" he shouts.

She shakes her head and narrows her eyes. "Cut *what* out?"

A stillness overcomes him, and he leans into her. His eyes dart around, ensuring the two of them are alone. And then he whispers in her ear, his breath hot against her neck.

"The Devil."

"He was about to cut off his fucking hand!" Claire whisper-shouts.

She is in the foyer with Peter. They have finally settled her father back into bed after much wrestling.

The commotion of her dad's outburst and subsequent injury woke Peter upstairs. Claire was relieved when he showed up in the kitchen. She's not sure how she would have contained her father without him.

"I don't understand," Peter says, sighing and rubbing his eyes. "He's never done anything like that."

Claire throws up her hands. "It was terrifying, Peter. He looked so disturbed, and then the blood..."

Words fail her as she replays the scene in her head. Peter reaches out, wraps his arms around her, and pulls her close. The gesture, while well meaning, is a remnant of another time. A time when they knew each other. Now, it feels stilted and awkward. They both sense it and pull apart only a moment later.

"So, what do we do?" Claire asks.

"What do you mean?"

"About Dad. What do we do now?"

Peter raises one eyebrow. "Well, it's two in the morning, so right now I think we go back to bed. He's calm in there. Asleep again."

Claire juts her chin forward and widens her eyes. "So that's it?"

"Look," Peter says, sighing, "he's never done that before."

"You mentioned."

"So I don't think we need to worry about it. He probably had a bad dream or something. We'll work it out tomorrow, okay?"

Claire's insides squirm.

After her brother-in-law returns upstairs, Claire spends an hour in the kitchen gathering every knife, pair of scissors, and wine opener she can find. Anything that could act like a blade. She places them all on a high shelf of the pantry beside the double ovens.

She spots the bloody shears glinting in the sink. Dread hollows her gut as she goes to work cleaning them, scrubbing harder than needed. She watches as the small amount of dark red swirls in the stainless-steel basin before slipping into the drain.

Claire again checks the locks of every door downstairs and then notices that the same window in the kitchen is unlatched again. Her father must have opened it. She closes it, secures the lock, and tests it three times before finally heading upstairs. When she quietly slips into bed beside Julia, she notices that the girl's body has moved again so that her head is back to the right place on the pillow.

The next morning, Claire sits at the kitchen table with Julia as the girl munches on crispy bacon and sips orange juice. Watching her daughter drink from an open cup is like waiting for a grenade to pop; any moment, the sticky substance could be all over her daughter and the floor.

Tilly joins them at the kitchen table with her own plate of food. "You don't want anything?" she asks Claire.

"Not much of an appetite."

Tilly nods. "Still upset about last night? Peter said you were pretty shaken."

"Uh, yeah," Claire says. She nods toward Julia, indicating she can't go into detail right now. "It was awful."

Claire had wanted to recap with both Peter and her sister, but Peter is already working in the upstairs office. He has some kind of engineering job that Claire doesn't understand. He secured it while in college in mainland Virginia, where he and Tilly both went. Once he moved back to the Eastern Shore, he was able to convince the company he could work remotely, so he crosses the bridge only once a week for meetings.

"I want a braid," Julia says with a mouthful of bacon.

"Okay," Claire says, seeing this as an opportunity. "Can you go upstairs and get the brush and hair ties?"

Julia nods excitedly and runs through the sunroom up the steps.

Claire turns to her sister. "How is Dad today?"

Tilly shrugs. "He seems fine. Same as usual."

"Tilly, this was—I mean, if I hadn't—I honestly think he would have hurt himself really badly—"

"I couldn't find the knives when I was making breakfast," Tilly interrupts. "Did you hide them?"

"In the pantry," Claire says, pointing. "I had to. I couldn't sleep unless I knew the sharp stuff was out of reach."

Tilly nods slowly. Clearly, something is on her mind.

"What?" Claire asks, her voice snippy.

"Nothing," Tilly says lightly. "Makes sense."

Claire wants to ask more but is distracted by Tilly's fingers grazing the charm of her necklace. It's a gold cable-link chain with a small firefly pendant, a bright emerald gemstone for the bug's light.

"You still wear that?" Claire asks.

Tilly nods and tucks the necklace under her shirt. "Every day."

Claire has one too, but it's back home in a drawer. Their mother got the three sisters matching necklaces one year for Christmas. She said the firefly charms reminded her of when they were little and spent summer nights catching fireflies. The sisters had oohed and aahed over the emeralds. For a long time, they never took the necklaces off.

Claire doesn't remember exactly when she stopped wearing hers. She only knows at some point it became a burden, feeling that chain around her neck, a constant reminder of what she had lost.

Gabby went missing two weeks after she turned eighteen. Bad luck, really. If she had still been a minor, the police would have been legally obligated to care. Instead, since Gabby was known locally as an outspoken, rebellious teenager, most people accepted she had run away. And that wasn't an altogether crazy theory—Gabby couldn't wait to get the hell out of Cape Chase. And once Gabby was gone, Claire felt the same way. Or maybe she felt a subconscious duty to carry out her sister's dream. The truth was, Claire always loved the Shore. But after Gabby, she had to leave.

She wonders if Tilly still blames her. After all, Claire was the only one home when Gabby disappeared. Tilly and their parents were in Virginia Beach at one of Tilly's dance competitions. Eventually, when it became clear that Gabby was not coming back, all eyes turned to Claire. What signs had she missed? What was she not telling them? Surely she must know *something*.

But really, it was just another weekend. Claire and Gabby hardly crossed paths; Claire was in tech rehearsals for the community theater show opening that week, and Gabby was working at the local ice cream shop. They saw each other only once, when Claire complained of Gabby's smell: She reeked of the too-sweet birthday-cake flavor. It was a short conversation.

Short, but loaded, she thinks.

Claire shakes her head. She has worked hard to forget those last words exchanged with Gabby. The ones she has never told anyone.

"So who do we call about Dad?" she asks, forcing herself back to the present.

"Call?" Tilly says. "There's no one to call, really. I mean, I'll tell his nurse what happened when she comes for her shift."

"I'm confused," Claire blurts out. "Dad tried to cut off his own hand last night, and you and Peter are acting like it's nothing."

"We're not acting like it's nothing," Tilly says. "But we've been dealing with Dad for a long time."

"Peter said he's never done something like this before."

"Well, no, he hasn't," Tilly says. Her voice is pointed.

Claire furrows her brows. "I can make some phone calls today. I have the time, and I think it's important we get him assessed."

"Jesus, Claire, you just got here. Let it rest, okay? We've got this."

TURN OFF THE LIGHT

Claire gapes. Her sister clearly has *not* "got this." But before she can say as much, Julia comes bounding down the stairs.

"Braid now, Mama?"

Claire nods as frustration tugs at the edges of her awareness. She is not overreacting, though of course that's what her sister thinks. But if she pushes it, she'll come off as too intense. Yet another thing Tilly has accused her of being over the years.

After Gabby's disappearance, Claire and Tilly adopted new roles in an altered family dynamic. Claire was the control freak who shaped her life around the desperate need to keep things from falling apart again. And Tilly became the people pleaser. The one who had to hold the boat steady and even.

So Claire swallows her words and plays her part, thinking that maybe this is the definition of *family:* a complex web of patterns that its members are doomed to repeat indefinitely.

5
EDITH

Edith sits by the window until the sun rises. When David wakes, she is already building up the fire.

"I'll tend to Jacob's crop first thing, before it gets hotter," David says. "You can pack my breakfast."

"Shouldn't I come?" Edith asks. "To replenish his boneset. I also wanted to try some joe-pye weed for the fever."

"Pack them," David says curtly. "I'll take them with me."

Edith tilts her head. "But I should advise about the dosage. And prepare the tea."

"I'm sure Grace is capable of brewing tea," David says, his voice clipped. "I'm minding Jacob's crop, but I need you here. I'm sorry the man is sick, but I can't let my own house fall apart in the meanwhile."

His protests are strange, perhaps even misplaced. Edith does not understand. But then, she rarely does.

She packs his breakfast of salted meat and bread alongside the medicinal herbs. She instructs him on how much goes into a cup and how long it should steep, but he is barely listening.

TURN OFF THE LIGHT

"Has Goodman Ward seen Jacob?" David asks. "Last I heard, he was in King's Creek. Someone should fetch him."

Edith deflates. Goodman Ward is the closest apothecary. Her husband's implication is clear: He does not believe her herbal remedies to be sufficient in easing their neighbor's sickness.

Lately, David has been downplaying Edith's knowledge even more than usual. When they first met, he himself fell ill. He grudgingly drank her teas and used her salves, though he seemed genuinely surprised when they worked. But recently he referred to her herb gardening and drying and steeping as *hobbies*. He even warned her that these *musings* shouldn't get in the way of *the real work*. His words stung; he was not only belittling her gift but also reminding her that she now needed her husband's permission to do most anything.

Edith is realizing that perhaps she was not built for marriage. It feels like a too-tight corset that will slowly suffocate her.

Now she watches as David leaves the house with his pack and heads toward the woods. Her husband is right about one thing: She does have other work. A full day of tasks to tend to in his absence. The clothes need washing; the vegetable garden needs harvesting; the eggs need gathering. She must bake another batch of bread, and it is time to make more soap.

But she will do many of these things with resentment in her heart. She is a healer, so her duty is with her neighbors Jacob and Grace. What a waste that she be here kneading dough when she could be tending the man's fever and sore throat. Even if she believes he will not survive the week, she can make him more comfortable in his final days. And isn't that worth much more than a bar of soap?

Edith is sitting by the edge of the creek, her hands raw from the washing, when she hears a voice call out from behind her.

"Edie!"

It's a child's voice, and when Edith turns, she sees Violet, her twelve-year-old neighbor to the north. She is the oldest of six brothers and sisters and is prone to wandering the woods on her own.

"Morning, Violet," Edith replies. "Where is your skirt?"

The girl is wearing only her petticoats and a loose linen blouse. She points to a fallen log, atop which rests a heap of brown cloth.

"It's too hot!" she laments in dramatic fashion. "My skin is going to melt off."

Edith can't help but laugh. If Violet's mother saw her traipsing around in her petticoats, it would take the breath clean out of her, for she is a tight-lipped woman of tradition. But she is currently pregnant with her seventh child, so Edith doesn't imagine she will be coming through these woods anytime soon. It's at least a two-mile hike to their property from here, and she'd not likely make that trip without a very good reason.

"Please don't make me wear it," Violet says, sidling up near Edith and the washing. She slips her feet into the shallow water of the creek. "I could dunk my head in that basin, that's how hot I am." She points to the wooden bucket Edith is using to clean laundry. Bits of soap and dirt float atop the water's surface.

Edith thins her lips and raises an eyebrow. "I do not advise that."

Violet leans forward, smells the water in the basin, and scrunches her nose in disgust. "I shall refrain," she says, then sighs and pretends to faint to the ground.

Edith laughs. She has always felt more comfortable around children than adults, and she finds Violet's flair for the dramatic endearing. She imagines the girl is a natural performer, but she is also one of six, soon to be seven, siblings. To get any attention in that family must require some effort.

TURN OFF THE LIGHT

"Are you shirking your chores, miss?" Edith asks playfully, flicking water from her fingertips onto Violet's face.

Violet sputters and sits up. "I suppose so," she admits, her shoulders sagging. The girl pulls her feet in closer and rests her elbows on her knees, her chin on her hands. A portrait of childhood. "It's too hot for chores, Edie."

Calling Edith by her first name — and not even her full Christian name at that — is another habit of Violet's that would seize her mother's spirit. But what does Edith care about all those formalities? And she likes the girl, who feels more like a younger sister than anything. They are, after all, only nine years apart, given Edith's age of twenty-one.

"I agree," Edith says, wiping her wet hands on her apron. "The heat is unbearable today."

"It is unbearable *every* day," Violet whines. "The air is so thick, I could slice it with a hatchet."

"Well, let's not go swinging hatchets, okay?" Edith smiles.

"I hate it here," Violet says, her voice quieter, her eyes cast down. She throws a small pebble into the water.

Edith remembers telling her father something similar when she was young. This was before she found a sense of purpose through her aunt's teachings. Her father's eyes had flickered, as if her words had been personally aimed at him. Then he told her those kinds of thoughts were meant to remain *thoughts*. Unspoken.

Edith looks at Violet, whose eyes are still trained on the creek. Sweat slicks her dark brown hair to her temples and neck; the long, braided pigtails hang limp. The girl's features are still soft like a child's, the gentle slope of her nose and the plump bump of her chin. But even at her young age, she shows signs of stress; there are dark hollows carved beneath her eyes.

"If you hate it here," Edith says, her voice soft, "where would you rather be?"

Violet looks up excitedly, as if no one has asked her this before. "Ooh, well, England, of course! London. The bustling city. Can you imagine?"

Edith snorts. "Have a talk with Grace about London."

The stories Grace has shared make it obvious that much of life abroad has been glamorized. Grace had been eager to embark on a new adventure in the colonies. Maybe, though, she would say something different now.

"Grace was an orphan, Edie." Violet dismisses the argument with the confidence of the naive. "Of *course* she wanted to leave. I'm talking about living on the grand estates. Wearing beautiful dresses and having conversations over tea with intellectuals."

Edith raises an eyebrow. "We've shared a pot of tea. What are you saying about my intellectual abilities?"

Violet rolls her eyes, annoyed. "You know what I mean," she says, drawing out the *n* sound for emphasis.

Edith laughs. "I do. I do know what you mean."

Violet smiles and returns to the visions in her mind. "Or if not London, maybe somewhere tropical."

Edith points to Violet's exposed petticoats. "Could you handle the heat of the islands?" she jokes.

Violet frowns. "That's different."

Edith briefly allows herself to imagine a life so unlike her own. A break from the harsh winters and disease-ridden summers of the Eastern Shore.

"It can be nice to think about sometimes," Edith says. "Escape. Adventure. Maybe one day you can go to those places."

"Do you think?" Violet asks as if Edith is proposing a trip to the moon.

"Well, why not?" Edith wrings out the last of the wash and dumps the water from the bucket into the shrubs. She directs Violet to help her hang the items on branches.

As the girl arranges a pair of breeches on a sunny spot, she says, "Mother teaches me how to cook and clean. I know how to make honey cakes. But what does that really matter?"

"I suppose if you want a family someday," Edith says, "it matters a great deal."

"But what if I don't?" Violet asks. She speaks the words carefully. "See, you have something *beyond* all that. You have your herbs and you can make sick people healthy again."

"Not always."

Violet flips one of her long braids behind her shoulder. "You know things! Things that matter. You don't even need to have babies."

Edith's breath catches in her chest. Violet may be a child, but she is astute; she already senses that her worth as a woman will be wrapped up in her ability to procreate. Already wonders if she could hold value beyond her reproductive organs.

As badly as Edith wants to agree with these statements, she cannot. It would make her a hypocrite. She has spent the past day obsessed with the idea of her infertility. A fear is growing within her that she will not measure up to society's expectations. That she will be seen as disposable.

She thinks again of David's comments this morning. His suggestion that Jacob and Grace consult the apothecary. His dismissing her healing abilities as a mere hobby.

And then she feels something. A small ember burning in the bottom of her gut. Like a forgotten dream that has been awakened.

"You really are interested in what I do?" she asks.

"Oh, yes, very much," Violet says, her eyes widening. Then she hesitates, slowly pushing a loose hair behind her ear. "Remember when my sister Aria was born?"

Edith does remember. This was five years ago, when Aunt Joan was still alive and toted Edith along on her healing visits. Violet's mother fell very ill during childbirth.

"We were afraid your mother would die," Edith says quietly.

Violet nods. "I was only seven, but I remember feeling so helpless. All I could do was watch. But *you*. You knew what to do." She sucks in her breath and then releases it as if sighing out the hurt and starting over. "If something like that were to happen again . . . well, I do not wish to be helpless next time."

Edith looks at the girl and smiles. "It's settled, then," she says. "I shall teach you about medicinal herbs."

6
CLAIRE

Claire sits on the couch in the sunroom and directs her daughter to stand in front of her. "There are a lot of knots," she warns, "but I have to brush them out if you want a braid."

"Okay." Julia sighs. She rarely has the patience for Claire to properly brush her hair.

To their right, floor-to-ceiling windows look out on the backyard and wooden path that leads to the beach. The bright blue sky is speckled with cotton-ball clouds.

Silverware clinking in the kitchen sink draws Claire's attention. The same sound she heard last night. She shudders.

"Leave the dishes," she calls to her sister, who is bent over the faucet. Claire can see her over the counter that divides the two rooms. "I'll do them when I'm finished."

Tilly turns off the water and dries her hands on a striped dish towel. "You sure?"

"Of course," Claire says. "Sit. Have your coffee while it's still hot."

Tilly refreshes her cup and joins them in the sunroom. She sits at the very edge of the armchair like a bird perching momentarily, ever ready for flight.

"Ow, Mama," Julia says. She grabs her hair and holds it. "That hurts."

Claire rubs her daughter's shoulder in apology. "Sorry," she whispers.

"Why is there a door in the floor?" Julia asks.

Claire stops the brush midway down the girl's head. "What?"

Tilly leans forward. "Are you talking about the cellar? In the living room?"

Julia nods. Claire puts a hand on each of her daughter's shoulders and spins the girl so she is facing her.

"Never go down there," she says sternly. "Never, ever. Okay?"

Julia nods again, slowly. "Okay. Why?"

"It's not safe." Claire grits her teeth and spins the girl back again. She brushes too intensely, and Julia complains.

Tilly smiles. "Your mom has always been scared of the cellar," she tells Julia with a wink.

Claire shoots her sister a look, but Tilly pretends not to see it.

"Why?" Julia asks.

"Because it's not safe," Claire repeats again, preempting any response from Tilly. "Auntie Gabby got stuck down there for three hours one time. You don't want to get stuck down there, right?"

Julia shakes her head adamantly.

The girl knows very little of Gabby. Claire has regaled her with stories of her sister's loud personality and fearless confidence, but she has not told Julia details of what happened. Only that they don't know where Gabby is.

"So, the nurse is coming by today?" Claire asks Tilly, keen to change the subject.

"Should be," Tilly says. "But she hasn't confirmed yet."

TURN OFF THE LIGHT

Claire's eyes remain fixed on her hands, busy braiding. "We should reach out. In case Dad needs an adjustment in his meds or something after last night. I can do it if you give me her number."

Tilly stares into her coffee mug as if it has suddenly become interesting, seemingly steeling herself. Then she stands and flits out of the room. "I'll do it," she says on her way out, her voice thin.

Claire weaves sections of Julia's hair together. She is reminded of her own childhood, when her dad would braid her wet hair after the shower. His hands were firm but gentle, working through the slippery, well-conditioned strands with ease. She always kept her hair long, maybe as a subconscious way of preserving the memory of that ritual between them, though these days it's usually pulled into some version of messy bun on top of her head.

"Mama," Julia says. "Is Auntie Gabby in the stars?"

Claire inhales so abruptly that she chokes on her own spit.

"You okay, Mama?" the girl asks, turning so that Claire can see the genuine concern furrowing her brows.

Claire secures the hair tie at the bottom of the braid and takes a deep breath. "I'm okay," she says. "I just — well, to answer your question, we don't know if Auntie Gabby is in the stars or not."

"It's a secret?" Julia asks.

Claire chews the inside of her lip. "Kind of like that."

"Why does she keep it a secret?"

Claire smiles a little, then sighs. "I wish I knew," she admits.

"I'm not allowed in the cellar," Julia says, shaking her head as she repeats the instructions from moments ago.

"That's right," Claire agrees. "Not safe."

Julia nods. "Auntie Gabby got trapped down there. So we don't go in the cellar. Nope. Not safe."

Claire remembers finding Gabby. They'd all assumed she was out with friends because it was the night after her eighteenth birthday.

But when Claire was tasked with getting something from the cellar, she opened the trapdoor to find Gabby huddled on the floor, shivering despite the heat. Her eyes got wide when she saw Claire.

"A kid," Gabby said, terrified. "A ghost."

Gabby was always pulling pranks on her sisters, so Claire didn't believe her. Not *really*. But she'd never liked the cellar anyway, so this solidified its creepiness for her, whether warranted or not.

As Claire reflects on that moment now, though, she can't help but think that the fear in Gabby's eyes then matched the fear in her father's expression last night.

Surely she is reading into things.

"Let's go see if Grandpa is awake, okay?" she says to her daughter.

Julia frowns. "But I wanna wear my dress."

Claire smiles. Her father has always complimented Julia on her sense of style, which is already becoming something unique and bold. He loves her combinations of flower prints with rainbow stripes, shiny cowboy boots with bright leggings and a tutu. Before, when they FaceTimed more regularly, he would remind Julia never to lose that spirit, that fearlessness to be so authentically herself.

"All right, you can change first," Claire says. "And then we'll see if Grandpa is awake."

Claire is eager to see her father in the daylight. She is not sure if he even recognized her last night. A part of her is nervous for Julia to be in the same room with him in case he becomes violent again, but she pushes the thought aside. Claire will be in the room too, and anyway, the whole reason they are here is to spend time with him.

As Julia runs upstairs to change her clothes, Claire's gaze flicks to the small table next to the couch on top of which rest her father's bird book and binoculars. Just outside the window are two large bird feeders and a fountain. He became an avid watcher soon after

Gabby's disappearance. He loved to go for long walks with a list, checking off names of the birds he saw.

Claire and Tilly used to tease him for his newfound hobby, ribbing him that it was for old people. But one day early on, their mother watched him wistfully from the window as he headed out alone. She shook her head when the girls laughed.

"I understand why he likes it," she said. Then she looked right at her remaining daughters. "He gets to search for things he can actually find."

Claire pries her eyes away from the bird book and sits back on the couch. She thinks again of last night, of her father's hunched figure, his hot breath on her neck as his strained voice whispered in her ear. What did he mean when he said he needed to cut the Devil out?

A hand grabs Claire's arm, and she yelps.

"Sorry, Mama," Julia says. She is wearing a soft long dress. A slip-on princess gown that is designed to be pajamas but that she insists on wearing almost daily.

"That's okay," Claire says, clutching her heart. "You just scared me."

"That's because I'm a monster!" Julia says, holding her fingers up like claws.

"Oh, no! A monster!" Claire squeals, grabs Julia, and slips her onto the couch, where she tickles her neck and armpits. "What have you done with my daughter?"

Julia screams and laughs and giggles, dissolving into pure childhood pleasure.

Claire's dad is awake when she enters with Julia, and he looks even more frail in the daylight. He nods slightly when he sees them, but there is no recognition in his eyes.

"Hi, Dad," Claire says. "Julia is here too."

The girl hides behind her mother's legs, but Claire keeps her eyes on her father. His gaze flicks toward the nightstand.

"Water?" she asks, pointing to the large hospital cup with a straw. "You want some water?"

She moves forward while Julia stays back. Claire grips the water cup by the handle and gently puts a hand behind her dad's back to help him sit up. He brings the straw to his lips, where two crusty sores have appeared. She didn't notice them in the frenzy of last night.

"That's all you want?" she asks when he pulls away.

He does not respond, so she returns the cup to the table. He seems worse today, if that's possible. His movements are stilted, like he has forgotten the choreography necessary to move his muscles. It hits Claire that she is too late. She has missed any meaningful chance to say goodbye. Her throat feels full, like she's going to cry. Or maybe puke.

She looks at Julia, who has retreated to the door. "You want to come over?" Claire asks.

Her daughter shakes her head and leans against the dresser as if she doesn't have the strength to stand on her own. One of the telltale markers that Julia is feeling vulnerable.

Claire's gaze travels to the window on the other side of the room. In front of it sits the blue corduroy armchair that softly creaks when it rocks. Her father used to sit there every night reading before bed; the arms where his elbows rested are worn to threads.

"Mama?" Julia asks, pointing to her grandfather with wide eyes.

The man's expression has changed. He seems fearful. He is sitting straighter now, his body shaking, and he points at the mirror directly across from him.

"No!" he says. "No, no! Get out!" He's shouting, his voice frantic and fraying at the edges.

"Dad?" Claire says. "Dad, it's okay."

She tries to lay a hand on his arm, but he bats her away and then turns to her. Where only seconds ago his eyes were filled with fear, now they glow with anger.

"Get him out!" he shouts, pointing again toward the mirror.

Claire turns out of instinct, but of course the only reflections in the mirror are herself and her father.

"I don't like it," Julia whines from the doorway.

"Go to the kitchen," Claire tells her. The girl shouldn't have to see her grandpa like this. "Go get your markers. I'll come draw with you at the table in one second, okay?"

Julia hesitates, but when Claire nods, her daughter slips out of the room.

"Get him out!" her dad says again. "Get the Devil out!"

Claire grabs one of the fluffy polyester blankets from the end of his bed. It's peach and looks like something he probably bought at Costco. She throws the blanket over the mirror so that her father's reflection is covered.

Almost immediately, he turns his attention to his hands, and his body calms again. Claire sighs. She thinks about sitting on the edge of his bed but worries it will make him nervous since he doesn't recognize her. But then, isn't this the very reason she is here? To be with him. To remind him he is loved.

She maneuvers herself onto the mattress near his hip. Then she places her hand next to him on the bed, palm up. An invitation.

They sit like this for a while. Claire keeps her hand there as she gazes out the window that overlooks the front yard and driveway. She remembers how, at Christmastime every year, these windows would be blocked by the inflatable Santa and Grinch and snowmen that her father put up as decorations. They would reflect the colorful lights that hung from the roof, lighting up her parents' bedroom like magic. The perfect spot to cuddle and watch holiday movies.

Just then, Claire feels her father's hand in her own. When she turns, he is looking at her, and the corner of his lip twitches slightly like he's trying to smile. When his daughters were growing up, he used to squeeze their hands three times, his way of saying *I love you*. He used to tell them: "Three squeezes for the words, three squeezes for my girls."

Remembering this, Claire squeezes his hand three times, but he does not respond. No squeezes in return.

Her tears come freely now. Her dad was always so capable, self-taught in so many regards. Curious and independent and driven. When she looks at him now, he seems to have been stripped of his identity. What remains is not him, just some poorly drawn rendition of him. A replica that misses the mark.

Suddenly self-conscious, she wipes her tears with her free hand. As she does, her father scratches at the bandage Peter applied to last night's cut. His forehead wrinkles in confusion at the gauze.

This feels like an opportunity. A window into her father's thinking. "You cut yourself last night," she says, pointing to the bandage. "Do you remember?"

He stares at her, eyes wide and blank.

"You went into the kitchen, Dad. Remember? Why did you pick up those shears? Why were you going to hurt yourself?"

Even as she pushes, she knows she shouldn't provoke him. But she can't help it. She needs to know what was going through his mind. What he meant when he whispered in her ear.

TURN OFF THE LIGHT

"And just now," she continues, "with the mirror. What did you mean when you said it was the Devil?"

For the first time, a flicker of recognition crosses his face. He opens his mouth and speaks, his voice dry and crackly.

"Don't drink the tea," he tells her.

Claire finds Julia drawing at the kitchen table. "Where's Aunt Tilly?" she asks.

Julia shrugs but doesn't lift her gaze from the paper. She continues to draw as if in a trance. Claire is used to this; her daughter adores coloring.

Claire pours herself a cup of coffee with a generous splash of milk. Then she leans against the counter to get her bearings.

The kitchen, like the rest of the house, has its quirks. Even though it has been renovated and modernized over the years, old bits remain. The low ceiling with exposed beams sags slightly. Beside the refrigerator is an old dumbwaiter shaft, permanently sealed. A floorboard near the pantry always pops up like an open mouth, as if the house itself needs to breathe. Claire figures this is from years of warping due to humidity.

She pops her knee and bounces her leg as she stands. Presses her thumbnail into the pad of her index finger. Replays her father's words in her mind on a loop. Last night could have been a one-off, a bad dream like Peter suggested. But how would that explain today's outburst? He mentioned the Devil again. And this was no dream; he was wide awake.

"Mama, do you like it?" Julia calls from the kitchen table. She holds up her drawing.

Claire sets down her coffee and moves to the table to see her daughter's artwork. It's a geometric flowerlike pattern with a circle around it. Like a wheel. Julia has decorated it with every color of the rainbow, but the drawing still turns Claire's blood cold.

"I told you not to go in the cellar," she says, her voice icy.

Julia frowns and bites her lip. "I didn't, Mama."

Claire picks up the picture and makes her way to the living room. There, she sees the trapdoor wide open. Livid, she turns to her daughter. "You have to *listen* to me!" she shouts. "I told you it's *not safe* down there!"

Claire hurries over and is about to close the trapdoor when she suddenly feels compelled to descend. A need to confirm what she already knows: that her daughter's drawing is a carbon copy of what waits down there.

"Stay back," she calls to Julia.

She flicks on the light, an exposed bulb hanging from a frayed wire. It flashes once, twice, then settles into a low yellow glow. Shadows hang in the corners like cobwebs. She hesitates before making her way down the uneven stone steps that have been worn smooth in the center from centuries of foot traffic. The air immediately shifts. It's different down here. Cooler, but also heavier, like the house is holding its breath.

Halfway down the steps on the wall to the left are irregular black soot stains. At the bottom, she looks up at the blackened wooden beams. Some of the wood down here has been replaced, but not the large center beam; it's much older than the others, its underside charred.

Evidence of a fire.

As a child, she asked her mother what happened down here and when. Her mom had only shrugged. "Old houses hide old stories."

The floor is mostly packed earth. There's an old drain in the center covered by a rusted iron grate and water stains along the base of the far wall. Around the edges, the stone foundation is exposed in places, irregular and blotched with lichen.

Claire spins so she is facing the steps, then again looks up at the center beam, which dominates the ceiling, thick and dark with age. Newer wood crisscrosses above it, but the beam itself is ancient, blackened and split. Its charred underside seems to swallow the light. In the wood on the side farther from the entrance, exactly as she remembered, is a small carving. Miraculously unburned, though the wood all around it is entirely scorched. It's as if the fire tried to burn it but couldn't.

She holds up her daughter's drawing to compare it to the carved symbol.

The images are exactly the same.

Proof that Julia sneaked into the cellar. How else would she have known this design?

Claire stomps up the stone steps and shuts the trapdoor tight behind her. She finds Julia hiding behind the couch. The girl is crying, folded into herself, just like she always does when she feels guilty.

"Promise me," Claire says, still angry but trying to soften her voice, "that you won't go down there again."

Julia sucks on her bottom lip and avoids eye contact.

"Please, Julia. This is very important. You could get trapped. Promise me you will not go down there."

"I promise," the girl says quietly.

Before Claire can say anything else, Tilly appears from upstairs. "All good?" she asks tentatively, clearly picking up on the fraught energy in the room.

"Julia went in the cellar," Claire says.

"I didn't!" Julia cries.

Claire sighs loudly. "Let's not lie about it on top of everything else, please."

There is a charged moment of silence as Tilly and Claire share a look.

Eager to change the subject, Claire asks, "Did the nurse get back to you?"

"Not yet," Tilly says. "I was about to head to the grocery store."

"We'll go for you," Claire says quickly. She needs to get out of this house. An uneasiness is beginning to creep like ants under her skin. "Julia can pick some snacks."

The girl perks up a little at this suggestion.

"All right, then," Tilly says. "That'd be helpful, thanks."

Though there are smaller markets closer to town, Claire drives to the major chain store that is thirty minutes from the house. She needs the time away. Plus, there's a lower risk at the big store of running into anyone she knows. Or *knew*. The last thing she wants to do is muster small talk with one of her mother's old bridge partners.

Claire drums her fingers nervously on the steering wheel and tries to calm her mind. From the back seat, Julia says very quietly, "Sorry, Mama."

Claire finds her daughter's face in the rearview mirror. The girl's sad expression immediately softens her. "I know, sweetie," she says. "Thank you for saying that. I'm sorry I yelled. I just got scared."

Julia nods and looks out the window. Claire relaxes a little. Her daughter is four. She is bound to do stupid things. Especially when told not to. Hopefully she understands now that she cannot go in the cellar under any circumstance. And anyway, the novelty has worn off now that she's done it, right?

Claire's mind turns to her father. He is not a religious man. He has never believed in the Devil, never before even mentioned the word. So why now?

But then she sighs. She is reading too much into things. Her father has dementia. He doesn't know what he is saying. It's all word salad. And as much as she wants to believe he is still in there, his actions indicate otherwise.

She should have come sooner.

Claire knew he was bad, but it's another thing seeing it. Actually understanding how all-consuming this has been for her sister. Tilly must be even more resentful than Claire realized. And what about Peter? Yes, he loves their father, but this is next-level commitment. Surely not how he imagined life with Tilly.

"Are we going to a playground?" Julia asks from the back seat.

The roads are practically empty, a stark contrast to Los Angeles. She waits at a red light with no other cars in sight.

"No playground, love," Claire says. "We have to get groceries, remember? For Aunt Tilly."

"Oh, and snacks!"

"That's right." Claire smiles. But guilt gnaws at her. Julia needs exercise. The travel has worn on them both. She decides if they pass a playground on the way, she'll stop.

But of course, they do not pass any playgrounds. In fact, they pass practically nothing. A gas station, a fish market that might or might not be abandoned, a weathered sign advertising a music festival that happened two years ago.

"When we get home," Claire says, "we'll do something fun, okay? Maybe we can go to the beach."

Julia frowns. "I don't want to go to the beach," she whines.

"Okay, then, we don't have to."

Claire knows how this game goes. There's no point playing into her daughter's exasperation. Better to let it run its course. Julia will likely feel different in an hour — or even in three minutes.

After parking, Claire looks up at the large blue letters of the store's name against the worn brown bricks of the building. Being back here, especially with her daughter in tow, gives her a sense of déjà vu. She came here countless times with her own mother. She remembers buying flowers here for Tilly's big dance performances. Remembers the summer she took a job as a bagger and then swore to herself she'd never work in customer service again. She even had her first kiss near the dumpsters around back, which is something she wishes she could forget. The location, anyway. The kiss was fine.

As Claire walks through the parking lot, her daughter's small hand in hers, she imagines her younger self walking just behind her. As if her shadow is the version of her from twenty years ago. Ever present, looming over her shoulder, following her around every turn to remind her of how much she has changed —

And how much she hasn't.

7
EDITH

Edith walks south along the shoreline. She is headed for Reeve's place, the local trading spot where she acquires tools for her healing practice.

She has been invigorated by the idea of teaching Violet. The locals turn to her only in times of need; they rarely acknowledge her talents unless it is relevant to their own health. So Violet's enthusiasm has awakened something in Edith. To be able to share what she knows, to have an eager and willing audience as she talks about the plants and their effects, is rare.

They walked together for an hour as Edith pointed out plants and told stories from her own childhood. Violet watched her with awe and curiosity, newly awake to the possibilities of what she could do and what her mind could accomplish in this lifetime.

When Edith was a girl and first expressed an interest in healing, her aunt Joan gifted her a soapstone mortar and pestle. The moment she got it, Edith ran her fingers over the visible wear patterns. She noted its dark patina from constant use. The history of the thing made it more special; this mortar and pestle had saved lives long before it landed in her hands.

And now she has decided to carry on that tradition for Violet.

She finds Reeve bent over his rustic table, a worn plank balanced on two old barrels. He wears his trusty wide-brimmed hat and pushes it out of his line of sight when he hears her approach. He stands to his full height, which must be more than six feet. His skin is weathered and thick like leather; a long scar runs from his left ear to the corner of his mouth.

"Goody Harris," he says, bending his head toward her.

"Afternoon, Reeve," she replies. "I have something for you." She reaches into her sack and pulls out a jar of red-tinged oil made from the flowering tops of Saint-John's-wort.

"What is it?" he asks, a bit suspicious.

"For the burning under your skin," she says, pointing to the spot on her own face where the scar slices his.

"Ye remembered," he says, reaching for the jar.

Last time Edith was here, Reeve complained of a ghost riding his bones. Pain with no clear source. He said it started in his scar and ran down his neck into his shoulder.

"Rub it into the painful spots whenever you need," she says.

David does not approve of Reeve. He calls him a drifter and is wary of the man's vast knowledge of the landscape. But Edith has always been drawn to the mysterious man. She feels a kinship with him. They are both more comfortable in nature than in the company of men.

Reeve spent years with the Accawmacke people, learning their customs and language, and he became an expert navigator of the creeks, marshes, and tidewaters, even in fog or dark. Now he trades in herbs, pelts, shell beads—and secrets.

"Thank ye, Goody Harris," he says, stowing the jar of oil away. "What can I get ye in return?"

She tells him, and he disappears into the woods and returns with a green granite mortar and pestle. Edith's breath hitches when she sees it. The stone is beautiful, made even more so by the uneven chips on its edges.

"Oh, Reeve," she says, running her fingers over the smooth inside of the bowl. "This is gorgeous. But I only brought this." She produces a neatly tied bundle of sage. "Is it enough?"

He pushes the sage away, then pats the pocket that holds the oil. "No need for anything more."

"No," she says, shaking her head. "That was a gift. For a friend."

Reeve pauses, clearly touched. Then he takes the sage. "I owe ye, then," he says.

"You do not owe me anything," she tells him.

She admires the green granite tools the entire walk home.

When she gets back from Reeve's place, it is nearly dusk. Edith's husband has still not returned, but she knows he will be starved when he does. She cannot allow him to arrive home to an empty table. That would elicit too many questions about her day.

At the creek, she rakes a sackful of oysters from the shallows. They will be thin and watery—it is August, after all, so the oysters are only freshly spawned—but crabs would take too long to gather from the traps. Since she cannot predict when David will arrive, she opts for the quicker preparation; she will throw the oysters into a simple soup to mask their lighter flavor.

At the house, she starts the fire and situates the oysters for steaming. As she waits for them to open, she prepares the carrots for the soup, cleaning them of dirt and slicing them longways. Suddenly, she hears something and pauses, straining her ears like a deer in the woods.

It's a *hiss, hiss, hissss.* Like someone is whispering in the corner.

She sets down the fat carrot she had been chopping and wipes her hands on her apron. She slowly steps away from the fire, and her feet carry her past the table toward the trapdoor to the root cellar. It is open, so she kneels near the top and listens. But there is no one. Nothing. She is about to lock the hatch and stand when—

Hiss, hisssss

Again. Like a whisper. But she cannot make out any words.

The hairs on her arms rise. A chill runs through her as if she has been struck by a breeze. But the air is stale, even a bit rank. As if maybe a jar of preserved garlic or onions has broken down there. She descends the stone steps and makes a cursory sweep of the space before abandoning her search. There is nothing down here, and she needs to finish the soup before David arrives. She cannot afford distractions.

When she returns to the hearth's fire, the water in the pot is boiling, and an oyster pops open. Perhaps this was the noise she heard? The oysters steaming in their pot? She bites her lip and hears her father's voice in her head: *That restless fancy will undo you.*

Still, she could have sworn it was a voice. An urgent whisper, like a clipped warning. And so as she finishes the cooking, she keeps one ear cocked to the rest of the house, waiting for it to return.

But it never does.

David comes home much later.

Edith hears the door open, and annoyance turns at her gut like a key in a lock. She would have liked to be in bed an hour ago; her day of teaching and cooking and cleaning has exhausted her. But she felt compelled to wait up for her husband to be sure he was safe. And now that she knows he is not floating dead in the creek somewhere, she can feel properly annoyed.

That annoyance dissipates, though, when she sees his haggard face and his shirt soaked with sweat. What a day he must have had, tending to another man's harvest. She wordlessly ushers him to the table and helps him remove his boots and change into dry clothes. When she places a bowl of oyster soup before him, he gulps it without a spoon. Eventually, she swaps out the small bowl for the pot itself.

"Grace asked after you," he says when he has replenished his body and returned to the land of the living. "She's in a hard way."

"Is she well?" Edith asks. "I mean, she hasn't fallen ill like Jacob?"

"No, nothing like that," David says. "But the stress of it all. The farm. What will happen when he dies."

"Did they use the herbs?" she asks.

Her husband nods without conviction. She does not press, though she suspects he did not relay her instructions. And while this stokes a fire of resentment within her, she extinguishes it by remembering her afternoon. The hours spent teaching Violet and discussing the importance of her work. Their little secret.

"Best not speak of this to your mother," Edith told the girl before she left.

"No," Violet said, shaking her head. "Mother would never let me come here if she knew. She wants me to be mending knickers or chopping parsnips. Not wasting time learning how to save lives."

Edith laughed at this, a quick bark at the surprise of Violet's words.

"Well, you might not always save someone's life," she told the girl. "But you can help with the transition."

"Can I come again tomorrow?" Violet asked, cleaning her hands with her skirt and then stepping into it and securing it around her waist.

Edith paused. "Okay," she said. "But if my husband is here, we must be discreet."

Violet nodded excitedly. Edith gave her a bundle of root vegetables to take home to her mother. At least she would have something to show for her absence.

Now Edith watches David finish the oyster soup. He smiles at her over the pot.

"Just what I needed," he says. And then she sees it: the glimmer in his eye, the slightly upturned right corner of his mouth. He is full, reinvigorated. And he wishes to bed her.

She lowers her gaze. "I am unclean," she admits.

His eyebrows shoot up. "Your monthly bleed has returned?"

"Yes," she says, her voice heavy. She inspects her fingernails, thoroughly scrubbed after her time in the garden.

He wipes his mouth with his hand, which somehow seems like the hand of a giant. Thick veins on fat, swollen fingers. They intimidate her, though she doesn't have cause to be frightened. Her husband has never been violent toward her. He has never threatened her. And yet she feels, at all times, a strong potential for danger from this man she has known less than a year. Much as she cannot see what resides under the ocean's surface, but she knows that a whole unseen world exists there.

"This means you are not pregnant," he says as if she hasn't had the thought ten times over already.

"That's right," she confirms.

He carefully places his hands on the table, palms flat. "Help me understand," he says. "You know all about these herbs. You help people who are sick. But you can't solve this problem in your own body?"

TURN OFF THE LIGHT

The words sting. "I do not know that there is a *problem*," she says.

"Then why have you not conceived?" he asks. "If there is no problem, and yet you are still without child, then what are you saying? Are you taking measures to thwart conception?"

Her jaw drops. She shakes her head emphatically. "I wouldn't do that. I don't know *how* to do that."

"How would I know what you can and cannot do?" he asks, throwing up his hands.

She stops herself from saying *You could ask.*

He continues to rant. "You spend all this time in your garden, in your cellar, crushing plants, working your sorcery—"

"I am a healer, David," she says, tears stinging her eyes. "You know that. Do not pretend I'm something else. Do not act as though you do not know me."

He falls silent. Hides his hands in his lap and stares at the empty pot on the table. Then he runs his fingers through his dirty hair. "Forgive me," he says, his voice quiet. "I am tired. Saying things I have not . . ."

He doesn't finish his sentence. Edith stares at the table, unsure how to respond, willing herself not to cry.

"I want to be a father," David whispers.

Edith looks at his face, his jaw slack and eyes soft, and her heart breaks for his vulnerability, the truth in his words. They all know their duty is to grow the colony, but David's confession goes beyond duty. It speaks to a personal desire, an individual longing.

Guilt tugs at her gut, dropping her stomach like an anchor.

"I know," Edith says. "I am trying. I promise."

Edith wakes with a start.

Her eyes pop open. The night is still. David snores beside her.

She heard footsteps. She is sure that is what woke her. But when she blinks into the dark, she cannot see anything out of the ordinary.

Still, she pushes herself from the bed and stands. She is certain she heard the pattering of bare feet on the wood-plank floor.

Thud. Thud. Thud.

As her eyes adjust, the room gets slightly brighter, and though she swivels her head in search of a shadowy figure, she sees nothing. The one-room house is empty save for herself and her husband, who continues to sleep on the straw tick.

She allows herself to be pulled toward the hearth like a tide responding to the moon. Her fingers run over the bricks, a kind of ritual that she has used in the past to calm herself. Bricks are rare here on the Eastern Shore; they are expensive and labor-intensive to make, so they are typically found closer to Jamestown and other cities. But the builder of this house was a bricklayer. Edith loves the crimson blocks with uneven edges. Each one tells a story, braiding into a patchwork of rusty reds and blackened corners worn from use and smoke.

A glint catches her eye. Something reflects a spear of moonlight that shoots through the wooden shutters. She approaches the table and finds the kitchen knife lying atop it. She stares at the half-rusted blade. All the other dishes are in their rightful places; she cleaned well even though the meal was late. Had she missed the knife? She picks it up, her fingers wrapping around the hickory-wood handle, and twists the blade in the light. The knife is clean. Which means she washed it and surely would have returned it to its designated spot on the shelf.

Edith frowns as she puts the knife away. Then she forces herself back to bed. The sun will be up before she knows it.

She might have imagined the footsteps, but how does she explain the knife? An uneasiness settles in her bones. There was someone in the house. She can *feel* it.

When she wakes again, the early-morning light is not yet shining through the slats of the wooden shutters. She rubs her temples. A dull ache is forming behind her forehead.

Beside her, David still sleeps, but he is nearing his typical wake time. Edith quietly exits the bed.

By the hearth, she moves about the space in her well-choreographed morning routine. She tries hard not to think about the knife as she wipes last night's soup pot and sets it over the fire to prepare the eggs.

And then she sees the blood. A single drop on the floor beneath the window. She bends down and swipes at it with her middle finger. The blood transfers; it is still wet. She widens her gaze to the rest of the floor and sees that there are more droplets of blood. A trail leading toward the hearth and cellar, where it stops.

Instinctively, she lifts her right foot and inspects the sole. Nothing. She switches and looks at the bottom of her left foot. Still nothing.

Whose blood is this?

When David wakes, she hands him a plate of eggs and salt pork before presenting the mystery. But he merely shrugs.

"From last night, I suppose," he says. "Just didn't see it in the dark. I worked myself ragged yesterday, no surprise there's a little blood."

He flips his hands and inspects his knuckles. There are multiple cuts and bruises.

Edith frowns. "But I also heard a noise. In the middle of the night. And when I got up to look around, I found our knife out of place."

He chews his pork loudly, the sounds of spit and suction distinct. "Are you sure you weren't dreaming?"

"I am sure of it," she says.

"So you are having trouble sleeping, then?" He stops eating and looks out the window, mulling something over in his mind. Quietly, to himself, he adds, "And trouble conceiving..."

She understands then what her husband is implying. That her restless sleep and infertility might be connected. That she might be the target of an evil spirit—or even the Devil himself.

A sour taste fills her mouth. She tries to swallow it down. "No," she assures her husband. "I have not had trouble sleeping. It was only last night. Likely just an animal that got in through the window. You're right, there's no need to be concerned. I will be sure to latch it tighter tonight."

Then she pulls the pot from the hearth and brings it to the table.

"More eggs?" she says, plastering a dutiful smile on her face.

8
CLAIRE

"Can we get this? What about that? Ooh, chocolate milk!"

Julia sits in the shopping cart, pointing to and grabbing anything she wants on the shelves. Claire has already agreed to a family-size bag of stick pretzels, a chocolate egg with a prize inside, and a pink, fuzzy pocket notebook.

"I think we have enough," she says, half distracted, as she tries to find the items on Tilly's list. She squints into the baking aisle, determined to find the sweetened condensed milk without having to ask. Claire does not cook much beyond the most basic of recipes, so the center aisles baffle her. She's more comfortable in the produce, dairy, and meat sections.

She is reminded of grocery shopping with her own mother when all three of the girls were little. Gabby used to help her mom push the cart while Claire and Tilly rode in the basket. They played a game of sneaking things into the cart when their mother wasn't looking. Tilly and Claire would point at the shelves, daring Gabby to grab various items, while swallowing down fits of giggles. Her mother was a good sport about it; if they managed to sneak something all the way to checkout, she would generally buy it for them.

One time, they sneaked a tube of vanilla cookie icing all the way to the front of the store. They were thrilled. But when they reached the cash register, their mother nearly doubled over in laughter, sharing a moment with the checkout clerk.

"Girls," their mother said between guffaws, "this is not icing. It's hemorrhoid cream!"

Claire had never seen her mother laugh so hard. Especially when she had to explain what hemorrhoids were to her blankly staring young kids.

Seeing her mother like that was rare. As an Englishwoman, she was never the warm and fuzzy type. But in the months after Gabby's disappearance, her mother's take-charge mentality turned out to be exactly what they all needed. Not only did she organize searches and liaise with the police and local news, she also sat on the couch for hours with Tilly's and Claire's heads in her lap. She'd assure them over and over that everything would be fine. It was an antidote to Claire's anxiety and unrelenting nausea and anger. She didn't need anything more than *fine*.

Fine would have been a godsend.

Her mother was already prickly by nature, but once they officially lost hope of finding Gabby, she became even more withdrawn. Their dad clung to a relentless optimism, convinced Gabby would return home any day. But he also began to let Claire and Tilly get away with things he never had before, babying them even when they were wrong, and this led to arguments with his wife. Resentment built between them, miring the guts of what had once bound them together.

And of course, the people of Cape Chase had their opinions too.

Every version of the story painted the Fern family as either incompetent or unloving. For those who insisted Gabby had been killed or had suffered some tragic accident, the family was neglectful and clueless. For those who believed Gabby had run away, the family was overbearing and unsupportive.

And even though the townspeople had few facts and knew nothing about the inner workings of the Fern clan, their whisperings mattered. Because here's the thing Claire has learned about outside opinions: They are like ivy vines on a wall. If allowed to grow at their own rapid rate, they will eventually suffocate the structure beneath them.

Claire had hoped the grocery store would bring her some calm. That the wide aisles and bright lights would distract her from what waits back home. But she is bombarded with memories in this place. She presses her thumbnail into the pad of her index finger. Then thumb to middle. Thumb to ring. Her breath is getting shallow, the air thin.

Julia reaches for something. "Can we have it, Mama?" she asks.

Claire nods, half absent. "Sure."

It's a lemon Bundt cake from the discounted-bakery-items display. While her four-year-old does not need the sugar, Claire doesn't have the energy to argue. So she lets her put it in the cart and turns toward the next aisle.

And that's when she comes face to face with a ghost.

Well, not a literal ghost. Rather, a ghost from her past.

Ethan.

The love of her life from ages seventeen to twenty.

His medium-long hair falls in black curls around his face. Stubble lines his round but well-defined jaw. So much of him is the same, though he has replaced his worn Timberland boots with sneakers and his oversize hoodie with a well-fitted tee. One that comes slightly distressed and tugs in all the right places.

He looks good.

"Claire?" he says, his voice full of surprise.

She stares and considers pretending she doesn't recognize him, then realizes that's ridiculous and thinks about playing it cool. Or maybe she should feign being in a rush and get away from here as quickly as possible.

"Claire?" he says again, because she has done none of these things and is instead staring at him in dumb silence.

"Ethan, hi, oh my God, wow." The words spill from her.

He takes her in. She imagines he must be shocked to see her on the Shore doing something as mundane as grocery shopping, like this might be her everyday existence. Then his eyes clock Julia, and he stares, curious.

"Are you here now?" he asks. "Have you moved back?"

"No, no," Claire says too quickly. "I just mean, no, we're visiting my sister. Or, really, my dad. He's sick."

"I heard that," Ethan says, and of course he did, because everyone knows everyone's business here in a way that makes Claire squirm. "He's doing okay?"

"Yeah," Claire says, nodding. Then she shakes her head, snapping out of it. "No, actually, I don't know why I said that. He's not. He's dying."

Why is she being so weird?

"Oh, shit," Ethan says, then winces and sends an apologetic look toward Julia. "Sorry. That's awful. He was so . . ."

"What?" she prompts, her voice eager, as if she's aiming to collect any memories of her father that are floating out there.

"Nothing, he was just always kind to me. Which sounds small now, or silly, I guess."

"No, it's not silly," Claire says. "It's nice." Tears push at the backs of her eyes, and she struggles to swallow them, then clears her throat.

She had gone to school with Ethan through all their years on the Shore. But they moved in different circles and didn't start dating until after Gabby's disappearance. Claire was drawn to him then, especially because he had known Gabby only tangentially. It was emotionally safer, somehow, easier to be around someone who didn't feel a gaping hole in the universe like she did. And emotionally powerful too. He'd gotten to know Claire when she was already the broken version of herself, and he still wanted her. So she let him in.

But Gabby was gone, and then two years later, her mother was too, back to her hometown. Claire was learning an important lesson: Anyone she let in would eventually vanish. It was only a matter of survival, then, to become the one who vanishes first.

"And this is . . ." Ethan asks, pointing to Julia. He smiles at her.

Julia, still seated in the front of the shopping cart, buries her face in her mother's torso.

"This is Julia," Claire says. "My daughter."

Ethan pauses. His thick eyebrows rise and fall above his deep-set eyes. Claire notes how dark his features are — his hair, his eye color, his tanned skin.

"I didn't know you had kids," he says.

"One. One kid," Claire corrects with a smile. "Just Julia."

"Well," Ethan says, "it's very nice to meet you, Just Julia."

Julia turns enough to eye Ethan from the safety of her mother's frame. She smiles a little. "That's not my name," she says playfully.

"It's not?" Ethan asks.

"Noooo. My name is *Julia*."

"Ohh," Ethan says. "Well, now, that's a beautiful name."

Julia smiles again, and Claire raises her eyebrows at Ethan. She gives him a thumbs-up and mouths, *Wow, that's big.*

"So is your husband here?" he asks, looking around.

"I'm not married," she says.

Ethan's face contorts into an expression of apology, as if he has misstepped. "I'm sorry, I shouldn't have assumed," he says.

"Oh, it's fine," she says. "We're not together. We were never married. We tried to make it work, but . . ." She lets her voice trail off, because why is she telling him any of this?

"Got it," he says.

"And you?" Claire asks. "You married? Girlfriend?"

"Ah, well." He runs his hand through his hair the same way he always did as a teenager. Claire's breath catches. "No. I'm single at the moment."

Claire senses a story. But she obviously can't ask. "What are you doing for work these days?" she says instead.

He smiles. "The yacht club. I'm a mechanic at the docks."

She nods, remembering how Ethan was out on the water almost every weekend, either fishing with his dad or bringing a group of friends out for water-skiing.

Julia whines. "I need to poop," she says.

Claire snorts and smiles awkwardly. "Out of the mouths of babes," she says to Ethan, who laughs.

"I'll let you go," he says. He hesitates, then adds, "Should we exchange numbers? I know you're busy while you're here with your dad, so I don't want to get in the way."

"No, yeah, let's get together," Claire says. "That'd be great."

"Yeah?" Ethan says, his eyes widening a little.

TURN OFF THE LIGHT

"Would be nice to catch up," she tells him.

As soon as his number's in Claire's phone, Julia cries out, "Mama, I really. Have. To. Poop." She pauses between each word for emphasis.

Claire nods apologetically at Ethan and scrambles toward the bathroom in the back of the store.

On the drive home, Claire thinks about how Ethan has changed. His look is more sophisticated, more put-together. But in all the ways that matter, he seems like the same person she loved all those years ago. His sincerity, his kindness, his calm. And at that time in Claire's life, those things were in short supply.

She has thought of him often over the years. Memories of Ethan are the only ones she lets herself revisit from that time. There was a stillness when she was with him. She had a sense of being held in place instead of floating away. In Los Angeles after Julia was born, Claire would be bone-tired in the middle of the night while nursing, and she'd remember the weight of his hand over hers in the dark. She'd allow herself to wonder, briefly, what it would've been like if she'd stayed. If they were still together.

But she never let herself dwell on the feeling. Because dwelling led to wanting. And wanting was a distraction, a dangerous desire that left her vulnerable.

Still, as she's driving home from the store, a small smile comes across her lips. She didn't expect to see him. And she certainly didn't expect him to still feel like a safe refuge.

By the time Claire pulls into the driveway, dread is once again gnawing at her ribs, feasting on whatever calm she conjured in the last hour.

Tilly helps unload the car, and the sisters work together in the kitchen to put the groceries away while Julia gets tablet time.

"Did you hear from the nurse?" Claire asks.

Tilly folds an empty paper bag. "Yeah, she can't come today, but she said she'll talk to the doctor about some options for meds."

"Oh, you asked about meds?" Claire takes this as Tilly's admission that she is worried, whether or not she will say it in so many words.

"Well, I told her what happened and that you're afraid of him having another episode. She said something about antipsychotics." Tilly shakes her head.

"What's wrong?" Claire asks. "Why isn't that a good idea if the nurse thinks medicine will help?"

"She hasn't seen him yet. She's just going by the story I told her. The story *you* told *me*."

Claire has been emptying groceries onto the counter for Tilly to organize, but now she pauses. "What is that supposed to mean?"

"Nothing, just that I wasn't there. Neither was Peter. We're going by your account of what happened."

"You say *account* like you think I'm making it up."

"I'm not saying that. It's just that antipsychotics are no joke, so maybe we take a beat before putting him on yet another pill." Tilly shoves the plastic container of grapes into a too-small space in the fridge. "You haven't been here, Claire. You don't know what other meds he's on, how he has been reacting to them. That stuff matters. Last time we switched his meds, he was queasy for a week. You can't just throw another thing in the mix."

"Well, if you ask me, it's worth risking a bout of nausea to prevent him from going full Edward Scissorhands."

Tilly stares at Claire, her jaw set and stern.

Claire sighs. "Okay. Fine. No antipsychotics. Want me to start on the attic later?"

"Jesus, Claire!" Tilly shouts, her voice rising in pitch.

"What? It needs to get done, and I don't know how long I'll be here."

"Give it a fucking *rest*. You've been here less than twenty-four hours, you realize that? My God."

"I'm offering for *you*," Claire bites back. "I didn't think sifting through all Dad's stuff up there was something you wanted to do alone."

"Why not?" Tilly says. "I've managed everything else."

She puts the water on full blast and starts rinsing dishes. Claire rolls her eyes at Tilly's back before taking a deep breath. She sucks on her teeth, steeling herself. Then she approaches the sink and stands by her sister's side.

"I'm just trying to be helpful," she says. "I swear."

Tilly does not look at Claire, but her shoulders relax. "Yeah," she finally says. "I know. Sorry."

They work together side by side to load the dishwasher. When some food gets stuck in the sink, Tilly uses her fingers to push it down the disposal.

"Oh my God, don't do that!" Claire shouts.

Tilly pulls back, surprised. "Do what?"

"Put your fingers down there like that!" Her whole body shudders.

Tilly laughs. "Why are you freaking out?"

Claire's face is serious, her eyes bulging. "Every time someone's hand is near the garbage disposal, I picture it turning on all of a sudden."

"By itself?" Tilly asks.

Claire raises her eyebrows. "It could happen! It'd be like sticking your fingers in a blender!" She shivers. "Ugh, it freaks me out."

"I think you've watched too many horror movies," Tilly says. She dries her hands and starts tossing items into the slow cooker. She's making chili for dinner.

Claire finishes folding up the empty paper bags. She looks over the counter and across to the sunroom, where Julia is plugged in with headphones to her tablet.

"Are you sure she went in the cellar?" Tilly asks when she sees Claire watching the girl.

Claire nods. "Yes. The trapdoor was open."

"But how would she even open it? Isn't it too heavy for her?" Tilly asks.

Claire shrugs. "I guess it's not." She reaches into her shorts pocket where she stuffed Julia's picture. She pulls it out, unfolds it, and shows it to her sister. "She drew this."

Tilly breathes in, sharp. "That's the carving, right? On the main beam?"

"Yep." Claire is about to elaborate but stops. Looks around. "Do you smell that?"

Tilly sniffs, then shakes her head. "I don't smell anything." She stares at her sister for a beat. "How about I bring Julia to the beach? You take a second to rest. Come meet us whenever."

Claire nods. She helps Julia get ready and waves them outside. "I'm right behind you," she tells them, and watches out the kitchen window as they head toward the water.

Now alone, she is again distracted by the smell of something burning. She's read that can be a sign of a brain tumor. But this scent is more sweet than smoky. She checks that all the burners are off as well as the oven. She opens the electric cooker, but, no, that's not it. And anyway, the smell is not concentrated in one place. It's everywhere, all around her.

TURN OFF THE LIGHT

She thinks then of Gabby. How she stank of birthday-cake ice cream the day they fought. The day she disappeared.

And then Claire is crying, because grief is neither linear nor logical. Grief creeps in when least expected, like water through a crack the moment a facade is broken.

9
EDITH

David is cold today. After dinner last night, he softened into her, sharing his deep desire to be a father, but this morning he is aloof. Edith is surprised when he invites her to Jacob's property with him. Yesterday, he practically scolded her for suggesting she come along, and now today, he is insisting.

Perhaps it was jarring for him to see Jacob so sick. Maybe David realizes that their neighbor and friend deserves medical attention even if the apothecary is not available.

"Show me what you are packing," he says as he descends into the root cellar behind her.

He has to stoop down here, his body comically large for the small space. His eyes ravage the shelves as he mentally categorizes the many jars and bundles tied with twine. Edith has never seen him like this. Normally, his showing interest in her collection would have excited her. But something about his intensity and hardened eyes gives her pause. Something is off between them.

She uses the lantern to shine light on the sassafras, which she is bringing in two forms, root bark and ground filé powder. "And this," she says, holding a small jar of liquid up to the warm light, "is witch hazel. It can help with any swelling."

Edith narrates her moves as she packs her sack for the journey, and David nods periodically. But his attention is elsewhere, and she is confident he would nod the same way even if she were spouting facts in a foreign tongue. He is not listening. Instead, his eyes continue to scan the shelves, searching for something. She cannot imagine what he is hoping to find.

They leave early, just as the sun is beginning to rise, before the unbearable heat takes hold. She is tired, the effects of her restless night setting in. But she cannot mention this without facing more questions, more insinuations about the reason for her sleeplessness. She finds herself wondering again if that trail of blood really was from one of David's injuries, as he suggested.

"You will tend to Jacob," her husband says, "and then return home. We are nearly out of soap."

"I started to make a batch yesterday," she says, then stops herself because she remembers why she got distracted — Violet. Yet another thing she cannot tell her husband. Her insides squirm as she thinks about the secrets mounting up.

"And?" he says.

She searches for an explanation. "The lye was too weak. It needs to be further boiled. I should be able to cook the batch today."

He nods, seemingly satisfied. Edith does not like having to hide parts of herself. It is taxing and does not come naturally to her.

She focuses on the path ahead. Since they have made this walk many times, a trail has been trodden through the woods between Grace and Jacob's property and their own. Sometimes after a strong wind, the course will be blocked by a fallen tree, but otherwise the path is a clear marker of direction.

She turns her eyes upward. The tall birch trees are thin but dense in number. The sun speckles through the foliage and, directly in front of them, paints the air in streaks like something holy descending from the heavens.

"A beautiful morning," she says, gesturing toward the light.

David does not respond, does not even lift his eyes from the ground, just continues to trudge along. Her mind returns to last night's conversation, when he suggested that she might intentionally be preventing pregnancy. Edith is shocked that he would think her capable of betraying him in that way, of deceiving him so wholeheartedly.

Is that why her husband joined her in the cellar this morning? Was he looking for some kind of clue that would prove his theory?

And the truth is, Edith has never wanted to be a mother. The idea of it has only ever been tied to duty. She knows it is her role within the colony to grow the population. She has never doubted that she would have children, but not because of some innate desire. No, simply because she has always known she *should*. It has always been an *expectation*. But if she had her choice, she would never be with child.

Is *this* how she has influenced the course of things? Could her thoughts hold so much power, enough to prevent a pregnancy? Surely not. It is preposterous, even heretical for her to believe she could have such influence over the natural cycle of life.

She shakes her head, clearing her thoughts, and returns her gaze to the sky. As much as she doesn't want to admit it, David's paranoia is getting to her. She can feel his doubt becoming her own, boring into her brain like a tick and digging in to take up residence.

Jacob is not well. He has the shakes. His chills are so strong that Edith worries he will crack his teeth.

David is out in the field already, tending to the crop. Grace sits beside her husband, holding his hand as he lies propped up in bed. Every few minutes, he rolls over and vomits into the bucket she is holding. Most of what comes out now is yellow bile; his stomach has been empty for days.

"Okay," Grace says in a whisper as Jacob pukes. "You're okay." She rubs his back in big, sweeping circles. When Grace looks up, Edith sees the sadness in her eyes. A resolution mixed with dread; she is coming to accept what is obviously inevitable.

Edith has boiled water with willow bark, and now that it's cool, she encourages Jacob to sip. His face is white and gaunt and dripping in sweat. They sit here for an hour or so, until Jacob's shakes subside and he gives in to sleep once more.

Edith sets a new pot to boil for more tea. She finishes just as there's a knock at the door. Grace opens it to find Margaret, her closest neighbor to the south, holding a loaf of bread. The woman is thin and made of harsh angles, with a square jaw and pointy elbows. Her eyebrows are thick and dark and animated as she inquires after Jacob's health.

When Margaret steps inside, she sees Edith. "Oh, hello," she says as though Edith is a stray dog that has wandered in.

Grace ushers them to the table for a snack of bread and cheese. Edith wants to leave.

"I wish there were more to be done," Grace says. Her eyes are wet with tears as she stares at a spot on the wall.

Margaret leans forward in a display of strength. "It must be God's will."

Edith is annoyed by Margaret's dismissal. Grace is allowed to feel disappointed or angry, regardless of God's will.

Grace sighs. "If Jacob's sickness is a test of his faith," she says, "well, he is one of the most devout men I know. So what does that mean for the rest of us?"

"It means now more than ever," Margaret replies, "we must pray."

Edith chews on her lip. "Sometimes people get sick and there is not a divine explanation," she blurts out. "Sometimes the blight comes to even the strongest stem."

Margaret wrinkles her nose and purses her lips like she has smelled something sour. "What are you talking about?"

Edith shrinks into herself, immediately regretting her outburst. Grace looks at her with mild amusement, or maybe gratitude.

"I think she means it as an expression," Grace says when Edith remains silent.

Margaret clucks and shakes her head. "I never understand anything she says," she tells Grace as if Edith is not sitting across the very same table.

Edith holds her elbows. "I only mean that Jacob is a devout Christian," she says, her voice small. "He will surely be met with the most enthusiastic greeting from God."

She senses she has entered dangerous waters.

Margaret ignores Edith's explanation and stares at her through narrowed eyes. "What is that there?" she asks, pointing to Edith's forearm.

"Hmm?" Edith pulls up her arm for inspection.

A bruise is forming near her elbow. It is almost an inch wide with dark, undefined edges that fan out like butterfly wings.

"Oh," Edith says.

"Did you fall?" Grace asks.

"No," Edith replies, shaking her head. "Not that I . . ." Her voice trails off. She had not noticed the bruise. When did it bloom? She thinks about the knife. The blood. The feeling that someone or something was in the house last night. Signs of the Devil at work.

And now, on the heels of her outburst, her insistence that not everything has a divine explanation, a mysterious bruise will make her seem even more suspicious in Margaret's eyes.

"Oh," Edith says, feigning a return of memory. "It must be from yesterday evening. I slipped while harvesting oysters for supper."

Margaret shoots a dubious look at Grace, who avoids eye contact with both women.

Edith deems it time to leave. She scrambles awkwardly out of the house, citing her chores as an excuse, and sighs with relief when she is alone in the woods. On the walk, she ruminates on the insinuation that Jacob's illness might be some kind of test or punishment. *What does that mean for the rest of us?* Grace had asked. Edith can't help but think of her own infertility... her uneasiness... the relentless heat that is making so many sick... and she wonders if maybe Grace is right.

Maybe God is punishing them.

She looks again at her forearm, where the bruise is getting darker. She presses it with her fingers and flinches. It hurts more than she would have guessed. She will need to apply some knitbone salve.

She spends the afternoon stirring lye and fat over the fire for soap. Once it has reached a pudding-like consistency, she will pour it into wooden molds. The work is a welcome distraction. Ever since this morning, she has been replaying the odd conversation at Grace's in her mind.

Violet has not turned up today, and Edith feels slight relief; after this morning, she is reticent about teaching the girl. First was David's nosiness in the cellar, then the beady-eyed Margaret eager to question her. It feels like she is destined to misstep wherever she goes, so she is grateful for some peace and quiet at the house.

While filling the first soap mold, she bumps her forearm bruise on an iron pot and yelps. The mold closest to her falls, spilling the mixture of lye and fat on the wooden floor and spraying her apron and legs. She curses loudly. Hours and hours of hard work lost in a second. Not to mention the waste of resources; they are running low on lard, and she does not have enough to cook a new batch of soap tomorrow.

She takes a breath. She can already see the evening laid out before her; she'll have to pick and scrape the waxlike soap off the floor, a painstakingly slow process. Or maybe she can cover it with the rush mat until she has time to address the disaster. Frustrated but desperate not to waste any more, she carefully pours the soap into the remaining three molds and carries them gingerly down into the root cellar, where they will cool overnight. Then she takes a breath and grudgingly returns to the spilled mess.

But it is gone.

Edith does a double take, trying to make sense of the scene. Only moments ago, the liquid soap mixture was spattered over the floor and front stones of the hearth. To prove she is not losing her mind, she pulls up her apron and inspects it in the light of the fire. The spattered mess is indeed still on her person. So how has the rest of it disappeared?

Edith gets down on her hands and knees and crawls about the room. She knows she must look ridiculous, but perhaps the liquid oozed through the cracks of the floorboards. Still, wouldn't it have stained, at least until the mixture dried? When she finds nothing, she leans back and sits on the floor, resigned.

"Edith?"

Her spine straightens. Someone has whispered her name. She looks around frantically but sees no signs of a visitor.

"Edith? Is that you?"

TURN OFF THE LIGHT

She hops to her feet with fear. But the room is still, the air hollow. Her body is weightless, ready to flee, her heart flapping like a hummingbird within her chest. She remains frozen like this for a long time, waiting for the voice to return. But it does not. Did she imagine it? Was it only a trick of the mind? Perhaps a cool breeze through the shutters that made the wood whistle just so?

She finally turns her attention to the fire, which continues at a low crackle, its hue a muted orange as the flames begin to recede. Edith stares into it, mesmerized by the unpredictable movements on the flames. Her fingers graze the bruise on her left forearm. She flinches again and looks down to find that it has doubled in size. Its color is a rich purple, its shape uneven. In her haste to get the day's work started, she forgot to apply the knitbone salve.

Edith acquires the balm from the cellar and situates herself in the rocking chair. She spreads the ointment onto her butterfly-shaped bruise and feels its cooling effects immediately. Once the salve is applied, she wraps her arm in linen cloth.

She is gravely unnerved by all that has happened in the past couple of days. The hissing, the breath on her neck, and now this — a mess mysteriously cleaned, her name on the lips of the wind. It is beyond curious. In combination with her wondering if God has more in store for the settlers of the Eastern Shore, it is downright terrifying.

Here, alone in this house and powerless, she feels like a pawn in someone's game.

10

CLAIRE

Claire walks through her favorite birch trees along the wooden path that leads down to the water. It's humid, and her hair sticks to the back of her neck. Dark clouds lurk over the sea. She guesses it will rain later. Weather in Virginia can turn on a dime, and August is usually one of the wettest months for the Eastern Shore.

She finds Tilly talking with Julia on the beach. "That's a crab pot," Tilly says, pointing to a buoy on the water.

"A what?" Julia asks.

"Under that buoy is a cage for catching crabs," Tilly says.

Julia spots her mother as she approaches. "Look, Mama! A crab bot."

Claire smiles. *"Pot,"* she corrects her.

"Are we going to eat them?" Julia asks.

"Not me," Claire says. "I'm allergic, remember?"

"Pee-pee pen!" Julia says, then runs and grabs her beach bucket. "I'm going to build a castle like Elsa did!"

Tilly raises an eyebrow and turns to Claire. "Pee-pee pen?"

"EpiPen," she says. "But nothing is funnier to a four-year-old than potty words."

They start down the shore, walking side by side.

"So, uh," Tilly starts, "I saw the blanket on Dad's mirror."

Claire nods. "Yeah. He got really freaked out by his own reflection this morning. Has that ever happened?"

Tilly half shrugs, half nods. "It can be normal for people with dementia. I've read about it. But still . . ."

Her body pauses with her voice. She stops and turns to face the water. Claire stands beside her.

"I don't know," Tilly continues. "I haven't seen him this agitated before. I mean, he has been steadily declining. That's why I called you. But this is different."

Claire nods. "I agree. There's something more going on. There has to be. Last night, he was looking around like someone was watching him. And this morning, he said to me, 'Don't drink the tea.' Do you have any idea what that means?"

Tilly tilts her head to the side and gives her sister a sad look.

"What?" Claire asks.

"His brain is sick."

"I know that. Of course I know that. But even you said this seems like a rapid decline, right?" Claire checks to be sure Julia is not within earshot. "He said he was going to cut off his hand to get the Devil out. I know this sounds crazy, but I feel like there might be something else going on. Besides the dementia, I mean. Something that accelerated his decline somehow."

Tilly stares at Claire, then raises her eyebrows, implying that the answer should be obvious.

"I don't get it," Claire says.

"Listen, I know I called you, and I appreciate you dropping everything to get here so soon." Tilly's words are rehearsed. "But

I wonder if maybe you shouldn't stay somewhere else? Since Dad seems so bothered."

"Oh my God," Claire says, incredulous. "You think he's worse because *I'm* here."

Tilly shrugs apologetically. "As soon as you got here, he changed. He's restless and violent and scared."

"I didn't even *see* him before finding him in the kitchen with the shears," Claire says, though it's not entirely true. She went into his room hours before and found him thrashing under the covers. But he didn't wake, did he? He didn't see her. And anyway, Tilly doesn't know about that. "Dad didn't even know I was here, so your theory doesn't hold up."

"I'm not saying it's *you,* it's probably just the change from routine, but for his own good—"

"We're not leaving," Claire says, defiant. "Fuck that."

She abandons Tilly and walks into the bay, feeling the lukewarm water on her toes and up to her ankles. It's so much warmer than the Pacific ever is. Like a bath. Warm ocean water means home. Or at least, it did at one point in her life.

Could her sister be right? Could something about Claire's arrival have triggered a fear in her father? A restlessness, as Tilly described? Claire looks down the beach and sees Julia dripping wet sand atop her castle for a drizzle effect, blissfully unaware of the angst happening mere feet away. Of the cloud that hangs over the Fern family.

Claire spent so much time out here on the beach after her sister went missing. At first, search parties met on these shores; half the participants fanned out toward the woods, and the other half trekked through the dunes. As the weeks and months wore on, fewer and fewer people came out to search. But Claire still went out almost daily, even alone. It had become a ritual. A part of her knew she'd never find Gabby that way. But she continued to walk through the woods and along the water's edge. Continued to hope that Gabby had left by choice and could therefore, someday, choose to return.

Being back in this place condenses Claire's perception of time, folding it like an accordion. She realizes that even after so many years, she is still the girl who checked the woods every day for months.

"What the hell is going on, Gabs?" she whispers. "Is Dad just sick or is he seeing something in the house?"

This is an old habit, talking to the sea as if it is her sister.

She thinks about Gabby's frightened face when she'd found her in the cellar. That was only two weeks before she disappeared.

"What did you see down there?" Claire asks under her breath.

"Claire," Tilly calls from behind her. She joins Claire at the water's edge, and the two wordlessly link arms.

They stare at the sea for a long time before Claire finally asks, "I'm too late, aren't I? That's what I kept thinking this morning in his room. I'm too late."

The left side of Tilly's mouth pulls tight in confirmation. Then she takes a deep breath. "I don't know. I hope not, but I don't know."

They stand in silence for a while longer. Claire takes a deep breath. "I want to stay here. I want Julia to see her grandfather before—"

"Yeah," Tilly says, waving off her words. "Stay. We'll see how the next couple days go, all right? Sorry I jumped to... It's been hard, you know? But I shouldn't have. Forget I said anything."

Together, the sisters wrangle Julia away from the beach, and they walk back toward the house. Claire's shirt sticks to her skin in the heat, and the impending rain gives the air a heavy quality.

"I want to stay on the beach," Julia whines. "Please?"

Claire and Tilly share a look; the girl sounds just like them at that age. When they were young, they spent countless hours crabbing and collecting shells and swimming. Summer was always marked by sand in the house.

"Maybe we'll come back after dinner," Claire says. A hollow offer, since she knows they will all be tired.

When they reach the back porch, Tilly points to the hose. "Rinse feet first," she sings.

Claire smiles, remembering her own mother endlessly begging them to rinse off outdoors so they wouldn't track the sand inside. "You sound just like—"

"Don't say it." Tilly stops her playfully.

Claire remembers how they used to prank their mother, turning the hose on her when they were meant to be washing their feet. Claire grabs the hose now and makes eye contact with Tilly, trying hard not to laugh.

"Oh, don't you dare," Tilly says, knowing what's coming, but before she can escape, Claire is spraying her. Tilly squeals and fights, turns the hose on Claire, and both of them go back and forth in the water war until they dissolve into laughter like they had so many times as children.

Claire grabs paper napkins from the pantry to help set the table for dinner. They are still in the same place her mother always put them: second shelf from the top, all the way on the left. As she reaches, the floorboard beneath her left foot moans. When she steps away, it *pops* up at the end, like it always does in the summer humidity. But a sharp prick on her bare heel makes her wince.

TURN OFF THE LIGHT

"What the hell?" she says as she sits down and inspects her foot. A small dot of blood beads.

"What is it?" Peter asks, bending down to help. Then he spots something. "Ah, the nail. Look. It's all bent and sticking out."

The distinctive square-shaped head of the nail is raised slightly. Claire runs her fingers over the piece of metal, and her skin catches on its rough surface.

"I'll fix it later," Peter says. "It's been popping up like that a lot lately."

"It's been popping up like that *forever*," Tilly adds from the island where she's plating bowls of chili.

"Yeah," Claire agrees. "This house is a mouth breather."

After cleaning the puncture and slapping on a Band-Aid, Claire joins the group at the table for dinner. She tells them about running into her former boyfriend at the grocery store.

"When's the last time you even talked to Ethan?" Tilly asks.

"Oh, jeez, I don't know," Claire admits. "Ages ago."

"Was there still a spark?" Tilly asks.

Claire laughs. "We dated fifteen years ago," she says.

Tilly raises an eyebrow. "So what? Is he single?"

Claire shakes her head. "I don't know. We didn't talk about that."

The words are out before she can consider them. She's not making a concerted effort to lie to her sister, but she finds herself annoyed by Tilly's suggestions. Any small feelings that popped up for Claire at the grocery store feel too personal, too *hers*. She does not want to share them, especially with her sister, who will insist on making something out of nothing.

"Is Dad coming for dinner?" Claire asks.

Peter shakes his head. "He's sleeping. We can make him a bowl when he wakes up."

Claire nods. Relief blooms in her chest, and then a heavy guilt. She should want to spend time with her father, but the past couple of visits have been anything but smooth. Add to that Tilly's accusations and apprehension, and Claire knows every interaction she has with her father will be under scrutiny.

Julia pushes chunks of chili around in her bowl with a spoon. A typical sign she's not interested in the evening's offerings.

"Want some toppings?" Claire asks, leaning toward her daughter.

Julia nods, so Claire adds sour cream and shredded cheese to the bowl, which encourages the girl to curate a small spoonful of the best bits.

"I ordered more diapers," Peter tells Tilly. "They should be here tomorrow."

"Dad's in diapers?" Claire asks, surprised.

"Has been for a while," Tilly says. Claire feels another stab of guilt that she didn't know this. Yet another reminder of how absent she has been.

Julia taps on Claire's arm. "Mama, did she say Grandpa wears diapers?" Her face scrunches up in confusion. "That's silly. *Babies* wear diapers."

Claire smiles at her daughter. "You're right, they do. But sometimes adults do too. When they have trouble going potty."

Julia laughs through her teeth as if Claire has said a bad word. "That's so funny," she says.

Peter pipes up. "This is really good," he says, digging into the chili for another bite. His attempt to change the subject is not subtle.

Tilly frowns and shakes her head. "It's not right," she says, staring into her bowl. "Something's off."

"It's delicious," Claire says. Although she's not a fan of the beans. She has been piling them up near the sides of her bowl. Whenever her father made the family chili, he cooked a separate pot for Claire that was bean-free. And while neither of Claire's parents were very skilled cooks, her dad's chili was Cape Chase–famous.

Tilly shakes her head again. "No. The spice isn't right."

"What do you mean?" Claire asks.

Peter pushes away his empty plate. "She's been trying to replicate your dad's chili. 'Secret family recipe.' But isn't the point, then, to share the recipe with your family? I don't get it."

"I'm sure he would have," Tilly says, a bite to her voice. "But I didn't think to ask until it was too late."

A heaviness descends in the wake of her words.

Claire looks out the window at the backyard with its clumps of wispy beach grass. Even the earth seems sick, overgrown with weeds and desperate for attention.

Peter reaches for Tilly's hand. "I'm sure this is normal," he says. "I bet lots of people think of things they wish they had asked when they had the chance."

The words slice through Claire's veins.

She watches as Tilly nods slowly and leans into Peter's chest. Suddenly, Claire feels like a voyeur. The moment is too intimate. She turns her attention to Julia, who looks up at her with a sweet smile. Claire senses the girl is about to ask another deep question about death or her aunt Tilly's sadness.

Instead, she brings her mouth to her mother's ear and whispers loudly, "Can I have dessert?"

"I'm thirsty, Mama," Julia says, already half asleep in bed.

Claire pads through the dark house down to the kitchen, limping slightly to keep the weight off her recently injured heel. She refills her daughter's water bottle with the refrigerator spigot. The dispenser is noisy, its internal gears clunking. But when the noise continues even after Claire has finished filling the bottle, she realizes it's not coming from the fridge.

It's coming from the dumbwaiter.

She places her hand on the wall in the center of what looks like a shuttered cabinet. Its borders are ornate but it frames only flat wood, the access door to the dumbwaiter that was sealed shut and painted over at least a hundred years ago. This one was a manually operated pulley system, a small freight elevator used to transport food and things from upstairs to downstairs and vice versa.

But again, it hasn't been used in a century. And yet . . .

Clink-clunk. Pause. *Clink-clunk.* Pause.

Metal on metal, muffled behind wallboards. The sound of old pulleys groaning. With her hand against the wood, Claire feels a slight vibration. Just like she might if the elevator were moving.

How is it possible?

She thinks of that last conversation with Gabby. They were standing right here in this kitchen:

"Oh my God, you stink," Claire said.

Gabby was still wearing her ice cream–shop uniform, a pale pink polo with red-striped pants. A real-life candy cane. Her boss claimed the cheery outfits helped bring in tourists.

"I'm about to change but I'm starving. Did you finish my kung pao chicken?" She was staring into the fridge.

Claire shrugged. "Oops."

Gabby was about to protest when she froze. "Do you hear that?"

"Hear what?"

"That!" Gabby said. She closed the fridge and stood still. Then she pointed toward the closed-off shaft. "Oh my God, is someone moving the dumbwaiter?"

TURN OFF THE LIGHT

Claire rolled her eyes. "Ha. Ha."

"I'm serious. I can hear the gears moving."

"I'm not twelve anymore, Gabs. You can't scare me with your bullshit stories."

But standing here now, Claire wonders if Gabby had been telling the truth that day. Had she heard the same sound that Claire just did? And if so, why couldn't Claire hear it then? Why is she suddenly hearing it now?

A lump forms in Claire's throat. Guilt, lodged like stubborn food. She should have believed her sister. Gabby might still be here today if Claire had only listened. But instead, the next words out of Claire's mouth, fueled by annoyance and cruelty, changed everything—

She drags her mind back. Doesn't allow herself to go there. The noises have stopped, so Claire pulls her hand from the wall and trudges upstairs to bed, her body still stuck somewhere between East and West Coast time, still ravaged from the travel and her sleepless night yesterday. When she slips into her room, she is surprised to find Julia still awake.

"Mama?" Julia whispers.

"I got your water," Claire says, placing the bottle on the girl's nightstand. Then she begins to slowly run her fingers through her daughter's hair. "I thought you'd be asleep by now."

"I don't want to close my eyes."

Claire frowns. "Why is that? Aren't you tired?"

Julia nods.

"Well, you have to close your eyes to sleep. Want to try?"

Julia shakes her head and bites her lip.

"What's up, sweetie?" Claire asks.

Julia looks up at the ceiling and then at the wall behind Claire. "Tell it not to watch me again."

Claire's fingers stop. She props herself up on her side, leaning her weight on her elbow. "What do you mean?"

"It's watching me," Julia says.

"What is?" Claire asks.

Her daughter looks at her with a blank expression. "The house."

Julia falls asleep within ten minutes of this confession, but Claire cannot calm her mind. She locks the door to their room and double-checks that the window is latched. Then she locks the door to the room on the other side of the adjoining bathroom. And pulls back the shower curtain for who knows what reason.

Her daughter's words echo in her brain. *It's watching me.* She thinks of her sister's fear in the cellar. The sounds of the dumbwaiter.

Back in bed, Claire lies on her side and stares at Julia, whose small chest moves up and down rhythmically. Her face is so peaceful, her lips puffed in a sweet pout.

Thup. Thup. Thup.

Claire's breath stops. She freezes, straining to understand the sound. It's the same noise as last night. A hollow, gentle thud.

Slowly, she sits up. Her head swivels as she surveys the room, but she finds nothing. Her eyes travel to the window. Maybe the sound is coming from an animal outside. But she sees no movement beyond the glass pane. No signs of life at all.

Pipes in the wall. It must be. The house is so old. It speaks a language of its own in creaks and cracks and thuds.

Thup. Thup. Thup.

She whips her head around. The sound came from close by. Right behind her. Just over her shoulder.

But the room is empty.

TURN OFF THE LIGHT

Claire releases her breath. Then inhales, fills her chest, and lets the air out slowly.

She needs sleep. Her mind is playing tricks on her. She's overstimulated, that's all. Worked up and hypervigilant. She forces herself to lie back down. But when she does, her head begins to throb. Her body feels like it's sinking into the mattress. And then: A figure. A dark figure, too shadowed to make out the details of, like a living unfinished sketch. She tries to scream, but her voice catches in her dry throat.

And then the figure is right beside her, its face — or the space where its face should be — close to her own. Claire's chest is tight, her breath restricted.

"It's just me," a soft voice says, and she feels something lift the covers and push down the mattress as it crawls into bed.

"Mama, you're bleeding!"

Claire's eyes pop open, and she winces against the bright light of the morning. When did she fall asleep?

"What happened?" Julia asks, staring at her with wide eyes.

Claire, half asleep, reaches for her daughter, hoping Julia will cuddle with her and allow her a few minutes of rest before blazing into the day.

But Julia dodges her mother's touch. "No, yucky!" she says. "There's blood on your fingers, *eww.*"

Claire rolls onto her back so that she can inspect her fingertips, a few of which are crusting with remnants of blood. Her left ring finger throbs, and when she touches the nail, it's loose; the whole thing lifts a little, and she can see underneath it.

This wakes her up quick. She jumps to her feet and goes to the adjoining bathroom, where she grabs the hand towel and presses her nail into her finger as if there's hot glue under there and this will somehow make it stick.

She looks around, searching for signs of a struggle or a streak of her own blood on the wall or floor or anywhere. But nothing is out of the ordinary. The bedroom door is still locked, as is the door from the toilet to the adjoining room.

"What happened?" Julia asks again, and Claire doesn't have an answer.

"Maybe I was chewing my nails in my sleep. That's silly, isn't it?"

Julia frowns, and guilt seizes Claire's chest. She is trying to keep things light, but her daughter is clearly unsettled.

"Why would you chew your fingers in your sleep?" Julia asks.

Well, look at you, you suck your thumb all goddamn night, what's the difference?

Claire catches herself. She gets irritable when she is sleep-deprived. If only she could have a few hours of deep rest.

Keeping the towel pressed against her finger, she kneels down in front of the sink cabinets so that she's eye level with Julia.

"Sweetie," she says. "What did you mean last night? When you said the house is watching you?"

Julia gets shy, dipping her chin toward her chest.

"Have you seen . . ." Claire shudders as she remembers the figure hovering over the bed. But she doesn't know how to describe it. It was more like a shadow. A silhouette. Not quite human. "Did you see someone in the room?"

"I don't know," Julia says quietly. Then she looks at Claire's finger. "Was it the house? Did the house hurt you?"

Claire sees the nervousness in her daughter's expression, knows she needs to be a pillar of strength right now for her four-year-old.

"Are you feeling scared?" she asks, her voice soft.

TURN OFF THE LIGHT

Julia nods, and Claire mirrors the movement.

"I get that. I do. It's okay to feel that way," she tells her daughter.

Julia leans into her, and Claire holds the girl's small body close to her own. Her teeth clench in that familiar feeling of deep, deep love. Like she could eat this perfect little creature.

"It's okay to feel scared," Claire says again. "But there's nothing to worry about. We're safe. We're safe."

She repeats the words over and over, though she isn't sure for whose benefit.

11
EDITH

Mercifully, the evening with David is uneventful. When he returns from Jacob and Grace's, he is exhausted and eats quickly, then washes up for bed. He tells Edith that he won't go there tomorrow because he cannot afford to lose another day of work tending to Jacob's crop.

She hides her bruise, keeping her sleeve over her forearm. But really, she needn't have thought about it. David has been in a world of his own from the moment he arrived, too distracted to notice. Dark hollows sink below his eyes, and his pointy nose is bright red at the end.

"I worry you are going to work yourself to death in that hot sun," Edith tells him as he opens his Bible for evening prayers.

"Join me?" he asks, kneeling beside the bed and pointing to the floor next to him.

He looks at her then, really sees her. The left side of his mouth slides upward in a half smile as he reaches his hand out for hers. She takes it, feeling how his skin has roughened from working the fields.

TURN OFF THE LIGHT

Edith kneels down beside him. He closes his eyes, and she follows suit. When he starts the prayer, she joins in, reciting the words she has said nightly since childhood.

"Lighten our darkness, we beseech Thee, O Lord; and by Thy great mercy defend us from all perils and dangers of this night..."

When they have finished their prayers, David climbs onto the bed and sits on its edge. His head hangs down slightly, his neck rounded, as he stares at his weathered hands.

"Things are looking grim," he admits. "The crop has hornworms. It will not last a week without Jacob. But tomorrow I must finish the boat for the Blackwells."

There is a tinge of guilt in his tone. Edith stays at her husband's feet and leans her head against his knees as if bowing to him.

"You have done what you can to help," she says. "You are right to stay home tomorrow. You cannot sacrifice your own work."

He nods slowly, taking in her words. "If you are correct about when Jacob will die," he says, "that means he has only three days left."

Something in Edith's heart squeezes. Here he is again, harping on her prediction of Jacob's dying day. His comment feels leading, like a test. Or a trap.

"I do not know the exact day he will die," she reminds him.

He raises an eyebrow. "We shall see." A pause. He seems to be holding his breath. Then he releases it and says, "Grace is worried."

He stares at her, maintaining eye contact for too long. What is he thinking? Did Grace tell him of their earlier conversation? Did she tell him that Edith suggested Jacob's sickness might be something more natural and less divine?

A panic awakens in her gut. A fear that Grace has watered the seed of doubt that was already planted in David's consciousness.

"It is natural for Grace to be worried," Edith says, trying but failing to keep her voice even. "She is about to lose her husband. Perhaps also the farm. Everything she knows."

Edith remembers a time when Grace admitted that her husband was angry with her. She told the story with a sly smile, a mild amusement. She confessed that changing the pattern of Jacob's thoughts was easy. "I just direct him toward the bed," Grace had told her with a chuckle.

Thinking of this and feeling on the precipice of danger, as if she might suddenly say the wrong thing, Edith slides her hands up David's thigh, close to his waist.

"I would be frantic. I cannot imagine losing you," she says.

She hopes the words sound more sincere than they taste on her tongue. She feels the need to steer away from conversation. Away from the potential to awaken the doubt within her husband that fueled his darting eyes and hungry gaze in the root cellar this morning.

She reaches for the waist of his linen pants and tugs, slides her fingers underneath and feels the heat of his overworked skin. He cannot have all that he wants, since she is still bleeding, but she can do enough to keep his hunger from turning cruel.

David wraps his own fingers around her forearms and pulls her up onto the bed beside him. She winces slightly at his grasp on her bruise, but she quickly hides the expression behind a suggestive smile and leans into him.

With her mouth on his mouth, she feels safe. With her lips occupied, she does not risk saying anything that might anger him. With his lips occupied, he cannot ask more questions. The darkness of the night envelops them, and she is confident that David will sleep soundly after they bed.

She hopes that the tenderness of her touch can convince him he does not need to look at her with such scrutiny. That the softness of her lips will remind him she is his trusted wife and partner and that she would never purposely poison their chances at growing a family, even if she herself secretly does not want one.

As her breath gets heavier and her skin flushes in excitement, she hopes that her body is saying all the things she does not trust to words.

Edith's prediction was correct: Her husband is sleeping deeply after their time together.

But she, of course, is not. She finds herself wide awake after only a short slumber. She is overly warm again, but freeing her feet from the blanket provides little relief. She pulls her linen shift up to her waist and fully exposes her legs, but the heat is still stifling. Edith feels as though the warmth is coming from inside her, like the temperature of her blood is *rising, rising, rising* of its own accord.

This is the witching hour. She can sense it. That time of night when spirits are most active. When she was a girl, she was taught that if she woke during this time, she must stay silent. The only words she should utter are those of the Lord's Prayer. And above all, she must not look out the window, lest she risk seeing a spirit and inviting it into her home.

Edith has no memories of her mother, who died shortly after giving birth to her. But she knows bits and pieces from Aunt Joan, who shared stories as they pressed and dried herbs.

"Your mother was a fitful sleeper," she told Edith once as they were laying out small chamomile flowers for drying. "No amount of chamomile could help her."

"Fitful?" Edith asked, young and unfamiliar with the word.

Aunt Joan rearranged the flowers, moving them closer together on the cloth in order to make space for more. The whole drying process would take a week, at least. Especially in the humid summer air.

"Anything would wake her," Aunt Joan said. "Someone could breathe heavily nearby and her eyes would startle open. She always slept with a Bible under her pillow."

"Why?" Edith asked, her little fingers delicately pulling the freshly picked flowers from her apron.

"For protection," Aunt Joan said. "Especially during the witching hour. Bad sleep can be a curse, you know."

Edith rolled her eyes. Yet another example of Aunt Joan's deep-rooted superstitions.

"I'm serious, girl," her aunt said. "If someone with the evil eye sets their sights on you . . ." Her voice trailed off as she shook her head ominously.

"Why would anyone curse Mother?"

Aunt Joan sighed. "We'll never know, now, will we? Maybe someone envied her. Beautiful woman. Successful husband. Baby on the way."

"So the bad sleep started when she got pregnant?" Edith asked.

Aunt Joan frowned. "Around that time," she admitted.

Edith understood then that she had somehow played a part in her mother's downfall. Whether from pressure within by harming her mother from the womb or from pressure without by making her mother a target.

As she lies awake beside her husband, Edith wonders if this is why she does not want a child. Maybe some part of her knows that having a child could be the end of her. Although *not* having a child could have the same result. In the eyes of the men of this colony, she is of little use if she cannot continue the family line.

Edith gives up the notion of sleep and abandons the bed. She lights a candle and gathers some rosemary. Then she burns the ends and waves the smoke around the room, cleansing the air and warding off any potential spiritual attacks. Her aunt's memory has awakened a minor superstition. And, really, what harm can burning some rosemary do?

When she finishes, she feels naked in only her shift and reaches for her apron hanging on a nail. As she ties it around her waist, her fingers graze the light fabric and feel the rougher spots where the splashed lye has hardened. She remembers the spilled mess that disappeared without explanation.

And then, without thinking, she wanders to the window and pulls open the shutters. At first, the landscape is calm, softly lit by the nearly full moon. But then movement flickers near the ground. An unsteady motion that Edith cannot pinpoint. And then she sees a shadow. A walking silhouette, distorted by the angle of the light so that it appears longer and lankier than a man.

Someone is here. On her property. Could it be Grace, coming to tell them of Jacob's death? But surely she would wait for daybreak. Could it be Violet, seeking help for her pregnant mother? Perhaps the woman has gone into labor. Edith frowns, trying to remember how far along she is, then abandons the thought because surely the woman would seek out the midwife who lives north of the creek.

So then who, and with what motivations, would come to her home during the witching hour? Could it be the same person who left the trail of blood last night? The same person who moved the knife?

The shadow goes still. Whoever it is has stopped walking and now stands in place. Given the trajectory of the shadow, the person is far in Edith's periphery. She could see who it is only if she goes out the front door, on the opposite side of the house. But Edith has no intention of going outside. Not now.

The shadow remains still, and Edith shivers as she thinks about an unknown person staring at the house. She is about to call out for David when, suddenly, the shadow disappears. Instantly extinguished. As if the person has vanished into thin air.

But of course, that is not possible.

She steps forward and leans out the window, straining to find the shape on the landscape. She is certain she did not imagine it. The light must have somehow shifted. The stranger must still be lurking out there, hiding beyond the edge of the woods.

Or maybe it is not a person at all.

Darkness envelops the house. Edith's heart hammers, and she steps back, slamming the wooden shutters closed. She forces herself to control her breathing, though she is shaking. Then she blows out the candle and tosses the rosemary into the ashes of today's fire. She turns toward bed and—

The candle is lit again, flickering softly.

Edith's breath stops. Her whole body freezes like a frightened rabbit in the woods. The air changes, and her blood is warming again, as if she is being burned from the inside. She imagines the shadow reappearing in the house, growing larger, overtaking her.

She quickly steps forward and blows out the candle, then squeezes her eyes tight shut. Somewhere in her brain, the words of the Lord's Prayer echo: *Lead us not into temptation, but deliver us from evil.*

Why did she look outside? What evil force drew her to the window in the first place? One minute she was burning rosemary, the next minute she was out of her body, being called to the landscape.

Edith draws breath in through her nostrils and releases it slowly through her lips. She opens her eyes, and the room feels normal again. The candle is unlit. The faint smell of burned rosemary hangs in the air like limp laundry.

TURN OFF THE LIGHT

She is about to turn to bed when—

␣ffwick!

The candle lights itself.

Edith is standing by the fire when David wakes at first light. She is staring into the flames, stirring their pot of breakfast mush. He clears his throat loudly, and her attention flicks to him.

"Hello," she says as if in a trance.

"Edie?" he asks. He rarely uses her byname.

"Forgive me," she says, "I am tired this morning." She shakes her head and abandons the spoon near the hearth.

"Did something happen again? In the night?" His forehead wrinkles as his eyes tighten in scrutiny. He looks around the room, perhaps searching for anything out of place.

"I have only been thinking about Grace and Jacob," she half lies. "About what you said last night. How she is worried."

David's face softens. "I know she is your friend, but you do her no service by lying awake thinking about her."

She nods.

Her husband's eyes travel the length of her body, noting the absence of her corset-like bodice. "Where are your stays?"

"Apologies," she says, only now realizing she is undressed. "I was so hot this morning. I will go dress now."

As she passes him, David grazes her arm. Something catches his eye, and in a quick motion, he wraps his fingers around her wrist and flips her palm to the ceiling.

"What is this?" he asks, then pulls his hand away as if he does not wish to touch what he sees. As if her very skin could poison him. The expression reminds her of Margaret's disapproving scowl.

Edith looks down at her arm and sees the welts forming there.

Hundreds of small bumps. Redness blooming like flower petals over her limb. She lifts up her linen sleeve and sees that the rash continues up to her shoulder and neck. Again, her blood burns hot, and she wonders if it really is boiling her from the inside.

"Poisoned weed," she says without missing a beat. "I was tending to the garden yesterday and did not see it until it was too late."

David narrows his eyes and nods. "Bad luck, that."

"Bad luck indeed," she says.

The lies are coming more easily to her now, as if they have been planted in the soil of her mind by something else. All she has to do is pluck them.

12
CLAIRE

Claire sits at the kitchen table and stares into her coffee. Asleep with her eyes open. Her right hand haphazardly picks at the Band-Aid she has wrapped around the nail of her left ring finger.

"Mama, can you fix Bunny?" Julia holds up her stuffed lovey, showing her mother where the small blanket is starting to detach from the bunny's paws.

"Mm-hmm," Claire replies automatically.

"Mama," Julia whines, elongating the last vowel with a dramatic tone of frustration. "Can you do it *now*?"

"Give me two minutes," Claire says.

Even if she really means ten minutes, she never says more than two. It's a catchall phrase for any amount of time in Julia's world. Just like *yesterday* means anytime before this morning and *nap time* means any moment Julia lies down to sleep, night or day. The four-year-old lexicon is its own brand of confusing.

When Tilly comes in from outside, Claire sends Julia into the living room with the tablet. "I need to talk to you," she tells her sister.

"What's up?" Tilly asks. Her hands are caked with dirt, and she rinses them off in the sink. "Saw some weeds out there and next thing I know, an hour has passed. I'm not sure homeownership is all it's cracked up to be."

"I think there's something going on here," Claire says. "In this house."

Tilly rips a paper towel from the roll and dries her hands. "What do you mean?"

"I woke up with this," Claire says, prying the Band-Aid from her finger.

Tilly winces at the sight of the loose nail. "Oof, that does not look good. I have a first aid kit if you need it."

She starts to go, but Claire stops her. "I got it while I was sleeping, Tilly. And I saw someone in my room last night."

"What?"

"Or, like, a shadow of a person. And I heard this noise. The same one I heard the other night when I found Dad downstairs."

Tilly blinks, trying to take it all in. "Wait, Dad was out of bed again?"

"No," Claire says, unsure how to explain everything. "I just mean—it's this weird hollow sound. And there was this face right in front of my face, and I couldn't move or scream."

Tilly's eyes go wide. "God, sounds like an awful dream."

"No, it wasn't a dream . . ."

But Claire's voice trails off because she realizes she doesn't remember anything after the figure sitting on the bed. The next thing she knew, it was morning. Does that mean it could have been a dream after all? But it felt so real. Visceral.

"I have some melatonin if you want it for tonight," Tilly offers.

"But even Julia senses it. She said the house was *watching* her."

Tilly raises an eyebrow. "Yeah, that's definitely creepy. But she also thinks unicorns are real."

Claire sighs. Her sister has a point. She probably shouldn't put so much stock in a four-year-old's comments. Especially since they are in a new place. Of course her daughter is feeling scared.

Another thought comes to her. "The dumbwaiter. Have you ever heard it moving?"

"That dumbwaiter?" Tilly points to the boarded-up wall beside the fridge. "The one that hasn't been used in over a hundred years?"

"I heard it moving last night. Behind the wall. And Gabby heard it too. The last time I saw her, we were right here in this kitchen, and she got freaked out. Said she could hear the gears moving."

"Wait, what? The last time you saw her? Why am I just learning about this now? Did you tell Mom and Dad?"

Claire feels her cheeks flush. "It didn't seem important at the time," she says meekly. She holds her breath as she waits for her sister's reaction.

Tilly sighs. "Was she telling the truth? I mean, you heard it back then too? With Gabby?"

Claire frowns. "Well, no. I didn't hear it then. I figured she was making it up."

Tilly deflates a little.

"But I definitely heard it last night," Claire says. Then she realizes how that must sound. "You think I'm crazy?"

"No," Tilly says. "I don't. But I do think you're sad and grieving. You're finally seeing how bad Dad is, and it's a shock. Plus, being back here brings up old memories. It makes sense."

"Gabby told me she saw a ghost in the cellar," Claire says, still insistent. Desperate for Tilly to understand. "The day she got trapped in there. Did she ever tell you that?"

Tilly sighs. "Gabby was kind of a dick, Claire. She was our big sister and took every chance she could to scare us. When I said I wanted to be an actor, she told me I needed headshots. Which I understand now are pictures, but she told me they were literal shots that all actors got in their heads. I was eight! And remember my tenth-birthday party? She gave us a Ouija board to try and then she hid in the closet and tapped on the wall. Two of my friends never came back to the house after that, they were so freaked out."

Claire had forgotten about that party. Tilly didn't speak to Gabby for a week afterward.

"Hey," Tilly says, touching Claire's arm gently. "Stop spiraling. I know it's weird being back in this house. It's weird for me too. But of all the things we need to be worrying about right now, I don't think ghosts in the walls is one of them."

Claire nods. She wants so desperately for her sister to be right.

Tilly looks at the clock on the oven and sucks in her breath. "The nurse should be here in an hour or so. I'm going to take Dad his protein shake."

"I can do that," Claire says. "It'll get my mind off things."

Really, she wants to ask him if he saw anything last night. Tilly's points are valid, but Claire still feels like there are too many coincidences to ignore.

Tilly hesitates, obviously uneasy at the thought of Claire being alone with their dad. But then she sighs and nods.

"Okay. Sure." She moves to the counter and mixes four different powders with some milk. "Hopefully he's awake. He needs sustenance. I'm not used to him sleeping this much. But Phoebe — that's the nurse — she says it's normal at this stage."

Tilly hands Claire the unappetizing brownish drink.

"Yum," Claire teases. "He'll definitely wake up for *this*."

TURN OFF THE LIGHT

Claire finds her dad asleep, so she settles on the worn armchair and scrolls on her phone, cleaning up her email inbox, which she has largely avoided since arriving. For the past six years, she has worked for an event-planning agency, and every year her enthusiasm for the position has waned. Being here, so far from her daily routine and commitments, only exacerbates that feeling. She is realizing how little she cares for the job. How tired she is of her micromanaging boss and entitled clients. She still enjoys the work itself — seeing an event through from inception to fruition — but the politics at the company have been grating on her for quite some time.

"Claire."

She looks up to see her dad staring at her. His eyes are alert, his body turned toward her on the bed. For the first time, he has recognition in his eyes. He has called her by her name. Is this a rare moment of clarity? She leaps up from the chair and sits carefully on the mattress.

"Dad! Hi."

His face softens, and she is overcome with gratitude. Maybe she will get a proper goodbye after all.

"Claire," he says again.

"Hi, Dad." She holds his hand. "I'm so happy to see you."

He smiles. "I wanted to tell you..." His face strains, like he is working hard to conjure the words. "I don't remember."

"That's okay, Dad. That's okay," Claire says.

She tells him about her life as if merely catching up on a routine FaceTime call. Since it's fresh in her mind, she talks about the problems with her job and admits she harbors dreams of starting her own business. She recounts the details of Julia's first plane ride.

She gushes about her daughter's talent for drawing and her growing curiosity about the world around her. Claire even tells him about running into Ethan at the grocery store.

Her dad smiles and nods the whole time, though she isn't sure how much he actually understands. He seems to be slipping in and out of awareness.

Finally, he stops her. "I need to piss," he says.

She winces, unaccustomed to him speaking crudely. "Of course. Do you need help?"

He waves her off, so she stands out of the way as he moves slowly. When she again offers her hand, he growls. His mood has flipped.

The entrance to the bathroom is only a few feet from the bed. It's more like a second room, with double sinks and a large jacuzzi and huge walk-in closet. The toilet has its own door at the back end of the suite.

Claire busies herself on her phone again while she waits for her dad. Talking about Ethan has brought him to the forefront of her mind. She'd like to chat with him more, hear about the past decade of his life. So she opens a blank text and, without giving herself time to change her mind, asks him to lunch today. For some reason, when she presses Send, her stomach flutters. She has no reason to be nervous, but she feels like a teenager again, waiting for a boy's approval. The three dots appear, indicating he's writing back, when—

She hears a loud *crash* from the bathroom.

Claire throws the phone onto the armchair and rushes in to find her father on the tile floor. A trickle of blood drips from his temple, where he must have hit his head against the wall on the way down.

"Oh my God, Dad!" She kneels beside him and assesses for more injuries. "What happened?"

He looks at her blankly, the recognition from earlier gone. "He... was here," he says.

"Who?" Claire asks. "Who was here? There's no one, Dad."

"The Devil." He is whispering, just like he did the other night. "I think I let him in."

Claire shakes her head. "What do you mean? How did you let him in?"

Her father grips her arm and pulls her closer to him. His breath smells like moldy towels. Claire is only inches from the crusty sores around his mouth. One of them produces a drop of yellow pus.

"I'm scared, Claire-y," he says.

Claire-y. His nickname for her in childhood. The sound of it is a gut punch. His eyes are pleading, trying to tell her something, begging for help. The drop of blood drips into his eye, and he blinks, then reaches with his shaky fingers to wipe at it. When he pulls his fingers away from his face, he sees they are wet with blood. He rubs his fingers together, then lifts his hand to the wall and paints a circle. Claire watches as he brings his hand back to his forehead, gathers more blood, and starts to fill in the circle with lines.

"What's going on?" Tilly's voice is frantic as she launches into the room. "I heard a crash." When she sees their dad on the floor, the blood on his forehead, she shrieks and pushes Claire to the side.

"Dad saw something," Claire says. "Just like Julia did. And Gabby, and me —"

"Claire, *please*," Tilly says, her voice biting. She helps their dad to his feet. But he falls back again, unable to regain his balance.

"Tell her, Dad," Claire says. "Tell Tilly what you saw. Tell her what you told me."

But he just stares at her as if she is speaking a foreign language.

"He's not stable," Tilly says. "We have to be careful, you can't get him worked up like this."

"It's not *me*. He's seeing things!"

Tilly holds up her hand to make Claire stop. "Later," she says.

Claire bites her lip and swallows her words. She tries to help Tilly maneuver their father to the bed, but Tilly refuses to let her, so Claire stays behind to clean up the bloody mess. She gathers paper towels and Clorox cleaner, but just before she sprays the wall, she freezes. There, painted in blood, her father has drawn the same geometric pattern that Julia sketched.

The same as the carving in the cellar.

It takes Tilly and Peter thirty minutes to get the old man back into bed. Claire waits in the living room with Julia. Eventually, Peter emerges alone.

"Is he okay?" Claire asks.

Peter looks worn out. "I have a feeling he won't be getting out of bed again."

"What do you mean?"

"The nurse told us this might happen. And since he hit his head, she's probably going to say it's safest for him to stay put."

The air leaves Claire's chest. The end feels even closer now.

She follows Peter into the kitchen. "Something is trying to hurt Dad."

Peter's reaction is minimal, which tells Claire that her sister has already given him a heads-up about her theories.

"Have you seen anything weird?" she asks. "Heard anything?"

Peter shifts his weight and leans back against the pantry door. "No," he says simply.

"Dad fell because he saw something that scared him. I think this is why he's gotten so bad so fast. It's not just the dementia." She holds up her phone and shows him a picture of the blood drawing on the wall. "See this? It's the same thing Julia drew."

Peter squints at the picture. "It *is* weird he used his own blood to draw on the wall. But do you really think it's the same design? This kinda just looks like a smudged circle."

Claire sighs. "Listen, I found a care facility forty minutes away. I think it'd be good for him to get out of this house. The place looks really nice, and he would be safe there. I already called, and they have an opening. He's freaked out, Peter. He needs to get away from this house."

She thinks of the desperation in her father's eyes. *I'm scared, Claire-y.* It's unnerving seeing her father in this state. In fact, she has never seen him truly frightened. When she was nine, they endured a category five hurricane and holed up in the house for a week. Her mother was frantic and barely slept. But her father was a steady force of calm the entire time, even when a tree fell mere inches from the house. It was like he just knew they would be okay. And when Gabby disappeared, he went through all the emotions — anger, desperation, sadness, blind hopefulness — but never did he seem scared. So Claire knows that whatever is happening to her father now must be truly terrifying.

Peter only sighs, his face full of pity. "Your dad hasn't made sense for a while, Claire. It sucks. And it's so hard. But I haven't been able to have a real conversation with him for weeks. That's the disease. Moving him won't change anything."

She looks at her brother-in-law and notices the dark hollows under his eyes. Has he always looked this tired? Or have they just gotten older? Maybe she is expecting to see the teenage Peter she knew so well. But Claire has been gone for years; life has continued on, and she no longer knows the people who once made up the entire fabric of her life.

"Have you thought about sleeping pills?" Peter asks. "If you don't get sleep, it'll just make all this worse."

His tone is careful, and she can read between the lines: *You're losing it.*

She shrugs and takes a deep breath. Trying to get Peter on her side has turned out to be a dead end.

"Yeah," she says, resigned. "You're probably right. It's all just a lot."

He smiles a little, one corner of his mouth curling up in sympathy. "I agree," he says. "It's a fucking *lot*."

Claire takes a hot shower and then stands in the guest room staring out the window. She is so tired. Her breath is shallow, her muscles too tense to allow for more expansion. The emotional exhaustion of the past couple of hours paired with the events of the past two nights are wearing on her.

She stares at the horizon. Through the tall, thin trees, she sees the bay and the sand and the sky changing colors from blues to pinks. She remembers the dark clouds yesterday and realizes that it never rained after all.

"Mama!" Julia says, barreling into the room.

Claire's attention is ripped from the window, and she turns and smiles at her daughter. "Hey, sweetie," she says.

"Mmm, you smell good," Julia says. "Because you took a shower."

"Sure did." Claire squeezes water from her hair with the towel. "We're leaving soon for lunch, okay?"

"But I want to stay here," Julia whines.

"No," Claire says. She might be overreacting, but she doesn't feel comfortable going out and leaving Julia in the house. Not until she knows for sure there's nothing going on. "We're meeting that nice man from the grocery store. Ethan. Remember?"

Julia's face lights up. She nods.

"See? Lunch with new friends. It'll be fun." Claire smiles.

They are meeting Ethan at a diner. She still hasn't talked to Tilly about their dad's accident. The nurse is running late, and Tilly has been holed up with their father as if guarding him. Claire will be happy to escape the suffocating walls of this house for a couple of hours.

Julia jumps on the bed as Claire works a comb through the knots of her own hair. She scrunches mousse into the ends and leaves it to air-dry.

"What were you looking at?" Julia asks.

"Hmm?" Claire says, inspecting herself in the mirror. She has opted for breezy linen pants and a loose cotton top. The look is more sophisticated than she feels, and she considers changing. Doesn't want to seem like she is trying too hard. Then she inwardly chides herself — she's not seventeen anymore. She's a grown woman. And anyway, who cares what she looks like? This is lunch with an old friend. Nothing more.

"The window," Julia says. "You were looking out the window."

"Oh." Claire's coral lipstick has escaped her makeup bag, so she bends over the suitcase in search of it. "I wasn't really looking at anything specific. Just looking." She finally finds it and sighs in relief. This is the only lipstick that can perk up her tired face.

"You still need to fix Bunny," Julia says, holding up her lovey.

Claire smiles apologetically. "You're right." She bends down to address the stuffed animal directly. "Sorry, Bunny. I'll sew you up as soon as we get back. Promise."

Julia takes Bunny and moves her so that the lovey gives Claire a kiss. *"Mwah."*

Claire laughs.

Then Julia turns Bunny toward her own cheek. *"Mwah."*

"Kisses for everyone!" Claire smiles.

"Mwah," Julia says a third time, pointing Bunny away from them and kissing the air.

"Who was that one for?" Claire asks playfully.

Julia freezes as if she has been caught doing something she shouldn't.

"What is it?" Claire asks.

Her daughter's demeanor changes drastically. She lowers her gaze, then lifts one shoulder toward her ear shyly. There's clearly something she doesn't want to say.

"Is someone else here?" Claire asks.

Her daughter stares at the bunny, wrapping her fingers in and around the little attached blanket. Claire sits on the mattress beside her and gently nudges her chin upward, encouraging eye contact.

"Julia," she says slowly. "Is someone else in the room?"

Julia looks over her shoulder, then shrugs and shakes her head: *No.*

Claire bites her lip. "*Was* someone else here? A second ago, when Bunny gave them a kiss?"

Julia looks up at her mother, her eyes large and round, and very slowly nods: *Yes.*

Claire is sure of it now: There is something in this house.

13
EDITH

Edith is worried. Ever since David pointed out the rash, her thoughts have been racing.

She should not have eaten that apple.

She should not have opened the window last night.

This is all on her: She has invited the Devil in.

She crawls on her hands and knees in the dirt harvesting the last of this year's radish crop. David is in the back acres hollowing out a cypress tree for a dugout canoe. She has not seen him since breakfast, but she cannot get the image of his shocked face and narrowing eyes out of her mind. His disgust has been seared there.

The rash is indeed shocking. Though she has wrapped it in witch hazel leaves, she feels it resisting the herbal remedy, burning and stinging as it asserts its power.

She wants to believe her theory is ridiculous. Letting the Devil in. It's something Aunt Joan would have said. Curses and evil eyes and Bibles under the pillow. But she cannot help wondering if this was what happened to her own mother. Maybe she had trouble sleeping because she, too, was being visited at night.

"That's a pretty dress," Edith hears someone say.

She sits back on her heels and wipes her sweaty brow with her uninjured arm. She looks up to find a young girl wearing a simple yellow cotton dress. Edith has never been adept at guessing children's ages, but she imagines this girl cannot be more than five. Violet's little sister, then. Or one of them, anyway. Edith cannot keep track of that growing family. So many children under one roof.

"Hello there," Edith says, shielding her eyes from the sun. It is bright already, though still hours from high noon. "And thank you."

She looks down at her own clothing. Her shift is stained with dirt, but she is wearing her favorite blue skirt. Most of the women here on the creek wear brown or gray. Edith and this girl are standouts in their summer colors. "I like yours as well," she adds.

The little girl smiles, grabs the end of her braid, and twists it this way and that. Perhaps she is feeling shy.

"How is your mother?" Edith asks. "Is she well?" She remembers the disappearing shadow from last night. How she thought for a moment that her neighbor had gone into labor. What a relief that would have been, to have such a normal explanation for the bizarre and frightening event.

"I don't know," the girl says, then giggles.

Before Edith can say any more, the girl is gone, running back toward the woods. Edith strains to see where she goes, but the sun is too bright, and she loses sight of her. In her wake, a cloud of small insects fly together like a school of fish.

When Edith finishes with the radishes, she pushes herself to standing. Her body is achy from the lack of sleep, her joints stiff, but it feels good to get her hands dirty. Working with the earth grounds her. Out here in the garden, she is in her element, capable and in tune. She trusts herself.

"Hi, Edie!"

TURN OFF THE LIGHT

Another girl's voice slices through the heat of the morning. This time when Edith shields her eyes from the sun, she finds Violet.

"Your sister was just here," Edith says as she gathers the vegetables to bring inside.

"She was?" Violet frowns. "Mother will have her hide, then. She's supposed to be gathering eggs."

Edith gestures for Violet to follow her as she makes her way toward the house. "She's so little to be wandering alone."

The girl shrugs. "We're used to it."

Edith marvels at how different Violet's life is from what she herself experienced. Edith was an only child without a mother who grew up with a cobbled-together family. Violet has a houseful of siblings and two very present parents. Edith feels a small tug of jealousy at the thought.

Inside, she places the radishes in a basket near the hearth so she can wash and cut them for the midday meal. Then she looks at Violet with excitement in her eyes. "Would you like to see my collection?" she asks.

Edith lights the lantern and leads Violet down the stone steps of the root cellar. When she presents the green granite mortar and pestle that she got from Reeve's place, the girl nearly falls over with gratitude.

"For me? Oh, it's so beautiful, Edie," she gushes. And then her eyes bulge with awe when she sees Edith's stash of herbs and balms and salves.

What's that? Where's this from? What does this one do? The questions invigorate Edith, who feels a strong sense of purpose when teaching. This is what she was born to do: heal people and help spread the knowledge.

She points to a bundle of willow bark. "The easiest way to remember what everything does is to memorize the rhymes."

"Rhymes?" Violet asks, leaning in for a better look.

"Willow can be used for fevers. So remember: 'If fever burns and shakes the bone, a tea of willow, cool as stone.'"

Violet tries to repeat the rhyme, and Edith corrects her. The girl says it a few more times until it sticks.

"Very good," Edith says. "Shall we make some tea with this, then?"

"That's not a waste?" Violet asks.

Edith shakes her head. "A healer must know every step of the process."

"It's just brewing some tea," Violet says. "I've done that a hundred times."

Edith smiles at Violet's overconfidence. "Mmm, I see. And how long must willow bark steep?"

Violet falters, then smiles, catching her own misstep.

They ascend from the cellar and spend the next hour cutting and shredding the bark into smaller pieces. After Violet helps boil the water, they steep the bark for twenty minutes. Edith pours a cup for Violet.

"It is important to know the taste as well," she says.

The girl takes the cup and sips, then immediately spits it out into the hearth. The fire sparks with the liquid.

Edith laughs. "Bitter, right? If you have honey, you can mask that." She continues to stir what is left in the pot over the stove. "For a more potent decoction, we steep for thirty minutes."

"More potent?" Violet cries. "I think I would rather have fever."

Edith raises an eyebrow. "You say that now."

As they wait for the tea to further steep, Violet helps Edith wash and prepare the radishes. Edith is grateful for the company; it is such a relief not to be alone with her thoughts. Even her rash feels calmer, and she works with Violet to switch out the leaves and apply a salve. She tells the girl the same thing she told David: She mistakenly got into poisoned weed.

TURN OFF THE LIGHT

And honestly, that is the most likely conclusion, is it not?

Still, she finds herself thinking again of the past few days' mysteries. The knife, the blood, the shadow. The candle lighting itself. The whispers. And it all started with that damned apple.

This gives her an idea. "You all planted an apple tree in your garden, right?" she asks Violet. "For cider. Was it two seasons ago?"

The girl nods. "Yes."

Edith is relieved. That is it, then. An animal carried the apple from Violet's garden. There is a logical explanation after all.

"But it got blighted," Violet continues. "Spots on the leaves. They all curled up and died. We have not gotten an apple from it in over a year."

Edith takes this in. Violet's family is the only one to have successfully planted an apple tree here on the Shore. So if the fruit did not come from their garden...

She bites her lip and wishes she had not asked.

Edith attempts to turn off her brain. To move with muscle memory through the motions of her life. She spends the afternoon harvesting and preparing David's favorite dinner, blue crabs with vinegar. When the water boils, she throws the live crabs into the pot. The largest of them struggles, flailing and tapping the edges of its claws against its confinement.

Hissssss — wheeeeeeee!

The crabs sing as their shells release steam. They get redder and redder, and their scrabbling for an exit eventually slows. Finally, the singing stops.

The crabs go still.

They are dead.

That evening, David's appetite is insatiable.

"Delicious," he says, twisting a small leg and snapping it from the crab's main shell. He sticks the end in his mouth and sucks out the meat. Then he licks his fingers and starts in on the next leg.

"How is the canoe coming?" she asks.

David frowns. "Taking longer than I expected. I promised it to Blackwell this coming Friday. But I finished the burn and scrape only today. I have yet to shape and seal with oakum. And with the rain coming..."

Edith lights another candle as the room gets darker. The sun has not yet gone down, but the sky was an angry gray while she harvested crabs. David is right. The rain is coming.

"Do you think you will finish in time?" she asks.

"I have no choice. A man is only as good as his word. And I promised him this Friday." He dips a large chunk of crabmeat into the vinegar and rips it with his front teeth. "But the weather does prove a challenge. I covered the wood with deer hide. Let's hope that is enough."

David wipes his mouth with his sleeve, and Edith winces. Why can he never use a rag? He makes for double the washing when he uses his clothes as a napkin.

"Do you not want some?" he asks, gesturing toward Edith's untouched plate.

The truth is, watching him eat has soured her own appetite.

His hands are slimy as he crushes another crab's shell with his swollen and callused fingers. Vinegar drips down his chin.

She shrugs. "More for you," she says with a thin smile.

That night, Edith sleeps.

But it is fitful, full of vivid dreams.

TURN OFF THE LIGHT

In one, she walks the shoreline, her feet bare on the sand, squishing indents that the water fills up. She wades into the shallows and moves her feet around in circles like a dance to very gentle music.

Her knees bend and bring her body to the water. She sits in the bay like it's a bath, the water warm after a storm. Edith closes her eyes and lies down; the entire back of her body is in the water now, only the front exposed. She feels warm and comfortable, as if she were birthed from this very bay and will return to it upon death.

And then another sensation cuts through the peace. A pinch. On the bottom of her foot. She winces, then wiggles her toes. Another pinch, this time on her right hip. She bats away the sharp pain and then feels something hard against her palm.

Edith sits up and sees —

The water is full of crabs. They are descending on her quickly, climbing over the top of one another to get to her faster. She tries to get away, to shift her weight and scoot her butt out of the water, but the crabs attack her hands. Their pincers poke and pinch her skin. There are too many to shake off. She cries out and pulls her hands in toward her stomach, but the crabs use the opportunity to migrate to the softer part of her torso. They stab her belly through her thin linen shift, knives to her gut.

Edith cries out again, but now there must be twenty crabs on her, burrowing as if they could bury her alive with their bodies. She feels all their legs, so many legs, scurrying over her own limbs and digging into her flesh. The weight of them pushes her onto her back, and when she tries to call for help, her mouth fills with water. She sputters and coughs.

But she does not taste salt water — she tastes vinegar.

The crabs let up from her upper body, and she manages to lift her head from the water for a breath. But her legs are paralyzed, weighed down by the small creatures. They huddle near her hips, gathering themselves at her groin.

And then she feels a *twisting*.

The pain is unbearable, otherworldly. The crabs work in tandem to twist her legs in their sockets, wringing and spinning the limbs until each muscle tears. She remembers David twisting the legs off the crabs at dinner and sucking out the meat, the juices dribbling down his neck and onto his shirt.

Spots light up her vision, and she is on the verge of losing consciousness. She opens her mouth and screams, but the sound is not a scream at all — it is more like a whistle. The same noise the crabs made when steam escaped their shells while she was cooking them.

Hissss — wheeeee!

All the crabs mimic her, opening their tiny mouths and whistling like kettles. The noise is so loud that she brings her hands to her ears, where she feels blood. Her nose is bleeding too. It's coming from everywhere. Darkening the water to an angry red. The water gets *hot, hot, hot* and burns her skin. Her own blood is boiling her from the inside.

When her right leg finally *pops* from the socket, more blood gushes out. The crabs *suck, suck, suck* the meat from her dismembered leg, and Edith sinks under the red water, her mouth filling with the taste of salt and copper and vinegar.

She wakes in bed, her clothes soaked through with sweat. It is the witching hour again, dark and brooding. She rubs her temples and billows her linen shirt for relief from the heat.

A nightmare. Anyone would tell her that this is a sure sign she is being ridden by an evil spirit. She needs to visit the minister. But she must go alone. She cannot afford for her husband to know the truth of what she is experiencing. For that matter, no one else can know. The people of the Shore already question and distrust her.

Sleep is impossible now, so she pads out of bed to the hearth. She sets a pot of water on for tea and thinks. Convincing her husband that she needs a private moment with the minister will not be easy. He has to believe the idea is his own. Going to the minister's home means a day of travel, and while normally he would not balk at the idea of her journeying alone, he has been so suspicious of her lately.

She needs him in a pleasant mood, so she decides to make his favorite honey cakes for breakfast. It is still early enough that she has the time. She spends the next hours mixing ingredients, shaping the dough into small flat rounds, and arranging them on an iron plate for the fire. When David wakes, Edith presents him with a plated cake, dripping the very last of their honey preserves as dressing with a flourish.

"What's all this?" he asks.

There it is again. That suspicion. Although this time it is warranted. She thinks about this cycle, how the more he distrusts her, the more suspicious she acts. Like someone mad in the head insisting she is not — and looking more mad as a result.

"I had a craving," she says, sitting down with her own plate. "And I know they are your favorite."

"You were not able to sleep again?" he asks.

She must tread carefully here. "I was too excited," she tells him. "I've had an idea. I was hoping we could visit the minister today."

He pauses mid-bite, his mouth full of sticky honey. "The minister? What for?"

Edith picks at her own plate and brings a small bite to her mouth. "I would like him to pray for us," she says as she has rehearsed in her mind all morning. "For the baby. It would help to have his blessing, would it not?"

"Of course, but we will see him at service this Sunday," he says. "We can ask him then."

She rehearsed this part too. "He is due up north this weekend, remember? He will be at Occohannock Creek. And he will not return for weeks. I would like to see him before he goes."

It is a risk, spouting this made-up story, but she does not mind looking a fool later. When the minister is indeed at service this Sunday, she will tell her husband she had been mistaken. That she heard a rumor that proved untrue.

"Occohannock Creek?" David asks. "Why up there?"

Edith shrugs and keeps her answer vague. "I'm not sure. I only heard from Violet, the Cotton girl."

"A girl? She could be wrong. I cannot afford to lose an entire day of work over unreliable information."

"That is true," Edith says. "Your time is too valuable." She nods slowly, then looks down at her cake. Though her stomach does not want it, she forces down another bite. She cannot stand the idea of wasting the rare ingredients. Both flour and honey are hard to come by.

She pouts for another minute or so, then pretends to get an idea. "What if I went on my own?" she asks. "That way, you do not lose time, and we can still get the blessing of the minister."

"You want to go alone?" he asks.

"Well, no, I certainly do not *want* to," she lies. "But if that is what is best for our family, I can brave it. I will take our canoe. I can be home before sunset."

David considers this. He leans back in his chair. "You know the way?"

She smiles. "You forget I am a native," she says.

It is true that every other woman her age on the Shore is from across the ocean, imported here to serve as a bride. But Edith was born and raised in Virginia. A rarity.

"And if it is storming?" David asks. "After all, the rain is coming."

"I do not mind the rain," she says. "It would only make the journey a little slower. And wetter." She cannot afford for him to worry about complications of the weather.

David thinks for a long moment, and Edith's heart dances in her chest. Finally, he curls his mouth in a half smile.

"It is a good idea to get the minister's blessing," he says. "And I am happy to see you eager to be with child."

"Of course," Edith says, flattening a crumb between her middle finger and thumb. "I want nothing more."

14
CLAIRE

Claire and Julia wait at the diner. It's new—or at least, new since Claire moved away. The booths have that sticky fake-leather fabric, and anytime she shifts her weight, she feels her skin peel from the surface with a tug and a pinch.

Julia sips fresh-squeezed orange juice as Claire's knee bounces incessantly. Her body is tired but her mind is alert with a strange mix of anticipation and fear. She doesn't know how much of it is driven by lunching with Ethan and how much by the realization that her childhood home is haunted.

They are in the back, far from the windows and entrance and crowd. Claire would like to be invisible in this moment. She orders a grilled cheese for Julia; better to have food on the table and preempt any feral hunger-monster meltdowns.

"Claire!" Ethan walks in long strides to the rear of the diner. "God, feels like we're doing something unsavory back here. Or we're in the Witness Protection Program."

"I just wanted some privacy," she says with a nervous laugh.

"Hey there, Julia." Ethan waves as he sits down.

TURN OFF THE LIGHT

"You are from the grocery store," Julia says.

Ethan nods seriously. "That's right, I am. You have a very good memory."

"I know," Julia replies. "I'm really good at finding things too. I'm good at lots of stuff."

"Is that so?" he asks.

Claire is suddenly struck with the strangeness of it all, sitting here with both Ethan and her four-year-old daughter. After she and Ethan order, Julia slides off the booth and onto the floor beneath the table.

"Hey," Claire says, poking her head down there. "What are you doing on the floor? Yucky, yucky."

Julia giggles and tugs on Claire's legs, then half climbs back up onto the booth for a sip of orange juice. She spills some down the front of her dress and cries. "It's all wet."

Claire cleans her daughter up in the bathroom, then settles the girl at a nearby empty booth with her small purse of treasures, little trinkets she collects, like hair clips, beads, small floss samples from the dentist. The more random, the more likely Julia has it. She is obsessed with small things, as if she could build an entire world to her size.

Claire allows herself to ease into the lunch with Ethan. They talk about her desire to start her own business and the challenges of balancing work and motherhood. She tells him about living in Los Angeles and what an adjustment it is from the Shore.

Ethan opens up about his ex-girlfriend, who he discovered was cheating on him with a coworker. They'd dated for three years, but when Claire asks if he'd wanted to marry her, he shrugs.

"Honestly, what happened was for the best," he says. "There were a lot of reasons we should have ended things sooner."

Claire nods. She knows a thing or two about that.

"What happened with Julia's dad?" Ethan asks, seemingly reading her mind.

Claire looks over at Julia to ensure she is still busy with her trinkets. "It's not a very interesting story," she admits. "We dated for a while. I'm not sure he ever took it as seriously as I did. And then I got pregnant, and he bailed."

"Any chance of you guys getting back together?"

Claire snorts. "God, no. We don't even speak."

"He doesn't want to be involved?" Ethan asks, looking over at Julia.

Claire swallows. This is a sore spot for her. "He made it very clear that he does not."

"Sounds like an asshole," Ethan says, and Claire can't help but laugh.

"Julia and I are good on our own. We make a good team." Claire looks at her beautiful daughter. "I wasn't trying to get pregnant. I was waiting for my doctor to refill my birth control. So we were smart; we used a condom. And even when it broke, I got Plan B."

Julia has gotten a refill on her orange juice and now holds the cup with both hands and brings it to her mouth with extreme concentration.

"Clearly, I was meant to have her," Claire adds. "And it's the best thing that ever happened to me."

Ethan smiles. "You seem like a great mom."

"I try," Claire says. And she means it. She really does try. But has being a good mother come at a cost? Has it meant becoming a lesser daughter? An absent sister? Is that the price anyone pays when becoming a parent?

"What is it?" Ethan asks.

Claire tries to shrug it off. "Feeling guilty about not being around lately. Taking care of Dad has been a lot for Tilly."

"Yeah, I bet," he says.

They sit in silence for a minute before Ethan leans in. "Is everything okay? I know we haven't seen each other in forever, but you used to get this look when you were worried about something. It's the same look you have now."

Claire's chest warms at the familiarity. It has been a long time since she has felt seen. She is about to answer when Julia calls out from the other booth.

"Mama! Can I get a chocolate muffin?" She points to a table talker that has a large picture of the menu's fresh muffins.

Claire sighs. Her daughter has barely touched her lunch. She needs more protein before housing a sugar bomb. But Claire is exhausted. She doesn't have the energy to fight her daughter on this.

"Sure," she says, to Julia's great glee.

Once the treat has been delivered, Ethan leans in again. "So, what's up? I mean, I understand if you don't want to talk about it."

"There's something in our house." The words spill out before she can vet them.

"Something like what?"

"A spirit. Ghost. Whatever you want to call it," Claire says.

Ethan leans back like he has been slapped.

"Hear me out," she says. Then she tells him about her father's head injury and the kitchen shears. His talk of the Devil. The sigil in the cellar and Julia's drawing and her father painting with his own blood.

"Jesus," Ethan says. "That's definitely weird. But you don't think it's the dementia? Isn't it normal to hallucinate toward the end?"

"It can be," Claire says. "But I keep thinking about Gabby's last days. Right before she disappeared, she was seeing and hearing things in the house too."

"Wait—really?"

Claire nods. "Even in my last conversation with her, she insisted she could hear the dumbwaiter moving."

"No shit. What did she think it was?" Ethan asks.

Electricity jolts through Claire's chest. "I don't know. I wrote it off. I didn't believe her," she admits, that familiar sensation of guilt hitting like a bout of vertigo. "She was always messing with us, so I figured she was making it up."

Claire does not elaborate. Does not tell Ethan exactly how she responded. The specific words that might have been the ones to push Gabby out of all their lives . . .

"So you think whatever happened to her could be connected to the house?"

Claire shrugs. "I don't know what to think," she says. "It's like I have all these pieces to a bunch of different puzzles. I can't work out how they fit. But I'm sure they do. Somehow."

Ethan bites his lip. "Any theories on who the ghost is?"

Claire seesaws her head back and forth. "No. I saw a figure over my bed. It seemed like a man, but I don't know. It's an old house. A lot of people have lived there."

"What do Tilly and Peter say? Are they seeing stuff too?"

Claire chews on a limp french fry. "No. They aren't. And Tilly blames me for Dad's episodes. She says he wasn't acting like this before I got here."

Ethan blows out a puff of air. "That's ridiculous. How could it be your fault?"

"I don't know. But if she's right, if me being here has somehow triggered something, then I need to fix it."

"Fix it?" he asks.

TURN OFF THE LIGHT

In the booth beside them, Julia picks out the large chocolate chunks from the muffin, digging tunnels through it.

"It's like he's being tortured," Claire says, "but he can't do anything about it because his mind is trapped deep in that broken brain, totally unable to differentiate between what's real and what's not. Whatever is haunting the house has made Dad's condition accelerate. It's literally killing him. Way faster than the disease would."

Her poor father. He was the one who held out hope for Gabby the longest, the one who fought the hardest to keep the family a family. And this is how he is forced to spend his last days.

Ethan frowns in sympathy. "It does sound awful."

"I need to figure out what's going on in the house," Claire says. "Dad can't die like this. It's not right. He deserves some peace before he goes."

Julia pops back into the booth with her small purse. "Can you do this, Mama?" she asks, fumbling with the zipper.

Claire reaches over like a zombie, her mind elsewhere, and helps Julia close the bag.

Ethan cracks his knuckles. "So you think if you figure out what's causing these episodes, you can help your dad?"

Claire nods. "Maybe if I know what's in the house, I can get rid of it." She swallows, already doubting her ability. "At least, I have to try."

The nurse is at the house when Claire and Julia return.

"You must be the sister," the woman says when Claire pops her head in her father's room. The nurse moves like a bulldozer to shake Claire's hand. "I'm Phoebe." She has a salt-washed southern accent, though Claire can't place from where exactly.

"Is Tilly here?" Claire says, looking around.

Phoebe tells her she's taking a shower upstairs. "You want to help with the stretches?"

The woman marches around the bedroom with the energy of an army general. It's not what Claire would expect from a nurse. Even so, something about her presence is comforting. Like she could hold up the roof if a tornado came through here.

"Sure, uh, okay," Claire says.

She stands on the opposite side of the bed and assists Phoebe in moving her dad's arms gently forward and down, then in circles above his head and toward the ground. Phoebe leans him forward to stretch his spine and works on loosening his neck.

"Tilly told me about his fall," Phoebe says matter-of-factly. "We need to monitor for a concussion. It can be tricky with patients like your dad, since he was already displaying some of the symptoms due to the dementia. But we'll keep a close eye."

Claire feels strange talking about him as if he weren't right here. "And she told you about the other night? With the kitchen shears?"

Phoebe nods. "You were smart to pack the knives away."

Claire sighs, a bit relieved. Tilly and Peter can ignore her concerns, but if anyone has to care, it's this woman. It's her job to listen.

"Dad is really freaked out," Claire says. "And Tilly is being so casual about it. She's not taking it seriously. He didn't just fall randomly. He fell because he saw something."

"What did he see?"

Claire pauses. She must play her cards carefully here. Her honesty with Ethan surprised even herself. But something about being with him made it easy to fall back into their old dynamic. She somehow felt confident he wouldn't judge her. This woman is a stranger, though.

"I'm not sure," Claire says. "But it really scared him."

TURN OFF THE LIGHT

Phoebe nods. "Hallucinations are quite normal at this stage."

Claire presses. "But Tilly said he wasn't this bad just a few days ago."

Phoebe looks at the old man in the bed who hardly even resembles Claire's father anymore. "Well, he's nearing the end. It'll go fast now."

"And what about the antipsychotics?"

Phoebe furrows her brow. "Tilly decided not to. Would you like to look into it?"

Claire shakes her head. Truthfully, she isn't convinced medication would help at this point. Her father isn't imagining the things he's seeing. She knows he's not. Meds won't change a thing.

"Could we move him? I don't think it's good for him to be in this house. I called, and they have an opening at Bay Lake Home near—"

"I don't advise that," Phoebe says. "Moving him right now would be very disorienting. Why shouldn't he be here?"

She stares, her eyes intense. Claire is about to respond when Tilly enters, wet hair wrapped in a towel.

"You're back," she says to Claire, her voice flat.

The sisters look at each other for a long beat, both waiting for the other to make a move. Phoebe, either oblivious to the tension or wanting to break it, leans toward Claire.

"We'll do the legs now," she says, nodding to the other end of the bed.

"Okay," Claire replies just as Tilly says, "I got this."

Tilly waves Claire away from the bed and puts her own hands on their father's leg. "You go be with Julia," she says without giving her sister another look.

Claire spends the next two hours researching from a beach chair while Julia plays at the shoreline.

She types her address into an AI chat app and asks for the history of the property. It brings up countless land patents, wills, deeds, and tax records. She squints against the bright light of the afternoon to scroll through dates and names. The first official patent for the house that she can find is from the 1660s. The owner is listed as the Harris family.

Claire finds a few detailed history books on the Eastern Shore, but none are digital and it would take over a week to get them delivered in hard copy. She tries to skim through some of the preview pages online, but those are mostly maps of the area and its many creeks. Her keyword search brings her to a college dissertation on the erosion of the Shore and the mass dying of oysters. She gets sucked into too many pages of what turns out to be a sad story.

Claire finds a newspaper article from the seventies that includes an interview with the house's previous owners, part of a "unique finds" piece on old architecture on the Shore. The article talks about the fireplace and root cellar, both in the original blueprint. Based on the stones used in the stairway, experts said the house dated all the way back to the early 1600s. There are photos of the owners in the cellar and close-ups of the burn marks on the walls. The journalist wrote that the deep soot stains indicated the fire had happened long ago.

Claire keeps digging. She reads about life as a colonial woman and the first white settlers of the Eastern Shore. There are few records from that time, but she learns what they ate, wore, drank. She even finds an article on witchcraft in the Chesapeake.

But nothing points to definitive answers about the house. She does not find any accounts of strange behavior or happenings, only tax and valuation data, ownership information, and sales history.

TURN OFF THE LIGHT

She sighs.

Claire looks up and out toward the water. Julia sees her looking and runs over. "Mama, isn't it *beautiful*?"

Claire smiles. It's adorable when Julia uses adult-sounding words. But then, why wouldn't she? She is a parrot of the world around her.

"Very pretty," she agrees. "Hey, sweetie. Can I ask you something?"

Julia nods.

"The other night, you told me the house was watching. Remember? And then you saw someone in the room with us. When those things happened, did you feel scared?"

Julia thinks about this and shakes her head. "Not really."

"No? It's not scary at all?" Claire asks, finding this hard to believe. "It's okay to tell me. I felt a little scared the other night too."

But Julia shakes her head again. "No," she says. "I was afraid at first. Because she surprises me sometimes. But she's not scary."

Claire freezes, her heart hammering. "Who is *she*?"

"The lady."

"What lady?" Claire asks.

Julia shrugs. "The other lady who lives in the house," she says as if it's the most obvious answer in the world.

When Julia returns to the large hole she is digging in the sand, Claire gets back on her phone. But her daughter's words continue to irritate her brain. If Julia has seen the woman . . .

Claire makes her way to the girl at the shore and kneels down in the sand beside her. "Hey, sweetie," she says. "Can you tell me what the lady looks like?"

Julia thinks for a minute, then shrugs. "I don't know."

Claire gets an idea and pulls up the photo in that article from the seventies, the one with the previous owners. "Is this her?"

Julia takes in the woman's gray curly hair and paint-splotched overalls. "No," she says. "She's old."

"The lady you see at the house is old?"

Julia sighs dramatically. "No," she whines, frustrated that her mother isn't getting it. "That lady in the picture is old. But the nice lady is not."

Claire thinks. A younger woman, then. "Can you describe her at all?"

"She wears dresses," Julia says. "Like me."

Claire nods, encouraging the girl. "Dresses. Good. Okay. And are they colorful like yours? Fancy?"

"Not fancy." Julia frowns. Then she smiles like she has just thought of a joke. "They look like our window curtains."

Claire wants to ask more questions, but her daughter's attention has returned to her sandcastle. Claire moves back to the beach chair and bites her lip in thought. She hasn't got much to go on: a younger woman with dresses. But the window-curtain detail is interesting. At home in Los Angeles, they have heavy blackout shades in Julia's bedroom, but in all the other rooms, they have light linen curtains.

The detail makes Claire think the woman is probably from older times. She decides to look up that early patent again, the one that lists the Harris family as owners.

She searches for anyone with the last name Harris in those early years on the Eastern Shore. The earliest patriarch mention is David Harris. A painting of him shows thick eyebrows and sunken eyes, a pointy, angular nose, and reddened cheeks.

Claire holds her breath. She zooms in on the screen, even though it's a photo of a portrait and only gets blurrier as she zooms. But the

TURN OFF THE LIGHT

blurry version of him is the one she knows. The shape of him, the outline. It looks remarkably like the figure that stood over her bed.

She shivers, a long snake traveling up her spine. Her fingertips tingle as if she is losing feeling in her hands, and she squeezes her fists to prove they still work.

David Harris, commissioner, the caption says.

She reads as much as she can on the man, though information is limited. He was a commissioner with the Accomack County Court starting in the late 1640s. He would have overseen legal matters and land disputes, been a respected member of society. He had a wife named Grace, and together they had three children. He lived to his fifties, which was rare at the time.

And then Claire finds a seemingly unrelated document with Harris's signature on it, a record of death for a woman named Edith. She died shortly before David married. Could this have been his sister? Or maybe a previous wife?

She searches for Edith Harris, but nothing comes up in the archives. Claire's AI chat app links to one lonely Reddit article from thirteen years ago. It's on the Eastern Shore of Virginia subreddit, which Claire can't even believe exists.

Edie of the Dunes, it reads. *Local ghost story. You guys heard of this one? They say she roams the dunes at night and pulls anyone in her path into the water. Drowns them. Anyone ever seen her?*

Another user said, *I've heard of this one — she was a witch, right?*

And someone responded to that with *LOL, so you mean she was an intelligent woman?*

But it's the last comment that gets Claire's attention. Her heart drops to her stomach. She rereads the comment, then clicks on the poster's profile. A local woman who claims to be a historian. A quick Google search confirms that she works at the Historical Society of Cape Chase.

Which means her intel is probably legit.

Claire calls Ethan. He answers after the second ring.

"Her name was Edith," Claire tells him. "Story was that she drowned. But..." She reads the comment again. Sucks in her breath. "They never found her body."

On the other end of the line, Ethan says, "So she disappeared?"

"Yeah," Claire confirms. "Just like Gabby."

15

EDITH

Edith shoves the canoe off from shore soon after breakfast. The rain is steady but light, more like a fine sheet of mist. In her sack, she has the remaining honey cakes as well as salted venison and dried peaches. She is thirsty, but she doesn't drink anything, knowing she has only a small flask of weak ale. Hopefully, the minister will have rations to offer.

In the canoe, she strips off her leather boots. Wet shoes mean blisters and heavy feet. Her internal temperature is already rising. She opted for the wool skirt and cape, since wool repels water well, but the pieces are unseasonably warm. Still, she does not remove them, because the linen shift and petticoats underneath would soak through immediately. Though the rain is light, it is persistent.

When she has balanced the boat on the water, she begins to paddle. Here, away from the protection of the trees, the rain is heavier — or perhaps the storm has worsened in the time it took her to prepare and climb into the boat. The rain comes in sheets now. She has to constantly wipe water from her eyes. She slides her sack of rations under her skirt for protection and takes a deep breath. The sky is darkening above her, the clouds overfull and bulging, pressing down on the marshy shoreline of the creek.

The first stretch of the trip, from Old Plantation Creek to King's Creek, leaves Edith feeling exposed. She tries to stick close to the shore, but the wind is picking up, bending the reeds on the beach. The canoe is sturdy but heavy and difficult to maneuver in the wind. With each gust, she is pushed farther out into the open waters of the Chesapeake Bay. The rain continues to lash at her, making it difficult to see more than a few feet in front of her face.

The waves are rising too. Edith fights against the current with each stroke of her paddle. Her arms are already fatiguing. When a large wave crashes into the canoe, slopping up and over the side, Edith is forced to pause her paddling to bail out the water. She uses a hollowed-out gourd that David has stored here for this very circumstance. But by the time she has successfully emptied the canoe — at least enough for her to feel confident pushing forward — the tide and wind have carried her significantly farther from the shore.

The rain is loud as it beats against the canoe and pummels the surface of the bay. Edith can barely hear herself think. And even if she could, her limbs are too exhausted to allow for any energy to be spent thinking. She moves only from muscle memory, her body already exhausted not even halfway through the journey.

The storm churns up debris, and Edith must navigate the canoe around a large floating log that would surely tip her if they collided. When she is finally closer to the shore, she realizes the water level is higher than normal. She must watch for the oyster beds that lie hidden in the shifting tide; the jagged reefs can scrape and weaken the canoe's belly.

And then she hears the dreaded rumble of thunder. Ahead, in the far distance, a cloud lights up momentarily. Lightning.

She used to love this as a girl. She and her father would open the shutters to feel the cool breeze that always accompanied an impending storm. The world looked more vibrant in those moments. The leaves and mosses and trees were greener. She never understood why; probably some trick of the light due to the darkening clouds. Even her own senses were heightened in anticipation; the air itself smelled different. When the rain finally came, her father would pour tea and close the shutters. They would then sit together by the low-burning fire and listen to the soft, muffled patter of water on the thatched roof.

Edith daydreams about those times as she fights tooth and nail to drag the canoe through the angry water along the shore. She is approaching King's Creek, and while she would love a break, she is afraid to lose momentum. She pushes past it and past Cherrystone Creek. There is one more long stretch of land without inlets, and then she will finally be at her destination.

Her skirt is properly soaked now, but she welcomes the heaviness of the wool. While she had been warm in the early-morning heat, she now notices her teeth chattering. The constant onslaught of water has chilled her to the bone.

She is almost to Hungars Creek when a wave slams into the canoe. She plants her paddle in the water, trying to fight the tide that wants to carry her out into the open bay. Edith pulls on the paddle with all her strength, but the wind is against her, and after she's made three heavy thrusts, the boat stops abruptly and she lurches forward. Thanks to the rain obscuring her vision, she didn't realize how close she was to shore.

And just as she feared, she has run up against an oyster bed. She can tell by the scraping noise, which is loud enough that she can hear it over the storm.

She curses under her breath and feels around with the paddle for a surface from which to push. The wind whips her hair, now loose from its braid, in all directions; it pokes her eyes and sticks to her cheeks. She groans in frustration as she pushes with the paddle, but every inch of bay floor below is covered with sharp oyster shells that threaten the integrity of her boat.

Edith finally manages to find some kind of surface and pushes hard on the paddle with both arms, but the boat does not budge. Instead, it tips, welcoming in a new gush of water as Edith shrieks. When the boat is steady again, albeit heavier with its added weight, she catches her breath. She nearly capsized, and that would be a disaster in this weather. She would not be able to recover the boat from the turbulent waves, and her heavy wool clothing would make it difficult for her to keep her head above the water. She could drown.

She loses what she guesses must be nearly an hour as she opts for a slow and steady method to free the boat, rocking it only slightly and pushing very gently to loosen the vessel from the oyster beds underneath. All the while, the rain beats down on her.

Finally, she is free. As she continues north, she allows the boat to drift away from the shore. It makes for more difficult paddling, as she must actively fight the tide and angry waves in the more exposed water, but she does not have to worry about running aground.

By the time she reaches Hungars Creek, Edith is spent. She drifts through the calmer waters protected by the high banks and thick forests. The wind still whistles through the trees, bending the branches and stirring the leaves, but she can finally take a breath. She drifts into a small inlet, drags the canoe ashore, puts her boots back on, and flips the canoe so it does not take on water during her visit. And at last, she collapses a few feet away from it, under the cover of a large tree.

Though the storm rages all around her, loud and unforgiving, Edith closes her eyes. Her teeth chatter. She is freezing. As much as her body wants to stay here on the ground and rest, she knows she cannot. She is shivering, which is a good sign, because if the shivering slows or stops, death is officially near. Edith knows that she must get dry. Must strip herself of these soaking clothes and find warmth by a fire. So with every bit of strength she has left, she forces herself to stand and make the remaining journey on foot to the minister's home.

With the sun hidden behind clouds, Edith cannot tell the time of day. She stumbles in the direction of the small house and soon sees the faint glow of an orange lantern in the window. She abandoned her wool skirt somewhere along the way, stripping it off as she walked. Under any other circumstance, she would be mortified to appear at the minister's in this state, half dressed, her boots squelching with every step. But nearly on the verge of death, she is not of a mind to care. Her body knows only to seek warmth and shelter and sustenance.

The modest home is made of rough-hewn timber, and water rolls off its thatched roof. She smells damp wood and smoldering embers, and she looks up to see smoke coming from the chimney.

When the minister opens the door, his face is illuminated by a single candle he carries in his hand. "Goody Harris?" he says, squinting into the dark of the storm. His expression turns to one of shock. "God above, what has happened? Come in before death takes you."

He steps aside to allow her to enter. She strips off her boots and is left with only her petticoats, shift, and bodice, which steam in the warmth of the room.

"Parson... Carter..." she starts, attempting to speak through the chattering of her teeth.

The minister guides her to a chair. "Sit," he instructs. "Speak when you are able."

Nathaniel Carter is a tall, severe man, the edges of him sharp and defined. But his eyes are soft and genuine. He readjusts a dark robe that hangs loose about the shoulders.

"Who is it?" a woman asks as she approaches from the hearth. It is Parson Carter's wife, Elizabeth. When she sees Edith, her lips form a surprised O. "My dear!"

Edith immediately senses the woman's suspicion. Her eyes narrow, and she crosses her arms in front of her chest. Her face, wrinkled beyond her years, contorts in an expression of worry. She has waist-length hair that is tied loosely at the nape of her neck, and she uses one hand to flip the hair in front of her for added protection.

"Hello, Mistress Carter," Edith says, though she is not sure if the words are intelligible through her shivering.

Elizabeth frowns, then points to Edith's wet clothes. "We should get those off you," she says. Reluctantly, she adds, "You can borrow some of mine."

The minister gives them privacy while Elizabeth helps Edith change her clothes. All the while, she clicks her tongue and shakes her head, muttering under her breath. "No good comes of wandering in the dark. And alone, at that. Where is your husband? Surely he has an opinion on all this."

Edith knows better than to respond. Elizabeth already regards her as a strange woman, and showing up now, sopping wet in the dark, is surely not helping to convince her otherwise. She is afraid if she tries to explain herself, she will only make things worse.

"D-do we have m-many hours y-yet t-till supper?" Edith asks.

"It's nearly time for supper now," Elizabeth tells her, annoyance in her tone. "We were about to sit down ourselves."

"Excuse m-me," Edith says. "I do not mean to disturb."

So it is nearly nightfall, which means Edith has lost the entire day to her arduous journey. She should have been back home by now. David will be worried.

Elizabeth must register the concern on Edith's face, because for one brief moment, her own expression softens. "Worry not. Eat. Recover." Her face hardens again. "Then you can tell us exactly what has brought you here in such weather."

The three of them eat fish and bread in relative silence, and Edith is grateful for the respite. Her body is finally warming thanks to the dry clothes—a fresh shift, a woolen sweater, and a petticoat that swallows her small frame. Her boots are drying by the fire. She will need to stay the night in Hungars Creek, but she cannot worry herself with those logistics now. Her mind is able to focus only on lifting her fork to her mouth and chewing the flaky fish.

"So," the minister begins as he leans away from the table, "what brings you here to us this evening? And in such a raging storm? What could not wait until service on Sunday?"

Edith looks briefly at the man's wife, who keeps her eyes trained on her plate. Edith needs to speak to Parson Carter alone, but asking his wife to leave would seem rude or ungrateful, especially after her show of hospitality. Still, Edith cannot open up to the man with Elizabeth listening. Half the Shore would know her business by next week.

"Could we . . ." she starts.

Parson Carter picks up on her hesitation. "You request privacy?"

Edith frowns. "If possible," she says quietly.

He nods toward Elizabeth, who is probably accustomed to dismissal. Many must request private meetings with the minister. Still, the woman harrumphs as she clears the plates, brings her husband tea, then busies herself at the hearth. Edith wishes she would leave entirely, but that is unreasonable, given the inclement weather. Edith will simply have to keep her voice low and hope the woman is not prone to eavesdropping. She can see Elizabeth tending to the fire with a tight grip on the poker, as if preparing to use it as a weapon.

"I am afraid," Edith finally tells the minister. She speaks in such a low tone that he has to lean halfway across the table to hear her.

He nods solemnly. "Tell me."

Edith swallows. This is it. There is no coming back from this, no retracting her words once she tells the minister what has been happening, tells him about the disappearing mess and the mysterious rash and the candles lighting themselves and the shadow behind her home. "I . . ."

The minister nods again, encouraging her to go on.

But Edith's gaze flicks once more toward the hearth across the room, where Elizabeth stands straight as a rod as she stirs a pot, her other fingers still wrapped tightly around the fire poker. She stands with one ear in their direction, obviously listening.

Edith has a bad feeling. She imagines her father rolling his eyes, chuckling, running his fingers through his beard. *What threat does that woman pose? Simply speak your piece to the man.* But her insides twist at the thought, so she swallows her true concerns.

"We . . . me and my husband . . . we want a child but have failed to conceive."

Parson Carter's fingers tighten around his cup of tea. "I see," he says.

Near the hearth, Elizabeth taps the spoon on the side of the iron pot.

"Search your heart, Goody Harris," the minister says. "Have you offended the Lord?"

Edith thinks about the apple. About all the events of the past few days that have convinced her she has been led astray. She thinks of Aunt Joan with her evil eye and a Bible under the pillow. *Your mother was cursed.*

Has she offended the Lord, as the minister suggests? Perhaps she offended him as a newborn child following the death of her mother. Perhaps she has been doomed since birth.

Edith rubs her eyes. Her head aches near the temples. Little makes sense to her right now, and the exhaustion of her journey is descending like a crushing weight.

"Let us pray together that the Lord may open your womb," Parson Carter says. "Then you shall sleep by the fire. We can discuss all in the morning."

Edith nods, grateful for the dry and warm place to rest. Parson Carter approaches and puts a hand on her belly before starting in on the prayers.

Across the room, Elizabeth watches through narrowed eyes.

16
CLAIRE

After her bath, Julia asks for a nap. A rarity these days, but the lunch outing and playing on the beach have taken it out of her.

Once Julia is down, Claire finds Tilly and Peter in the kitchen. The energy shifts the moment she enters the room. Tilly has barely said two words to her since this morning.

"Hey." Peter nods when she enters. Then he finishes telling his wife a story about one of his coworkers, someone who partied too hard at a weekend conference and is likely getting fired. Peter speculates on when it will happen.

"I feel bad for him," Tilly says. She's hovering over the slow cooker.

"He took acid on a work trip," Peter says. "I'd say he brought this on himself, no?"

But Tilly isn't paying attention. She brings a spoon to her mouth. "God," she says, exasperated. "It's still not right!"

Peter joins her and takes a bite. "I think it's even better than last night's," he says.

Tilly shakes her head. "It's not like Dad's. It's different. Less spicy. I mean, Dad's wasn't spicy. What is it? It's less . . . smoky than his." She turns to Claire. "Did he use some kind of smoky spice that I'm missing?"

Claire has no idea. And, more important, her sister is doing the trademark Fern-family avoidance thing. Claire honestly could not give two shits about replicating her father's chili when he is being tortured by wayward souls trapped in their house.

"Paprika!" Tilly exclaims. Then she gets another idea. "Ooh, or maybe *smoked* paprika."

"Yes, good, very good," Peter says, returning to the kitchen island with Claire. "What have you been up to today?"

"Beach," she says. "I'm waiting for Julia to wake before we go out."

"Go out where?" Tilly asks.

Claire hesitates. "I, uh, need to stop by the historical society."

She hadn't planned to tell them this, but after discovering the Gabby connection, she thinks they should know. So she lays it all out — the research, Julia's sightings, the fact that Edith also disappeared.

"And that design in the cellar" — Claire is speaking faster now, eager to share all she has learned — "you know, the one Julia and Dad both drew? It's called a daisy wheel."

She pulls out her phone to read from the website she found.

"Or a hexafoil. It says they were 'common in early colonial homes to ward off evil. Carved into wood near doorways, fireplaces, or *root cellars* to protect against witches or the Devil.'" She looks up at them excitedly. "Dad has been talking about the Devil! And the ghost story says Edith was a witch."

"I don't get it," Tilly says, frowning. "You think this woman is haunting our house?"

"Maybe. Or maybe she was haunted too. Maybe whatever is here has been here for a very long time."

Peter tugs at his T-shirt, which is too tight around the belly, then chews on his thumb cuticle. "I still don't see what this has to do with Gabby."

Claire takes a breath. "This woman, Edith—she went missing. All those years ago. She disappeared, just like Gabby. There has to be a link."

Peter and Tilly share a look that makes Claire want to scream.

"They lived hundreds of years apart," Tilly says. "How can there possibly be a link?"

"Maybe the same thing happened to Gabby that happened to Edith. Maybe whatever is in this house hurt them both." Claire can see they think she's insane, but she needs them to understand. "There are too many coincidences to ignore. And Gabby even told me she was seeing stuff. Hearing things."

She should have believed her. Why didn't she believe her?

"Hmm," Tilly says.

Peter shrugs and runs his tongue over his teeth.

Claire barrels on. "If we can figure out what's going on, we might get answers about Gabby. We might have a shot at saving Dad."

This gets their attention. "What?" Tilly says at the same time Peter lowers his chin and says condescendingly, *"Claire."*

"You said it yourself, Tilly," Claire says. "Dad got much worse recently. It has to be because of all this stuff. It's freaking him out."

"Dad is sick," Tilly says, her voice biting.

"I'm not denying that," Claire says, "but this house is making him worse. I think if he could get away—"

Tilly grabs the ladle from its rest and brandishes it for emphasis. "Oh, I know exactly what you think. Phoebe told me all about how you called a care facility. How you told her it's *not good* for him to be here. I'm sure you can imagine that led to some pretty probing questions from Phoebe, which was humiliating. You know

TURN OFF THE LIGHT

what she thought? She thought you were implying elder abuse. Said she didn't believe it but was obligated to ask the 'tough questions.' Really, Claire? Really? Peter and I have given up our lives to take care of Dad for the past year, and you show up and suddenly, two days later—"

"I never said that to her," Claire says. "Seriously, Tilly, I never meant for her to—"

"I don't care what you meant!" Tilly shouts. "You come in here like a tornado and insist on all these changes and tell us how to do things. You haven't *been here*! You don't have the first clue about Dad's care or what's going on with him. You didn't give a shit about Dad until I called you and said he was dying."

This stings. Partly because it's unfair and partly because it's true. Guilt winds itself around her neck like a too-tight scarf.

Peter uses the silence to step closer to Claire. "Are you okay?" he asks. The question is loaded, like he knows that she is far from okay.

"What do you mean?" she asks.

His eyebrows come together in concern. "This is how it started with your dad, you know? He wasn't sleeping well. Got confused. And then a couple months later, he had full-blown dementia."

"Okay," Claire says warily, "but I don't have dementia, Peter."

She does wonder, though, briefly, how that works. If it runs in families. If she could be developing an early-onset form of the disease.

Tilly bursts into tears, and Peter crosses to her and puts a hand on her shoulder. "I thought we'd have more time," she says between sobs. "I thought he'd get to be a grandpa."

Heat explodes in Claire's chest. "He *is* a grandpa," she says.

"You know what I mean," Tilly retorts.

"No, I really don't," Claire says, defensive. "Julia doesn't count because—why? Because she's far away?"

Tilly shrinks. "I just meant . . ." She shrugs off Peter's hand, and he winces in response. She wipes her tears, then sniffles and pushes her hair behind her ears. "I can't do this right now." And she leaves the room.

Claire and Peter stand in silence. He rubs his eyes and sighs loudly.

"You have to agree that was a fucked-up thing to say," Claire says to her brother-in-law.

"Just lay off all this Gabby stuff, okay?" he says, his tone firm. "It's hard enough with everything going on with your dad. You're making things incredibly difficult for your sister."

Peter follows Tilly, leaving Claire speechless. She has never heard him talk like that. Whatever is in this house is starting to come between them all.

Claire pulls into the parking lot of the historical society. She and Julia marvel at the home that has been reclaimed and renovated by the group. It's gorgeous. Two stories with a wraparound porch that is partially screened in on the left. The siding is light pink and the trim off-white; one distinct triangle in the roof is painted bright teal.

"It's like a dollhouse, Mama," Julia says, eyes wide with awe.

They exit the car and head for the front door. Claire wipes sweat from the back of her neck. The humid air causes wisps of her hair to stick straight out from her head like a lion's mane. Allowing her waves to air-dry might work fine in Los Angeles, but here in the humidity of the Eastern Shore, it's a disaster.

Inside, the downstairs is set up like a museum for browsing. The walls are covered in photos of the Shore from over the years.

"Howdy, folks," a man says from behind the corner desk. He wears shorts and a cardigan. Claire cannot imagine how he is still standing in this heat.

"Hi," she says as Julia sets off to touch all the antique furniture. "I'm looking for"—she pulls out her phone and checks the name—"Penelope Wickman."

The man whistles through his teeth. "Poppy? What do you want with Poppy?"

"She works here, right?"

The man shakes his head. "Used to. Not for years, though."

Claire deflates. "The website says she still does."

He laughs. "Aw, we ain't updated that thing in ages."

Claire sighs, annoyed. "Okay, then. Is there some way I can get in touch with her?"

He narrows his eyes. "What for?"

"I'm looking into the history of my family's home, and I think she might know some things. She was mentioned in an article I read." Claire does not tell him the so-called article was actually just a Reddit comment.

"Oh, yeah, Poppy knows more about this place than anyone. Her family goes all the way back to the earliest days on the Shore."

This piques Claire's interest. "Really?"

The man gushes about Penelope "Poppy" Wickman, who was one of the founding members of this society and is now retired. He tells Claire about the crab-grab fundraisers that Poppy ran every year and the restoration projects she helped spearhead up and down the coast. Claire listens patiently, hoping to get in the good graces of this guy and convince him to share the woman's contact information.

"Mama!" Julia comes running up. "This place is so *cool!*"

It's her daughter that clinches the deal. The man is wooed by her adoration, and he winks as he hands Claire a handwritten phone number on a piece of paper.

"You tell her Richie sent you," he says.

Claire tries the number that afternoon but gets voicemail. She leaves a pleading message and hopes for the best. The remaining hours of the day pass by with the two sisters largely avoiding each other.

Finally, Claire slides into bed next to an already-sleeping Julia. The moment she touches the sheets, she feels sand under her hands and in her mouth. She spits it out, then runs her hands over the mattress. There is sand everywhere, despite Julia taking a bath. Claire cringes as the sand grates against her skin.

Julia is spread out like a starfish, her right thumb in her mouth, her other arm out wide. Her legs are wide too, one under the covers and one exposed. Her skin looks particularly soft and flawless in the subtle moonlight. All at once, Claire is slammed with emotion. Sometimes, when her daughter is at her most vulnerable, like right now during sleep, Claire's brain turns to worst-case scenarios. She thinks of children whose lives were cut short by accidents or school shootings or illness, and her heart suddenly cannot contain the ache. It's like the bones of her chest will shatter, *need* to shatter, to relieve the pressure built up there. She sneaks a little squeeze of Julia's arm, as if trying to prove to her nervous mind that her daughter is safe beside her. That she has not vanished into thin air like Gabby did—without warning, without answers.

Claire finally settles down and rolls over to face the windows. Her eyes are heavy, and her body is too, like a sack of bricks. Immovable.

Thup. Thup. Thup.

TURN OFF THE LIGHT

That same noise again.

Her heart picks up its pace. She keeps her eyes closed, hoping to avoid another encounter with the hovering figure, but her body still registers the nerves. The anticipation of his appearance. Her heartbeat swirls and pulses in the ear that's pressed against the pillow.

And then her head begins to throb, just like it did last night. Her body feels like it's sinking into the mattress.

He's here.

She squeezes her eyes shut even tighter, refusing to see what she can now sense is only inches from her face. The room is silent, but it's the kind of silence that screams. The kind of silence that envelops like a blanket over the head, amplifying the small sounds that normally go unnoticed.

His nose is close to her forehead. She can feel the breath, the steady in-and-out.

Do ghosts breathe?

And then that voice. "It's just me," it says softly. She again feels the mattress dip, and now she is worried for Julia. She slides her hand along the sandy bed.

"Get the feet," the voice says. This time the tone is harsher. An order. Nothing soft about it.

Claire feels hands grip her ankles and squeeze.

She sits bolt upright, her shirt soaked in sweat. The room is empty. Julia sleeps next to her, blissfully oblivious.

Claire bends her knees to her chest and hugs her legs. With one more lingering gaze at Julia, she crawls out of bed. Whatever is haunting this room at night seems to be interested only in Claire. It might even be safer for Julia if Claire isn't here. She silently makes her way out the door and across the room to the stairs.

When she reaches the kitchen, Claire fills the electric kettle and flips the switch. The kettle gets louder and louder as the water heats, at first a dull static like a white-noise machine, then turning into a roiling roar, like train wheels on a metal track.

She opens the fridge and stares into the light. The cold air bites at the edges of her consciousness. Her eyes scan the contents of the refrigerator and land on the brownies that Tilly made a few days ago. She takes a thick square from the pan and spreads cold cream cheese on top, a favorite childhood shortcut for frosting.

Her eyes flick more than once toward the boarded-up dumbwaiter, but it's silent tonight. She pours hot water over a green tea bag and settles at the kitchen table. It's dark, but moonlight through the huge windows is enough for Claire to see pretty clearly. Outside, the world is still, the heat and humidity oppressive enough that everything seems crystallized.

Scraattchh

Claire freezes. She shifts her gaze from outside the house to inside, and her eyes take a moment to adjust.

Scrit-scrit-scratchhh

She squints through the kitchen toward the sunroom, even trying to see through to the dining room and foyer. But it's all shadows and dark corners.

She abandons her snack and tea and follows the sound. It leads her toward the dining room. Across the foyer is her father's closed door. Her heart sinks as she realizes the sound is coming from his room.

Scratchhhh

No, actually, not from his room. It's coming from her right, somewhere in the living room. Maybe an animal in the chimney.

Claire walks through the dining area toward the couches. The noise is like claws or a tool scraping wood. Erratic. Desperate. The animal must be trapped.

TURN OFF THE LIGHT

She frowns. The sound becomes more muffled, but she can still hear it, can still sense something relentlessly boring its way through wood or stone or—

The cellar.

There is something in the cellar.

She stops.

She backs away from the latched trapdoor and almost trips over the small step up into the dining room. Claire turns quickly and hurries to the kitchen. She can't go into the cellar defenseless. She opens drawers in search of a blade before remembering she hid them. She reaches high in the pantry and pulls down a large chef's knife.

She grips it tightly with both hands like it's a gun and holds it in front of her chest. Then she stalks slowly back toward the trapdoor. Imagines what might be waiting for her in the cellar. Could it be the same thing that made Edith and Gabby disappear? A spirit? The Devil, like her father keeps saying? She shivers. She can't even begin to picture what that would look like.

Claire works her way around the dining table, heart slamming against her chest. She steps down into the living room, her hands sweaty.

Then she pauses. Waits. Straining to hear the scratching.

But there's nothing. Only silence.

She continues to wait, holding her breath. She tells herself she'll go down there if she hears it again. She will.

But after some seconds of quiet, she has a moment of clarity. Sees the large knife she's holding. Thinks of her father trying to cut off his own hand with kitchen shears. Then thinks of what Peter implied, that Claire's mind might be deteriorating like her dad's.

Claire shivers.

She returns the knife to the pantry. Then she carries her tea up to the playroom, far from the locked cellar. The liquid is cool now, and the darker bits have settled at the bottom. She uses a spoon to stir the tea. The *clink-clink-clink* of the metal makes her think of the mysterious *thup-thup-thup* she has been hearing nightly. And finally she can identify the sound: a spoon in a wooden cup. Stirring.

She brings the mug to her mouth and almost takes a sip before hearing her father's voice in her head.

Don't drink the tea.

She hesitates, then abandons the cup.

For a long time, she stares into the dark of the night, waiting for something to emerge.

17
EDITH

Despite Edith's crushing exhaustion and desperate need for recuperation, her eyes pop open once again in the middle of the night. It is the witching hour. She is sure of it. She can feel it in her bones.

For a moment, she does not recognize where she is, and fear sets in. But everything quickly comes back to her: She is reclined in a chair by the hearth in the minister's home, a warm blanket wrapped around her torso and legs. She looks at the fire, which is dead save for one burning ember. Edith squints and blinks as her eyes adjust. The home is very dark. She does not hear rain, but a very distant rumble of thunder groans through the atmosphere. The storm has passed, then.

Edith looks away from the fire toward a window. And that's when she sees something. Movement in the corner of the room. Dark and looming, just like the shadow she saw outside her house. And then it rises, same as before. Edith brings her hand to her mouth in fear, bites down on a finger to keep herself from screaming. Her eyes dart about for an exit or at least something with which she can protect herself.

But a second later the figure steps forward, and Edith sees it is not anything supernatural.

It is the minister's wife, Elizabeth.

Still, fear brims under the surface of Edith's skin. Her limbs have been activated in preparation for flight. The rate of her heart does not decrease; there is no relief when she sees the woman. Because Elizabeth has a dark scowl on her face. And she holds the fire poker from before.

"What have you brought into this house, woman?" she spits in a nasty whisper.

"S-sorry?" Edith stutters, and she hates herself for showing her fear. But she is helpless in this unfamiliar place. She would not know how to defend herself if the need arose.

"No one brings business to our home at such an ungodly hour. And to travel through the rain and wind. *Alone.*" Elizabeth stabs the air with the poker for emphasis. "You may have difficulty conceiving, aye, but that is not why you are here. You would not endure such pains for as simple an ailment as that."

Edith swallows. "It is not simple," she says, her voice small. "It has been nine months."

"And for what reason, then, does the Lord deprive you of your purpose in this way?" She levels the poker at Edith's chest. "You know very well the Devil enters through doors left open. So what is it, Goody Harris? What have you done?"

Elizabeth can see it. She can sense the weight that Edith carries, the darkness that has latched onto her.

"I do not know, Mistress Carter," Edith says. Her voice cracks, and she stares at the sharp iron tool. One good thrust, and Edith would have a stake through her heart.

TURN OFF THE LIGHT

"I shall tell you, then," Elizabeth says. "It is your pride. You think you can play God with your balms and salves. You think you can change the course of His will with your herbs." She says the last word with disgust, as if the plants are something truly abhorrent.

"Surely you misunderstand me," Edith says, holding her hands up in surrender. "Never would I assume to know the will of God, much less try to change it. That is why I am here, Mistress Carter. To consult with your husband, to understand the path God has chosen for me. My medicines are only to help others in the meager way I know how."

"A smooth tongue you have," Elizabeth says, still wielding the poker, ready to pounce. "You are good with words. Or perhaps that is the Devil speaking through you."

"Should I leave?" Edith asks. "Is that what you want?" She slides forward an inch in her chair, dropping the blanket to the ground.

"Do not move," Elizabeth spits.

Edith freezes. She does not want to spook the woman, who seems unpredictable now, jittery as a cornered animal.

"What I want," Elizabeth continues, "is the truth. The real reason you sought counsel from my husband."

Edith hesitates. She never should have come here. The minister cannot help. She came only because she had her aunt's voice in her head. And her father's. Everyone else's instructions always screaming louder than her own, even within the confines of her own brain.

But there it is again, the doubt her husband planted that has taken root and grown through all the shadows of her mind. A nagging question. Elizabeth is as godly a woman as they come. If she believes Edith carries the Devil on her shoulders, then how can Edith convince herself otherwise?

"I should not have come," Edith says. "Forgive me." She stands and makes a show of retreating as she heads to the table to grab her sack. "Please," she says, speaking slowly and deliberately so as not to startle her adversary, "if you allow me to wear these clothes home, I will clean them before Sunday's service. I can return them to you at the parish."

"Keep them," Elizabeth says, her shoulders finally relaxing as she steps aside so Edith has a clear exit from the home.

"Thank you," Edith replies, her whole body exhaling.

"I give them to you not out of kindness," the woman clarifies with a biting tone. "Only because I dare not hold something against my person that has been on the back of the Devil."

Cast out, Edith stumbles in the near-total darkness. Though the storm has passed, the lingering clouds still hang low, obscuring the stars and moon. She attempts to retrace her path back to the inlet where she abandoned her canoe. Perhaps she can reclaim the skirt that she removed mid-journey.

But the lack of moonlight makes the walk more difficult than she anticipated. She steps gingerly, feeling the marshy ground for soft pockets that could trap her feet. The humid air is heavy, and from the wet earth emanates a stench of decay. More than once, Edith's stomach roils, and she bends over to retch, tasting remnants of her fish dinner.

What will Elizabeth tell her husband in the morning? Surely she will not admit to casting out their visitor in the middle of the night with no provisions or lantern. Perhaps she will feign surprise when she finds an empty chair by the hearth. Perhaps she will tell her husband that she expected nothing less: *That woman was never to be trusted.*

TURN OFF THE LIGHT

And now what will Edith tell David? Parson Carter managed to say a prayer over her empty womb, but the rest of it... Word will travel to him. It always does. He will discover that his wife disappeared into the night like a vagrant. And what will he assume then? Edith could tell him the truth, but wouldn't Elizabeth's accusations feed the wariness that already gnaws at her husband's gut? She fears that he would not laugh off the woman's suspicions but rather find some kind of proof in them.

Edith finally reaches the inlet. She hears the waves crashing farther away, where the creek opens up to the bay. The tide must still be rough after the storm. She considers putting her flint necklace to use and starting a fire, but the wood is too wet.

Smack!

She slaps a swamp fly against her cheek. The rain has left puddles of still water, the perfect breeding ground for the stinging insects.

Smack!

This time, a sting on her wrist.

Smack!

Her neck. Her ankle. Her forehead. Her scalp.

The worst of them are gathered near the marsh reeds. She tries to escape, to maneuver herself farther into the woods and away from the inlet. But they follow her, an eager swarm of nearly invisible demons.

She thinks about the cows on the farm where she grew up, how they would stomp their hooves and toss their heads when the flies tormented them. This is how she must look now, flailing her body against the biters.

Her skin flares in response, each bite swelling into a sizable welt. If only she could build a fire. The smoke would drive them away.

But since she cannot, she finds the nearest cypress and claims her spot for the night. Edith stamps all around the base of the tree, ensuring no snakes are coiled in its roots. Then she curls herself into a small shape and gets as much of her exposed skin under Elizabeth's heavy wool sweater as possible. Water from the branches above drip-drip-drips onto her, and she continues to scratch at her bites until she bleeds.

And yet, as miserable as this night has become, these are elements she is prepared to fight. She grew up in this land. She is accustomed to the swamp flies and venomous snakes and aggressive wild boars. She is no stranger to damp ground and marshy waters and crawling insects.

The things that truly scare her are back home.

And so, oddly, a part of her would rather be out here, as uncomfortable as it is, than back at the house where shadows lurk and manipulate the world around her.

It is there she feels out of her depth.

The trip home after sunrise is, mercifully, uneventful. Edith's hunger claws at her from the inside, but she is grateful for the smooth waters and calm sky. She makes the trip in just over an hour, much quicker than the exhausting daylong affair of yesterday.

When she arrives home, David is not there. He is likely working on the boat in the back forty acres of their property. Alone, she feels no shame as she ravages the food pantry: dried pork, salted venison, fresh peaches she jarred last week. She eats until her stomach aches, washes it all down with light ale. Then she forces herself to the basin to bathe before collapsing into bed.

It is high noon when she is awoken by a loud *clink-clink-clink*. A steady and rhythmic banging of iron on iron. She makes her way to the front door, where she finds David standing on a chair and hammering something into the wood outside.

TURN OFF THE LIGHT

"Fixing damage from the storm?" she asks.

David nearly falls from the chair at the sound of her voice. Edith grabs his thighs to help him steady.

"Heavens above," he says when he has caught his breath. "You startled me. I didn't know you were home."

"You were not at the house when I arrived, and I was so tired that I fell asleep. I do not even know how long ago . . ."

David climbs down from the chair and takes in her appearance. She is grateful she has had time to nourish and wash herself; he would have been gravely concerned had he seen the state she was in a few hours ago.

"You were due back last night," David says. His voice lands somewhere between concern and accusation.

"Yes," Edith says. "But with the storm, I only made it to Parson Carter's just before supper. I was compelled to stay."

"At the minister's?" he asks.

Edith nods. "He insisted. It was very kind of him." She looks at David's hands, which are dirty from work. Then she looks above the doorway, where he has been hammering.

There, squarely centered above their threshold, is an upward-facing horseshoe.

"To bring prosperity," he says as he wipes his hands on a linen rag. Then he uses the same rag to wipe sweat from his brow.

Edith swallows. Looks back to the horseshoe. It is true that some families use it as a good-luck charm, but she is confident that is not what drove her husband to nail it here today.

More commonly, settlers use horseshoes to ward off evil.

Spirits.

Witches.

"That girl came looking for you yesterday," David says. He brings the chair into the house, his work here done.

"Violet?" she asks, following him in.

He shrugs. "The Cotton girl. Why does she come around here?"

Edith's heart picks up its pace. "Oh, I think she gets bored. Her mother always wanting her to do chores. You know how it is."

He squints, then pours himself an ale. "She seemed real disappointed you weren't here. Had you made plans with her?"

Edith hesitates. Is this a test? Does David already know the answer? Is he laying a trap for her? "Plans?" she says. "What kind of plans would I have with a twelve-year-old girl?"

He chugs the ale in three long gulps, then slams the cup on the table. He wipes his mouth with the dirty linen rag and tosses it haphazardly on a chair.

"I want rabbit stew for supper," he announces.

She raises an eyebrow. "We do not have any rabbit."

"So catch one," he says loudly.

A second later, he is gone.

Edith stands there, stunned. It seems her husband is purposely requesting something unreasonable. As if testing her obedience.

She suddenly gets the notion to check her herb cellar. And sure enough, the jars are all out of order. David has clearly rifled through the contents. The violation makes her shudder. This is her sacred space, and he has ravaged it with uncaring hands.

She double-checks that nothing is missing, though she has skimped on her detailed records lately, what with Violet's training and the emergency trips for Jacob's illness. She cannot be sure what quantities she should have of each.

Edith begins to panic. Did Violet reveal something to her husband yesterday? She can hardly blame the girl; she is only a child, after all. She would not understand the dire importance of remaining discreet.

TURN OFF THE LIGHT

Nervous and a bit distracted, Edith gathers her tools and sets out on a ridiculous quest to catch and kill a rabbit for supper that very night. As she leaves the house, she looks again at the horseshoe above the door. It gleams in the bright sunlight that has replaced the dark, bulging clouds of yesterday. The iron plate winks at her.

Just before she turns again, she feels the familiar sensation of her blood warming, her insides awakening. The rash on her arm, which for two nights has been calm, ignites again. Every bug bite from her hours in the marsh lights up, making her entire body itch. She drops her tools and scratches at the worst of them, mostly around her ankles.

Edith looks up at the horseshoe again, angry. It represents all that she is fighting against and the worst of her husband's assumptions. She can't help it; she raises a fist toward the thing and curses under her breath, *"Be damned!"*

And just like that, the horseshoe slips loose of one of its nails, so it hangs half secured over the door, swinging back and forth, back and forth, as if a strong wind has blown it from its place.

18
CLAIRE

Poppy Wickman returns Claire's call the next morning.

Claire does not let on that she is worried about a haunting. Instead, she says she is passionate about Eastern Shore history. When she mentions the name Edith Harris, she hears Poppy's sharp intake of breath.

"Can you come over later today?" the woman asks. "I have some things I can show you."

After the call, Claire passes through the living room and spots Peter hammering something into the wall beside the hearth. She hasn't spoken to him since their weird encounter last night, but she assumes it will be one of those things they never discuss. A blip.

He points to a framed photo resting on the floor. "It fell down," he says.

"On its own?" she asks.

He shrugs. "I guess. I saw it swinging on the nail."

The picture is a new addition since Claire moved out. Her mother was never one for family photographs in the home. She said they were tacky. But there are now a few scattered through the house, so Claire's father must have put them up once her mother left. The thought brings a smile to her lips. She likes knowing that her dad wanted to be surrounded by their faces.

Peter looks at the photograph. "I remember when you guys got this taken," he says.

It is the only official portrait the family ever took together. Odd to think about it now, since they did it only months before Gabby disappeared. She was getting senior photos anyway, the kind every girl on the Shore commissioned her last year of high school. White, pressed blouse, tight blue jeans, hair straightened to oblivion and blowing in the beach wind. The pictures were always on the dunes, with the subject lounging on the sand or gazing out at the water. Claire's mother decided that since she was already paying an arm and a leg for those pictures, she might as well pay a little more and get a proper family portrait.

The only thing Claire remembers from that day is the moment Tilly had to pee. They still had forty minutes left in the session, and there was no bathroom in sight. Gabby suggested Mom and Dad take a few solo shots, and the photographer had *aww*ed at Gabby's thoughtfulness. Then the three sisters climbed up over the nearest dune, and the two older ones kept a lookout as Tilly peed in the sand.

"Oh, no, I got it on my pants!" she cried, and her sisters nearly choked on their laughter.

In the rest of the photos they took that day, either Gabby or Claire was strategically placed in front of the pee spot on Tilly's jeans. In the photo that Peter pointed to, it's Gabby.

"That was a fun day," Claire says, picking it up.

Peter goes back to hammering the picture hanger. Claire wonders how such a heavy picture would have suddenly fallen. It was on the wall closest to the cellar entrance, and her gut drops as she remembers last night's scratching.

"Hey," she says to her brother-in-law, "I heard some weird noises last night. I thought they were coming from the cellar."

"Hmm?" Peter says. He is right next to her but apparently hasn't heard a word. She wonders what has him so distracted.

She repeats herself, and he asks, "What kind of noises?"

"Something scratching," she says.

She expects him to roll his eyes and shrug this off as another hallucination. But he deflates. "Oh, no," he says. "I bet we have mice again."

"Mice?"

"If they're in the cellar, they might be in the walls. Maybe that's why the picture fell. Shit. Don't tell Tilly, okay? She's stressed enough as it is. I'll check it out when I get a chance."

Claire does not think the scratching was produced by mice. And now this: the family photograph on the ground. It's like some kind of message.

"It'll be fine," Peter says, more to himself. "I'll go through the crawl space and set some traps."

"Crawl space?" Claire asks.

It's a dumb thing, a tiny thing, but she lived here for ages and never knew they had a crawl space. Peter has lived here less than a year and knows the house better than she does. He belongs in a way she does not. The feeling irks her.

"We dealt with mice when we first moved in," Peter says. "I thought I'd taken care of it, though."

Claire nods and leaves him to his work. She cannot help thinking about all the things she has missed over the past fifteen years. All the time spent away. All the relationships that have fallen through her fingers like forgotten sand.

TURN OFF THE LIGHT

Claire has a few hours before her meeting with Poppy, so she sets Julia up with a movie in the playroom and gets started on the attic alone. If Tilly doesn't want to be a part of it, that's fine. But Claire needs to busy her hands, needs to feel productive.

It's no wonder her sister has not been in a hurry to get up here. Why clean the attic unless they are selling the house? Tilly clearly assumes she is staying. That she and Peter will get to move in, automatic owners of waterfront property. Dread settles at the back of Claire's throat as she thinks about the financial conversation she has been putting off.

The attic is large, spanning the length of the upstairs, and is stuffed full of what appears to be junk. Claire is not surprised; her mother and father probably squirreled things away up here for decades. She starts in on the first box, and before she knows it, she has spent an hour sifting through old toys, discarded furniture, outdated gadgets and chargers and wires.

"It must be a hundred degrees up here."

Claire looks up to see Tilly, who has just ascended the ladder to the attic.

"At least," Claire agrees. She's sweating from hauling and dragging heavy boxes back and forth.

Tilly approaches sheepishly and sits beside her sister. "God, what even is this stuff?" she asks, poking around in a box.

Claire waits, wondering if they're going to talk about the blowup yesterday. And Tilly must sense as much, because finally she says, "I'm sorry for what I said about Dad not being a grandpa. I wasn't thinking. And really . . ."

When she doesn't finish her thought, Claire prods. "What is it?"

Tilly hesitates but then opens her mouth, her gaze fixed on the floor, and says, "Honestly, it was more a dig at Peter. He decided he doesn't want kids."

This information hits Claire with a smack. Tilly has always wanted to be a mother. "What?"

"Yeah," Tilly says. "I don't know what to do. I told him I was ready to start trying a few months before all this happened with Dad. And then when we had to move in here, we put the conversation on hold. But when I brought it up again recently, he told me he's officially decided he doesn't ever want to be a father."

"Jesus," Claire says. "What the fuck?"

"Yeah," Tilly says sadly. "Pretty much my thoughts exactly."

Claire's heart aches for her sister. Peter has put his wife in an impossible position. "Did he say why?"

Tilly shrugs. "Something about his shitty relationship with his own dad. Doesn't want to repeat history or whatever."

Claire remembers that Peter's father was an alcoholic. He never talked about him much, but the understanding was that Peter was always at their house because he didn't want to be at his own. "Do you think he'll change his mind?"

Tilly shakes her head. "He's adamant. And I don't want to force him into fatherhood. He would only resent me."

"But you want kids. So doesn't that mean you'll spend your life resenting *him*?"

Tilly sighs. "I don't know. I really don't. I'm still processing it all."

Claire nods. This tension between Tilly and Peter must be why he has seemed so distracted lately.

The sisters work in silence for a while before Tilly spots a box of Christmas decorations.

"Oh, man, look. It's all Dad's old stuff," she says.

Their father used to line the front of the house with light-up inflatables. Reindeer, candy canes, elves, the Grinch. The sisters thought it was so magical. That is, until they were old enough to be embarrassed by them. After that, they gave their dad a hard time every year as he spent hours assembling the display. But he kept it up despite their complaints, and Claire smiles now at that thought. Good for him.

It makes her sad to think of the teenage version of herself being too cool to take part in her father's childlike joy. Julia would have loved it, and she wishes her daughter could have experienced her grandfather in his prime.

"I haven't seen these in ages," Tilly says, looking at the decorations. "Dad stopped putting them up after Gabby."

"No, he didn't," Claire says. "I was home for two more Christmases after that, and . . ."

Her voice trails off. She is certain her father continued to hang the lights and blow up the figures even after his daughter disappeared. Didn't he even say something about it? How he wanted the house to look like home in case Gabby returned?

"Seriously?" Tilly says. "You don't remember?"

"I do," Claire insists. "He at least put them up until I left for college."

Tilly shakes her head. "He definitely did not." She gets a faraway, sad look. "It's weird how memory works. I've been thinking about that a lot lately. With Dad being sick and all. Isn't it wild we both have concrete memories of the opposite thing? We lived in the same place and have two totally different versions of how things went."

Tilly is right—it *is* wild. Claire can hardly believe what her sister is saying. And such a simple thing too. A benign disagreement over holiday decor. But what other things, more important things, are they misremembering?

"What do you think happened?" Tilly asks.

"I told you, he put up the decorations—"

"No," Tilly interrupts. "I mean with Gabby. We never talked about it."

Claire knows exactly why they never talked about it. She can't share her theory of what happened to Gabby without admitting the terrible things she said to her sister that last day. Claire is certain that she drove Gabby out and away — that she pushed her to make a rash decision that turned deadly.

But really, no one in the family shared their theories. Conversation was not encouraged, and it's only now in adulthood that Claire realizes how unhealthy that was. To avoid further pain, her family became adept at talking *around* the important things.

Tilly fiddles with a bit of packing tape hanging off the box beside her. "You really think it could be something with the house? Like a ghost?"

"I have no idea," Claire says, which is partly true. Since returning to the Shore, she has become even more confused about what might have happened to Gabby. But she can't deny that part of her hopes the ghost theory is right. If the house is responsible for Gabby's demise, that could alleviate the guilt Claire has felt for a decade and a half. More than fifteen years spent thinking her sister's disappearance was her fault.

But she can't say any of this. So instead she asks, "What do *you* think happened?"

Tilly chews the inside of her lip and says, "I think she ran away."

Claire waits for more, but her sister does not offer it. "So you think she's out there somewhere just living her life?"

"No," Tilly says. "Gabby was impulsive. I think she ran away and then got into some kind of trouble before she could come back. Maybe she was hitchhiking or some other stupid thing and got herself killed."

Claire is astonished by her sister's theory. It is nearly identical to her own. She never imagined Tilly had such a well-constructed hypothesis, but then, of course she did. They all did. They just never shared them. And Claire knows this was an act of self-preservation. Talking about the thing would have made it real.

"I've watched a hundred documentaries about missing girls," Claire says.

"Me too," Tilly says quickly.

"Really?"

Her sister nods. Claire's heart breaks a little more as she sees all the missed chances for connection. How she and her sister were living parallel lives with parallel pain and never reached across the divide.

Tilly looks at the boxes of holiday decorations. "Mom couldn't handle it. I mean, she couldn't handle the grief of Gabby, yeah. But she also couldn't handle Dad."

"What do you mean?" Claire asks.

"He was so convinced Gabby was going to come home. And he had always been the optimistic one, but after a while, Mom thought it bordered on delusional. She said it was unhealthy, the way he held out hope. And eventually she didn't believe his optimism. She thought it was performative. Like he was hiding behind a fake exterior that she couldn't get through." Tilly leans back on her hands. "I think he meant it, though," she says. "If he was deceiving people, it's because he was deceiving himself too."

Claire looks at her sister, taking in the blond wisps of hair that stick to her sweaty temples in the heat of the attic. Her oversize graphic tee that makes her seem childlike. The bright eyes that, Claire is only now noticing, have dimmed in the past couple of days.

"How do you know all this?" Claire asks, amazed.

Tilly smiles sadly. "I just paid attention, Claire."

Ethan meets Claire outside Poppy's house.

"No Julia?" he asks as they climb the front steps.

"Tilly offered to watch her," she tells him. Since she has never left the girl with a babysitter, this is a foreign feeling for Claire. But after mending things with Tilly, it felt cruel to deny her sister quality time with her niece.

Plus, she won't be gone for more than an hour.

"Thanks for coming," Claire says to Ethan as they approach the door.

He runs his hand through his dark hair. "Yeah, sure. I'm curious. It's not every day you get to research a haunted house."

Claire snorts. "True."

Poppy answers the door and leads them into a sitting area. She is a large woman in every sense. Round with long limbs and exaggerated features—wide eyes, a big nose, long fingers. She wears pigtails that would be better suited to a toddler than her seventy-year-old self, but she exudes an air of self-confidence.

"Anything to eat? Drink?" she asks as she ushers them to a couch. It's got a floral cover that must be a remnant of the nineties, with pale pink flowers that look like they belong on teacups rather than furniture.

The room is full of trinkets and photos and stacks of books, not a bit of empty space around them. It walks the line between *homey* and *hoarder*.

"No, thank you," Claire says, sinking into the well-worn cushions. She expected the seat to be firm, but it feels like the couch might swallow her whole.

Poppy situates herself across from Claire and Ethan on an armchair with thick blue stripes. It clashes horribly with the couch. All the furniture in here is off, like this is some kind of cartoon version of a real house.

"So, Richie sent you my way," Poppy says, commencing the meeting.

Claire nods. "He said your relatives were some of the earliest settlers on the Shore."

"That's right," the woman says. "And you live in the Harris house?"

Claire nods. "I never knew that, though. Just learned about David Harris yesterday."

"Some real interesting history in these parts," the woman says. Then she turns to Ethan. "And who are you?"

"Oh," he says, shifting self-consciously on the couch. "Ethan. I'm a friend of Claire's family."

Poppy nods, as if sizing him up. "Can you grab that box?" She points across the room.

Ethan stands awkwardly, retrieves a heavy cardboard box, and sets it on the table between them.

"These are the things I've gathered over the years," Poppy says as she invites them to look through.

"And you said you know a little about Edith? The woman who lived in my house? The one who disappeared?"

Poppy nods. "I'm a direct descendant of a woman named Violet Cotton." She pulls out a few scrapbooks. "I pieced together her old recipes from various diaries and things."

"Wow," Ethan muses. "A cookbook from the 1600s."

"No," Poppy corrects, "she was a healer. Her recipes are for burn salves and fever teas, things like that."

Claire flips through one of the bound journals. The handwriting is modern, so Poppy must have rewritten the information in one place. "This is amazing," Claire says as she reads through the notes. Then she lands on something called Edith's Nighttime Balm. Her breath catches, and she holds up the page for Ethan to see.

"That's right," Poppy says, leaning forward. "Edith was Violet's mentor."

"So Edith was a healer?" Claire asks.

Poppy nods. "Yep. She's the one who introduced Violet to the practice." She leans back and crosses her ankles. She's wearing khaki shorts, showing off pale legs covered in bright blue veins.

"And what about David Harris? Was he related to Edith somehow?"

"Her husband," Poppy says. "Edith was his first wife."

Claire nods. "Is there anything else? Maybe notes or something about what happened to Edith?"

"Nothing," Poppy says. "Although Violet did mention a fire."

Claire perks up. "In the cellar," she says. "There are burn marks on the walls and beams. I've always wondered."

"Well, I don't know much about it. She refers to it in the diary only in passing. Says she didn't have access to Edith's herbs because of the fire."

"So she kept her herbs in the cellar," Ethan says.

Poppy nods, her pigtails bouncing. "She likely would have. That was typical of the time. Unfortunately, Violet didn't write much personal stuff down. Her notes were all about patients and doses. But from the little she wrote about her life, it seems like she missed Edith greatly. She admired her. If you ask me . . ."

Claire leans forward. "What?"

"Well, it's just a theory," Poppy says. "But I think they killed her."

"*They* who?" Claire asks.

"The town. I think they were suspicious of Edith. You know how they looked at women in those days. Especially intelligent women."

TURN OFF THE LIGHT

Claire remembers the comments on the subreddit thread. One person said he'd heard Edith was a witch, and someone responded that *witch* was code for "intelligent woman."

"Could they have killed her in the fire?" Claire asks.

Poppy considers this. "It's possible. Violet's diary never suggested that, though. She only referred to Edith as missing."

Claire nods. She shares a look with Ethan.

"Is this about your sister?" Poppy asks.

Claire nearly drops the journal in surprise. "You know who I am?"

"Of course," Poppy says. "I don't let strangers into my house without doing a little digging first. I knew your name sounded familiar. Everyone on the Shore remembers when Gabby disappeared."

Claire bites her lip. She doesn't know what to say.

"You thinking it could be meaningful?" Poppy asks. "That Edith went missing and then, all those years later, your sister did too? In the same house? That why you're asking these questions?"

Claire swallows. "You probably think I'm nuts," she says, blushing.

"Not at all," Poppy responds. Then she leans in conspiratorially. "You ask me, everything's connected."

Later, Claire stares out the back window of the kitchen. The marshy reeds bend in the breeze. The clouds are an angry gray again, and she wonders if today, the long-anticipated rain will finally come.

Her mind is on Edith, imagining a million different scenarios in which her beloved stash of herbs could end up in flames. She wonders how scared the woman must have been. Did she know the town was turning against her or did they catch her by surprise? Claire considers descending into the cellar to feel the uneven edges of the wood, to trace the outline of the burn scar and hunt for clues. But even in the daylight, she finds that the idea of going down there makes her queasy.

A *tap-tap-tap* on the glass of the window brings her attention back to the now. A small bird paces on the kitchen windowsill, staring at her. He looks like a mourning dove but with a soft orange-and-peach-colored chest. His beady eyes are also rimmed with bright orange.

"Hi there," Claire says quietly.

Just then, her phone buzzes with a text. It's from Ethan: *What now?*

She knows what he means. She has figured out who lived in the house and even what might have happened. But where does she go from here?

Claire sucks on her upper-right incisor. *I think Edith is trying to tell me something,* she types.

Claire looks back at the bird, who continues to stare and pace on the sill, as if patiently waiting to be let in.

And I just need to pay attention.

19
EDITH

Edith did not catch a rabbit for supper. Of course she didn't. She is not a skilled hunter; she knows how to work traps and clean animals only after they have been caught.

So now she stands over the fire and cooks vegetable stew. She managed to bake some cornmeal muffins and hopes these will appease David. It's no rabbit dinner, but it will have to do.

As the liquid in the iron pot gurgles and spits, Edith leans against the wooden counter for support. Her body is exhausted. Spent. And her insect bites still itch. In fact, in most places, she has scratched them so fervently, the skin has broken. A few have already begun to scab.

Her eyes feel heavy, and she almost falls asleep while standing. But suddenly there's a loud noise — she can't identify it — and the sensation of something in her hair. She flails her arms hysterically, convinced some kind of large insect has fallen on her. Her hand bumps against something with a light thud. She hears a whipping and a flapping. Feels air pulse around her temples and neck.

Edith instinctively ducks, bending her knees and holding her hands over her face for protection. When she is able to steal a glance between her fingers, she sees the offender. A wild pigeon is on the kitchen table, cooing and pacing on the wooden boards.

"Shoo!" Edith says, lunging for the bird.

It is not uncommon for birds or other critters to wander in through open windows, but that does not mean it is convenient. The last time a bird flew in, she spent hours trying to direct it back outside and found remnants of its poop for days.

When Edith lunges for the pigeon, he simply hops out of harm's way, then flaps his wings, arcs above her, and lands across the room near the hearth. He looks at her with a steady gaze, then blinks a few times, his bulging eyes rimmed with orange. His little neck moves as he coos.

Edith sighs. She does not have time for this. David will be home imminently. She decides the bird will have to find his own way out. After all, he came in of his own accord, so he can manage the leaving too.

She covers the muffins with a rag, then shoos the bird away from the hearth again. He hops just once on the edge of the hot pot, and Edith's own heart hops with him when she imagines what would happen if the bird were to poop in the stew.

But then she smiles. A small, devilish grin. The idea of serving her husband bird-poop stew is, admittedly, somewhat satisfying. He was so callous earlier, insisting on rabbit for their meal. Rifling through her herbs. Hanging that horseshoe for all their neighbors to see. He would never notice if his dinner happened to contain a unique garnish . . .

And then her thoughts turn darker. For one brief moment, she imagines slipping spotted cowbane into his bowl. Some call it poison parsnip, because its root looks just like the vegetable. David would never suspect; it would blend right into his stew. He would know something was wrong only moments later, with the start of the fits. He would clutch his heart, then fall to the floor as his body convulsed in uncontrollable movements. Like a fish on dry land.

She takes a deep breath and erases the image from her mind. Why would her thoughts take her there? Lately, her mind does not feel like her own. She does not usually entertain such dark fantasies. And the few times she has, she has never derived pleasure from them. She thinks suddenly of Elizabeth's disgusted look and upturned lips when she proclaimed she would never wear something that had been on the back of the Devil.

By the time David returns to the house for dinner, the bird has left. Edith imagines how she must look: disheveled, hair a mess, hands covered with dirt from the garden's vegetables. She has spent the past hour chasing the pigeon within the confines of her home, an act that she realizes must be akin to a physical representation of mental madness.

She confesses to her husband that she could not deliver his requested supper, and she says it with regret in her voice. True regret, for she knows this was a test and she has failed.

But David smiles with half of his mouth, and his shoulders relax. He looks at the vegetable stew, then at her, taking in her haggard appearance, and he nods. She is certain of it: He is relieved.

She does not understand how, but she has passed the test.

"Stay close, now," Edith calls to Violet. "We are here for something specific. I'll show you where it grows."

They are in the woods, as Edith has decided it is too risky for them to train at her house under David's watchful eye. In fact, Edith would have given it all a rest, at least for a while, had the girl not shown up this morning in a fit of excitement. Edith did not have the heart to turn her away. And truthfully, she enjoys their sessions as much as the girl does.

The ground remains soft from the rain, the woodland still and humid. Heat presses in from all sides, infused with the scent of damp pine needles. Edith's eye is sharp as she scans the wildflowers that poke up through the ferns. On their walk so far, she has already pointed out goldenrod and yarrow, but neither is the focus of today's lesson.

"Here," Edith says, waving Violet over. She has spotted it. She kneels in the scrubby underbrush and parts the ferns to reveal a patch of small, daisy-like flowers. "This is feverfew."

Violet crouches beside her. "Feverfew," she repeats, tasting the word on her lips.

"Feel the leaves," Edith instructs. "See how they are thick and leathery? Almost like wax."

Violet nods as she runs her fingers over the plant.

"It is not just for fevers," Edith says. "It calms the blood but also clears the mind. Too much, though, and you make the head spin."

"How do you know how much to give, then?" Violet asks, frowning.

Edith considers. "Well, there are many factors. These leaves are plump and lush, so it is a good time to harvest. They are fresh and potent, so a few leaves will do for a fever that is not too high." She looks around and spots a relatively flat rock. She goes to it, spreads the leaves on its surface, and pulls her knife from her apron.

"I will show you how to measure," she says. Edith cuts the leaves very fine, which releases their pungent scent of crushed citrus peel and musk. "These we brew in tea. If someone is greatly suffering, they can chew on the leaves. That works much more quickly, but the taste is not pleasant." She slices the last leaf with the knife. "Never too much, though. Too much can overwhelm the body."

TURN OFF THE LIGHT

"Would the person die?" Violet asks. She joins Edith by the rock. They sit close enough that Edith can see something new crop up in Violet's eyes. Something akin to fear. Edith knows this feeling well: the razor-sharp edge between healing someone and potentially harming them.

"They could," Edith admits. "You have to consider the individual. Are they very young or very old? Are they very sick or generally healthy? The size of the body and its condition will inform your dose."

Edith rubs the leaves between her fingers, then smells the scent that lingers there.

"You must let the plant speak to you," she tells the girl.

Violet snorts. "Plants don't speak."

Edith smiles. She expected the girl to have that reaction, but instinct is a large part of the work. "Not in our language, no. But they have their own." Edith looks around the woods. Listens as a small animal scurries in the brush. A whole world happening out here — one that makes sense to Edith, unlike the man-made world she is forced to navigate daily.

"I examine the plant," she continues. "Smell it. Feel its energy. Soon, you too will develop a sense of which plants are stronger based on the season and how they have grown. One batch may be more potent than another."

Violet's eyes go wide. "It seems complicated."

"Don't feed that self-doubt," Edith says. "You will understand with time. And experience."

Violet lies on her back, staring up at the branches. Edith finishes harvesting the feverfew and secures it in a small pouch that she brought in her apron. She should be getting back to prepare midday meal. The thought of it deflates her enthusiasm. Her days run into one another, the monotony of preparing meals and cleaning the house and doing the washing. All cycles that never end. And for what purpose?

"I heard you went to the minister's," Violet says.

The words pull Edith from her thoughts immediately. "What?"

Violet picks at her shoe, apprehensive, as if she has divulged a secret she knows she shouldn't have. "I heard Mother and Father talking," she admits.

"About me?" Edith asks.

"They were whispering after supper last night. I was meant to be in bed." Violet sits up. "They said you traveled in the storm. That you were nearly dead but Mistress Carter took you in and cared for you."

Edith snorts. So *that's* the version of events the minister's wife is spouting. But then worry tugs at her chest as she wonders what other stories the woman is spreading. "Did they say anything more?"

Violet chews her lip. "I think they were talking about you having a baby. Mother kept rubbing her belly."

Edith can picture Violet's mother cradling her own swollen belly, whispering under her breath all the reasons why the strange healer woman next door is not yet with child.

"Is that all?" Edith asks. She senses there is more; the girl seems nervous, like she has worked her courage up all morning to broach the topic.

"They said," Violet says, "a woman who walks the shore in the moonlight has no business among decent folk."

Edith slowly nods. She feels a shiver light up her spine despite the thick, humid heat. She has never enjoyed being the center of attention. But now, she fears, she is going to understand truly how much she hates it.

TURN OFF THE LIGHT

When Edith emerges from the woods alone, her training session with Violet concluded for the day, she hears voices. Men's voices.

She follows the low tones to the front of the house, where she sees David standing near a horse. The rider is obscured by the large animal, but Edith cannot imagine who it would be. No one on the Shore can afford a horse except for George Clark all the way up at Nuswattocks Creek.

Edith approaches slowly, hesitant to interrupt the men but curious about the unannounced guest. David spots her almost immediately.

"We could not find you," he says, waving her over.

When Edith joins them, she is surprised to see that their visitor is the minister. His eyes flicker when they land on her, and she has the feeling the two men have been talking about her. Then she remembers that only moments ago, she was discussing the minister with Violet. Her muscles tense. Did he overhear? But no, that is ridiculous. She would have noticed a man on a horse lurking in the brush.

"Good day, Parson Carter," she says. "Is something the matter?"

She has learned over the years that only bad news comes with such urgency.

The minister bows his head slightly. "I have borrowed Goodman Clark's horse to help spread the word," he says, his voice solemn. "Jacob Littleton has passed. Early this morning, he succumbed to the fever."

Edith's insides sink as she thinks about Grace. Though Jacob's death would have been no surprise, the grief would be grabbing on tight now. Not to mention she has to deal with the matter of sorting through the logistics of landholdings and farm maintenance. So much on Grace's shoulders.

"I am sorry to hear it," she says.

Parson Carter's gaze flicks toward the horseshoe over the doorway. It is hanging properly again, so David must have fixed it. Edith wonders if he thinks she vandalized it.

"A wise precaution with today's uncertainties," the minister says, nodding toward the good-luck charm. He shares a look with David. It is quick and subtle, but Edith is sure some unsaid thing has passed between them.

"I agree," she says, placing a hand on David's arm. "My husband is a wise one." She almost winces at the words. Surely they will see she is trying too hard.

But the minister is already gathering his reins and hoisting himself atop the horse. "I must continue on if I am to get to everyone," he says. He tips his cap to them. "Goodman Harris. Goody Harris. I will see you this afternoon for the burial?"

He looks at David, who nods. Again, Edith gets the sense there is more being conveyed here. But she cannot discern what.

"We will be there," she says.

When he has left, David pulls his arm from Edith's grasp. "Parson Carter told me he prayed over your womb," he says.

"He did," she confirms. "I am very grateful."

"And where were you just now? You were not in the garden nor at the creek. Can you imagine how it looked when the minister came calling, and I could not find my own wife?"

She bites her lip. "I was in the woods gathering feverfew."

"You are done with all that!" he shouts.

Edith shrinks away from his booming voice. She is not accustomed to David yelling.

"Gathering herbs and making potions," he spits.

"They are not potions," she replies, her voice childlike in its defensiveness.

He waves his hands in the air. "Do you not hear what they are saying? Do you not understand the danger you put us both in? And to what end? Jacob is dead. You are not a healer if you cannot heal."

This stings. Her husband knows full well that some sicknesses cannot be cured. Still, her own guilt gnaws at her, reminding her of all her failed attempts to save others—not only Jacob but the other patients she has lost along the way, including her own father and aunt.

She is about to say something when David holds up a hand, as if a new thought has come to him. He seems to be doing some kind of internal calculation.

"Wait," he says. "Jacob died this morning. Which means . . . how many days has it been?"

She is afraid of his train of thought.

"How many days since you first visited the man?" he repeats.

"Six," she says, her voice small.

"Six days," he says. "Jacob died in six days. Exactly as you predicted."

He stares at her for a long moment, his hands in fists at his sides. And then he turns on his heel and heads back toward the house.

Edith stands in place long after he has gone. The sun breaks through the clouds and fixes on her alone, the rest of the world dimmed away. As if her life is merely a piece of theater for someone else's enjoyment. And as she stands, she thinks of only one thing. The very fear she has been fighting against since finding that apple. But now it is here, not only an existential question but a real, visceral threat.

She must convince her husband she is not a witch. She must convince him—and, truthfully, herself as well—that she has not been possessed by the Devil.

20
CLAIRE

Claire's dad spends less and less time awake, and she worries she will lose him before she can solve the mystery of this house. She wants to free him of whatever hold this place has on him. And, admittedly, it has become more than that. She has been harboring a growing hope that the house is connected to Gabby. That she will finally get an answer about her missing sister. And in doing so, she can deliver to her father the ultimate peace before he dies: closure.

She spends the afternoon in and out of his room helping Tilly with laundry, refreshing his water, even though he has barely taken a sip, fluffing the pillows, and even wiping down the windows. It strikes her that she and her sister are both looking for ways to be productive. Ways to help, because the truth is, this disease has left them feeling helpless.

When all the chores have been completed, Claire slips away for a walk on the beach. The tall birch trees are still in the warm evening. She walks the boarded path until her feet hit the sand.

The lowering sun breaks through the clouds and shines down

TURN OFF THE LIGHT

like a spotlight. She hears water lapping at the edges of the shore and crickets chirping. The bugs are always more vocal when the weather is warm; their sounds make up the chorus of the dunes. She learned as a girl that only male crickets make noise, and they do it by rubbing their wings together. How bizarre that an insect can produce such penetrating tones with such a gentle gesture.

Just as she slides out of her flip-flops and feels the sand on her bare feet, a chill snakes up her arms. She has the sensation she is being watched. She turns back toward the house, scanning the landscape, but there is no one. The dunes are empty.

Claire wraps her arms around her torso and looks back to the sea. The sun is dipping quickly, its color melting into a burnt orange that reflects off the bay's surface. She thinks about the life cycle of a drop of water, how after all these years, she's probably looking at an entirely different bay than the one she grew up on.

By the time she walks back to the house, it is dark enough that she triggers the motion-detector light above the garage. It startles her, and she freezes. Then she catches sight of her odd shadow. Long and distorted across the backyard. Her head almost touches the tree line. Even though she knows it is her own shadow, it still spooks her. It looks alive, like it might peel itself from the ground and stand on its own, growing taller and taller until it towers over her.

She stays there, staring and still, for so long that the light shuts off. Her shadow disappears — *poof* — in a millisecond.

As if it had never been there at all.

After dinner, the sisters work on a puzzle in the sunroom. It's a thousand-piece puzzle depicting a café in some European-looking country — flowers spilling from hanging pots, intricate designs in the iron backs of the chairs.

Nearby on the floor, Julia draws. "You like it?" she asks, holding up her picture. It's a variation of what she always draws: a rainbow, three small unicorns, clouds, and a sun.

Claire squints to see more clearly. The sun is different. It's still a circle, but it does not have its usual rays. Instead, Julia has again drawn the sigil from the cellar and this time colored it yellow and orange.

"Beautiful!" Tilly gushes, and Julia beams.

But Claire can't stop staring at the daisy wheel. Why does her daughter continue to draw it? She wants to believe it means nothing, but dread accumulates at the back of her throat.

Before she can say anything, Peter flits through the room.

"Oh, hey," Tilly calls to him. "Can you put those in the wash?" She points to a pile of his dirty clothes by the side door, pants and a long-sleeved tee covered in brown dust.

Peter looks up from his phone, distracted. "What?"

"The clothes that have been sitting there all day," Tilly says, voice clipped.

"I've got to go back under the house," Peter says. "No use dirtying up two sets of clothes. I'm looking up what part I need . . ." His voice trails off as he returns his attention to the phone.

"They're gross," Tilly says. "And they stink." When Peter doesn't reply, Tilly pushes again. "What are you doing under the house, anyway?"

Peter throws up his hands dramatically. "We've got mice again. And I'm sorry that, between keeping up the house and caring for your dad and working my full-time job, I left a dirty shirt on the floor."

Tilly softens. "I didn't know. Why don't we hire someone? You shouldn't have to worry about that stuff."

"No," Peter says quickly. "I don't want to spend money on something I can easily do myself."

TURN OFF THE LIGHT

"It's not about that, though," Tilly says. "You deserve a break. You've got enough going on."

"I was fine until you started griping about the clothes!" Peter stomps out of sight, heading toward the front of the house.

Claire sits awkwardly, pretending that her attention is still squarely on the puzzle.

Julia shakes her head. "Uncle Peter is *not* happy," she whispers loudly.

Claire would laugh if she didn't know Tilly was so upset.

"He's really on edge the past couple days," Tilly says, frowning.

Claire doesn't admit that she has been largely avoiding him since he lashed out at her the other night, and even more so after Tilly's confession that Peter doesn't want children. Claire is harboring her own resentment toward him on behalf of her sister.

"I'll go talk to him," Tilly says, and she's gone.

Julia sidles up beside Claire on the couch and looks at the puzzle. When she leans on the table with her elbows, some of the pieces get stuck to her forearms and then fall to the ground.

"Uh-oh! I'll get them," Claire says. She bends under the glass table to pick up the pieces.

"I want my treasures," Julia says, referring to her small collection of knickknacks that has somehow doubled in size since they arrived in Virginia.

"I think it's on the living-room couch," Claire tells her as she sits back up.

Julia rushes into the other room. As Claire returns her attention to the puzzle, she feels something tickle her neck. She bats at it, thinking a mosquito has gotten inside. But then she feels it again. A light puff. Breath on her neck and cheek. A presence.

Claire freezes.

She looks up, her vision blurring as she tries hard to see something that is not there.

And then her nose twitches with a familiar scent. That earthy smell of burned—what? Recognition clicks in her mind. *Apple.* That's what it is. It smells like overcooked apple pie or apple slices crisping in a pan. But subtle, only the remnant of the scent hanging in the air, like a memory or an afterthought.

"Mama!" Julia cries from the other room. Her voice is desperate; she sounds like she might be hurt.

Claire jumps up and runs to the living room, but Julia is nowhere in sight. And then she sees that the trapdoor to the cellar is open.

"Julia!" she yells.

She makes it to the cellar in three long strides and looks down to find her daughter at the bottom of the steps, frowning.

"I dropped my treasures!" the girl says. She gestures to the floor of the cellar, where her collection is fanned out around her.

"Why are you down there?" Claire asks, quickly descending. She scoops up the child and immediately carries her up the stairs.

"My treasures!" Julia cries, reaching for the spilled knickknacks.

Claire sets the girl on the couch. "What part of 'Don't go in the cellar' did you not understand?"

Julia frowns. "But I wanted to help."

"Help? Help what?" Claire asks. She has no patience left. How does she get her daughter to understand how dangerous it is down there?

"The girl," Julia says. "I wanted to help the girl."

The hairs on Claire's arms prickle. "What girl?"

"I heard her crying," Julia says. "She was crying in the cellar."

"You saw a girl?" Claire asks, remembering Gabby's frightened face when she described seeing a child down there. Looking back now, Claire can see all the signs she missed: how jittery Gabby was in those last two weeks, how she avoided the cellar, how she spent less and less time at the house.

TURN OFF THE LIGHT

Julia shakes her head. "I didn't see the girl," she says. "I only heard her. But she sounded so scared. And sad."

Claire can't sleep. She feels tantalizingly close to answers, yet they are still out of reach. Her thoughts circle frantically in her mind.

Her father afraid he let the Devil in; the hexafoil carving and her father's and daughter's replicas; Gabby seeing a girl in the cellar; Julia hearing a girl crying; the dumbwaiter gears clunking to life; the smell of burned apple; the sensation of being watched.

How does the girl in the cellar fit into Edith's story? Is she another ghost from a different time? Did she disappear too? Is the house harboring centuries of lives lost under its roof?

Claire thinks about the visions she has had in this room. The men surrounding her, David instructing the others to "get the feet." Her limbs heavy and paralyzed. She thinks about the sound of the spoon stirring. Her father's warning: *Don't drink the tea.* The revelation that Edith was a healer. Poppy's hypothesis that the woman was murdered because people feared she was a witch.

And then it hits Claire: What if Edith's husband poisoned her? He could have used the very herbs that she kept for healing to kill her. He could have put them in her tea, waited for the effects to take hold, and then pulled her from bed to finish the job.

Is this what Edith wants Claire to know? What she *needs* her to know?

Claire does a double take on her thoughts, as if catching them in the periphery of her vision. Just a few days ago, her biggest concern was traffic on the 405. How has she gone from that to believing in ghosts? And not just believing—desperately searching for hidden messages in their communication.

She shakes her head at herself and checks on Julia, who, per usual, sleeps unbothered. Claire arranges the pillows around her daughter so she won't fall. Then she heads downstairs to her father's room. He, too, is sleeping peacefully. She sits in the armchair near the windows, watching as he breathes in and out.

She remains here for so long that, eventually, the sky outside lightens. The pale blues give way to long, thin pink clouds. She thinks of the adage she learned in childhood. *Red sky at night, sailor's delight. Red sky in the morning, sailors take warning.*

Claire looks at her father's mirror. Scans the perimeter of his bed. Stares at the windows' long panes of glass. She has been doing this for hours, running her eyes around the edges of the space. Like she is daring the ghosts to come out and show themselves.

She remembers a time when she was very little and had a stomach bug. Her father lay on the floor next to her bed, sleeping in ten-minute increments, poised and ready with the bucket anytime Claire even stirred in her sleep. His large fingers held back her hair as she vomited. Then he would gently wipe her mouth clean and guide her tiny body back onto the mattress. When she was settled again, he'd rub her back in giant circles.

Now, she keeps vigil over him like he once did for her. But she still fears she is failing him. That he will die before she can give him the truth for which he has been so long searching.

Sometime later, he stirs. Claire joins him on the bed. They sit in silence for a while before she gets an idea. "I'll be right back," she tells him, then rushes out to the sunroom and retrieves the bird book.

When she returns, she holds the large encyclopedia-type book that her father used to reference for his bird walks. The hobby that grew into an obsession after Gabby's disappearance.

"I saw a beautiful bird yesterday," she tells him. "Shall we try to find it together?"

TURN OFF THE LIGHT

It's a heavy, thick tome filled with pictures and information about thousands of bird species. Claire flips through the pages, showing her father the photos as she searches for the bird that stared at her yesterday through the window.

"It came right up to the glass," she tells him.

His eyes are only half focused. She does not know if he's following her, but she talks anyway, desperate for some semblance of connection.

"I swear he was staring at me," she says. "I'm sure you would know exactly what bird it was if you had seen it."

She scans pictures of finches and doves. "Hmm." She frowns. "None of these. The bird I saw had a longer neck. Its chest was kinda orange, and it had crazy-cool eyes."

Her father brings his right hand to his face, then circles his eye with his index finger. Around and around the eyeball.

"Yes!" she says, excited that he seems to understand. "The bird had orange circles around the eyes."

Her father nods, then points to the book and gestures for her to keep flipping. But as she scours the pages, she shakes her head, disappointed. She can't find the bird. Part of her deflates as she realizes her father's gestures were likely meaningless. But then he snaps his fingers and makes that signal again: *Keep going.*

"Back here?" she asks, getting to the last pages of the book.

And then, to her shock, she finds a picture of the exact bird.

"Holy shit," she says, staring. "You were right. Hell yeah, Dad, you still got it."

She smiles at him, then looks at the page featuring her bird friend. It's called a passenger pigeon. It was once the most abundant bird in North America, but now . . .

"Oh, wait," Claire says, frowning again as she reads. "This can't be right. The passenger pigeon is extinct."

She stares again at the photo. She is sure of it—this is the exact bird she saw on the windowsill yesterday. The features are so distinctive: beady, rimmed eyes, the wings and back a steel blue, the chest and belly a palette of oranges and peaches. But how is that possible if the bird went extinct over a hundred years ago?

"So, what?" she asks. "I imagined it?"

Just then, Claire's father flails, and the back of his hand hits her cheek with a hard *smack*.

The shock of it sends her off the bed and onto her feet. She blinks hard, trying to rid her vision of the floaters that have popped up there. Her cheek throbs. She brings her hand to the spot where he hit her.

She sees something register in his eyes, like he feels guilty for what he has done, and she doesn't want that. He didn't do it on purpose.

"It's okay, Dad," she says. "I know you didn't mean to."

He looks at her, his mouth parting slightly and then closing again, his tongue licking his cracked lips over and over.

"Time," he says. "It's time."

"Time for what?"

He lurches forward, eyes wide and glassy. Then he starts screaming, high and raw, spit flecking his chin. The words come out in pieces, chewed up by his failing brain. They are half-formed sentences, curses that don't belong in his voice. It's like witnessing him becoming possessed in real time. Like something is dragging itself up through his throat and trying to wear his skin.

21

EDITH

Edith gathers items for the sack. They will be leaving shortly to head to Grace's home for the burial. She is bringing dried meats and fruits as an offering; she wanted to bring a sweet treat, but she used up the honey preserves on David's cakes.

She feels a harsh *sting* on her left cheek and instinctively slaps her hand against her skin. A swamp fly. She looks at her palm and sees it squashed there, dead, a single streak of blood smeared across the wrinkles of her hand. She wipes the insect off on her apron and scratches her cheek, which is already beginning to swell. Oddly, her skin stings with the pain of the slap more than the pain of the bite.

Edith decides to also pack some herbs for Grace, wild cherry to help her sleep and black cohosh for the sadness. She starts to gather the roots and bark, then pauses. She hears a quiet internal ringing, like some distant alarm. Should she not bring Grace herbs? Her husband's words slither through her consciousness. *Do you not hear what they are saying? Do you not understand the danger you put us both in?*

But Grace is her friend. And as a healer, Edith can help ease the woman's grief. How can she deny her friend that help, even if she fears the repercussions?

The nerves in her body are alight, warning her against it, but she slips the herbs into her apron anyway. Best to keep them separate from the items in the sack in case she needs to deliver them in private.

She turns to exit the cellar when a faint scarring in the wooden beam above catches her eye. It's not shaped by rot but a deliberate carving. One that wasn't there yesterday.

Her eyes narrow as she tries to make sense of it. At first, it looks like a simple circle, but as she approaches, the pattern reveals itself: lines arcing and interlocking, like a wheel. Her breath hitches. She knows this symbol. A ward. Yet another charm against witches.

Her throat tightens. *David.* The grooving is shallow but fresh, recently carved, not worn by time like the ones she has seen hidden in other barns and hearths on the Shore. She struggles to swallow. The air is suddenly thin, as if the house itself is warning her to *get out.*

Edith heads for the stairs when a sound cracks through the silence. She flinches, dropping her skirt and stepping back in fear.

Thnnnnk-thnnnnk-schluuuup

Her eyes flick upward to the source of the sound. Something is being dragged across the floor above her. Getting closer, approaching the opening to the cellar. She cowers, stepping back slowly until her spine hits the wall. But her eyes do not leave the cellar's opening.

Thnnnk-schluuup-thnnnnk-schluuup

She slides down to the floor and huddles in the corner, as if she could hide from whatever is getting closer. Is this the very demon or spirit that has been riding her? Is it about to descend and swallow her whole?

THUD-THUNK

THUD-THUNK

Like heavy footsteps on the stairs. Something being dragged down into the cellar, one step at a time, landing with a thump on each stone. But she can see only the flickering of a silhouette. The shape of something appearing.

And then the sound stops abruptly.

Edith holds her breath, straining to listen. Her heart hammers, and she can feel a presence, can sense some *thing*.

"You ready?"

Edith yelps at the sound of David's voice. Her body must jump an inch off the floor.

"Edith?" he says. The silhouette above is now clearly her husband's tall figure.

She knows how this must look. How strange it must be for him to find her huddled down here in fear, her cheek swollen and red from the swamp fly bite, her eyes beady and darting.

"Did you hear that?" she asks. "Were you dragging something?"

David stares for a long minute before sighing loudly. "We mustn't be late," he says. "They are expecting us."

The words turn sour in midair on their way to her. Edith can smell the danger in them. Of course the neighbors are expecting them. Why spell it out like that?

She notes her husband's fingers drumming his thighs, his shifting feet, his unwillingness to make eye contact.

And she has no choice but to follow him up the stairs and out the door to Grace's house, even though she is beginning to feel like it is some kind of trap.

"Brethren, we are gathered here in the sight of God to commit the body of our departed brother Jacob Littleton unto the earth from whence we all were formed."

The minister speaks, standing beside the grave that is situated in a clearing near the edge of the woods. Edith notes the evening light turning amber and long over the trees, casting the group into shade. Jacob's body lies in the grave, wrapped in a simple linen shroud.

She had expected only herself, David, and perhaps Margaret, Grace's neighbor to the south, but she sees more faces than that. Even Violet's mother, bloated with child, is here, standing toward the back of the group, fanning herself and cradling her heavy belly with her free hand. Edith cannot imagine what compelled the woman to come; given her condition, no one would have expected her at the burial. But her husband is here as well, so that means the children are too. Some, including Violet, sit at their mother's feet, while a few of the youngest are at the far end of the clearing, tumbling and laughing. Every few minutes, their giggles carry over to the gravesite, and Edith finds it refreshing. A reminder of the cycle of life. But the parents shoot aggravated looks in their direction.

Edith tries to share a smile with Violet, but the girl will not look at her. If Edith were to give in to paranoia, she would say the girl has been avoiding her since the moment she and David arrived.

"Who among us can stand before Him and demand more days than He has appointed? Who among us can claim righteousness enough to escape the grave? Not one."

David swats at a fly in front of his face. Elizabeth, the minister's wife, stands at the front of the group and surreptitiously pulls at her skirt, unsticking it from her skin. Even though the sun will soon be setting, the heat is unforgiving. The high temperature paired with the pungent scent of churned-up soil makes Edith feel suddenly nauseated. She swallows, forcing herself to keep her breath even.

She is tempted to take a step away from the grave, away from the strong scent of tilled earth and recent death. No one else can smell it, she imagines. After all, the man is newly deceased; his body is not yet rotting. But Edith's senses are attuned to that faintly sweet yet sickly smell. The flies know it too. They are beginning to gather in and above the grave.

"Let us not be troubled as the heathen who know not the Lord. Let us weep as only those who mourn. For we know that the grave is not the end. If a man believes in Christ, though he die, yet shall he live . . ."

Edith pulls at her collar. Her shift feels too tight around her torso. She opted for long sleeves despite the heat to cover her bites and rash. But now she regrets the choice, because she can feel beads of sweat dripping down her back and sides, getting trapped in crevices and folds and making her itch.

Elizabeth steals a glance at her from the front of the group. The woman looks once, then again, lingering on the second stare. Eyes are on Edith. She feels them from behind too, like hands on her back. She resists the urge to turn. Instead, she looks at the ground near her feet, gently lowering her lids. Anyone watching might think she was praying, though in actuality, she is willing her insides to stay on the inside. Any moment now, she fears the contents of her stomach will be on the ground. She brings her left fingers to her mother's flint necklace and rubs the thumb against the smooth side of the pendant, quieting the bats in her stomach.

". . . His true home is not here among the dust and shadows. If he was faithful, as we know he was, he rests now in the bosom of the Lord. He is freed from all suffering . . ."

Edith cannot help herself; she looks again toward Violet. And this time, she catches the girl staring. When they make eye contact, Violet looks away immediately, then begins worrying the end of her braid between her fingers. That is, until her mother slaps her hand and tells her to keep her eyes on the minister.

"Let us now commend our brother to the earth. The flesh perishes, but the soul belongs to the Lord. 'For dust thou art, and unto dust shalt thou return.' Let us pray."

Edith's insides did *not* stay on the inside.

She stands now at the far end of the clearing, still at the edge of the woods, as far from the group as she could get before the burning liquid made its way up her throat and out into the world. She has tried her hardest to be discreet, but she knows they are all watching. Judging.

When she feels properly emptied, she leans against a sturdy tree and wipes her hands and mouth with a linen cloth from her apron. While fumbling for the cloth, her fingers graze the small pouches of roots and bark she brought for Grace.

She feels driven to leave this place as soon as possible, to set out on the trail home before it gets dark. She resolves to find Grace, give her the herbs, and leave. Edith hopes David will agree, given how tired he must be from helping to dig the grave in this heat.

But when she looks back toward the group, only the minister remains. The crowd must have relocated. Perhaps they are at the house? Edith bites her lip. This seems unusual. Food offerings were made before the burial. What other business do they have at the house? After all, this is not a social gathering.

She heads toward the home. Two of Violet's younger siblings cross her path, chasing each other and shrieking in youthful delight.

It's a boy and a girl, maybe five and seven. Edith tries to get a good look at them, as she realizes now she has not seen the girl who appeared in her yard the other day. The one in the pale yellow dress. But then, the Cotton children have been spread out since arriving at the Littleton household, never staying in one place. Edith cannot imagine how their mother manages to keep track of them.

Still, something about this bothers Edith. That she has not yet identified the girl she saw on her own property. Was that not a Cotton child after all? But if not, to whom did that little girl belong? The Shore is vast, yes, but not in number of people. And given her work as a healer, she has had to travel a good deal. She always assumed she had a grasp on the residents, including servants and their children.

But then, her world has shrunk since getting married. A heaviness settles in her chest as she thinks about the ways in which the circumference of her life has gotten smaller.

As Edith approaches the house, she hears voices. And as she turns the corner, she finds David with William Cowdery, Margaret's husband. William is complaining about a stolen hog.

"I heard a gunshot, then saw the man hightailing it out of there with a fat hog in his arms," William says. "He left the ears behind. Mutilated, they were, but still bearing the mark of my livestock. The gall of it!"

"Did you prove it?" David asks.

"Of course," William says, standing taller. "And he had to pay me three hundred pounds of tobacco."

Edith looks around again for the little girl. She sees two boys fighting with sticks closer to the woods, and around the other side of the house, she sees Violet's father with the littlest of the clan. One is barely walking, and the other is closer to age three, running circles around her father. But again, no sign of the girl in the yellow dress. Or any of the women from the funeral, for that matter.

Edith is about to wander off when she feels David's hand on her arm. "We should be going home."

"Yes, of course," she says. "I just want to give something to Grace."

David starts to reply but is interrupted by a second chapter of William's story. Edith uses the distraction to go in the house. She wants to say goodbye to her friend and slip her the herbs.

The air in the home is stifling. Her eyes take a moment to adjust to the darkness, but soon she sees she is alone.

The house is empty.

Edith returns to her husband. "Where is everyone?" she asks.

A curious expression crosses his face. "They are not inside?" he says. "Odd, that."

His response does not sit well with Edith. She senses he is hiding something. But a second later, William is saying his goodbyes, and David is ushering Edith toward the path home.

The walk is long. She pushes up her sleeves for relief, because the bug bites have been rubbed raw all day by the fabric.

When they finally approach their house, she exhales.

But then she sees that the door is open.

She is certain she latched it when they left. Has someone broken in? Her heart flutters as she remembers the dragging sound on the cellar steps. Has some spirit stuck around? Is it waiting for them inside?

Edith looks to David, but he is not bothered. His eyes remain trained ahead, his steps deliberate and labored. And this is when she knows she should run. Her husband is up to something. Every fiber within her pulls her in the opposite direction. Like a thousand voices calling to her from behind, Sirens on an island in the sea. But her feet betray her and continue in step with her husband to the house.

David stops at the threshold. He gestures toward the open door, and though she knows she is doomed if she continues, Edith cannot stop herself. She walks right through.

The women from the burial are here. *Here,* inside *her* home.

Edith thinks about that look she saw between her husband and the minister. She thinks about Violet avoiding her at the burial. David's comments that everyone has been talking.

Her eyes flit around the room, taking it in. No one says a word.

The door to the root cellar is open. Edith knows even without looking that they have traipsed through her holy space. She imagines them roughly and carelessly tossing around her bundles of herbs, shoving her jars to the side, lurking and peeking in corners meant for only her.

So David's violation was not enough, then. He enlisted the women to search as well. Neighbors, some of whom Edith has treated and helped, now here to do her husband's bidding. It stings. Even though Edith has long known these people do not like her, she wrongly assumed they at least respected her.

Violet is the first to make eye contact. And there is something akin to fear in her expression. Or maybe trepidation. Either way, it takes only a moment for everyone else's eyes to follow, and now their collective gaze is on Edith. She wants to shrink beneath the floorboards. There is Elizabeth, with her pursed lips and arms crossed over her chest; there is Violet's mother, seated by the table, her arms resting on her belly as if it were a tray; there is Margaret, her edges harsher than ever as she stares intently at Edith. Violet retreats to the hearth with two of her younger sisters.

And then there is Grace.

The silence lingers for a moment too long before Grace approaches. "Goody Harris," she says, and the address is like a knife to Edith's ribs. Since when does her friend, her *only* friend, refer to her with such formality? As if they are strangers. Grace places her hands on Edith's elbows and gives her a pitiful look, as if Edith is the one whose husband has just died.

"You must be wondering why we are all in your home," she says.

Before Edith can answer, she hears the door click behind her. Elizabeth has situated herself between Edith and the exit, latching the door and securing it tight.

Locking her in.

"We just need a moment," Grace says, then she pulls an empty chair to the center of the room. "Please. Sit."

22

CLAIRE

The rain has finally come. That old adage about a red sky in the morning turned out to be true. This time, anyway.

Claire sits on the porch, which provides full protection overhead with its solid roof. The sides are more exposed with mesh-like screening, but this is a typical Virginia summer rain. No wind, just a straight downpour from dark, angry clouds.

"Do you want some ice for that cheek?" Ethan asks.

She called him to come over. She hasn't been able to quiet her mind since finding Julia in the cellar, and the discovery of the extinct bird followed by her father's violence has only made her more anxious. She needed to tell Ethan about the developments. Not only because she wanted to try and puzzle it out with him, but also because she was in dire need of his calm. His quiet, steady confidence. Even after all these years, she can spill her heart to him without the fear of being judged.

Tilly is in with their dad and an aide. They called Phoebe, but she wasn't available, so she sent someone else from her center. Tilly told them it was an emergency because Dad had gotten violent; he needed to be restrained or at least calmed down. Peter emerged from the office only long enough to help Tilly contain their dad. As soon as the aide arrived, he retreated back upstairs. He is so on edge.

Claire texted him shortly before Ethan came over. *Everything okay up there?* She saw three dots appear, disappear, reappear, disappear again. It's only right now, as she is sitting with Ethan on the porch, that a text comes through. *Not feeling great. Taking the day off.* The stress is getting to them all. Claire senses they are dangerously close to some kind of breaking point.

The only one who seems unfazed is Julia. She sits in the sunroom watching *Frozen* on the iPad, mouthing the dialogue of the movie she has seen at least forty-seven times.

"Claire?" Ethan prods. "Ice? For your cheek?"

"Oh," she says, instinctively bringing her hand to her face. "Sure."

He returns with a small pack of frozen corn and sits beside her on the couch, their backs to the sea. The sound of pummeling rain echoes all around them. Claire always loved being out here during a storm. As long as the winds weren't too high, the porch remained mostly dry, and there was nothing like a summer rainstorm on the Shore.

She admits to Ethan that she misses the weather. Life in Los Angeles is one long sunny dream, with the days blending into one another until it's disorienting. There's barely a difference between March and October. At least it feels that way to her, coming from a place with seasons.

"Are you happy there?" Ethan asks.

"In Los Angeles?"

He nods.

"Yeah," she says. She leans back against the couch cushion and presses the cold bag into her cheek. "I think so."

"Can I ask you something?" Ethan turns so that he is facing Claire.

"Of course," she says.

He runs his hand through his hair like he always did as a teenager, then presses his lips together as if he's deep in thought. "Why did you end things between us?"

Claire's chest tightens. She wasn't expecting this. "I was moving across the country," she says, as if the answer is obvious.

He shrugs. "So? You never asked if I wanted to go."

She rolls her eyes. "Come on."

"What?" he says. "I'm serious. We never even had a conversation about it. You just said you were leaving and that meant we were done."

"Well . . ." She holds her arms out and gestures to the world around them. "You're still here, aren't you?"

"I haven't had a reason to leave," he says.

She tilts her head to the side. "I knew you'd never leave the Eastern Shore. Or if you did, you'd end up resenting me for it. So I ended it before that could happen."

He shakes his head.

"What?" she asks.

"I figured," he says.

"You did?"

He shrugs a little, almost apologetic. "That was kinda your pattern, you know?"

She frowns. "My pattern?"

"You needed to feel in control."

She fights the urge to be defensive. It's not the first time someone has called her controlling. She thinks about Tilly's accusation that Claire came here like a tornado, immediately trying to change things. Then she remembers her coworker's comment about over-independence being a trauma response.

Claire knows this about herself. Ever since her sister's disappearance, she has been fighting an unwinnable battle to make sure life never surprises her again. But knowing this and hearing it from someone else are two different things. It stings more coming from the outside, realizing that others can see her flaws as clearly as she can. That she has, in fact, *not* done a decent job of hiding them.

"You're saying you would have left with me?" she asks.

"It would have been nice to have the choice. But it was so long ago. I don't mean to rehash it," he says. He pauses before he adds, "I'm mostly worried you're doing it again."

"What do you mean?"

"Trying to control something you can't."

She flattens her lips. "How so?"

"I know you want to help your dad find some peace in his last days," he says. "But there's no denying it's the disease that's killing him. You can't save him, Claire. And I don't want you blaming yourself when he goes."

She looks down at her hands, presses her thumbnail into the pad of her index finger. She watches as the indentation slowly disappears, then reappears when she presses again.

"I'm afraid of that too," she admits. "I know he's going to die no matter what. But if I can figure out what happened to Gabby before then—"

He shakes his head slowly.

"You don't think I can?" she asks.

"Maybe," he says. "It feels like a long shot. You know? It's been nearly twenty years. I'm not saying to give up. I'm just saying be careful. If you spend your dad's last moments worried about Edith and Gabby and the house, you might miss your chance to say goodbye."

TURN OFF THE LIGHT

Claire presses down with her thumbnail even harder, watching as the finger pad turns white and then red. Ethan is right, of course. But she has become attached to the idea that she can bring her father closure. Even if she can't rid the house of whatever lurks here, she can still give her dad what he has been wanting for nearly two decades: answers about Gabby.

Truthfully, she is being selfish. Deep down she knows that doing this for her father is her way of atoning for having disappeared. For running across the country and putting three thousand miles between them. For robbing him of a meaningful experience as a grandfather when he was still healthy enough to enjoy it.

Claire looks at Julia in the sunroom, her eyes fixed on the iPad in front of her. Guilt stabs at Claire's chest. She has let down not only her father but her daughter too. Julia has also missed out on a key relationship.

"Julia was in the cellar again," Claire says. "She went there because she heard a girl crying."

"The same girl Gabby saw?" he asks.

Claire shrugs. "It must be. But Julia didn't see her, she only heard her."

"So you think there could be something in the cellar? Like, whatever hurt Edith and this girl also hurt Gabby?"

Claire bites her lip. "My mind keeps going there. But I think Edith has been showing me her death. Those are the visions I've been getting at night. I think her husband poisoned her. Used her own medicine against her. Mixed it into her tea so she was paralyzed, then dragged her body somewhere."

Ethan thinks. "So he reports her missing, and the record says she disappeared—"

"But really, she was murdered," Claire says. "Like Poppy always thought. Except now we have a real theory as to who might have done it. The only problem is, I have no idea how that connects to the other stuff. The cellar, the dumbwaiter, the girl crying."

Ethan raises an eyebrow, then leans back against the cushion. He stares at the low table in front of them, chewing the inside of his cheek.

"You think I'm losing it?" Claire asks.

"Maybe we both are," Ethan says. "You have to admit, this is all—"

"I know. I *know* it is. But I don't have a choice. Normally I'd force myself to ignore the noises and the visions—I'd chalk them up to bad sleep or stress or grief. But Gabby was talking about the same stuff before she disappeared. And I can't possibly ignore that."

Ethan nods thoughtfully and scratches the stubble on his chin. "Then maybe we're asking the wrong question. Maybe it's less about *what* and more about *why*. Why is Edith telling you all this? What's the point?"

Claire thinks. "She wants her story to be known? Wants to set the record straight?"

"But even so, how could you prove it? Officially, I mean."

Claire thinks about her missing sister. How the lack of closure drove everyone in her family mad. They were aware that there was only one way to know for certain what happened.

"We would need a body," she says.

Ethan nods as if he has been thinking the same thing.

"Bones," he says. "You would need to find Edith's bones."

Ethan leaves for work at the yacht center a short while later, so Claire goes inside. She tells Julia that screen time is over for now. Julia acquiesces with a sigh and a groan and then is quickly on to the next thing. Claire is inwardly relieved; a year ago, taking away the iPad would have led to a fifteen-minute tantrum.

TURN OFF THE LIGHT

This is one of the strange things about motherhood: Claire is, of course, delighted to avoid the tantrum, but the fact that her daughter no longer totally loses her shit when the movie is stopped means Julia is maturing. Getting older. And when Claire thinks about that, she has a habit of slipping into nostalgia for things she still has. Because motherhood is a constant anticipation of everything changing. These phases are blips, barely registering on the long timeline of life. Claire is so afraid she is going to forget the specific sound of Julia's four-year-old voice or how she smells right after a bath or how she says *froggy* instead of *foggy* and *spider ribs* instead of *spiderwebs*.

These thoughts and fears slam into her without warning, hard enough to make her knees buckle and her throat thick with grief. It's especially bad lately as she witnesses her father's decline, forcing the inevitable cycle of life to the forefront of her thoughts. She wonders what memories and tidbits from her own childhood are trapped within her father's mind. What pieces of her will die with him. What pieces of her have already escaped and fled abroad with her mother, forever lost.

"Mama, I want a snack," Julia announces.

They have migrated to the floor of the playroom, where they are building with some old blocks Claire found in the attic. She is half asleep. She hasn't properly slept since they arrived in Virginia five days ago. Or was it only four days ago?

"Mama," Julia says, louder this time, "I want a snack!"

Claire shoots her a look, and the girl's expression softens.

"Please?" Julia adds.

"Okay, okay. I'll go grab something. What do you want? Cheese?"

After a lengthy back-and-forth, Julia agrees to sliced apples and peanut butter. But the second Claire descends the back stairs, she knows something is off. Tilly is in the kitchen, standing over the stove. Her apron is covered in red and brown stains; she looks like a manic, murderous butcher. The counters are covered in packages of raw meat. Seasoning packets and emptied cans of beans litter the space. Four different pots are cooking at once, with another set of bowls nearby, all filled to the brim with chili.

"Oh, no," Claire says as she takes in the scene.

"I have to get it right," Tilly says. She removes a lid from one of the pots and stirs with conviction. "I have to. It's not right."

"Is the aide still here?" Claire asks, and Tilly nods. "What about Peter? Where is he?"

"Upstairs." Tilly gestures toward the ceiling. "He's useless. So checked out. It's like he . . ." Her voice trails off as she focuses on another pot, tasting and then salting its contents.

"It's like he what?" Claire asks.

"Hmm?" Tilly says, looking up as if noticing Claire for the first time.

A pot gurgles and spits, splashing its contents over the rim so that a glob of chili lands *plop* on the stove. It burns, smoke escaping from under the pot.

"Tilly, stop," Claire says. "Come here."

She approaches her sister and attempts to turn her around into an embrace. But Tilly resists, pushing Claire away with force, then turning back and knocking a pot handle with her elbow, sending the whole concoction careening to the floor.

Tilly is doused with piping-hot chili, and she yelps, instinctively jumping back, flailing her left hand in an attempt to knock off the hot food that is stuck there. She pivots to the sink, turns the cold water on full blast, and shoves her hand under the stream for relief from the burn. Then she crumples to the floor.

Claire joins her there.

TURN OFF THE LIGHT

"I don't want him to die," Tilly says, crying now. They are in the corner of the kitchen, backs against the cabinets, butts on the hard wood.

Claire's heart collapses, folding in on itself. "I know," she says. Tilly lies down with her head in her sister's lap, and Claire strokes her hair and rocks her back and forth. "I know. Me neither."

Grief radiates from Tilly's body like a tangible thing. Above them, the pots of chili continue to gurgle on the stove.

"It's just," Tilly says between sobs, "it feels like it happened so fast."

"It does," Claire says, holding her sister like a child. "And it brings up all the Gabby stuff. Grief triggers grief."

She hasn't realized that until this moment, until she says it out loud. But it's true: The more she grieves her father, the more every moment of grief from her past resurfaces. As if the sadness is muscle memory. Or flaring up like an old rash.

Claire rarely sees her sister like this. Tilly never falls apart. Seeing her so raw and vulnerable feels like a cosmic typo.

"And everything with Peter," Claire continues. "His deciding not to have kids — you're going through so much, Tills."

Tilly wipes her eyes with the backs of her hands. "I keep thinking about all the times I picked fights with Dad over the dumbest stuff. Or how I took Mom's side after Gabby. I feel like . . . I don't know, like I missed out on so much time with Dad. And now . . ."

Claire turns her sister's head in her lap so that they make eye contact. "Are you kidding? You have been the best daughter. You've been taking care of him this whole time." She swallows. Thinks about all her own regrets. "I'm the one who's never here. Who barely calls. Julia hardly knows her grandfather, and that's my fault."

Tilly pushes herself to sitting, holding Claire's hands in her own. "But at least you were brave enough to go *do* something. To leave this place."

It strikes Claire in this moment that what she has perceived as Tilly's resentment or judgment might have been something closer to envy. Maybe even awe. The thought makes Claire nauseated.

"Brave?" she asks. "I don't think so. I mean, I took a risk moving across the country, yeah. But did I do it because I was brave? Or did I do it because I'm a coward?"

Tilly sniffles. "A coward?"

Claire bites her lower lip. She has never admitted this out loud, though it has been on her mind for years. But something about Tilly's vulnerability has cracked Claire open.

"I was running *from* something," she says. "Not toward it. After Gabby disappeared, I was so angry. I was angry at Mom and Dad, who I thought should have been able to fix it. They were our parents. I thought they could solve anything. I was angry with Gabby for leaving or dying or whatever. I was angry with you for still being so perfect even when life was fucking horrible. And I was angry with myself for not being able to be perfect like you."

Tilly stares at her sister, her eyes wide.

"Now, having a daughter, I'm terrified something will happen to her like it did to Gabby," Claire says. "That I'll look away for one second and she'll be gone. Or that there will be some horrible accident. The playground is terrible. I just see danger everywhere. Places where Julia could fall and crack her skull or snap her neck. I'm so worried about what might happen that I can't enjoy what's actually happening. It's like the worst of both worlds."

Tilly nods very slowly. "I wonder if that's how Mom felt."

"What do you mean?" Claire asks.

"I wonder if that's why she left. If it got to be too hard. Like maybe she was scared something would happen to us too, and it was easier if she was the one who left first."

If this is true, then Claire and her mother are more similar than she ever realized. For the first time in a long while, she feels close to understanding her mom. The resentment she has long felt about her abandonment does not dissolve entirely, but the edges of it soften.

She thinks about Tilly too. How desperately she wants to be a mother and how the person she loves might keep her from that.

Claire realizes in this moment that motherhood is more complex than the idea of "having a child." Perhaps motherhood is defined as much by what someone has lost as by what she has.

In fact, Claire's entire identity as a mother has been built on loss. She didn't lose only her sister; she lost her trust in the world. And this is a lingering wound that has shaped how she parents. The fear. The clinging. If she doesn't figure out what happened to Gabby, she risks passing this same legacy down to Julia. She risks bringing her daughter into a world where she, too, never feels safe. Whatever darkness followed Gabby in her last days is still in this house. Claire's desire to understand the past is not simply an obsession with finding the truth—it's also a desperate attempt to stop history from repeating itself.

Later, Claire forces her sister to relax. She sets Julia up with some paints at the kitchen table and starts in on the mess of the kitchen. Spilled chili has hardened on every visible surface; empty packs of meat leak their raw juices on the counters; smudges of spices and smears of greasy oil abound. Claire finds bright yellow gloves under the sink and gathers a few cleaning tools, including a greenish spray and some paper towels.

She addresses the floor first. The chili went everywhere when her sister knocked the pan from the stove. The dark mixture is splashed up the cabinets, along the floorboards, and even under the toe space. It's like blood spatter at a crime scene.

Claire gets on her hands and knees to scrub the hidden spots, and that's when she finds another mess. This bit is thicker and oddly congealed. It doesn't look like chili. It's hardening, almost like wax. She frowns at it, then figures it must be discarded fat or grease from the ground beef and attacks it with her gloved hand. It takes some work, but the mixture finally lifts.

Just as she finishes the floor and is about to move onto the cabinet doors, she is overcome with the smell of burned apple again. This time, it's stronger, potent enough to drown out the chemical scent of the cleaning spray. The last time she smelled apple like this was when Julia sneaked back into the cellar.

Claire's heart almost stops, and she turns quickly toward the table. But Julia is there, quietly painting, focused on her project. Claire pauses, still. Listening. She looks over her shoulder. Whispers into the empty space.

"Edith?" she asks quietly. "Edith, is that you?"

But no one responds. Nothing happens. And after another minute, the apple smell dissipates entirely.

"Mama," Julia calls from the table. "Why do you say it's a secret?"

Claire stands there, still distracted by the smell. She gathers the cleaning supplies and moves to the cabinets. "Huh?"

"Aunt Gabby. You said you don't know if she's in the stars. Because she keeps it a secret."

Claire senses a heavy conversation and abandons her task to join Julia at the table. "That's right," she says. "We don't know where she is because she disappeared."

Julia frowns. "But you told her to go."

Adrenaline surges in Claire's veins, bringing her body to high alert. "What do you mean?"

"You told her to leave."

Claire tries to swallow but can't. "I don't understand."

Julia sighs in typical dramatic fashion, like her mother just isn't getting it. "Auntie Gabby said she didn't like it here, and you told her to 'fucking leave already.'"

Claire coughs, choking on her own spit. It's not possible. This is the one thing Claire has never shared with any living person. Her last conversation with Gabby. The last words she ever spoke to her older sister. The words that ultimately drove her away and to her demise.

"Oh my God, is someone moving the dumbwaiter?" Gabby said.

Claire rolled her eyes. "Ha. Ha."

"I'm serious. I can hear the gears moving."

"I'm not twelve anymore, Gabs. You can't scare me with your bullshit stories."

She wishes now more than anything that she had believed her sister. But Claire was tired of Gabby complaining. She was never satisfied. She always wanted more than their life on the Eastern Shore. And in wanting more, she made Claire feel judged. Less than. Claire loved it here. But what did that say about her? Compared to Gabby, Claire was complacent. Simple.

"The house isn't haunted," Claire said. "You just want your life to be a horror movie because that's easier than being bored."

"Sorry that I don't want to scoop rocky road for all eternity."

Claire felt something growing inside her. A resentment that she had never allowed to bubble over, since she had always looked up to Gabby. But things were changing. They were getting older, and Claire realized her sister didn't have all the answers. Not even her parents did. There was something terrifying but also freeing in this. Claire was allowed to be her own person. Separate from her sisters. But every time Gabby complained that she needed more from life, she made Claire feel smaller in comparison.

And Claire was tired of feeling small.

"God, Gabby, I get it. We all get it. You hate it here."

"Don't you?"

Claire threw up her hands. "No, I don't! But maybe that's because I don't look at everyone here like I'm better than them. Like I was born into the wrong family or something."

"It's not that, Claire. Really." Something in Gabby's eyes softened. "It just feels like this place is going to swallow me whole."

"Then fucking leave already!" Claire shouted.

Gabby blinked like she'd been slapped.

"No one's keeping you here," Claire continued, unable to stop herself. "Just go. Run away. Disappear, if that's what you're so desperate to do. None of us would give a shit anyway. It'd be a relief from all the complaining."

She has thought about that conversation so many times in her life, shame wrapped in every word. Gabby had stared, shell-shocked, then walked out the front door. Never seen again.

But Claire has never told anyone about this. She couldn't.

So how does Julia know?

"I saw you talking to Aunt Gabby," Julia tells her. "In the kitchen earlier."

Claire's head swims. "But . . ."

"You looked different," Julia says matter-of-factly, still focused on her painting. "Like the picture."

"What picture?" Claire asks.

"By the fireplace."

She must mean the portrait from the beach. The one they took as a family shortly before Gabby disappeared. The same one that spontaneously fell.

Claire makes her four-year-old clarify it three times. She asks her to stand where she saw Gabby standing. She makes her repeat as many of the words as she can remember. She makes her describe Gabby's tacky ice cream–parlor uniform, which Julia has never seen in real life or photos. By the end of it, Julia is probably regretting having told Claire at all. She just wants to return to her art.

But it becomes certain: Julia saw the moment that Claire lived almost two decades ago. She watched the conversation between teenage sisters play out.

Claire's shock fights with her shame. Her daughter witnessed the worst moment of her life. Julia heard Claire shout at Gabby to leave. Will Julia blame Claire the way Claire has blamed herself? Does Julia see her mother differently now?

Claire is too confused by what is happening, though, to dwell on the emotional repercussions. Her thoughts burn her skull, as if they are firing so rapidly, they cannot be contained within the confines of her body.

Gabby saw a girl in the cellar.

Julia heard someone crying down there.

An extinct bird landed on Claire's windowsill.

Julia witnessed her teenage mother fight with her older sister.

Her father slapped her and insisted, *It's time.*

"It can't be," Claire mutters to herself, a realization taking shape. Then she looks around for her phone. She needs to call Ethan.

Claire is upstairs in the guest room. She's got a million tabs open on her computer and Ethan on the phone on speaker. They've been hashing it out for thirty minutes already.

"Okay," Claire says, scanning an article on her laptop. "So Einstein's theory of relativity tells us time can stretch and compress depending on speed and gravity, right?"

"Yeah," Ethan confirms. "Like how at a black hole, time nearly stops."

"Yes. Or like how a clock on a fast-moving spaceship ticks more slowly than one on Earth."

Claire has always been fascinated by this stuff but is not naturally gifted at it. She had to read the last paragraph of this article four times to make it stick. But she's getting closer to understanding what's happening in this house. She knows she is.

"So," Ethan says, "we shouldn't think about time as linear, as a straight line of past, present, and future."

"Right."

She watches Julia from the corner of her eye. The girl is playing in the adjoining room, building a home for Bunny with cardboard boxes previously destined for the recycling bin.

"So then we get to the block universe theory, which basically says that the past, present, and future all exist at once," Claire says, continuing to read and work things out aloud. "We experience life one moment at a time, but all the other moments still exist simultaneously."

"That one's harder for me to grasp," Ethan admits.

"Same," Claire says. "But I think that's what's happening here."

"How so?"

Claire bites her lip in thought. She flips through the tabs of articles and personal accounts and blogs and stories. "Picture time like a blanket," she tells him. "We have always thought of it like a smooth surface, an arrow pointing in one direction. But now imagine throwing that blanket on the bed. It's not going to land perfectly flat, right? There will be ridges and folds and places where the fabric lands on top of itself."

"Ahh," Ethan says, getting it. "So if you take right now and then back in the 1630s with Edith, we'd normally think of them as four hundred years apart. But if time folds on itself, those two moments could compress, like two different spots on the blanket."

"The two timelines bleed together," Claire confirms. "Even if only briefly."

"Wild," Ethan muses, fascinated. "So that bird you saw. It's extinct today, but it did exist in the 1630s. So that bird was really here, you didn't imagine it. And it was also in the past at the same time."

"I was seeing a moment from Edith's timeline," Claire adds. "She was probably looking at that very same bird in that very same moment. And the girl that Gabby saw in the cellar when she was trapped down there? That wasn't a ghost. It was Julia. She was seeing my future daughter—who was lured to the cellar by Gabby's cries. Gabby was crying when she got stuck down there."

"So it's like a version of time traveling."

"Kinda," Claire says. "But not in the way we usually think of it. Just like gravity can bend light, certain forces must be able to bend time. Echoes of the past slip into the present. And vice versa."

"What forces do you think bend time?" Ethan asks.

"Not sure," Claire admits. She scans another article that posits something similar. "Emotional intensity? Trauma? Seems like no one knows. There's this scientist I'm reading about now—she has a theory that two timelines can become entangled. What one does can influence the other, choices rippling through time. Not in a cause-and-effect way so much, but like... maybe I lose an object in the present, and Edith finds it in the past. Or a candle goes out in the present because a door has closed and created a draft in the past."

They stay on the phone together, reading in silence, too excited by what they are finding to stop searching.

"Oh, this is interesting," Ethan says of something he has found on his own computer. "It says some people think certain *places* may be conduits. Like, geographic locations where time folds more easily. Places that hold deep human experience with lots of history. You know, like deaths and emotions imprinted on the land."

Deaths. Claire shivers as she thinks about Edith. As she wonders about Gabby. Then she gets another idea.

"What if... okay, you know how people always think about ghosts as remnants from the past that have stuck around? Well, if we accept that time moves the way we are saying it does, then there's not really any such thing as ghosts. In reality, those are just the moments that time is folding. If you hear footsteps in the other room, it's not some spirit lurking around. You're quite literally hearing the person in the other room, but they exist in another time. Either before or after you."

"Oh my God," Ethan says. "It's so true. And if you think about it, people usually report ghosts when benign things happen. Like when they hear whispers or a TV turns on randomly or something falls in the corner of the room—"

"Because usually when time crosses, it's just an ordinary moment," Claire adds. "A trail of footprints left behind from muddy feet twenty years in the future. Someone turns off the light in another timeline, and yours goes off too."

She has never thought about hauntings in this way, but the idea is exhilarating. It feels right. This is what's happening here. She's sure of it.

"It's almost like you and Edith are communicating," Ethan says.

Claire frowns then, something bothering her. "But I still don't understand why only some of us in the house are seeing and hearing these things. Why not Peter? Why not Tilly?"

"Yeah..." Ethan says.

Claire can tell by his tone that he's holding something back. "What?" she asks. "You have a theory?"

"Not *my* theory," he clarifies quickly. "But I read something."

"Okay?" Claire prompts.

Ethan hesitates. "Well, apparently some people think you're more open to seeing these things when you're close to transition. Like your dad, since he's close to death. And Julia, since she's close to birth. They're more open. More receptive."

"That sounds a little woo-woo, doesn't it?" she asks.

"Yeah, but it does explain it. And same with Gabby. She was experiencing this stuff only in the last week before she disappeared. You were both standing in the kitchen, but only *she* heard the dumbwaiter moving."

The truth of this hits Claire. "So you're saying she was able to hear it because she was close to death?"

"If this theory is right," Ethan says, a hint of apology in his voice, "it holds water."

"Wait." Claire does the mental math. "I couldn't hear the dumbwaiter then. But I can now. So does all this mean *I'm* close to death right now?"

Ethan breathes into the phone. "Maybe you're just more receptive in general," he says, not convincingly.

A lump forms in Claire's throat. She has never thought of herself as receptive. She never saw ghosts or felt spirits before this trip. And while she has never particularly feared death, the idea of leaving her daughter behind makes her nauseated and vengeful all at once.

"The truth is, we don't know," Ethan says, clearly trying to calm her. "Just like we don't know the exact trigger that is making time fold. Or why your house is more susceptible to it happening. But, Claire, it feels like you've really figured this out. We finally understand what's going on in the house. This whole time, you thought Edith was haunting you—"

"When really," Claire finishes, "we've been haunting each other."

23
EDITH

Edith sits in the center of her home, which is far too small for so many bodies. The chair feels hard and unforgiving beneath her tailbone. The air in the room is thick with sweat, everyone's nerves on edge. The burial may be over, but the atmosphere is still heavy with grief. Or — what was grief this afternoon but has now twisted into something else. Something sinister.

Grace has receded into the shadows beside the hearth. Elizabeth takes charge, stepping away from the locked door and approaching the center of the circle the women have formed around Edith.

"We must be certain," Elizabeth says.

Edith looks around the room, pulse quickening, but everyone avoids eye contact. Instead, like Elizabeth, they step closer, walls of suspicion blocking her in.

"I don't understand," Edith says.

The women step forward again, their movements measured and methodical.

"You went to the minister," one of them says.

"You have been seen in the woods at night."

"You can predict death to the day."

"Your herbs are bewitched. Cursed."

"You cannot bear children."

The voices overlap and step on one another as the women become more anxious and excited.

Hands find her sleeves, roll them up past her elbows. The fingers are sticky and prodding. Edith tries to turn toward Grace, to plead with her eyes, but hands jerk her head forward. When Edith tries to stand, Elizabeth nods to Violet's two young sisters, who fall at Edith's feet and restrain her ankles. Anger flares in her chest that they have gotten the children involved.

She keeps her breath measured, afraid that if she shows even one sign of discomfort, they will use it against her. Claim it as proof of their theories. She knows what they are doing: They are looking for the witch's mark. A place on her body where the Devil has suckled, has been allowed in.

And the truth is, she has a nagging fear they may find one. Just last week, she would have scoffed at the idea. But not anymore. Not after all the things she has seen and cannot explain.

She wonders if she has been too meek. If she has allowed this to happen to herself. Perhaps the Devil prefers quiet hearts, as they do not scream when he slips inside.

"What is this?"

It is Margaret, again questioning Edith about the bruise on her forearm. The one for which Edith has no explanation. What was her excuse the other day? She cannot remember in the chaos of this moment.

"A bruise," she says. "From an iron pot in the kitchen."

Margaret clucks. "A different story from before." The woman looks at Grace. "What was it Goody Harris told us?"

TURN OFF THE LIGHT

Edith cannot see Grace, who stands behind her. This brief moment of silence buoys Edith's hopes. Perhaps her friend is coming to her senses. Perhaps she will tell them this is ridiculous and cruel.

But then Grace's voice floats above the tension of the room: "She said she fell harvesting oysters."

Edith's throat tightens.

Elizabeth says, "Well? Which is it, Goody Harris? Did you bump into a pot or did you fall gathering oysters? Or perhaps it is from something else entirely?"

Edith starts to answer but flinches as fingers press into the purplish spot on her arm. "Ouch!"

"It hurts?" Elizabeth asks. Then she frowns. "Not the witch's mark, then." She nods toward the women, who resume their search.

Hands again roam Edith's body, this time frantically moving over her scalp, beneath her hair, behind her ears, along the back of her neck. Someone tugs at the laces of her bodice, exposing the hollow of her throat, the curve of her collarbone. Edith instinctively reaches to conceal herself, but Elizabeth leans in and smacks her hands away.

"We will have to restrain you, Goody Harris," the woman spits, "if you cannot stay still."

Edith looks down at the young girls holding her feet. Neither one can be more than eight years old. She could easily kick them off, but she doesn't want to risk hurting them. Which is by design, of course. Her stomach rolls. Remnants of her own vomit are still on her tongue and lips, and the taste of it threatens to bring up even more.

The hands work their way down Edith's body, now lifting her skirt, examining her ankles, and exposing her calves. Fingers slide all the way to her upper thigh. Edith squirms, but someone from behind—it must be Grace, *Grace, of all people*—presses her palms against her chest, confining her to the chair.

It's disgusting, the way these women stare at her, violating her with their hungry eyes. Their dirty hands all over her skin. The places where, before this moment, only her husband had ever touched. Tears prick her eyes, but she refuses to cry. She wants to spit and shout and scream and throw punches but she cannot move. She is frozen with shame. How can she ever face these women again? How can she exist in a place where all her neighbors have run their fingers along her soft belly, scraped their nails along the grooves of her crotch? How can she sleep and cook and live in the very room where she has been tortured?

Overwhelmed, she leaves her body entirely, floating somewhere in the corner of the room and watching as a detached observer.

Someone asks about her bug bites. When Edith does not reply, another woman points out a bite on her own ankle. Swamp flies. Not a witch's mark.

They continue to poke and pinch and prod, and each time, Edith reacts with a jump or a yelp of pain, proving that she is not under the control of the Devil. That she can still feel human hurt. Her rash, which is now a series of pink, scaly patches, becomes a topic of great debate. They talk about her as if she is not here. And maybe that is right, because she does not feel like she is even in this room anymore. She is somewhere far away. Pruning chamomile flowers with Aunt Joan.

Sometime later, Elizabeth says something about supper. Margaret mentions an impending storm, the need to get home. The women begin to disperse, saying nothing of Edith and what was found or not found. They act as though none of this has happened.

Edith assumes they are finished. They have not discovered

anything to prove their theories. But she is too overcome with humiliation to feel any relief. She sinks into herself, tugging at her remaining clothes to cover her body the best she can. Her shirt is ripped, her bodice loose.

"We better see you at service on Sunday, then," Elizabeth says. Her voice is pointed but rote, as if she has not just conducted a symphony of assault.

Edith nods.

24

CLAIRE

The house sleeps.

Claire sits with her father. The nurses will come daily now. Everyone can sense it: They are on deathwatch.

Claire stares as her father's chest moves in shallow ups and downs. Then she slides her fingers between his bony ones. Desperate to connect, even if only for a couple of minutes. What she would give for a lucid conversation. Just one. There are so many things she wants to say, so many ways in which she'd like to apologize for disappearing. For running away after he had already lost one daughter.

She thought she was getting so close to answers, but now she is not sure. If what Ethan proposes is correct, that people near transition can sense the folds of time, then Gabby is dead. And Claire may not be far behind. But how did Gabby die? Was this house a part of it? Did Edith witness Gabby's death, much like Julia witnessed that conversation between Claire and her sister?

Claire's body is restless. Cannot be contained. She itches all over, and she scratches like maybe she can break free of her own skin. She considers making a cup of tea, but all she can think about is the clinking of the spoon in the wooden cup. David poisoning Edith with her own healing herbal remedies.

She moves to the living room, her feet a steady metronome to the incessant thoughts clicking through her mind. Time is bringing these two women together for a reason. She can sense it. It feels like Edith needs her. But for what?

We would need a body, Claire told Ethan. The only way to prove Edith's story.

Claire stands in the living room and looks out the window at the moonlight illuminating the front yard. A bat squiggles its way up from the trees and zigzags through the sky.

Scrit-scrit-scratchhh

There it is again.

That scratching from the cellar.

She stops breathing.

She looks over to the trapdoor ten feet away.

Scrit-scratchhh-scrit-scrit

A desperate scraping with no predictable rhythm.

Claire forces herself to take a breath. She remembers Peter hanging the picture by the hearth, remembers him crawling under the house to set the mousetraps. The scratching could be small rodents.

Or it could be Edith.

Or Gabby.

Under that door right now. Waiting. Watching.

She is frozen, caught between lunging forward and running away. The idea of seeing her sister's face, unchanged after all these years, hits her like a punch to the sternum. Her guts twist. Bile rises up in her throat, hot and bitter.

Claire takes a step forward. Then another. A floorboard creaks, sharp and sudden. She flinches. A jolt of electricity goes through her veins.

Another step.

What if Gabby has been down there all along? What if Gabby... isn't really Gabby anymore?

Claire's fingers tremble as she reaches for the latch.

But then something *pricks* her hand, and she yelps in surprise. A stinging sensation on her nail. She drops the latch and brings her left hand up to inspect the ring finger. Her eyes widen as her focus narrows. With her right thumb, she presses on the nail and it *slides* off the skin.

She holds the nail up to the moonlight. It is almost see-through against the backdrop of the window. Something stringy hangs from the edges. Hair? Or is that...

Skin.

Bits of Claire's skin hang from the nail like tentacles on a tiny jellyfish.

She shudders, rushes to the downstairs bathroom, and throws the detached fingernail into the toilet. She flushes and watches it swirl twice before being sucked down the hole. She almost feels relieved—until she sees it return, resurfacing. She frantically flushes the toilet again and again until the nail disappears for good.

Then she stares at the raw skin on her left finger. The exposed flesh where her nail has been ripped entirely clean.

The scratching... the desperation... the damage to her nails...

A narrative forms in Claire's mind. A story that begins to take shape.

Edith was poisoned. Assumed dead, though David would not have known how the medicinal plants worked, would he? He would not have known how much was needed to heal or kill.

Maybe he thought she was dead, but really, he buried her alive.

Locked her in the cellar, where she cried for help, where she tried to scratch her way out. Then perhaps he burned it for good measure.

Which means if there's anything left of Edith's bones...

It all comes back to the cellar. That's where the answers are. Julia has been drawn there repeatedly for a reason. The house has been pointing Claire here all along. *Come inside,* it seems to be saying. *Come down into my guts and find the truth.*

Claire moves quickly so that she does not have time to change her mind. She pries open the warped door of the cellar, flicks on the dim light, and descends the uneven stone steps.

The soot stains along the walls look like smudged handprints dragging downward. She looks away from them, staring forward and watching her footing so she doesn't fall. The light buzzes, a dry electric hum that stutters and then resumes. Something creaks overhead as she descends, like a weight is shifting or wood is straining.

She looks around the space in a way she never has before, as if seeing it for the first time. She doesn't know what she is searching for, but the familiar feeling of dread begins to snake itself around her limbs so that she nearly freezes. She hates being down here. That much hasn't changed.

Wooden shelves line the walls. They are mostly empty now, though clearly warped from years of heavy work. She spots an old coiled garden hose and a pile of mildewed rags. To her left is a cobwebbed cabinet of unknown purpose with mismatched drawers. On top of it rests an oil lamp, unlit, its glass clouded with age.

Claire runs her hands along the floor, feeling for any loose bricks or stones. She touches the walls too, but nothing budges. Nothing moves. She brings her hands to the steps, feeling for anything out of place. And then—*loose grit*. She is sure of it. Right on the back corner of the bottom step.

She gets on her hands and knees and dips low, squinting into the cracks between the stones. And then she notices a dark void behind the bottom stair. Not just a shadow, but a hollowness. A hole.

She sweeps away dust and what looks like old mortar. And then a smaller stone in the corner shifts. It's not fixed, but set loose, like a lid. When she lifts it, she sees blackness stretching beyond. *Space.*

She lies flat, pressing her cheek to the cool floor, sticks her fingers into the crack, and pulls against the larger stone beside the opening. And it budges. She pulls harder, until the entire front of the bottom step is removed, revealing a hole just large enough for her to crawl through.

Claire shifts onto her forearms and belly and army-crawls through the opening and into the space under the house. She turns the flashlight of her phone on and shines it in front of her.

The air down here is stifling, making her breath damp and heavy. Her vision is narrow. Darkness presses from all sides, only partially stamped out by the feeble light her phone provides. At best, she can see a few inches in front of her. All wooden beams and dirt and cobwebs. So many cobwebs. She swipes at her hair, where they cling and tickle her temples and neck. One gets stuck in her eyelash, and she frantically swats it away, only to bang her knuckles on a beam.

"Shit," she says, pausing as she tries to get her bearings.

Here, under the house, the earth is cool but damp. Muddy in some spots, dry and dusty in others. Something scuttles away from her in the darkness. That must be one of the mice. Panic sets in as she wonders if there are snakes down here. Her whole body shudders in fear as she pictures a long, slithery reptile sliding its way toward her, its tongue flicking in the darkness, searching for her by scent. Preying on her fear.

She can't think about that right now.

Outside, the cicadas scream. But down here, it's like they are underwater. Half a world away.

Claire sneezes. It's so dusty. Her allergies are going haywire. She sneezes again and then gets a whiff of something rotten. A coppery tang. Maybe it's rust. As she continues forward, she hears a *crunch* under her forearms and freezes.

Reluctantly, she shines the flashlight on the dirt just under her arm and sees the remnants of a small animal carcass. Its bones have snapped under her weight.

Claire almost hurls. She drops the light, which shines upward to reveal sagging insulation and dirt-caked pipes.

Then — a shift in the air.

Not a breeze. There is no wind down here.

No, a true shift. A *change*. Like something is here with her. Breathing right beside her.

Claire freezes.

A prickling crawls up her spine. Like a dozen fingers trailing along the back of her neck, pressing against her shoulders and upper arms. A pinch. A poke. She even feels the lower part of her shirt lift —

"Fuck this," Claire says, swinging the light around to see the path back out. But the narrow tunnel of dirt and wood she came through now seems longer, the opening at the bottom of the cellar stairs farther away somehow.

Another poke. This one harder, right against her ribs. She gasps and twists toward it, but her neck is jerked back in the other direction as something pulls her hair. "What the fuck!" she yells.

Claire contorts her limbs in a million pretzel variations to turn herself back toward where she came. All the while, she feels them. Eyes. Hands. Pressing into her skin, grabbing and pulling.

She screams, then lunges forward and hits her head on a beam. Blood trickles down. She blinks it out of her eye. But she can't stop now. She can't stay still. If she does, she will be overcome by whatever is reaching for her, ripping her clothes, violating her with every touch.

Finally, her fingers find the edges of the opening and grasp at the undersides of the stones that make up the cellar steps. She pulls herself forward and out, scrambles to her feet, then runs up the uneven steps and slams the cellar door shut without a second thought.

She falls to her hands and knees, breathing heavy, her chest tight and burning. Her shirt is torn, like an animal got to it. Her pants are filthy. Her skin is covered in bites, as if she were bitten by a hundred mosquitoes.

But the strangest thing of all is the fingerprints.

Her skin is covered with them. Dozens, all over her arms and legs and belly. They are stamped onto her skin, glowing like a crime scene under a black light.

"I don't understand."

"Why now? Why were you down there?"

"You couldn't wait?"

"What exactly were you looking for?"

Peter and Tilly are interrogating Claire. Turns out, she woke her sister with her scream, which traveled through a vent connected to the crawl space. The eerie echo bounced up the shaft to the second-floor bathroom where Tilly was peeing, half asleep.

TURN OFF THE LIGHT

Peter is especially agitated. He paces in front of the couch where Claire sits, only feet from the entrance to the cellar. "What were you thinking?" he presses.

Claire is too shell-shocked from her time under the house to do anything but stare blankly in response.

They are all freaked out by the fingerprints. Tilly wonders if they need to call the police. Peter is adamant they do not. "There is no one under the house," he insists.

And Claire knows he's right. The police can't help them. She suspects this was a crossover moment. A bleed in time. All those hands on her skin were probably also on Edith's skin, though she can't imagine why. Horrible scenarios play out in her imagination.

"So you think," Tilly says, joining Claire on the couch and nodding toward the trapdoor, "that Edith is down there somewhere?"

Claire nods. "I do." She does not add that answers about Gabby might be down there too. Not only does she lack the words to explain her theory, but, more important, she doesn't want to get her sister's hopes up.

Tilly's eyes scan Claire's body, and Claire senses a shift in her sister. Maybe because she has real evidence now. Tilly heard the scream. Can see the ripped clothes and pinch marks and fingerprints.

"Then we should call someone," Tilly says, resolved. "Who do you call for ancient bones? Like, an archaeologist or something."

Peter rolls his eyes. "Jesus, we're not calling an archaeologist. It's nearly one in the morning."

This time, Tilly rolls her eyes. "Not right this second, Peter, God. Tomorrow morning. We need someone who can preserve the burial site, you know? It's honestly good you weren't able to search thoroughly," she adds to Claire. "You could have compromised the site somehow."

"Do you hear yourselves?" Peter asks, his voice rising. "Claire has been having some bad dreams, and now you're both convinced there's a woman buried under the house? Wouldn't she have been found by now? Like, I don't know, during one of the thirty or forty times this house has been rebuilt over the centuries?"

"Ancient bones are found all the time!" Tilly argues. "And these aren't just dreams. Look at her, Peter. Even you can't explain those fingerprints. Claire is telling the truth."

Peter takes a breath, steadying himself. "I'm not saying Claire is lying. There's obviously something weird going on here, I'll give you that. I just don't think we should jump to such massive conclusions. We're going to pay someone to come rip the house apart for bones that *might* be down there? Do you realize how much that will cost? We don't have that kind of money, Tilly."

"There have to be grants or something," Tilly says, her voice losing conviction.

"Even if there are bones down there," Peter continues as if he hasn't heard her, "so what? It's a random woman none of us even care about."

Claire's chest tightens. "I care about her," she says.

Peter waves his hand in the air. "Yeah, sure, okay."

"Maybe we just all need some sleep," Tilly says. She disappears into the kitchen. Claire hears the water turn on and assumes her sister is setting in on the dirty dishes in the sink. They had all agreed to attack them tomorrow morning for the sake of an earlier bedtime.

"What are you doing?" Claire calls from the couch.

When Tilly doesn't answer, Claire leaves Peter and crosses to the next room, where she finds Tilly scrubbing one of the large pots that, only hours ago, was full of grief chili.

"It helps me relax," she admits. "My heart is pounding. I need something to busy my hands."

Claire sits on a barstool at the end of the island.

"It's creepy, you know?" Tilly continues as she puts the water on full blast for a rinse. "To think all this time... right under our feet..."

Peter enters the kitchen, joins Tilly at the sink, and grabs a dish towel to help dry. "There's no need to be creeped out," he says. "We don't know for sure that anything is down there."

His voice is calmer now, but Claire notices a vessel in his throat thumping. Like he is working hard to maintain this cool composure.

Tilly shoots him a look. "I believe Claire."

Peter sighs loudly. "Okay, can we just agree to drop this until morning? None of us are going to make well-informed decisions right now. We're tired and agitated."

Claire can't argue with this. He's right.

The two of them continue to work at the sink as Claire fiddles with a dish towel on the counter. She works the fabric between her fingers. Bends the harder edges against themselves, then thinks of the analogy of time folding like a blanket and Ethan's suggestion that she can experience all these things because she is "open."

Or—the other possibility—that she is close to death.

When Gabby started seeing things, she had less than two weeks left.

What does that mean for Claire?

Nausea sends bile up the back of her throat. She is not ready to die. She has a daughter to raise. Is it possible she can change the course of events? If she helps find Edith's bones, will her own life be spared?

"So who do we call in the morning?" she asks, but no one answers her. Peter seems in a daze as he dries a large baking sheet. His hands work the towel as he stares listlessly. Tilly cleans the sink, pushing food down the drain and squinting to see if she has gotten it all. The light over the sink isn't on. She nods toward the switch.

"Can you get the light?" she asks Peter.

He nods, but in an absent way, like he has only half heard her. He reaches for the switch.

The next moments move in slow motion. Claire's brain registers all the parts: her sister bent over the drain; Peter, distracted, reaching for the wrong toggle. But she cannot put these parts together in time to stop it.

There is a sudden, deafening grind as the garbage disposal's blades slam and tear into Tilly's flesh and muscles and tendons.

25

EDITH

The minister's wife is heading for the door to leave when it starts.

A deep, gut-churning rumble engulfs them. Like the growl of a creature waking from within the earth's core.

Edith, freshly violated, is still sitting in the center of the room. But she looks up when the world shakes. All of the women freeze.

A clay cup rattles, vibrates its way toward the edge of the table. Through the window, Edith sees marsh grasses in the distance ripple like waves, though there is no wind. A tree crashes to the ground. She cannot see the chickens, but she hears their frantic clucks.

Electric energy courses through Edith's body as if preparing her for some Herculean task. Is this real? The very thing that is meant to remain steady—the earth beneath their feet—is shaking and rumbling and rolling. She has heard of this only in stories.

Elizabeth looks around, her eyes wide with fear. Then she turns to Edith. "What is this?" she asks. An accusation.

Edith does not know how to defend herself. After all, the timing is impeccable, is it not? Fate is mocking her, picking this very moment to shake the earth. As though the Devil himself has arrived to say, *Yes, you are right, I am here.*

The others echo Elizabeth's sentiment, demanding answers, squirming and shrieking with fear like trapped rats. And then the earth heaves again. The wooden walls creak and groan as if the structure itself is twisting. Sparks spit from the fire in the hearth as the stones in the chimney shift and shower the floor with grit. Edith places a hand on the table for stability as a fresh roar travels up and through the soil.

Herbs hanging from the rafters above them quiver, and dust shakes from the wooden beams. And then —

A burst of sound and a spattering of *wet*.

Liquid splashes them all, spraying them with what feels like water. A few women scramble for shelter under tables and chairs, shocked and confused. Edith looks up, wondering if the roof has collapsed. Where else could the water have come from?

But then she catches sight of her own limbs. She holds up her hands and arms. Inspects her torn white sleeves.

Everything is spattered with red.

The water isn't water at all.

It's blood.

Pandemonium breaks out as the women yell in confusion, staring at their hands and wiping the red splotches furiously from their bodies and clothes. Edith looks around, searching for the source. She even pats down her own body, but she has no injury that she can see or feel. The blood seemed to come from the center of the room. When she looks, she sees no one doubled over in pain, only panic-stricken faces.

The tremor has passed, but the house continues to groan and croak in low laments as the women squawk in fear. And then a guttural scream ascends above the mayhem, sharp and agonized.

TURN OFF THE LIGHT

It is Grace. She stands by the window, holding something up to the light. Edith worries she is hurt, but then she sees that Grace's expression is not one of pain.

It is one of horror.

"This is—where did—" Grace cannot finish the sentence. She bends over and vomits on the floor, her retching even louder than the house's protests.

Edith rushes to Grace's side and immediately spots what the woman was holding only seconds ago. There on the ground, mere inches from the runny, rapidly spreading puke, is a fingertip. Its full nail is still intact. The bone is cleanly cut just below the first knuckle, as if chopped with a butcher's knife.

"Grace!" Edith cries. "Let me see your hands!"

The woman complies, though she keeps her face to the floor and continues to dry-heave. But when Edith inspects her fingers, she sees that the found appendage does not belong to Grace.

"Whose is this?" she asks the group, holding up the bloody flesh and bone. Whoever is hurt will need the bleeding stanched, the wound sewn shut. All the women look at their own hands in horror, but no one claims it. Shockingly, no one is hurt. The severed fingertip does not belong to anyone in this room.

And if she wasn't sure before, Edith is absolutely sure now: The Devil is here.

26

CLAIRE

"They aren't blades," the nurse says. She is in her forties and has soft, silky-looking skin. Her hair is very short, tight wiry curls that extend less than an inch from her head. Salt-and-pepper-colored. More salt than pepper.

"I'm sorry?" Claire says. She is sitting in the waiting room of the ER, bundled up in a thick sweatshirt to cover the bruises and fingerprints from earlier.

"The garbage disposal," the nurse clarifies. "People often think they're blades, but they're actually spinning impellers."

"Uh-huh," Claire says.

Tilly is being treated, and Claire will be able to see her soon. The doctors are still debating whether she needs surgery. If she does, she will be in the hospital for a couple of days.

When the nurse leaves, Claire searches the internet for *spinning impellers*. Inside the disposal is a circular metal plate—appropriately called the grind ring—that turns at superhigh speeds. Attached to this are more spinning metal lugs. When the disposal is switched on, the grind ring turns, and the impellers fling food scraps outward against the serrated grinding chamber, which pulverizes the food into a slurry.

She thinks about how the disposal strained against the mass of Tilly's bones and jammed up quickly. But not before Claire and Peter were showered with spattered blood. When Tilly pulled out her hand, she screamed with horror, her brain trying to comprehend the damage. As Peter called an ambulance, Claire fished around in the sink for Tilly's fingertips. She found three and secured them in a small ziplock bag that she put inside a cooler with some ice. She wonders now where that missing fingertip is. If they'll find it rotting under the refrigerator in a few days. But why would it be anywhere other than in the sink?

Outside, the sun is rising. People float in and out of the waiting room like moving water. The receptionist fields frantic inquiries while the morning news drones from a corner-mounted television.

"I didn't mean to," Peter says.

They are all sitting in the waiting room now. Peter drove Julia here the moment she woke. When the EMTs arrived after the accident, they said Tilly could have only one person in the ambulance, and she had quietly asked Claire to come. Claire couldn't refuse, even though she didn't like the idea of leaving Julia behind.

When her daughter finally arrived with Peter, Claire was so relieved that she let her pick whatever she wanted from the vending machine. Julia chose Frosted Strawberry Pop-Tarts, which probably expired a year ago and are now crumbling all over her lap.

"I didn't mean to," Peter says again.

"Of course you didn't," Claire says.

"I *didn't*," Peter repeats as if she has disagreed with him.

"I know." She sighs.

Nearby, the automatic doors of the ER insist on reopening every thirty seconds, even when no one is around. They must be broken.

Peter rambles on, his voice bordering on hysterical. "I can't believe—I'm such an idiot—how did the—she said get the light, I reached for the switch—"

"Is it yummy?" Claire whispers to Julia.

The girl nods. Then she frowns. "Aunt Tilly got hurt, Mama," she says.

"Yes, sweetie. I know. But the doctors are going to make her all better. They might do surgery."

"Surgery?" Julia asks.

"The doctors need to fix her hand," Claire says.

Outside the hospital, two nurses are talking. One laughs at something the other has said.

"When will they know if she needs surgery?" Peter asks.

"Soon, I think," Claire says.

Julia finishes her Pop-Tarts and licks her fingers with a flourish. Claire grabs a wipe from the bag she told Peter to bring and sets in on cleaning her daughter's small hands.

Peter leans over with his phone. "Look," he says, pointing to an article. "Bones don't just break. They shatter. And the disposal was literally pulling Tilly's hand *in* while she was trying to pull it *out*."

"You have to stop googling," Claire says, as if she wasn't doing the same thing an hour ago.

"Do you think they'll have to amputate?" he asks.

"Amputate what?" she says. "The surgery would be to put things back on, not take them off."

"What is *amputate*?" Julia asks.

This is how the next two hours go as they await more news. Claire had hoped to visit her sister, but Tilly is still being evaluated by the surgeons. Claire is losing steam. She needs food and a shower and maybe, God willing, a nap.

"Can you hold down the fort?" she asks Peter.

He looks up from his phone. His eyes are sunken, and the dark hollows below make him look ten years older than he is. His color is off too. Claire can't believe this is the same man who answered the door when she showed up less than a week ago. He looks terrible.

"Are you okay?" she asks.

He stares at her. "My wife's hand was just mangled by sharp blades"— *They aren't blades,* Claire thinks, *they are impellers*—"and it was my fault. So, no, I'm not okay. Plus, you've managed to convince her that a body is buried under our house"— *"Our house," like it already belongs to him*—"and we, for whatever reason, should dig it up, because somehow that has become our responsibility. As if locating the bones of a four-hundred-year-old stranger is going to magically fix your dad or something."

"That's not—" Claire starts.

"So I'm not doing great, no. Things are pretty fucked up right now. Just try not to dig up any dead bodies while Tilly and I are here at the hospital, okay?"

"Right," she says, quite literally biting her tongue to keep herself from sniping back. "Text me if there are any updates."

Then she promises Julia they can stop at the doughnut shop on the way home— *What's another twenty grams of sugar?*—and they leave.

27

EDITH

Within seconds of Grace finding the severed finger, the women flee, shouting at one another as they all scramble to exit first.

"That thing didn't just appear! She conjured it!"

"She didn't scream when the earth moved. She knew it was coming!"

"That woman walks in two worlds! God has finally revealed her for what she is!"

The hysteria takes over the room, filling it to the walls and threatening to burst the wooden beams of the roof—and then it flees with the women. The house is empty and still, mocking Edith with its serenity.

She looks down at the severed fingertip in her hand, and she shudders. She, too, needs to escape these four walls. She no longer feels safe inside her own home. Or even her own skin.

When she goes outside, Edith is alone. The women have scattered into the woods, each in their own direction homeward, and David is nowhere to be found. The sky looks apocalyptic, an angry orange and red as the sun starts to set.

TURN OFF THE LIGHT

Her feet carry her toward the bay. A helplessness settles into her bones, making her ankles and feet heavy. She feels like she is dragging her body through space.

Will there be a trial? They found no witch's mark, but the rest of it is evidence enough. The shaking earth, the spattering of blood, the mysterious finger. She cannot help but feel this will be the death of her. She has heard of women being acquitted, but only for those cases in which the husband comes to the rescue. Testifies in the woman's defense. She knows that would not be her privilege. Her own husband fears her; she saw it when he hung the horseshoe, and she saw it again today when he led her into that trap.

As Edith approaches the bay, she notices there are no swamp flies out this evening. No bats. No small creatures scuffling in the beach grass. It is eerily silent in the absence of the crickets' nightly singing. The animals must have fled after the trembling. She doesn't blame them for hiding.

And then a large *splash* echoes from the water.

Edith stops, squinting.

Another *splash,* like someone surfacing, sinking, and resurfacing, gasping for breath. She strains to find the source. No one is drowning, but something large under the surface is pushing the water above it up and out to curl like a wave. A wall of motion barreling toward the shore.

And then a rhythmic scratching. A scuttling.

A tide of crabs, hundreds of them, push up from the waterline, their shells glistening in the setting sun, their many legs scuttling in a chorus of taps and scrapes.

The wet sand sucks at Edith's heels as she backs away toward the dunes. The crabs trudge forward as if they are coming for her. So many domed shells, their round bodies nearly the size of basins, two feet long including the tails. They look otherworldly, with their sharp spines. Like heavily armored spiders. But that's not all. There are blue crabs, too, and other ones that look like blue crabs but are even larger. All of their pincers are raised to the sky, clicking angrily like gnashing teeth, their beady eyes shining black.

Her old rash lights up, fire on the skin of her right forearm all the way to her elbow. The crabs are getting closer, so many of them that it looks like the ground itself is writhing. They scramble over one another in their hurry to exit the sea, some of them thrashing with long, spiky tails. One flips over, and its legs continue to run in the air. Little strips of accordion-like organs billow in and out as it breathes.

She has never seen so many at once. Two or three gathered after a storm, maybe. But this? The earth's shaking must have disturbed them. That's what her logical mind wants her to believe. But really, she fears this is the ultimate sign from God. She has somehow betrayed Him. She has affected the natural order of things, enough to draw crabs from the water and severed fingers from thin air.

Why her? In what ways has she so offended God that He must take such extreme measures to call her out? It must be because she teased her aunt for all her superstitions. Because she has relied on her senses when healing people rather than turning toward prayer. Because she has felt more grace in a patch of wildflowers than in a year's worth of sermons.

She cannot stand idly by. This is her doing, and she must make it right. She can think of only one way to prove her loyalty to God. Her fingers grasp her firestone necklace as she pivots on her heels and runs back toward the house.

28
CLAIRE

Claire is resting in the playroom when she hears Peter return from the hospital. She half opens her eyes to check the time on her phone. It is almost two o'clock in the afternoon. She calculates she dozed for only twenty minutes, which means Julia is still in bed. The girl crashed after all that sugar and their emotionally taxing morning.

Claire allows herself to float in and out of a snoozing state for another ten minutes before joining Peter downstairs in the kitchen. He is eating a takeout sandwich at the kitchen table.

"I grabbed you one," he says, gesturing toward the counter. "I also told Phoebe she should take a break and go out for lunch."

"Good call," she says. Claire had checked in with the nurse when she arrived back from the hospital, but she forgot about her in the following exhaustion. She's grateful Peter sent her out for a break.

Claire joins him at the table, grabbing her sandwich on the way. It's a white-paper-wrapped garlic bagel with chicken salad, her favorite order from the hole-in-the-wall bagel shop downtown.

"Sorry about earlier," he says. "I don't know. I'm kinda losing it, Claire."

Surprised by this sudden moment of vulnerability, Claire pauses, the sandwich halfway to her mouth. "Yeah?" she says.

He nods. "I feel so bad."

And then he is crying. Not free-flowing tears, at least not yet, but one single drop that he wipes away feverishly between large bites of food. Like he thinks maybe keeping his mouth full will stave off the waterworks.

She half smiles in sympathy. "I get it," she says. "It's such a weird time." She doesn't know what else to say, so she takes a bite of her sandwich to busy her mouth. It tastes exactly as she remembers from childhood. "But it wasn't your fault," she tells him between bites. "I mean, we're all so out of it right now. You just flicked the wrong switch by mistake."

"No," he says, shaking his head, "it's not just that. I mean all of it. I feel so bad. I should have — I didn't know how —"

"It's okay," she insists. "Seriously. No one blames you. We don't get a manual for dealing with this stuff." She's not sure how much she should say. Does he know that Tilly told her about him not wanting a baby?

Claire coughs a little. A piece of bagel has lodged itself toward the back of her throat, scratching.

"I just wish you could have let this whole thing go," he says.

She looks at him, confused. "Let what go?"

He slurps from his takeout cup of soda. "It was bad enough being back in this house," he says. "I hated it. But I figured once your dad died, I could convince Tilly to move."

"Move?" Claire says, surprised. "She loves this house. I thought..." She clears her throat again. The bread is really lodged in there. But now her neck is starting to feel hot, too, and her throat is getting itchy. She tries to scratch it with the back of her tongue.

"I can't live here," he says. "It's constant. It's all I can think about. Like I'm being haunted."

Claire almost chokes on her excitement. Peter is finally admitting to experiencing something in this house. "Wait," she says, swallowing, though it's a struggle, "so you *are* seeing Edith?"

"Not Edith, goddamn it!" Peter explodes. *"Gabby."*

"Gabby?" Claire repeats dumbly. "You're seeing Gabby?"

Her vision spins. She looks down to regain her balance and sees that hives are popping up on her right arm. A trail leading toward her elbow.

"Peter," she says, realization dawning, "is there crab in this?"

But he knows about her allergy. Some kind of restaurant mix-up, then? No, that can't be. The chicken salad tastes exactly like it did when she was young.

"I don't want this," Peter says, fully crying now.

Claire is confused, her brain fogging. She is clearly having an allergic reaction, but to what? She has eaten this sandwich a hundred times before. And Peter is crying. Not about Tilly, but about Gabby. What is she missing?

"I don't understand . . ." Claire says. Words are difficult. Her lips feel fat and swollen. The dizziness gets worse. "Peter, I need my EpiPen. It's upstairs."

But Peter does not move. He only looks at her sadly, like the terrible thing has already happened and there's nothing he can do about it.

"You just couldn't let it go," he says, now swinging toward anger. "You even went into the crawl space. I mean, seriously? You were never going to find Edith's bones while mucking around down there. Why couldn't you just lay off? Your dad is going to die any day now. If you could have just let him die, we would have buried him, you'd have gone back to Los Angeles, and everything would be normal again."

"Peter," Claire says, reaching for him, but he pulls away. Her stomach is starting to cramp now, and she doubles over in pain. A second later, she vomits on the floor, right between her and Peter's feet. "Please . . . my EpiPen . . ."

"You were never going to find Edith's bones," he repeats, his tone bouncing from frustration to insistence.

And Claire finally realizes why Peter is not running for her EpiPen. The chicken salad tastes like chicken salad because he spiked it with only the smallest amount of shellfish. It wouldn't take much. Peter is so upset that she went digging into the history of this house that he is going to kill her. And the only reason that would make sense is if there *are* bones in this house. Bones he *knows* are here. Bones he *put* here.

Not Edith's bones.

Gabby's.

Peter's hand is on her arm. Claire tries to stand. She needs to get to the back steps, crawl through the playroom, and grab her EpiPen that is tucked into the pouch of her suitcase.

But she does not have the strength to fight Peter.

"Please," she says, "think of Julia. Don't do this. We can . . . find another . . . way . . ."

"I've thought of all the ways," Peter says. "I don't want to do this, Claire! I don't!"

He's crying again, and Claire hates him for it. Like she's supposed to feel bad for the guy who is killing her. She has never known anyone more cowardly.

Julia sleeps above them in the guest room. What will Peter tell her? What will he tell Tilly? They'll find the EpiPen in her suitcase; they'll wonder why she wasn't able to get to it in time.

Or maybe he'll hide it. Destroy it. Pretend she left it back in LA. *In her hastiness to pack for her father's impending death, she wasn't thinking about herself...* Claire vomits again, this time all over her own lap because Peter is holding her down, pinning her to the table and chair. She is so weak. Her body shudders with the violence of the retching. The world spins. Three Peters lean toward her.

"I didn't kill her," he says. "I want you to know that. Gabby, I mean. I didn't kill her. It was my dad. She gave me a ride home that night. He was drunk. As always. And when he took a swing at me, she stepped in front. Tried to stop him. She was trying to help. And that pissed him off. It wasn't meant to happen. None of it was meant to happen."

Claire's vision gets blurrier. Her whole body itches on the inside, in that layer between the outer world and her internal organs. The thin space between her insides and her skin. Tingling and tickling and burning.

"He only hit her once. Just once. But she hit her head on the way down, snapped her neck. And then Dad made me put her here. He said no one would ever check the house. We knew the layout from working here that summer, we knew the hidden spots, and—God, it was awful, Claire. I hated myself every second. And now, being back here, I've had to think about it every day. I didn't think I could survive it. But I did. I *did*. Until you got back."

Claire can't even lift her head. Her chest is tight, her breath shallow. Her lips have ballooned to twice their size; they feel awkward as she lolls her tongue around in what used to be her mouth but now feels like a straw-tight hole.

This is it. She is going to die. This is why she has been vulnerable to time's gymnastics. She was near transition all along, just like Ethan suggested. She is going to be murdered, just like her sister was.

She expects to see scenes from her life play before her. But instead, she thinks only of the future moments with her daughter that she will miss: Julia losing her first tooth, beaming with a gap-filled smile; Julia being teased or bullied, no mother to hold her as she cries herself to sleep; Julia seeing snow for the first time — how is it that her daughter has never seen snow?

"I'm sorry, Claire," Peter continues, though she can barely hear his voice now. "I'm sorry, but this ends here."

She stares at Peter's hands on her. The knuckles are white from his applied pressure. She is losing circulation in her arms. She feels on the verge of passing out, her body itching all over, the rash lighting up on her right arm, a bruise already blooming under Peter's tight grip.

29
EDITH

She must burn the Devil out.

Her herbs and knowledge, once a comfort, now feel like tools that have been weaponized against her. She must use flame to drive the Devil from her home and, in turn, exorcise him from her body and soul.

She stands by the hearth and stares down into the cellar. Her favorite place that, over the course of only a few hours, has now become a sore spot in her vision. The reason for her husband's mistrust. The cause of her neighbors' suspicions. A place that once felt holy but is now tainted by fingers that roved its shelves much as they roved her skin. Callous, uncaring hands.

Edith thinks about the countless hours spent pruning and harvesting the herbs and plants. Her heart aches at the thought of all that hard work going up in flames. But if these jars and bundles have been touched by the Devil, what then? If she herself has been compromised by evil, how can she trust her own hands to care for another? Perhaps they are not her hands at all.

She thinks again of the severed fingertip and shivers.

A fire is the only way to cleanse this place. To start over with a clean slate. "Better to lose my craft than my soul," she says to herself, resolved.

Edith retrieves a linen rag from the hook by the door, then twists it into a ragged wick around a large wooden spoon. She reaches for the firestone around her neck — the one that once belonged to her mother — and strikes. Once. Twice. Sparks spit into the darkness, a promise unfulfilled.

Her fingers shake with anticipation. She looks around the room and sees the spatter of blood on the walls, up the sides of the table, on the planks of the floor. There is a darkness in this home. One that whispers in her ear and crawls through the folds of her brain.

She strikes the flint again, and this time, the spark catches. A small bloom of fire sputters to life. Edith feeds it the dry cloth and wood, and the fire grows, a torch in her hands. She lifts it in front of her face, feeling the growing heat as the flames lick the air, eager to catch and spread and destroy.

"This ends here," she says to the darkness.

Then she throws the torch into the cellar.

The fiery bundle arcs through the opening, hits the shelves, and bursts. The smell of singed chamomile and sage quickly becomes overwhelming. A jar shatters and explodes from the sudden heat.

Edith wants to shout at the heavens, *See? See what I have done for you?* She wants to pound her fists and scream off the edges of the earth. Her healing was never a gift. It was only ever a curse dressed in rosemary and rue. What good is knowledge if it opens the door to hell?

Smoke billows fast as guilt consumes her. The same leaves that healed babies and mended bones are now curling in flame to pay for her sins. She bends over, sobbing and choking on her tears and spit and shame. The dried herbs act like tinder, the oils catching, flaring, reaching into the air like fingers grasping for escape.

30

CLAIRE

BEEP-BEEP-BEEP

"What the hell?" Peter asks, his eyes wide.

It's the fire alarm. Claire smells smoke.

Peter jumps to his feet in shock, searching for the fire. "What the fuck?" he whispers. He disappears from Claire's field of vision toward the front of the house.

She must get upstairs. She must get to the EpiPen and to Julia before the house burns. Peter went toward the front door, mercifully at the opposite end of the house from where Julia sleeps. But Claire does not know how long it will be before the fire spreads. She has to move fast. She uses the momentary freedom to throw herself from the table, sputtering and coughing and gasping. She clasps her throat, which feels tighter and tighter by the second.

She heaves herself toward the back steps, the ones that lead from the sunroom up to the playroom, and crawls on all fours like a wounded animal. Lurching up, one, two steps at a time, thinking of nothing but her daughter and the EpiPen. She knows she is so close, but when she looks up, the staircase extends like a tunnel, the top getting farther and farther away. Can she ever reach it?

"Mama?"

Thank God, the smoke alarm must have woken Julia. Claire hears but cannot see the girl. Is she hallucinating? Her brain is going now, her blood pressure must be dropping. There is a sense of calm coming over her that she knows logically cannot be good but that *feels* right, feels like maybe it could be a good thing—

No. Stay with it, she tells herself.

"Mama?"

Julia's voice again, and she still can't see her, still doesn't know where she is on the never-ending staircase, but she says to the emptiness anyway, "Get—outside. Fire—"

"What's wrong, Mama?"

Claire shakes her head. "Crab—" She scratches her neck but wishes she could tear it open and scratch her throat.

"Pee-pee pen?" Julia says.

Claire's heart flutters with hope. She has explained to Julia what the EpiPen is, has shown it to her and demonstrated how it works. She didn't want her daughter to be afraid if Claire had to use it in front of her. But Julia is only four, her memory unreliable.

A flash of something moves in Claire's periphery. Julia has retreated, disappeared into the tall tunnel of the stairs. Claire is sinking, sinking, down into some unknowable realm. She stops moving, or maybe she stopped moving minutes ago. She doesn't know. Up and down look the same to her now. She has no sense of direction. Her breath is so shallow—tiny, raspy, desperate gasps for air.

"Mama?" she hears again, then feels something long and hard shoved into her limp hand.

TURN OFF THE LIGHT

Claire sits in the sunroom flanked by two EMTs. They gave her oxygen, administered antihistamines, and pumped her full of steroids.

"We strongly recommend a follow-up at the ED," says the younger one. He looks like he can't be more than nineteen. "You could have something called a biphasic reaction, a second wave of symptoms. Even hours later. It's safer for you to be monitored."

"It's okay, I understand, I'm fine, thank you," Claire says, trying to wave him off.

Julia hasn't left Claire's side. She leans into her mother, balling herself up in her lap as if she could fit back into the womb. Claire runs her fingers through her daughter's knotted hair. She doesn't need more hospitals and IVs and beeping machines; she needs quiet and calm for her little girl.

"I'll be sure to call you guys if any symptoms start up again," she says to the wary EMT.

"You'll keep an eye on her?" the kid asks Ethan, who showed up a few minutes ago.

"Of course," Ethan says. Then Claire signs a refusal-of-care form, which basically waives her right to sue them if she croaks in the next twelve hours.

The EMTs haul their equipment back to the ambulance as the police hover. They are questioning Phoebe, the nurse who returned from her lunch break only minutes after Claire got her EpiPen. Apparently, Phoebe witnessed Peter speeding away from the house, headed north in his SUV. When she got inside, she found the cellar in flames and put it out with the fire extinguisher. She then found Claire's father in hysterics, shouting unintelligibly and thrashing around in bed. She had to inject him with an antipsychotic to sedate him.

Claire is so exhausted. Her body is weak. Drained. When she holds up her hands, her fingers shake. Her forearm is bruised, a dark shape that fans out like butterfly wings. A lingering mark from Peter's grip that pinned her down. She clears her throat, which no longer feels swollen but is still sore and irritated. Her brain is foggy. The rash still faintly burns.

"I can't believe..." Ethan says. He doesn't finish the sentence because he doesn't need to.

He can't believe Claire's brother-in-law tried to kill her. He can't believe the man they've known for decades confessed to burying her long-lost sister in the foundation of her own home.

Claire told him the abridged version over the phone. The EMTs had already arrived by then, but her body was still in full fight-or-flight mode, and she needed another adult here that she trusted in case they insisted she go to the hospital. Someone needed to be here for Julia.

And really, if she's being honest, she needed someone here for *her* too. Not just anyone, but Ethan. The person who sees her, all of her, and still makes her feel safe. Like she doesn't need to control everything, because he's got her hand in his. Steady in a world built on uneven pilings.

Ethan shakes his head. "Jesus, Claire. You almost..."

He doesn't say the *D*-word, since Julia is curled up on Claire's lap.

One of the cops approaches. His name is Jimmy Young, and he and Claire were in preschool together. She still sees him as that four-year-old. Like his police uniform is actually some elaborate Halloween costume, and he's going to start picking his nose any second.

"If it's all right with you," he says, "we'll get the cadaver dog in here."

"Okay," she says. "Thanks."

"Lucky that cellar caught fire and distracted him," Jimmy muses. "Or you probably wouldn't be here to tell the story."

"Any idea how it started?" Ethan asks.

"Not a clue," Jimmy admits.

Claire shares a look with Ethan. Was this another fold in time?

"And of course we've got officers looking for your brother-in-law. He won't get far, I assure you," Jimmy says.

Claire nods. In reality, she knows that he cannot assure her of anything. But it's comforting to pretend like he can.

When Jimmy has excused himself, Claire turns to Ethan, anxious. "How do I tell Tilly?"

Her sister is still at the hospital. Probably in surgery now, or maybe just getting out of it. She has no idea that any of this has happened. That her husband is not the man she thinks he is. That their sister's bones have been under their feet all along.

"I don't know," Ethan says, shaking his head. "I don't know."

"Mama," Julia says, sitting up, "can I have a snack?"

"What would you like?" Ethan asks, rubbing his hands together. "Turns out I am very skilled at making snacks."

One corner of Julia's mouth goes up in a sheepish smile. "I don't know."

"A surprise, then? I'm also very good at surprises." He winks at her and sets off toward the kitchen.

Claire squeezes her daughter tight. "You were very brave, you know that?" she whispers into her ear. "Very brave."

Without Julia, Claire would not have reached the EpiPen. Thank God her daughter knew what she needed. Julia brought her the medicine just in time.

As they wait for Ethan to return, Claire watches the world move around them. The police officers gather by the back door, murmuring to one another as they check their notes. One gets a call on the walkie-talkie and steps outside. Jimmy gives Claire a little wave when he sees her watching. She smiles.

Claire leans her head back on the couch. For a second, she closes her eyes, but the terrifying encounter plays in her mind on repeat: Peter's knuckles whitening as he pinned her in place, the tears on his cheeks as he admitted what he had done all those years ago.

And the thing that saved her. *The fire*. In the very cellar that had already burned once.

Jimmy Young briefs the cadaver dog's handler outside. The man is buff, his arms practically bursting from his sleeves. Claire looks at them through the window. It's like watching a silent movie, easy to imagine all the things they are saying, though she is grateful she cannot actually hear them. She has no desire to listen as her preschool playmate and a gym-rat dog trainer discuss her dead sister.

Ethan suggests they get away, maybe take Julia to a playground. And it's a good idea. A sane one. But Claire can't leave. Not now. Not when they are possibly moments from solving the greatest mystery of her life.

Earlier, before the dog arrived, Claire asked Jimmy if he needed something of Gabby's. "That's how it works, right? It needs to follow her scent?" she asked.

Jimmy frowned. "It's a cadaver dog," he said, and Claire immediately felt like an idiot.

This wouldn't be a search like they conducted fifteen years ago. This would be a search for human remains. If Gabby's body is under the house, it no longer smells like Gabby. It smells only of decay and rot. A mixture of anger and anguish twists Claire's stomach into knots.

The police escort them out of the house to watch from near the shed. They allow Phoebe and Claire's father, who is immovable in bed, to stay. They have all decided not to tell him what's going on, though Claire doubts he'd understand them anyway, especially while high on whatever Phoebe shot into him to calm him down.

The dog walks the perimeter of the house, sniffing the foundation. The team made it clear he needs space, something about strong smells interfering with the dog's task and contaminating the search. Claire is happy to keep her distance. She'd rather witness it from afar.

She waits in the front yard with Julia and Ethan. The girl holds tight to her bunny lovey, sucking her thumb and looking at old photos on Claire's phone. Ethan twists and picks at grass in silence. What can any of them say right now?

Claire watches as the handler holds up his hands in various positions to direct the dog. Then they climb the stairs to the main entrance.

"He's going inside to smell the floors," Jimmy calls to her.

"Did they find anything outside?" Claire asks.

"We just have to let them do their thing," he says. "I know it's not easy, but we need to be patient." He follows them inside.

Claire cranes her neck to look through the living-room windows. "Can you see anything?" she asks Ethan. "There's a glare."

She can make out only vague shapes moving behind the panes. But then — stillness.

"I think the dog stopped," Ethan says.

"Oh my God," Claire says, repositioning herself so she can see through the largest window. "He's pawing at the cellar door."

The doctor explains to Claire that Tilly will be discharged today but she'll need a skin graft to replace lost tissue and reconstructive surgery on some tendon or nerve. Claire doesn't catch the name of it; she's listening — she *is* — but she is also internally mapping out the impossible conversation she needs to have with Tilly. Trying out phrases and explanations while the doctor's lips move. So she misses some of the details.

Tilly looks good when Claire gets to her room.

She does not look good after Claire tells her about the attempted poisoning and Peter's confession.

"I don't understand," Tilly says, her face turning white. "This all happened in the past few hours? How?"

Claire sits on the edge of her sister's bed. Julia is in the waiting room with Ethan. Downstairs, they ran into the young EMT who'd advised Claire to come to the hospital. He was putting something into the ambulance, hands full of what looked like instant ice packs, and he greeted Claire enthusiastically. She actually felt a little bad when she explained that she had not, in fact, changed her mind and taken his advice. She was here for Tilly, not herself.

"I know it feels impossible," Claire says to her sister.

"I can't believe it," Tilly says, shaking her head.

"I know—"

Tilly's voice harshens: "No, I *can't* believe it. It can't *be*."

Claire swallows. "They found her, Tilly. They found Gabby."

Tilly freezes. The only thing that moves are her eyes, which widen to an impossible roundness before fat, juicy tears bubble to the surface. A single trail of wet runs down her cheek.

"They did?" she whispers.

Claire nods. "They still have to technically confirm it's her, match the dental records and stuff, but . . ." Claire's voice cracks. The words are stuck in her throat like dry crumbs. "The firefly pendant was still around her neck."

This unravels Tilly, which unravels Claire, and the sisters lean together, gripping each other like life rafts.

"Does Dad know?" Tilly finally asks through tears.

TURN OFF THE LIGHT

Claire shakes her head. "He was hysterical after the fire. Phoebe said he probably smelled the smoke but couldn't make sense of it and panicked. She gave him a shot of something, so he's been out of it for the past few hours. He doesn't know anything."

They sit interlocked for what feels like an eternity, until Tilly leans back, settling against the hospital bed. She rubs her eyes. "How did I miss this?" she asks. The inevitable question.

"We all missed it," Claire says. "We were all close with Peter. He has always been like"—she almost chokes on the words—"like family."

"Where is he?" her sister asks, the fear setting in. "Is he going to come back for us? Will they catch him?"

"They will," Claire says without hesitation, because that is what her sister needs to hear.

"I feel disgusting," Tilly says, wiping at her skin like she wants a new suit of it. "I loved that man. I gave him everything. And the whole time... why? Why did he marry me? I don't get it. Why didn't he just run as far as he could from this place?"

Claire takes a deep breath. "I don't know," she admits. "I really don't know. I guess in his own fucked-up way, he loved you?"

Tilly snorts.

"Yeah," Claire says. "He's a piece of shit. Thank God you didn't have a kid with him."

"Unanswered prayers," Tilly agrees. She stares at her hands for a minute, then looks up suddenly, like she has just gotten an idea. "God, Claire, how are *you*? I didn't—in all the—you almost *died*. Jesus."

"I know. It was..." Claire shudders. "I was so scared. I couldn't stop thinking about Julia."

Tilly's eyes go round in sympathy. "Where is she?"

"With Ethan in the lobby."

Tilly nods, then bursts into tears again. "I'm sorry," she says. "It's going to take—I don't know how to process all this. It doesn't feel real. It can't be real. Can it?"

"I wish I could say this was some post-surgical hallucination."

"Do you think he did this on purpose?" she asks, holding up her injured hand.

Claire considers this, the idea that Peter intentionally mangled his wife's hand in the garbage disposal. But even after all the horrible things he did, she believes this one was a genuine mistake.

"I don't think so," she says. "It freaked him out. I think it might be what put him over the edge, honestly."

Tilly shakes her head and bites her lip. She presses her good wrist into her eye sockets one at a time, damming the tears.

"Are you hungry?" Claire asks.

Tilly nods. "Starved, actually."

"Should we order from the cafeteria? Or I could get takeout somewhere?"

"Anything," Tilly says. Then she catches herself. "Well, anything but chili."

Claire gives her sister a look.

"I'm serious!" Tilly insists.

And then they both break, howling with laughter.

Sometimes a good cry calls for a good laugh.

31
 EDITH

The smell of smoke still clings to Edith as she runs through the woods. It is in her lungs, on her hands, in her hair. The trees blur past. She is headed north, away from her burning home, away from Jacob's fresh grave to the south. She knows not where she goes, only that she must keep moving.

Her mind struggles to cobble together some kind of plan. She must convince her husband to move. That's the only way. As much as she would like to leave the man, everything she has is tied to him. So they need to abandon the Shore together and head for mainland Virginia.

He will understand. He must. She cannot conceive a child if she is worried she will have to stand trial. She cannot continue to live in a place where if she looks at someone the wrong way, she will be declared a witch. Where they will hang her from the nearest tree limb or banish her from all she knows.

As she runs, something tugs at her consciousness, a bug burrowing in the back of her brain. Latching on and slowly, quietly emitting waves of doubt. *Your husband is on their side. You'll never convince him.*

But she needs him. Her basic survival depends on him. The very roof over her head. She is legally, socially, and economically tied to the man, especially now that she has no remaining blood relatives. Her whole identity has been absorbed into that of her husband. Without David, she is merely a liability.

She must earn back his trust. Assure him that he has nothing to fear. And she is willing to work for it — private lessons with a minister, daily prayer sessions, extra tithing to the church. Surely the fact that she burned her herbs will prove to him that her pleas are in earnest.

She stops to catch her breath and looks back, searching for signs of smoke. There is only a faint wisp in the air, which seems odd. If the house was still burning, there would be more evidence in the sky. Did someone stop the fire? Has David returned home?

The little bug burrows deeper in her brain. *You cannot go back there until you know the Devil is gone.*

She resolves to keep her head down and continue running. But then she hears a whimpering. A muffled cry from behind the bushes. Not the cry of an animal; no, the sound is distinctly human.

Edith peeks through the foliage and spots Elizabeth collapsed near a fallen log. She is clutching her leg, her stocking soaked through with blood.

Edith pauses. She should keep running. This is the very woman who accused her of horrible things, who cast her out into the night with little more than a sweater, who forced Edith's friends and neighbors to violate her in her own home. Even if Edith were to help, Elizabeth would still point at her and cry *witch*. She is sure of it.

She is tempted to turn away and ignore the woman's cries. She is confident Elizabeth would ignore hers if their roles were reversed.

But Edith is, first and foremost, a healer. She cannot disregard this woman's pain. If she can help, then she must. It's a compulsion within her, the only way she knows how to operate. So she lunges forward, crashing through the foliage. "What happened?"

Elizabeth looks up, her face twisted in pain and white as linen. "S-s-snake," she says.

Edith drops to her knees beside Elizabeth, and the scared woman tries to scuttle away like a beetle.

"I know you don't trust me," Edith says. "But I am your only chance. You could die out here."

Elizabeth takes this in, her frightened stare traveling between Edith's face and her own swelling leg. Something within her must surrender, because she jerks her foot slightly, allowing Edith to peel back the fabric of the stocking to reveal two deep puncture wounds. The flesh around them is a canvas of angry reds and purples. Blood runs in thin rivers down her calf and ankle, mimicking the landscape of the creeks around them.

"It feels like fire," Elizabeth says.

Edith suspects this is the work of a copper-scaled snake. The woman probably stepped on it in her haste to flee Edith's home. The adder would have blended in with the leaves.

"Is it gone now?" Edith asks, looking around for the slithery offender.

Elizabeth nods. Her eyes close a little as she holds her head steady. "Dizzy," she mutters.

"Okay, try to stay still," Edith instructs. "Movement spreads the venom." She rips cloth from the hem of her shift and wipes the bite.

Elizabeth winces and takes a breath in quickly through her teeth.

"Don't move," Edith says. "I'll be right back."

She stands and surveys the plants around her. Along the path, where the soil is the most disturbed, she finds plantain. Its broad, veined leaves and tall seed stalks make it easy to spot. She snatches a handful and returns to Elizabeth on the ground.

"I'm going to chew this," she says as she puts a leaf in her mouth. As soon as it turns to a bitter pulp on her tongue, she spits it into her palm. "Now, this will sting. But it draws out the poison." Edith presses the poultice into the bite.

Elizabeth winces again, tears streaming down her cheeks. "I don't want to die," she moans.

"You won't," Edith assures her. She wipes the wound clean again and binds the poultice in place with the cloth. Tight, but not too tight. Her hands move by instinct, the way Aunt Joan taught her.

The way she will have to forget.

"Come," she says to Elizabeth, slowly helping the woman to her feet. "The Cotton house is closest. I will take you there."

At Violet's house, Edith spots one of the other children, a boy, maybe ten years old, carrying a basin toward the creek.

"Wait here," she instructs an exhausted Elizabeth.

The sun is low on the horizon now. Soon it will be dark.

"You, boy," Edith whispers as she approaches the child. "We need your help."

He jumps, startled, dropping the basin. He raises his fists in front of his chest, acting older than he is. Like a lion cub attempting to roar.

"I don't want to hurt you," Edith says. "Do you see that woman?" She points to Elizabeth, who is quietly moaning to herself in pain. "She was bitten by a snake. She needs to be cared for. I have applied plantain, but the wound needs to be properly cleaned and wrapped."

"I know you," the boy says, his eyes narrowing in suspicion. "I seen you at Goody Littleton's. You're the witch."

TURN OFF THE LIGHT

The word hits her with a slap. This child's accusation is a testament to how deep the Shore's hatred for Edith goes.

"Please," she says, "take the woman inside. She is the minister's wife. Your sister Violet will know how to care for her."

The boy continues to stare with rocks for eyes as Edith retreats toward the woods. She passes Elizabeth and tells her the same thing. "Violet will be able to help you."

Elizabeth opens her mouth but struggles to speak. She gestures for Edith to lean in closer. "I still pray for your soul," the woman says, clinging to her worldview. Then she lets out a breath. "But today, I owe you my life."

The woman's face does not soften. Her voice still carries the edge it always has when speaking with Edith. But her words suggest a crack, a small opening to allow for ambiguity.

Edith nods in return. A simple gesture of gratitude. She is shocked by the concession, but she holds in her emotion, for the boy is still staring suspiciously. She needs to retreat before he gives in to his fear and alerts his family to her presence.

She scurries into the woods until she is mostly hidden by trees, where she watches the boy rush to Elizabeth's side and help her hobble toward the house. The door opens and closes with little fanfare. Edith is now left to trust Elizabeth will get the care she needs. It feels unnatural to her, leaving the injured woman, but she has no choice.

She continues farther into the woods until she finally gives in to exhaustion and nearly collapses against a white oak tree. It is massive and gnarled, its bark deep-ridged like weathered skin. A squirrel flees at her arrival, abandoning a small pile of acorns. Edith leans back against the sturdy trunk and closes her eyes. The wilderness is still more quiet than usual, given the recent shaking of the earth, but it is slowly returning to normal. Like the blush of life blooming back to a fevered face.

Now that Edith's body is still and her mind calm, a thought begins to form. If Edith was still inhabited by the Devil, would she have stopped for Elizabeth? If she was as evil as her neighbors would have her believe, would she have risked her own safety to help the very woman who posed the biggest threat to her?

Edith looks at her hands, stained with blood from working on the woman's wound. She rubs her fingertips together, callused from pruning and gardening and mashing herbs for remedies. She traces the many lines on her palms. As she does, she thinks about how these hands have saved lives. How they have worked tirelessly to bring relief and healing and salvation.

Can the Devil really work through hands as kind as these?

For the first time in what feels like forever, she sighs, releasing days' worth of stress and worry. Surely Elizabeth will tell the others what happened. Soon enough, David will know the sacrifice she made. He will understand that she deserves another chance.

She will be okay after all.

32

CLAIRE

A forensics team spends the rest of the afternoon taking pictures and documenting evidence. Gabby's body is removed and transported to the medical examiner's office. She was found in the crawl space, just beyond where Claire was forced to turn around last night. The dog went haywire in the cellar, alerting at the bottom of the stone steps. When the handler led him into the crawl space, they found the wrapped body tucked behind and under old foundation stones.

Tilly is discharged from the hospital, and Claire asks Jimmy Young to post a police officer at the house in case Peter decides to come back. This is the only way she feels safe with her daughter under this roof.

"You all can be here," Jimmy says, "as long as you stay in the unaffected areas of the house. I should technically cordon this whole place off, since it's a crime scene, but I'm being flexible because of your dad. I know it'd be tough to move him at this point."

"Thank you," Claire says. "Really."

Jimmy Young is right. According to Phoebe, their father is already transitioning. There'd be no way to move him now, and Claire no longer feels the need. Something about the house feels different now that Gabby's bones have been found. Maybe it has shifted the energy somehow. Surely the worst is behind them.

Claire and Tilly sit with their father in his room. Phoebe adjusts his blankets and then gathers her bags. "I'm heading out," she says. "But I'll see you in the morning."

"Thank you for everything," Claire says. "I know this has all been traumatic." Phoebe certainly didn't come to work today expecting to be interrogated by the police. "And thank you again for putting out that fire so quickly. If you hadn't . . ."

Phoebe waves off the gratitude and merely shrugs. Nothing seems to ruffle her feathers. Or maybe she just refuses to let them see it.

Tilly pipes up, her voice small: "Do we tell him?" She nods toward their father. "About Gabby, I mean. Should we tell him they found her body, or would that be too upsetting?"

Phoebe raises an eyebrow and takes an audible breath. "I think it's whatever you're comfortable with. If I'm being honest, I don't think your father is registering much of what we say to him at this point."

Tilly nods sadly.

Phoebe's body softens in a way Claire has never seen. "I think tomorrow will be the day. I'm telling you because there's a lot going on. And I want you both to be prepared."

When Phoebe leaves, Tilly opens her mouth to speak but is stopped by Claire's phone vibrating loudly on the dresser.

"Sorry," Claire says. "One second."

She steps out of her father's room to answer the call.

"It's Jimmy Young," says the voice on the other end. "We got Peter."

TURN OFF THE LIGHT

Her heart flutters and her fingers tingle, as if her body is finally releasing a long-held store of adrenaline.

"We got him, Claire," he says again.

She promised Jimmy she would stay in the unaffected areas of the house, but she needs to go into the cellar. She must.

The overhead light flashes twice before settling into its muted glow. As she descends, she senses the shift in the air that she always does, but it feels different this time. Like seeing a spooky maze attraction the next morning, all of its tricks exposed in the daylight.

Smoke residue still lingers, stale and acrid. Ash dusts the steps like a thin layer of frost. A spot of charred bricks shows where the fire licked up one wall before sputtering out. When she reaches the bottom of the steps, she looks up, examining the center beam above, blackened and split. She moves closer to the warped yet solid beam. And then her stomach flips.

The daisy wheel is still there.

That same symbol tucked near the base.

Still miraculously unburned. Untouched.

In fact, the strangest part about the cellar is how familiar it looks. Nothing has changed. None of the smoke stains are new. The burn scar is exactly as it was before the fire. The same uneven splotches beneath the stairs, the same scorched ring in the far corner. Not similar. *Identical.*

Which means the fire that happened today had already happened. The two moments, past and present, were *one*. Somehow, the fire from centuries ago saved Claire today.

Claire breathes deeply; the lingering smoke makes the back of her throat itch. Instead of feeling watched by the house, she feels she is watching with it. Instead of feeling fear, she is filled with gratitude. Hope. Awe. She does not know how it is possible, but this place that she thought was torturing her has actually given her the gift of life. The gift of mothering the daughter she couldn't stand to leave behind. The gift of an answer to the lifelong mystery of her broken family.

She places a hand on the charred wall as if to say, *Thank you.*

They sleep in Tilly and Claire's childhood room. Julia is on the air mattress on the floor; Claire and Tilly share the bed. They need to be together.

After Julia falls asleep, the sisters huddle close, facing each other and whispering from their pillows.

"What do you think will happen to Peter?" Tilly asks.

Claire tries to stifle a yawn. "Jail?"

Tilly nods slowly. "Is it weird that makes me sad?"

"No. It's not weird."

They lie in silence for a while.

"She saved me," Claire finally whispers.

"Who?" Tilly asks. "Julia?"

"Yes, her too," Claire says, "but I meant Edith. She started that fire. I'm sure she did."

"Edith was here?"

"No," Claire says, "she started it back then. But it's the same fire that happened today. I know because the burn scar hasn't changed. It's the exact same it's always been."

Tilly takes this in. "So the fire happened in both timelines." She rolls onto her back and stares at the ceiling. "That's amazing."

Claire's eyes get heavy as she floats on the edge of sleep. She tries to nod, tries to murmur some kind of agreement, but she is weightless. The pillow so soft beneath her head. Her body is, at long last, giving in to the exhaustion.

And, finally, she sleeps.

The energy in her father's room has shifted. Phoebe thinks this is because death is near. And maybe that's right. But Claire thinks it's something else too.

She imagines that her father finally slept as well as she did last night.

When Peter suggested Claire was trying to save her father by solving the mystery of Edith, he wasn't far off. She had hoped that freeing her father from the time folds might somehow bring him back. But seeing him now, she knows that was never possible. Her father is dying. By the end of the day, he will be gone. And all the things she never got to say or do will remain regrets.

But she does have one last gift for him. Even if he can't hear her, even if he can't understand, she has to speak the words. It's the least she owes him.

She and Tilly take a private moment with him after breakfast. His eyes are closed, his hands cold. Claire slides her fingers up his arm and feels that he is frigid up to the elbow. She lies beside him on the bed, her head on the pillow next to his. Tilly does the same on his other side, and the sisters hold hands over his chest.

"We found her, Daddy," Claire says in a barely audible whisper.

Tilly's eyes close. "Gabby was right here all along," she adds.

Their father's breath is shallow and does not change. His blue lips do not move. His jaw remains slack.

"We got a lot of things wrong, you know? All of us," Claire says. "But I'd still pick you to be my dad. Every time."

Tilly opens her eyes, her tears staining the sheet beneath.

Their father's hand moves. Delicately, his cold fingers find theirs on his chest. Claire and Tilly share a look — their father is here. He understands.

And then, slowly, very slowly, he pulses his fingers against theirs.
Three squeezes for the words.
Three squeezes for my girls.

A few hours later, Claire and Tilly stand over their father. The air is sour.

"We are nearing the end," Phoebe tells them. "The respiratory rate has slowed. The pulse has decreased."

Their father opens and closes his mouth like a fish. His fingers are turning purple. The sisters sit on either side of him, each one holding a hand. Effortless tears slide down Claire's face and into her mouth, where she tastes the salt.

The pauses between breaths become longer. Beside Claire, Phoebe quietly counts the seconds between each one.

"That was a full minute," the nurse says.

They continue like this for a while. Maybe five minutes, maybe thirty. Her father's last breath sounds more like a wistful sigh. And then his face goes slack, like someone has flicked a switch.

"He's gone," Tilly says for no one's benefit, because they all know it already.

Phoebe waits another ten minutes to officially declare the death, and then the sisters move aside so the woman can do what she needs to. As she adjusts the body to wash it, a sound emerges. Like their father is exhaling again. Like he might still be here after all.

But it is only extra air leaving the lungs.

TURN OFF THE LIGHT

The house feels empty. Hollow.

The place that only twenty-four hours ago was bustling with police officers and EMTs and nurses and forensics teams is now silent.

Their father's body has been transported to the funeral home.

Gabby's body is at the medical examiner's office.

Peter is in custody.

Only Claire, Julia, and Tilly remain.

Ethan brings over a large, greasy pizza that they eat together at the kitchen table. Claire has her feet tucked under her on the chair. They use paper plates that Ethan brought from the restaurant, and hers is already soaked through with grease. Tilly sits beside her, her pizza untouched. Julia is at the end of the table picking pepperoni slices off the pie and eating them. No one says anything. No one minds.

Claire finishes telling Ethan what she told Tilly last night. How the burn patterns in the cellar did not change; how the evidence of a fire from centuries ago is the same evidence of a fire from yesterday. How she believes they were the same fire all along.

"So you think that's the reason time crossed? So she could save you?" Ethan asks.

"Or I just got lucky," Claire says. "Who knows."

Tilly frowns. "Why were you seeing all that stuff about her husband, though?" she asks. "The tea and the guys in your room."

Claire runs her hand along the edge of her pizza slice and gathers a big glob of cheese between her fingers. "I've been thinking about that," she says. "I have this feeling she needs my help too. She saved me, and now I'm supposed to save her. But how can I? Her life already happened. It's already written in history."

Ethan shakes his head. "You can't think about it that way. The timelines are folding in random places. It's not linear. We don't know what has happened for her yet."

Claire tries to wrap her head around this idea.

"But you haven't sensed her lately, right?" Tilly asks. "No more figures over your bed?"

Claire shakes her head. "I slept well last night for the first time since getting here. And nothing weird has happened today. The house feels back to normal."

This is what she wanted all along, but part of her feels cut off now that she can no longer sense Edith. Like she has unfinished business. All this time, she saw Edith as a sign of darkness within the house, but now she feels, strangely, like she has lost a friend.

She can't be sure, but she thinks she was able to sense time bending only because she was close to death. Now that Edith has saved her, she is no longer close to transition. She can no longer sense the overlapping timelines. This is the only explanation she has, even though it sounds absurd. Everything about her life the past week feels like a dream.

"So she's gone?" Tilly asks.

Julia, who has now eaten all the pepperoni, looks up. "Who's gone, Mama?" she asks.

"The other lady who lives here," Claire says, referring to Edith the same way Julia has in the past.

"Oh," the girl says. "But she's not gone."

This gets the adults' attention. "She's not?" Claire asks.

Julia shakes her head. "I saw her this morning. In the yard."

Claire's heart rate accelerates. *Of course* Julia can still see her. Why wouldn't she?

Twenty-four hours ago, this would have freaked Claire out. But now, after all that has happened, she feels relieved. This means they might still have a chance to help Edith.

"We have to warn her about her husband," Claire says to the group. "She doesn't know what he's got planned. Julia has to tell her."

Tilly asks, "Have you ever talked to the lady, Julia?"

"Mm-hmm." The girl nods. She is peeling off long, stringy chunks of cheese. The pie looks like a raccoon has gotten to it, random chunks taken by small hands. "She's nice. She said my yellow dress was pretty."

"Wow," Ethan says under his breath. "I wonder what was going through her mind. If she knew Julia was from another time."

"Is the nice lady in trouble, Mama?" Julia asks. Her expression is soft, genuine concern in her eyes.

"I think she might be, sweetie," Claire admits.

Julia sits up straighter. "I can help her!"

Claire can't believe that she is about to enlist her four-year-old daughter to help deliver a message to a woman from four hundred years ago. Last week, Claire wouldn't even let Julia climb the playground structure for fear she'd fall and hurt herself. She has opted out of countless playdates, nervous that Julia would have a meltdown or an allergic reaction to something when Claire wasn't around.

And now she's practically giving her daughter instructions to travel through time.

Because, really, what can she control, anyway?

"Okay," Claire says, taking a deep breath. "If you see the nice lady again, here's what you need to tell her . . ."

33
EDITH

Edith is still leaning against the white oak when she hears a rustling in the brush. Her mind immediately skips to David, who must be looking for her. But for the first time in many days, she is not frightened. She is hopeful. The future no longer seems bleak. She is on the verge of winning back the favor of her neighbors and friends. And maybe, if time allows, she can even return to her healing practice. After all, an endorsement from the minister's wife will mean something.

But it is not David. Nor is it any of the women from this afternoon's terror. Instead, it is a small girl. The same one Edith saw days ago. The same one she was searching for at Jacob's service. She is wearing the same yellow dress, but this time her hair hangs loose to below her shoulders.

"Hello there," Edith says.

"Mama told me to come," the girl says.

Edith's heart flutters. So Violet's mother has sent this little one to retrieve her. To usher her back to the house and back into the fold. Elizabeth must have spoken to the family, then.

TURN OFF THE LIGHT

"She did?" she asks, unable to hide her excitement.

"She says you are in trouble."

Edith's forehead creases in confusion. "Trouble?"

The girl nods.

Edith doesn't understand. Is she referring to this afternoon? The witch's mark? The blood? The severed finger? Or does Violet's mother know about the fire?

Edith is reminded, then, of the woman's growing belly. Maybe *she* is the one in trouble. "Is your mother having the baby?" Edith asks. "Does she need me?"

"Baby?" the girl repeats, her own face now contorting in uncertainty.

"Yes, the baby in your mother's belly. Is it coming now?"

The girl shakes her head. "There's no baby in Mama's belly."

Edith takes a breath. "Let's start at the beginning," she says. "What is your name?"

"Julia," the girl says proudly.

"Julia," Edith repeats. "Okay. And your sister Violet—"

"I don't have a sister," Julia says. "My mama is called Claire. She has a sister. Her name is Aunt Tilly."

Edith's head swims. She has never heard these names. But that seems impossible here on the remote Shore. Everyone knows everyone.

"Okay," she says again, trying to piece it together. "So your mother, Claire—she says I'm in trouble?"

"Yes." Julia nods enthusiastically. "She says you need our help. Can I tell you something?"

"Of course," Edith says.

"In your ear," Julia adds. Then she whispers, "It's a secret."

Edith bends forward, moving hair from her ear. The girl's breath is hot against her skin.

"David is a bad guy," says the small voice.

"What?" Edith says, pulling back.

Then the girl frowns. She looks down and talks to herself. "What was it?" she mutters. "There was something else."

But Edith is stuck on what this mysterious stranger has told her about her husband. "How do you — why does your mother think my husband is a bad man?"

"I don't remember," Julia says. She stares at her bare feet.

Edith wonders if this girl is lost. She is so small. Surely a parent somewhere must be worried about her. But then, she knows David's name. So her message must be intentional.

"Where do you live?" Edith asks.

Julia looks up again. "In California."

Edith frowns. The word sounds like a legendary land, as distant and enchanted as Eden.

"But right now," Julia continues, "we are at Aunt Tilly's. That way." She points in the direction of Edith's house. "There's a cool door in the floor and a secret room underground."

Edith's heart squeezes. "The cellar? But the fire—"

"Oh, yeah," Julia says, nodding. "Phoebe made the fire go away."

Who is Phoebe? Yet another name Edith has never heard. And how does this girl know about the fire?

Edith is getting hot. The sun has set, but that does not discourage the heat. The night bugs are beginning to wake, singing and chirping in the humid air. Edith feels clammy in her own skin. She wishes she could dismiss the girl's comment about David, but it has awoken something in her gut. The same way the apple did all those days ago. This girl in her yellow dress, reappearing now — this is an omen too. It must be.

"Is Phoebe your friend?" Edith asks.

Julia shakes her head. "She was helping Grandpa. Before he went to the stars. Oh! *Tea!*" she shouts, as if she has just gotten a bright idea. Her eyes light up as she flails her arms in excitement.

"I remembered! 'David is a bad guy,'" she repeats, as if reciting a phrase she has memorized. "'He is going to put something bad in your tea'! That's what it was!"

Edith crouches below the window where Violet sleeps. She has been waiting for the house to go dark. Just as it does, she hears the front door open. She leans out from the bushes, far enough to catch sight of whoever is exiting the Cotton home.

She squints as she tries to see the figure in the darkness. A tall, masculine frame with slightly hunched shoulders. He wears a posture of exhaustion, his steps labored and heavy. As the man approaches the woods, Edith's breath catches. She knows the shape of him, the way his edges cut through space. It's David.

What business does he have at Violet's house? And how long has he been here? Was he here earlier today when she brought Elizabeth over? Edith considers calling out to him or at least following him into the trees, but something stops her.

David is a bad guy.

She is here for Violet. She needs to talk to the girl.

Once her husband's figure has disappeared into the woods, presumably heading home, Edith turns back to the window. She spots Violet brushing her hair and gets the girl's attention subtly. She puts her finger to her lips and points toward the back of the house: *Meet me outside.*

As Edith waits for Violet, she thinks again about Julia. The strangeness of her. Even her yellow dress, which, in the glare of the sun on that first day, Edith assumed was a simple one. But today she noticed details she has never before seen on a garment. Delicate stitching and shiny accents. Does the girl come from incredible wealth?

Edith cannot identify what seemed so odd about the child. But she was somehow different. And she claimed to know something that would happen in the future. How could she possibly know such a thing? The question shivers Edith's spine and cools her blood.

"Edie," Violet whispers. They meet just inside the trees. "I am not supposed to talk to you."

"I won't get you in trouble. I promise," Edith says.

Violet swallows, then slowly nods.

"How is Elizabeth?"

"Better," the girl says. "Her breath is steady and the swelling has gone down. But..."

"What is it?" Edith prompts.

"She expressed doubt to Mother. Said that perhaps you are not the witch they thought."

Edith's heart lightens. "That's good."

Violet looks sad. "No, Edie. Mother did not believe her. She said only the Devil or someone working for him would have the knowledge that you do. She said this was your way of tricking them. That you were probably responsible for the snake bite in the first place."

Edith deflates. It occurs to her in this moment that she never stood a chance with these people. They decided her fate long ago.

"The finger," Violet starts, the fear in her eyes matching that in her voice. "Whose was it?"

"I don't know," Edith admits. "I have no idea."

"I'm scared," the girl says.

Edith wants to lighten the girl's load, but words of comfort feel false right now. "Your mother knows now, I suppose? That I have been teaching you? And my husband must know too. I saw him leaving. Why was he here?"

The girl stares for a moment before breaking down. She falls to her knees, in tears. "I'm sorry," she repeats over and over.

TURN OFF THE LIGHT

"Violet," Edith says, "why are you sorry? What's going on?"

"He... they asked me to..." She struggles to get out the words.

Edith does not want to rush the girl, but she knows they have little time. She cannot risk someone inside realizing that Violet is gone.

"What did they ask you?" Edith presses.

"They made me explain it," Violet says. "Goodman Harris, he... they made me tell them what to put in your tea. Mother forced me to... she forced me to prune it and show them a dose that would kill."

Edith's world tilts. She had expected accusations, had even expected a trial. But this? Her husband plotting with the neighbors, forcing a child to participate in murder?

David is a bad guy. He is going to put something bad in your tea.

"Thank you," Edith says, placing a hand on Violet's shoulder. "Thank you. You did nothing wrong. You are only a child. They never should have..." Her voice trails off as she fights back tears. "Just promise me one thing."

Violet looks at her with sadness and regret. Then she nods. "Anything."

"Never be like them," Edith instructs. "Never use what I've taught you to harm. It should only ever be used for good."

Violet leans in to Edith for a hug. "But I still have so much more to learn," she says.

Edith pulls away, tucks a strand of hair behind the girl's ear. "Go to my home," she says. "There, under the straw tick, you will find my journals. I moved them from the root cellar when I saw David getting suspicious. You will find all my recipes there. Everything I know."

Violet's eyes fill with tears. "What will you do now?"

Edith looks out toward the bay, the light from the rising moon glistening off the surface of the ever-moving water.

"I have to leave," she says, resolve settling within her. "Tonight."

Edith heads for the creek, questions swimming in her mind. When did David plan to kill her? Tonight? How would he dispose of her body? What would he and Violet's mother tell the others? Did Elizabeth know of the plan? Did the minister?

She climbs into the boat and pushes off the shore. She navigates the shallow creek along the bottom with her paddle. Finally, she reaches deeper waters. The air is thick, clinging to her skin, but mercifully, the moon is bright and the sky clear. She internally maps out her hasty voyage. It is a relatively direct path to the mainland, though it might be treacherous. She has never crossed the Chesapeake Bay, which she estimates to be fifteen to twenty miles of open water. She will be vulnerable out there, alone and exposed—but she is determined. She can find safety only on the mainland, of that she is sure. There is nowhere to hide here on the peninsula.

Edith aims west-southwest and glides easily through the low wetlands and barrier sands. As she reaches the mouth to the bay, a hiss of wind whips across the water. Her shawl lifts. And then—a *crack*. The hull jolts. The boat lurches forward, scraping against a sandbar beneath. She has just enough time to shift her weight backward, but as she does, her knee slams into a rib of the canoe. The prow twists.

No longer under the narrow protection of the creek, Edith is hit like a slap by a squall. The sharp wind catches the side of the boat. Water sloshes over the gunwale. She reaches for the paddle, desperate, but the boat rolls. Dark water swallows her in a single gulp, pulling her away from the sandbar and into the depths. Her skirt tangles around her legs, getting heavier by the second. She kicks upward, but the effort is futile. Her shoe is caught on something unseen, and her body is yanked below the surface.

As she fights against the angry bay, she imagines her canoe floating back to shore. Her husband coming upon it. Putting the pieces together, knowing that his wife tried to run away and failed. She imagines David sighing with relief at the sight of his own boat capsized, his broad shoulders relaxing.

Well done, he would think. *She did the deed for us.*

Under the water, Edith screams. Tiny bubbles emerge from her open mouth and dance, carefree, to the surface.

34

CLAIRE

Claire stands in the receiving line at the funeral. Initially, the service was meant for only their dad. But they decided to wait until the medical examiner released Gabby's body so that she could also be part of the ceremony. Two coffins are arranged near the church altar, side by side, separated by a large, framed photo of Gabby and their dad. In the picture, Gabby is sixteen, throwing a peace sign to the camera. It's her first day as a licensed driver, and their father strikes a comedically nervous pose beside her.

The barn turned church is all browns on the inside. The pews and podium are modern, but the building itself is old. An odd mishmash of styles. The original structure has more character than the run-of-the-mill furniture that has been shoved in here.

"I'm just so sorry," says an older woman with kind brown eyes.

Claire knows this is a loaded statement. It's not just about her father and Gabby; it's about Peter too. Word has spread quickly on the Shore. Who knows what version of events this woman has heard. She likely has only bits and pieces of the truth. Scraps that will eventually need sewing into something substantial.

TURN OFF THE LIGHT

"Thank you so much," Claire tells her.

The lady side-eyes Julia as she notes the girl's outfit. Rainbow leggings and a unicorn dress. Claire smirks to herself. She knew this would happen if she let her daughter come to the funeral like this. But she also knew it was exactly what her dad would have wanted, since he loved her fashion sense and unadulterated originality.

As Claire shakes another person's hand, she feels a tug on the black skirt she has borrowed from Tilly. She looks down to find Julia staring up at her.

"Is Grandpa in there?" the girl asks, pointing toward a coffin at the front of the church.

Claire kneels down beside her daughter. "His body is, but Grandpa is gone, sweetie," she says. "Remember? This is just to celebrate his life. For people to say goodbye."

"A party?" Julia asks.

Claire smiles. "Yeah. Kinda."

"A party because Grandpa is in the stars."

"That's right," Claire says as she squeezes her little girl.

Tilly sits with Claire and Julia in the front pew. "There she is," Tilly says, looking toward the back of the church.

Claire turns and finds her mother standing near the doors. She wears a black dress better suited for a board meeting than a funeral. Her hair, which she has allowed to go fully gray now, is clipped at the base of her neck. Tilly waves, and their mother nods. Then she slips out of sight into the last pew.

"Do you think she'll come to the house after?" Tilly asks.

Claire raises an eyebrow. "I'd be shocked." But for once, she doesn't feel that familiar tug of anger. Instead, she feels sympathy. Claire can't imagine losing Julia. It would quite literally tear her apart until she no longer recognized herself. She knows that the cells deep within her, cells necessary for her core survival, would shrivel and die. As a mother, she now sees her own mom in a new light. What was once frustration and hurt has softened to sadness and pity. Claire looks around the church. "I don't even recognize half these people."

She shouldn't be surprised that so many locals she doesn't know are here. That's how it goes in Cape Chase. You live here, you show up.

"They've come to see the circus animal," Tilly says, pointing to herself. "They're wondering how I fell for it. How I married the same guy who hid my sister's body in the cellar."

"That's a self-preservation technique," Claire says. "You know that. They have to believe you missed something. Because then they can convince themselves they would have known. Otherwise, they live in a world where their own husbands could be killers."

"Yeah, well, this is Cape Chase, not Chicago. Statistically speaking, one murderer is probably all we've got."

"You never knowww," Claire sings, which makes Tilly laugh. Behind them, a pair of old ladies snicker at their levity.

The church gets louder with murmuring and indecipherable conversations as everyone waits for the service to start. There's a comfort in the hum. Claire holds her daughter's hand on one side and Tilly's on the other. She spots Ethan, who is helping to usher guests to the crowded pews. She catches his eye, and he smiles. She smiles back.

The house is alive with the reception. The kitchen is bursting with potluck offerings, and cars are parked along the street as far as the eye can see. Their mother did not come back to the house. In fact, she kept a low profile at the funeral and slipped out before anyone

TURN OFF THE LIGHT

noticed her. Claire understands. Their mom doesn't want to mourn with people who have become strangers. Her grief is hers and hers alone.

Instead, they will get together tomorrow, just the four of them, and Claire's mom will meet Julia for the first time. Claire is giddy at the thought and oddly grateful that her mother has never met the girl before. It feels now like they might have a real chance at some kind of relationship, whereas before, Claire was too bitter. Too resentful and angry and confused. She is still all those things, of course. But she now also understands on a primal level that her mother did what she needed to survive.

Claire has spent the day reuniting with faces from her past. She thought she would hate it—these are the kinds of reunions she usually avoids—but she was surprised at how much she enjoyed it. Something about the lively spirits of old friends filling the space between these haunted walls has brought back the happy image of her childhood.

Before Gabby disappeared.

Before her parents fell out of love.

Before she and Tilly fractured apart.

Claire walks toward the beach. As much as she loves to see the house this full, something is bothering her. A recurring thought she has had since this morning that she can't shake.

She walks through the grass of the yard, between the tall trees, and down the wooden pathway to the beach. She slides out of her shoes and sticks her toes in the sand. The sun is just starting to set, its oranges and reds and yellows fanning out in long streaks across the sky. She thinks about evening walks with her father. Morning polar plunges with her sisters. The illegal bonfires she warmed herself by as a teenager. This beach has shaped her life in so many ways.

She sits in the sand and runs her fingers through the granules.

"You good?"

It's Ethan. He approaches slowly, like he's ready to bail if she waves him off. "Okay if I join you? Or do you need some space?"

"Please," Claire says, patting the sand beside her. "Sit."

He does, and for a while they listen to the water calmly lapping at the shore.

"There's a thought I can't shake," Claire finally admits.

"Oh?" Ethan asks.

She plants her feet in the sand in front of her and rests her arms on her upper thighs, still staring at the water. "I keep thinking about Edith. Julia hasn't seen her since she gave her the message. She's just gone."

Ethan's body mirrors Claire's. He watches the bay as he speaks. "Well, maybe it's like what happened to you."

"What do you mean?"

He turns toward her. "You stopped sensing Edith once she saved you. Once you were no longer 'close to transition' or whatever. So maybe it's the same for her. Maybe you saved her, and now she's not crossing anymore."

Claire takes a deep breath and shakes her head. "I don't think so. I did another deep dive. I even called Poppy and checked back in with the historical society. Nothing has changed. Everything we learned about Edith—it's still the same. She's still listed as *disappeared*."

"Hmm," Ethan says.

"If we saved her—I mean, if Julia's message had worked—wouldn't that have changed?"

Ethan frowns. "I don't think we can rewrite the past like that."

"I had that thought as well," Claire says. "Like, all right, this was always how it was going to happen. We can't change the past because the past is happening now. None of it's linear. But if that's the case, is it my fault she disappeared? I always thought she went missing because her husband murdered her and hid the body. But her bones aren't under the house. I was wrong about that. So what if Julia gave her that message, and Edith, I don't know, tried to save herself? Ran away or whatever and got hurt. Died. Disappeared. *Because* she was trying to get away."

Claire fights back tears. The guilt she feels reminds her of the guilt she felt over Gabby all those years. All that time she'd spent thinking her sister ran away because Claire told her to.

Ethan lets out a long breath. "I guess it's a possibility."

"So she saved me, and I killed her."

"We definitely don't know that."

"I think we do," she says. "That's how it always happened. That's how it was always going to be. But still, if I hadn't sent Julia with that message, maybe Edith would have lived."

"Or maybe Edith would have been killed by her husband," he says.

Claire chews her lip, then runs her fingers through the sand. "I hate the not knowing."

Her mind is going in circles, imagining all the ways in which this could have played out. But no matter how she alters the timeline, in her head, it always ends the same way, with Claire destroying the very person who saved her.

They all sleep in the sisters' childhood room again that night. Claire cuddles with Julia on the air mattress this time. She traces circles on her daughter's back. Anytime she takes a break, Julia whispers, eyes still closed, "A little more," and Claire starts the tracing again.

There is so much to be done. Claire's mind swirls around the never-ending to-do list. They must decide how to handle the house.

Tilly can't imagine living here after all that's happened, and Claire doesn't blame her.

Claire is feeling unmoored too. She doesn't want to go back to Los Angeles. Perhaps this shouldn't be a surprise: She went there only to seek refuge, to hide from something that followed her like a shadow on the Eastern Shore. But now she can begin again. She could start that business she has dreamed of, finally leaving the job she has grown to hate. She could stay in this place that she always loved and that she abandoned only because she was afraid.

She's done running from her fears.

Which brings her to Ethan. They haven't discussed what happens next, but she can't imagine saying goodbye. She feels pulled to him. They are meant to be in each other's lives, she knows it. She just doesn't yet know in what capacity. And maybe that's okay. Maybe instead of making plans and anticipating problems and desperately grasping for a sense of control, she can finally accept that it's all a mirage. The past, the present. None of it is real. Not in the sense she has always understood. All that truly exists is the *now*. So she might as well try living in it.

She closes her eyes. Listens to her own breath and the breath of her small daughter. Feels Julia's back under her hand move up and down as she falls asleep. Claire wraps a finger around a wavy piece of the girl's hair and rolls it between her index and thumb. Smells the coconut conditioner they used earlier from Tilly's shower. Then she cuddles in closer to her daughter and feels the girl's soft, warm exhales against her skin.

This.

This is all that is.

And for once, that thought is not suffocating. In fact, she feels freer than she ever has.

35

EDITH

The squall had been a blessing.

Edith lost most of her belongings, and her clothes are soaked and torn, but she is largely unharmed. At first, she tried to recover the boat, but it had taken on too much water. She thought again of David finding it, realizing what had happened. Assuming his wife had tried to flee and failed. Resigning himself to the fact that her body had been swallowed by the bay.

And then she realized this could work to her advantage. If she had merely disappeared into the night, per her original plan, David might have been compelled to search for her. But finding her crashed boat would make him believe she'd died. She could be a truly free woman. No one looks for the drowned.

So she decided to change course.

Now, she holds her soaked leather shoes and walks barefoot along the shore to the low, muddy point of Reeve's inlet. When she arrives, she does not see him, only the crude table where he brokers deals, that weathered plank balanced on two old barrels that is usually covered with rabbit pelts or duck eggs or copper wire. But now, in the middle of the night, the table is empty.

Edith walks farther inland. She thinks Reeve lives in a lean-to between the marsh and the tree line. Though he does not appreciate visitors, she is desperate and has to try.

She stops when she finds his wide-brimmed hat hooked on a driftwood peg. And next to it, his home. She marvels at the structure. It is tucked into the edge of a low bluff where scrub pine meets wet reed. The bones of its frame are shaped by driftwood and camouflaged with windblown seaweed and hanging moss. The front is open but shielded with sun-bleached sailcloth strung between stakes and hanging like a curtain.

The closer she gets, the stronger the smell of salt and smoke and old leather. Edith finds the scent comforting. It conjures happy memories with her father.

"I hear ye," warns a gravelly voice from behind the flapping sailcloth.

"It's Edith," she says. "I lost my boat."

Reeve climbs out of the lean-to. It does not appear that Edith has woken him, though the hour is late.

"Sleep with one eye open," he says as if reading her mind. "Can never trust the woods."

He takes in her haggard appearance and gapes.

"What you got yourself into, lady?" he says, but his tone is light. Friendly, even.

"I have to leave," she says. Then she gestures toward her bare feet, her soaked clothes. "I was trying to do it discreetly, but—"

"The bay won." He laughs. "For the best. Can't imagine you would have made it across on your own. You never navigated the open water, now, have ye?"

Edith shakes her head.

"Right," he says. "So you need a ride, do ye?"

She nods.

"Must be running from something bad," he muses.

She couldn't explain it if she tried. A stranger's message is driving her from her home. Anyone else would have questioned the girl's reliability. But Edith had a feeling. And that feeling was confirmed by Violet's confession.

Edith is done ignoring her instinct.

"This may seem indecent," she says, "but I need...well, if my husband comes asking..."

"I never seen ye," Reeve says. Then he looks around as if reading the wind somehow. He stands bone-still, listening for—well, Edith doesn't know what. But listening for something.

"Weather might be on our side," Reeve finally says. "You're in a hurry, I guess."

Edith nods. "I don't have anything to offer. But I can fetch something when we get to the other side."

Reeve holds his hand up to stop her. Then he points to the scar on his face. "No pain since you brought that balm. I owe ye."

Edith swallows so that she doesn't cry. This man is showing her such kindness when her own husband would rid her from the earth.

"Thank you," she chokes out.

"*Friends,* you said, remember?" Reeve sets to work gathering rations for the trip. "We better be off soon. Can take five hours to cross if a storm crops up."

As he pulls together his supplies, Edith looks around. Breathes in the briny air, rich with salt and marsh rot and green things breaking down. Death and life entangled. The moon casts silver across the trees and slick eelgrass, which wave to her like fingers in the dark. In the near distance, the tide murmurs, lapping soft and slow like breath. This place is alive. And it is saying goodbye.

People call Edith unnatural, but she has never felt more known than she does right here, right now. She does not regret the fire. It was a necessary rebirth. A release. But not from the Devil. No, it was never the Devil who held her. It was only her own self holding her back. Afraid of her own power.

But not anymore. On the mainland, across the wide Chesapeake Bay, she will be free — not only from the people of the Shore, but from herself.

"You got a name?" Reeve asks.

She frowns. He knows her name. "It's Edith."

Reeve shakes his head and laughs. "Not anymore it ain't."

36

CLAIRE

Claire is putting away groceries when her phone buzzes with a text from Ethan.

It's a photo of a portrait of a small group of women and girls. Behind them is a crude sign that reads APPLE HOLLOW.

Then her screen changes with an incoming call.

"What is this picture?" she asks.

"Can you show it to Julia?" Ethan says. He sounds excited, his voice practically jumping through the device.

"Uh . . ." She wanders out of the kitchen and into the sunroom, where Julia is making a fort from pillows and blankets and furniture. "You're on speaker," Claire says to Ethan.

"Hey, Julia," Ethan says, and the girl perks up. "Can you look at the picture your mom has on her phone?"

Claire pulls up the portrait.

"Do you know that lady in the middle?" he asks. "Does she look familiar?"

"Ohhh," Julia says, recognition immediately lighting up her face. "That's the nice lady. That's Edith."

Claire's chest gets tight. She sits down on the couch for support. It's powerful, finally putting a face to the name. "Where is this picture from?"

She takes Ethan off speaker as he explains.

"She didn't disappear," he says. "I mean, she technically did. From her life on the Shore. But I found her on the mainland. Near Jamestown."

"Wait, slow down," Claire says, barely keeping up. "This painting is from . . . *after*?"

"I kept thinking about what you said," Ethan tells her. "How you thought it was your fault. So I was looking everywhere near that area for female healers, and she popped up in some diary entries from the mainland. Logs that included recipes for her salves, and they match exactly the recipes that Violet Cotton recorded on the Shore. The ones that Poppy showed us. I took pictures of them so I could compare. Exactly the same."

Claire brings her hand to her mouth. Tears well in her eyes.

"So she survived," Claire says.

"Not only did she survive," Ethan says, "but she went on to start her own hospital. That's what the portrait is from. Those other women are her apprentices. It seems like she worked out of her home, slowly built it up. She called the place Apple Hollow."

Claire laughs, euphoria spilling from her. "She got out!" she says. "She did it."

Claire shakes her head as she marvels at the woman's ingenuity. She faked her own death and then went on to save other people. The strength it must have taken in that time to completely start over somewhere new. The chutzpah.

"And, Claire," Ethan says, his voice changed.

"What is it?" she asks as she watches her daughter crawl into her handcrafted structure and pull out a bottle of kids' nail polish to paint her nails.

"She changed her name," Ethan says. "The recipes were still referred to as Edith's, but she called herself something else."

Claire nods. "I guess that makes sense. She would have had to."

"Guess what she went by?"

Claire sticks out her bottom lip as she thinks. "I don't know, what?"

"Julia."

Claire smiles. Relief pulses through her veins. Julia's message was a good thing. Claire had not killed the woman who'd saved her.

After hanging up, she returns to the groceries. She needs to finish putting them away, then she'll hop in the shower. She and Julia and Tilly are meeting her mom in an hour. An excited, nervous rush surges through her chest at the thought.

The last thing she pulls from her tote is the compostable bag of apples. She pauses. Remembers fleetingly that she used to smell apple whenever she sensed Edith was near. And now she knows the woman called her hospital Apple Hollow. What inspired the name? Did it have some deeper meaning?

The flimsy produce bag slips from her fingers. The fruit thuds and bounces on the floor, rolling.

Julia runs into the kitchen to help her mother. "It's okay, Mama! It happens."

Claire smiles as she hears the words she has so often spoken to her daughter repeated back to her.

When they've gathered the stray pieces of fruit, Claire notes there are only four. She looks around. Five. There should be five. She is sure of it.

She crawls on her hands and knees, swiveling her head like a searchlight, but the fifth apple is nowhere to be found.

She stands, shrugging. Maybe she miscounted. After all, an apple doesn't just disappear into thin air.

Does it?

Claire smiles.

ACKNOWLEDGMENTS

wholeheartedly: Writers would kill to have someone like you in their corner. I am so lucky.

There is not a lot of information about life on the Eastern Shore of Virginia in 1630, so I am exceptionally grateful to have found and been able to reference the following texts: *The Formation of a Society on Virginia's Eastern Shore, 1615–1655* by James R. Perry; *Witchcraft in Colonial Virginia* by Carson O. Hudson Jr.; *An "Uncertaine Rumor" of Land: New Thoughts on the English Founding of Virginia's Eastern Shore* and *Another Day: More Stories from the Early Colonial Records of Virginia's Eastern Shore* by Jenean Hall.

Thank you to Keith Hayes and Pete Garceau for the cover of my dreams. I am obsessed. Thank you to my copyeditor, Tracy Roe, who taught me the difference between *spattered* and *splattered*. Thank you to production editor Karen Landry, who must be oh-so-tired of authors pushing deadlines. Sabrina Callahan and Liv Ryan: I haven't gotten to see you as much this time around, but I'm always grateful for your enthusiasm. Thank you to Darcy Glastonbury and Emma Littel-Jensen for your support on the publicity and marketing front. And thanks to Gretchen Koss for your expertise and publicity prowess. Thank you to Jen Patten-Sanchez for believing in me to record the audiobook for *Dearest* and letting me return to record for this one. There's no one I'd rather be cooped up in a booth with!

Thank you to my soul sister, Whitney Fern, for lending your surname. Thank you to my daily cheerleader and partner, Poppy Montgomery. Thank you to early readers JoAnneh Nagler, Marc Morgenstern, Amy Asay, Julia Erwin-Weiner, and Katrina Ryan.

Thank you, Mom and Wayne, for taking inspiration photos on the Eastern Shore. (And for being my absolute number one hype guys wherever you go!)

And thank you to YOU for picking up this book. If an author writes a manuscript and no one reads it, does it even exist? I owe you everything.

Acknowledgments

They say writing books is like having children—each novel [has its] own process, its own personality. Well, if that's the case, th[is] book's personality was defined by its desire to try and kill n[e every] chance it got. I had to write three full manuscripts before [arriv]ing at the version you have just read. Version One was an a[maz]ingly violent summer camp massacre story (maybe this will [make] a comeback someday). Version Two had our characters and s[etting] but took place entirely in the present day with a wildly dif[ferent] plot. And now, Version Three: *the* version, which I think is f[inally] the book *Turn Off the Light* was meant to be.

All that said, this process was brutal. So, thanks first and forem[ost to] my husband, Marco, for his understanding. He had to watch my [brain] melt inside its skull three times over—all while offering extra [help] to manage our little ones. Chiara and Francesco: Thank you for [your] patience. I couldn't have been more blessed had I special-ordered y[ou].

And thank you especially to my editor, Helen O'Hare, [who] heard my idea for Version Three and allowed me the extra tim[e to] make it happen. As with *Dearest,* some of my favorite parts of [Turn] *Off the Light* are thanks to your impeccable and brilliant notes.

Thank you to my agent, Richard Abate, who read Version [One] and kindly ushered me back to the drawing board. I mean [that]

About the Author

Jacquie Walters is the author of *Dearest* and an Emmy-nominated screenwriter. She has placed projects at Apple TV+, ABC Network, Paramount Plus, Legendary, iTV, and others. In all, she has written and produced over one hundred episodes of television. Walters graduated from the novel-writing program at Stanford University and is passionate about layered mysteries, psychological anomalies, and characters with everything to hide. She lives in Los Angeles with her husband, two children, and beloved golden retriever.

Acknowledgments

They say writing books is like having children—each novel has its own process, its own personality. Well, if that's the case, then this book's personality was defined by its desire to try and kill me any chance it got. I had to write three full manuscripts before arriving at the version you have just read. Version One was an alarmingly violent summer camp massacre story (maybe this will make a comeback someday). Version Two had our characters and setting but took place entirely in the present day with a wildly different plot. And now, Version Three: *the* version, which I think is finally the book *Turn Off the Light* was meant to be.

All that said, this process was brutal. So, thanks first and foremost to my husband, Marco, for his understanding. He had to watch my brain melt inside its skull three times over—all while offering extra hands to manage our little ones. Chiara and Francesco: Thank you for your patience. I couldn't have been more blessed had I special-ordered you.

And thank you especially to my editor, Helen O'Hare, who heard my idea for Version Three and allowed me the extra time to make it happen. As with *Dearest,* some of my favorite parts of *Turn Off the Light* are thanks to your impeccable and brilliant notes.

Thank you to my agent, Richard Abate, who read Version One and kindly ushered me back to the drawing board. I mean this

ACKNOWLEDGMENTS

wholeheartedly: Writers would kill to have someone like you in their corner. I am so lucky.

There is not a lot of information about life on the Eastern Shore of Virginia in 1630, so I am exceptionally grateful to have found and been able to reference the following texts: *The Formation of a Society on Virginia's Eastern Shore, 1615–1655* by James R. Perry; *Witchcraft in Colonial Virginia* by Carson O. Hudson Jr.; *An "Uncertaine Rumor" of Land: New Thoughts on the English Founding of Virginia's Eastern Shore* and *Another Day: More Stories from the Early Colonial Records of Virginia's Eastern Shore* by Jenean Hall.

Thank you to Keith Hayes and Pete Garceau for the cover of my dreams. I am obsessed. Thank you to my copyeditor, Tracy Roe, who taught me the difference between *spattered* and *splattered*. Thank you to production editor Karen Landry, who must be oh-so-tired of authors pushing deadlines. Sabrina Callahan and Liv Ryan: I haven't gotten to see you as much this time around, but I'm always grateful for your enthusiasm. Thank you to Darcy Glastonbury and Emma Littel-Jensen for your support on the publicity and marketing front. And thanks to Gretchen Koss for your expertise and publicity prowess. Thank you to Jen Patten-Sanchez for believing in me to record the audiobook for *Dearest* and letting me return to record for this one. There's no one I'd rather be cooped up in a booth with!

Thank you to my soul sister, Whitney Fern, for lending your surname. Thank you to my daily cheerleader and partner, Poppy Montgomery. Thank you to early readers JoAnneh Nagler, Marc Morgenstern, Amy Asay, Julia Erwin-Weiner, and Katrina Ryan.

Thank you, Mom and Wayne, for taking inspiration photos on the Eastern Shore. (And for being my absolute number one hype guys wherever you go!)

And thank you to YOU for picking up this book. If an author writes a manuscript and no one reads it, does it even exist? I owe you everything.

About the Author

Jacquie Walters is the author of *Dearest* and an Emmy-nominated screenwriter. She has placed projects at Apple TV+, ABC Network, Paramount Plus, Legendary, iTV, and others. In all, she has written and produced over one hundred episodes of television. Walters graduated from the novel-writing program at Stanford University and is passionate about layered mysteries, psychological anomalies, and characters with everything to hide. She lives in Los Angeles with her husband, two children, and beloved golden retriever.

RAISING READERS
Books Build Bright Futures

Thank you for reading this book and for being a reader of books in general. We are so grateful to share being part of a community of readers with you, and we hope you will join us in passing our love of books on to the next generation of readers.

Did you know that reading for enjoyment is the single biggest predictor of a child's future happiness and success?

More than family circumstances, parents' educational background, or income, reading impacts a child's future academic performance, emotional well-being, communication skills, economic security, ambition, and happiness.

Studies show that kids reading for enjoyment in the US is in rapid decline:

- In 2012, 53% of 9-year-olds read almost every day. Just 10 years later, in 2022, the number had fallen to 39%.
- In 2012, 27% of 13-year-olds read for fun daily. By 2023, that number was just 14%.

Together, we can commit to **Raising Readers** and change this trend. How?

- Read to children in your life daily.
- Model reading as a fun activity.
- Reduce screen time.
- Start a family, school, or community book club.
- Visit bookstores and libraries regularly.
- Listen to audiobooks.
- Read the book before you see the movie.
- Encourage your child to read aloud to a pet or stuffed animal.
- Give books as gifts.
- Donate books to families and communities in need.

Books build bright futures, and **Raising Readers** is our shared responsibility.

For more information, visit **JoinRaisingReaders.com**

Sources: National Endowment for the Arts, National Assessment of Educational Progress, WorldBookDay.com, Nielsen BookData's 2023 "Understanding the Children's Book Consumer"